THE WARRIOR

A DANTE WALKER NOVEL

PRAISE FOR THE COLLECTOR

"Hey Winchesters, there's a new guy in town who's as hot, sarcastic and obsessed with souls as you are. But Dante's playing for Crowley's team and he's Hell's best."
—Justine Magazine

"Witty, and so intriguing. I started reading and didn't want to stop. Victoria Scott is a fabulous new voice in YA."
—C.C. Hunter, author of the New York Times bestselling series SHADOW FALLS

"Dante Walker is the kind of guy I wish I'd met when I was seventeen. And the kind of guy I'd kill if my daughter brought him home."
—Mary Lindsey, author of ASHES ON THE WAVES

"He's mouthy, he's arrogant, and he's here to reap your soul for the bad guys, but you still can't help but love Dante Walker, loud and proud, from page one. His is one of the most unique voices I've read in a while and I could not put the book down!"
— Heather Anastasiu, author of GLITCH

"Victoria Scott's smokin' hot paranormal debut, The Collector, left me breathless at every turn with its sizzling anti-hero."
—Mindee Arnett, author of THE NIGHTMARE AFFAIR

"Dante Walker's bad—swaggering, sexy, cocky, charming, soul-collecting, bone-deep, anti-hero bad. And Victoria Scott's witty, dark debut The Collector is so very, very good."
—Eve Silver, author of RUSH

THE WARRIOR

A DANTE WALKER NOVEL

❖ VICTORIA SCOTT ❖

Entangled Publishing, LLC
2614 South Timberline Road
Suite 109
Fort Collins, CO 80525
Visit our website at www.entangledpublishing.com.

Edited by Liz Pelletier

Ebook ISBN   978-1-62266-279-1
Print ISBN   978-1-62266-278-4

Manufactured in the United States of America

First Edition May 2014

For Royce and Linda Scott, who have become a second set of parents to me.
Sorry for all the curse words. Dante made me do it.

"Remember tonight…for it is the beginning of always."

—Dante's Inferno

Working for the devil turns you into something unfixable. It makes you a demon, forevermore. It teaches you to feel anger before anything else, and to fight dirty for those things you believe yours. But I don't work for the devil anymore. I work for the good guys, even if I don't act like one. My job now is to protect my girlfriend from my former boss, and to rescue my friend from hell.

No, I don't work for the devil any longer. But I am still the man he made me. I am still angry, and volatile, and dangerous. I don't like the things he's done, and I'm not about to sit back quietly. After all, he taught me better than that. He loved me with the kindness of a serrated blade, and fed me from a spoon dipped in terror.

He made me into a monster.

But I will bite the hand that fed me.

—Dante Walker

PARADISE (IS GONE)

"In the middle of the journey of our life, I came to myself within a dark wood where the straight way was lost."
—Dante's Inferno

⇥1⇤

DINNER WITH A DEMON

If war is coming, I make it look damn good.

I am: sharp eyes for hunting, broad shoulders for fighting, strong hands for gripping a weapon. I am built for this. I will protect Charlie, and I will rescue Aspen from hell. There's nothing I wouldn't do for my girls, and I plan to do it all. Blood will spill, and I will spill it without a second thought.

I am a machine.

Like a sinister boxing match, the rivals lie ready. In one corner, we have five collectors, people who work for the underworld administering sin seals to those still alive. Working alongside them are dozens of humans who do their bidding. These dirt bags are called sirens.

In the other corner, we have seven liberators, people who work for the heavens that can dissolve sin seals on living humans. We all wear cuffs, called dargon, which allow us to walk the earth after death and to sense each other if we're nearby. But that's where our similarities end.

The collectors want Charlie, my girlfriend, and Aspen, my friend. They want them because an ancient scroll said they are a savior and soldier sent to fight in a brutal war between heaven and earth. They have Charlie's soul, and Aspen… Well, they have all of her. This is what I like to call a crap storm situation. Because if the liberators have the savior and the soldier—body and soul—on our side, we'll most likely triumph over hell. Otherwise, we'll be grossly outnumbered and outmatched by the collectors and their swarm of human soldiers.

Since hell has Aspen, *and* Charlie's soul, things aren't exactly stacked in our favor. To make matters worse, a victory for hell could tip the delicate scales between heaven and hell in the latter's favor, making it possible for demons to walk the earth unrestricted. Que chaos and suffering for all mankind.

The bottom line is that war is imminent, and Kraven, the self-proclaimed leader of our group and juiced-up liberator, says soon there will be a sign. After that sign, war will arrive within two weeks. Good thing since sirens are lingering outside our humble abode. Who knows when they'll finally decide to break down the door?

"Dante?"

Spinning around, I find Charlie standing against the bathroom doorframe. Here is the girl who will save us all. The girl destined to fight in this battle alongside Aspen and whose charity will usher in Trelvator—a hundred years of peace on earth. Blond hair spills over her shoulders, framing a heart-shaped face. Her skin is porcelain, her smile is bottled sunshine, and her body is sick in a good way. She is perfect.

She's perfect because I made her that way, because I talked her into signing a contract in which she traded her soul for beauty. Even though I've fought to change the person I am, the person who did that to her, I'm still a demon at heart. Big Guy may be Lord of the Heavens, and I may have gold dargon wrapped around my ankle, marking me as a liberator, but inside, deep down, a demon growls.

Sometimes I still feel the old cuff around my ankle.

The one I wore as head collector.

Charlie wraps her arms around my waist, and her fingers clutch my back. My armor falls away in an instant, and I'm no longer what I was a moment before. Now I'm sharp eyes for watching her, and broad shoulders for easing her worries, and strong hands for holding her tight.

"Are you ready?" I whisper against the crown of her head.

"Yes," she answers. "I'm excited."

I doubt that's entirely true. Cancer ate her Grams until nothing remained. Aspen, my first assignment as a liberator, gave her body and soul to Rector, to hell, so that I could escape with Charlie's soul. Only after I surfaced from the mouth of Hades with what turned out to be *my* soul did we learn that Charlie and Aspen were the savior and soldier we needed to win the war. So, yeah, I think Charlie may not be as *excited* as she claims.

Then again, I've pulled out all the stops tonight. Dinner by candlelight, food made by my own hand, and me as company. Pow! Charlie's mind may be filled with sorrow, but soon, it'll be filled with the awesome that is Dante Walker planning a date. In a Hive. Of angels planning for war. But whatev. It'll still be better than bacon, which is serious.

I tilt her head up and move my mouth close to hers. Then I speak so that our lips brush against each another. "I'm going to make you forget."

"Forget?" she says, confusion lilting her voice.

"Yeah, I want you to be with me tonight. No thoughts of what lies outside these walls."

Sirens.

Everywhere, sirens.

Humans who work for demons, who want to steal Charlie away.

"I can forget," she answers. "If you hold onto me, I can do it."

I wrap my hands around her cheeks and press my mouth to hers. Her head falls back, and she mimics the movements of my lips. The warmth of her, the feel of her tongue, washes over me. It makes my heart feel like a missile.

Her hands climb higher up my spine, over the dragon tattoo covering my back. Her chest grazes against me, and her hips connect with mine. For a moment, I contemplate killing the date idea and carrying her back to my bedroom. Yes, there is impending war. Yes, the girl I think of as a sister is in hell. But blood still burns through my body, and right now—always—it burns for Charlie.

"What are we having?" she mutters, breaking our kiss. "I guess I *am* hungry."

"We're about to have each other. Screw food."

Charlie laughs lightly, but she also takes a backward step. I'm not even sure if she does it on purpose. It's been a week since I returned from hell. A week since I left Aspen behind. In that time, Charlie hasn't so much as slept in the same bed as me. Granted, I'm not sure Big Guy would be real pleased that we ever did this in the first place, but what do I care? It's not like he and I have a relationship. Not like him and Kraven do, apparently.

The last seven days, all Kraven has done is walk around muttering to himself. If before he was Mr. Clean in his ever-present white clothing, now he's Mr. Clean sniffing the fumes from his own products. Valery says he's waiting for the sign that will determine the day of war. I say he's bat-shit crazy, and we need to skedaddle before he makes like the Unabomber and blows us all to kingdom come.

"I made you dinner with my own two man hands." I cup Charlie's chin. "So you need to prepare yourself for the mind freak that is my culinary skills."

"Should I call Wolfgang Puck?" she asks, smiling.

"And tell him he's out of business? Yeah, you might want to give him a heads up. It'd be the honorable thing to do."

I take her hand and press a kiss into her palm. Her fingers curl over the place I touched like she's self-conscious of her hands. She shouldn't be embarrassed. Fierce? Yes. Badass? Check. Anyone who saves me from hell by shooting blue lights from their hands and into the belly of a demon is A-OK, even if I don't know how said blue light works or if it'll make another appearance. Even if it does unsettle me to my core that Charlie has this untapped *power* that I never knew about.

As I lead Charlie toward the Great Room, I pretend everything is okay. We need this. What I don't show her is what lies inside my mind.

You left Aspen in hell.

You are selfish.

Coward.

I do my best to push these thoughts down. I'm doing a decent job quieting those voices when we turn a corner and see Blue. Before I do anything else, I glance at Charlie. She radiates like the North Star, like she's never been truly happy until now. It feels like a sucker punch.

"Blue." Charlie lets go of my hand and rushes toward him. Blue looks up from a book he's holding and sees Charlie coming toward him. He drops the novel to his side and opens his arms to her.

I want to break his arms.

Then I remember he hates me because I left the girl he's crushing on, Aspen, in hell, and I want to break my *own* arms.

Blue wraps Charlie in a hug, but it's different than he's done in the past. He doesn't cling to her, he just holds her for a moment before letting go. When he eyes me over her shoulder, he grabs onto Charlie's nonexistent biceps and gently pushes her away. It's as if he thinks I've trapped him somehow. Like I used Charlie as bait.

"I've missed you," Charlie says, gazing up at Blue. Her words sting, though I don't know why. Blue's attention is elsewhere now. On a different girl. It just so happens that girl is in hell.

"What are you looking at, prick?" Blue snarls in my direction. "I told you to stay away from me."

Blue's stance reminds me he's not the guy I met months ago

in Peachville, Alabama. He's neither lanky nor goofy. Not since he died fighting Rector to save Charlie. Not since he came back with a liberator cuff around his ankle. Now he's tall and strong and doesn't look half bad, for a dude. Even with big, dopey eyes and a head full of blond curls that makes him look in the way of canines.

I have so many things I want to say to him right now, but I can't find the words to defend myself. So instead, I move forward and take Charlie's hand again.

"I'm not going to apologize." My voice is firm when I meet Blue's gaze. "Not to you. I don't owe you anything."

"What about her?" Blue's top lip curls in disgust. "Did you owe Aspen anything? A fighting chance, at least?"

"Blue," Charlie says. "You know he didn't have a choice."

"Like hell he didn't." Blue points at me with the book in his hand.

"He thought he was saving my soul," Charlie whispers.

Blue's gaze whips to her face, and his own features soften.

"Come on," I say to Charlie. "We have a dinner to get to."

Blue's anger resurfaces as we move past him. "Enjoy your dinner, Dante. I'm sure you can forget what happened down there easily enough." And then, quieter, "Selfish asshole."

All I think when I hear his last remark is, *I want this pain.*

When we get to the Great Room, Charlie's eyes widen, and her mouth upturns in a smile. She touches two fingers to her lips like she's wondering how it got there. Her other hand loosens in my grip.

"Grams would want you to try and be happy," I say.

"Grams wouldn't want any of this." Charlie moves toward the table. When she turns toward me, her face is still pulled into a smile, but it isn't real. Seeing her this way, pretending to be happy, it's like spotting water in the dessert.

Before I even know what I'm doing, I'm crossing the distance between us. I pull her chair out, and she sits, tucking a purple skirt the Quiet Ones dressed her in beneath her. The Quiet Ones are liberators as well; two girls that have chosen to serve the savior and soldier in complete silence rather than fight. I'd say this is copping out, but what are you gonna do?

"I'll have you know," I say, doing my best to sound cheerful, "that every last course tonight is red."

"Seriously?" she says. "You created an entire dinner around our favorite color?"

"I aim to please."

A human shuffles out from the kitchen area with two plates in his hands. I've questioned Kraven a dozen times on how it's okay that they've brought humans into the Hive. He assures me they don't know what we are, but I have my doubts. I also have my doubts on whether dying by the hands of a siren or liberator is a reasonable occupational hazard for anyone to risk, especially if they don't know about that hazard.

The man, a guy in his mid-fifties with grey pants positioned way too high on his waist, sets down our first course. Charlie picks up the smallest fork and pierces a leaf of red cabbage coated in raspberry vinaigrette. Before she puts it into her mouth, she pauses.

"What is it?" I ask. "It can't be that bad. You haven't even tasted it."

She lowers her fork. "I just thought we could…"

"Could what?"

"Pray."

Boom. I didn't see that coming. I want to tell her to forget it. That I'm not boys with Big Guy and never will be. But she raises her chin and squares her shoulders, and I know I can't deny her this. One, because I'd do about anything to make her happy. Two, because she has blue, glowy hands that make me wary of pissing her off.

"So we'll pray." I straighten in my chair.

Charlie smiles. Then she lowers her head and closes her eyes. I watch her for a moment, and then catch one of her eyes slipping open.

"Why aren't you praying?" she asks.

"I thought you did it out loud," I respond.

"I'd rather do it quietly, if that's okay."

I open my hands as if to say, *whatever does it for ya.*

"You have to close your eyes," she says with a playful quirk of her lips.

I want to kiss her again.

Charlie lowers her head, and this time I do, too.

Dear Big Guy, way to abandon my ass in hell. Where were you? I thought you were all-powerful. Not for the likes of me though, huh? Guess I don't blame you. I don't do crap for you, so why would you do anything in return? No biggie. I'm a lone wolf, Big Guy, howling at the moon. I don't need your help rescuing Aspen, and I don't need help protecting Charlie. I'll do it myself. Pow!

I stop praying and glance at Charlie.

Her eyes are closed. Her lips move in this gentle, quiet way, like she's really talking to someone. All the worry lines I've come to memorize have vanished. Gone is the tension in her shoulders. All that remains is this peace that seems to hum, like rain falling outside.

I'm envious.

I always knew Charlie was religious, but I've never seen her pray. The way she's concentrating, you'd think she truly believed Big Guy was listening. That it's as simple as that. Open your mind and talk to him.

Bullshit.

I don't want to rupture her fantasy, but he's not there. Not really. Big Guy has his own agenda and having a real relationship with Charlie isn't part of that. Something dark yawns awake inside of me thinking about him fooling her this way. It begs for me to break something, to destroy this peace like a lion attacking his prey.

But then my sweet girl raises her head.

And I wonder if I am wrong.

She seems in this moment like someone who has something she didn't before. I want that something. I don't want that something.

I just want to freaking eat.

"Ready to dig in?" I ask, suffocating the darkness.

"Thanks for doing this, Dante. It means a lot." She takes a bite of the salad.

And then, somewhere outside the Hive, through the cold January snow—

A trumpet sounds.

⇥2⇤

TRUMPET

At first I think my salad is just that bomb. That my menu selections require trumpets and marching bands.

Then Valery races in, all breasts and curves and red hair. She looks like she was sleeping with full makeup on. Not surprising. My head fills with a soft buzzing as the cuff on my ankle senses hers. She trots up to us wearing a yellow nightgown that falls mid-thigh. It's a bad color on her. Redheads and yellow don't mix.

"Hey, Red." I stand from my dining chair. "You going to bed at 8:00 these days? Wouldn't surprise me considering your age and all."

She jabs a manicured nail in my direction. I'm wondering who's doing her nails in the middle of nowhere, in a piecemeal house on the edge of an ocean cliff. "I'm like five years older than you, Dante."

"More like ten."

"I am not—" She stops and shakes her head. "Did you hear that noise?"

"The sound of your heavy breathing? Yeah, I heard it a mile away. You had to run, what, thirty feet to get here?"

"I heard it." Charlie comes to stand beside Valery. "It was like a blast of sound, like a musical instrument."

For the first time, a chill tiptoes down my spine. I thought I'd imagined what the sound was. That it was actually Kraven outside, setting off one of his bombs in a trial run. Valery lays a hand upon her chest. She does that a lot. I'm not sure whether it's an unconscious tic or one she does because it's so Hollywood starlet. I'm guessing the latter.

Red opens her mouth to say something, but Max interrupts her.

"What are you doing out here, Val?" he asks, striding across the room. His usual lopsided grin is gone. Max is my best friend, my boy, my brotha from another motha. But lately, he's been less friend and more Angry Fiancé Who's Not Allowed to Marry His Girl. I guess Big Guy still hasn't given the ex-collector a full pardon. I'm sure I haven't been given one, either. Difference is I don't care. And Valery does. She won't marry Max until Big Guy stamps his approval on the deal.

Lame.

"Did you hear the sound?" Valery asks him.

Max nods, but his glassy eyes never leave her yellow nightgown. I guess for him, a redhead in yellow is the equivalent of a bong hit.

"So we all heard it," I say. "What does it mean?"

Valery smiles too quickly, and the gesture says everything she doesn't. "Nothing. It's probably just the sirens messing around."

"The sirens?" I step closer and lower my voice. "You mean the hundred or so humans clinging to the ocean cliff outside the Hive like freaking cockroaches? The ones who work for the liberators? The ones who want to slaughter us in our sleep?"

"Don't be so dramatic." Red flips her hair off her shoulder. Max watches her hand fly through the air with fascination. Like she just did a magic trick and he can't believe his eyes.

"What was that sound, *Valery*?" I say, making sure to emphasize that I'm not using my nickname for her.

"It could be that…" she starts.

Charlie lays a hand on Valery's forearm. "What is it?"

"It's the sign Kraven's been waiting for," I say, suddenly understanding, and also wondering why it took me this long. "They're signaling to each other. And maybe to us."

Valery's head snaps in my direction.

"What's going on here?" a new voice booms through the Great Room.

Kraven. He strolls in with his ever-present quiet, unsettling demeanor. Kraven is the kind of guy who doesn't speak unless he feels it's absolutely necessary. He's the polar opposite of my Charlie.

"Well," I say, "Charlie and I are trying to have a date here, and the sirens are making all this racket with their war-starting. Valery and Max are sexually frustrated, and you are creeping everyone out with your slinking and mumbling."

Kraven locks eyes with Valery. She tilts her chin up, and he nods. It's a silent communication between the two of them, as if the rest of us don't exist.

"Not cool, Mr. Clean." I motion for the guy who served our first course. He plods over. It looks as if his pants are even higher than they were before. "Can we take these in our room?"

He bows low, and I wonder just how serious his wedgie is, because there's no way he made it out of that bow without serious butt floss.

"Aren't you concerned about the trumpet, Dante?" Valery asks.

"I'm concerned about a lot of things, Red. But mostly, I'm concerned with putting this food down my gullet."

And I'm concerned that the sound we heard might mean war is two weeks away.

And that my time with Charlie is now more precious than ever.

I take Charlie's hand and motion toward the hallway. She jerks her fingers out of mine and glares at me with accusation. "We can't pretend this isn't happening," she says, her voice unwavering.

I turn my whole body toward her. "Yes, we can. Every day for the past four months, something is always watching, always coming. I'm tired of it. We heard a blast. I'm sure it has significance. But the sirens are outside. And we're in here. Right now, at this very moment, we're not in any danger. If we want to take action, I'm in, but my guess is Kraven is going to say…"

I wave my hand toward him as if that's his cue. He stares me down, not at all pleased with my theatrics, but like the predictable dick lick he is, he says, "I must wait on a message from our king."

I roll my eyes and turn back toward Charlie. "There ya go. Always farting around and waiting, so we might as well enjoy one more night before they ransack this place. Please, Charlie, have dinner with me."

What I don't tell her, what I don't tell any of them, is that I'm going to single-handedly figure out what else is on our ancient scroll. The one Big Guy created millennia ago and gave to his angels, and the twin one he gave to hell. Kraven assures us there's more to the message than what Charlie read; the one that declared her the savior and Aspen the soldier. I haven't figured out how I'll uncover the rest of this invisible message, but there are too many sirens surrounding the pad for my tastes, and that scroll is my only hope.

And we need hope. Because if the collectors and sirens succeed in capturing Charlie, they'll have everything they need—Charlie and Aspen, body and soul. With those girls in their grasps, they could tip the scales in hell's favor, which will cause the ground to open and demons to spill out upon the earth without the use of dargon. No biggie. But if we win, we can save Aspen and beat the collectors and sirens back into the underworld where they belong and bring about the hundred years of peace Charlie's charity is meant to trigger.

So, yeah, I want a night of relaxation before either option happens, because for the love of bacon, I have a plan.

Charlie takes my hand. "It's just a night," she tells Valery.

Valery presses her lips together in a tight line, but she almost seems relieved. Like me brushing off the sound of a trumpet blasting through the Hive makes her feel more at ease. Max touches Valery's back and then shoots a death stare at Kraven. He moves to leave the Great Room and bumps Kraven's shoulder on his way out.

Kraven doesn't even glance in his direction. He's got that comatose thing going on again and looks a bit like someone's grandpa who's been sippin' the sizzurp.

I walk by Kraven and hold my clenched hand up. "Fist bump?"

Kraven looks at me with confusion.

"No? Aight. Check ya later, Una."

Charlie and I move toward the hallway, and I feel Kraven behind us. I *sense* him because we both wear liberator cuffs, but I also sense him the way I do a storm cloud. Kraven's got serious pent-up anger, and remembering the way he threw a siren off the cliff a few days ago makes me wary of having my back to him at all.

I speed up, but pause when I hear Annabelle's voice from behind me. Annabelle is Charlie's best friend, and has stuck by her side through everything. She even gave my ass half a chance when everyone else thought I was bad news, which I was…*am*. Girl's also decent on the basketball court. I'm better, naturally. But she's good enough.

"What's going on?" she asks.

Spinning on my heel, I find Annabelle looking back and forth between me and Charlie. Then she glances in the opposite direction and finds Kraven standing still as stone. His eyes rake over her. Inwardly, I groan. These two have been dancing around each other ever since we arrived at the Hive. Not sure why they can't admit they have feelings for one another. If it were me, I'd come out and say it. Then again, I'm a dude who's secure with his disgustingly present, it's-all-Charlie's-fault emotions.

Kraven's thing for Annabelle started when he realized she wouldn't back down from his intimidation tactics. He didn't want a human who wasn't necessary staying at the Hive, and she refused to leave Charlie's side. Heated arguments ensued, but Annabelle held her own against him, tit-for-tat. It wasn't long before Kraven's anger toward Annabelle morphed into intrigue. And lust. Definitely lust.

"Hey, K-Town," Annabelle tells the head liberator, "how's the meditation going?"

Kraven takes a small step toward her, and though Annabelle is doing a great job of pretending to be unaffected by him, her breath catches.

"You should go back to whatever you were just doing." Kraven's voice is deep with authority.

"No," Annabelle says. "Shan't."

Kraven moves toward her in the space of a single heartbeat. "Go back into that room and lock the door."

"Don't tell me what to do." Annabelle takes the last step that's left to take between them.

"Jaysus," I interrupt. "Sexual tension, much?"

"That's not what this is." Annabelle grimaces, her eyes never leaving Kraven's face. "He just thinks I'm going to get myself in trouble again. Won't let it go. That mess happened weeks ago."

"It happened nine days ago. And that siren could have killed you." Kraven grabs her wrist, and that's when I step in.

"Back the hell up, Kraven," I say. "Take your hand off her. I get that your trouser snake is angsty, but keep your temper in check."

Kraven's head whips in my direction. Then he looks back at Annabelle. "She shouldn't be here." He growls and leans in close to her. "*You* shouldn't be here."

"Oh, trust me," she says. "I don't want to be anywhere you are."

Kraven says something else, but his words are lost to me.

A sudden movement has caught my eye—a shadow at the end of the hall.

It's there, and then it's gone.

❧ 3 ❧

SHADOW WALKER

My jaw clenches and frost courses through my veins. It's like my entire body has broken through ice, and now I'm sinking, drowning in the winter sea.

"Kraven." I try to get his attention without speaking, but he keeps on keeping on with Annabelle. "Dude!"

"What's wrong, Dante?" Charlie squeezes my arm.

"I saw something," I answer, louder.

Kraven stops harassing Annabelle and turns his attention on me. "Are you sure?"

"Yes."

No.

"I saw a shadow." I cock my head in the direction of where I spotted it.

Kraven straightens and motions for me to follow. Screw that. I don't follow anyone. I'm not a sheep, I'm a shepherd with swag. I step in front of the mute meathead and start walking. Kraven and I both stop when we realize the chicks are following us.

"No," I say.

"Not happening," Kraven adds.

"I can help." Charlie raises her hands as evidence.

"We don't know if it will work again. Please, stay here. It's probably just Blue, lurking like a freak." But even as I try to shrug it off, adrenaline slithers through me like a viper. Whoever it was is getting away, and we need to go after them now.

"What is this, the 1950s?" Annabelle adds. "Girls belong in the kitchen and crap?"

"You'll just distract us," Kraven sneers.

"Bite me."

Kraven bites the air at her, and Annabelle's face opens with surprise. Then she socks him in the chest and storms in the opposite direction.

I turn to Charlie. "Please, babe."

Damn. If looks could kill.

Charlie storms after her friend. I want to go after my girl, admit it's not *her* that I doubt. I doubt myself. Look what I did to Aspen.

Kraven heads down the hallway. I move beside him, our shoulders nearly brushing the dark walls beside us. The floor beneath our steps is made of wood, and each step sounds like Albert Pujols cracking one out of the park. Right about now, I'd like some decent lighting, and I wonder at the Hive's Torture Dungeon design style.

When I first arrived here, I thought the Hive looked like a place built by carnies. It's like someone took eight different houses and pushed them together and on top of each other. The end result is a labyrinth of strange hallways and attics and rooms you wouldn't expect. Red says the house was built in a rush, but that it also serves as a safety precaution. The thought is that if a siren or collector broke in, they'd be much more likely to get lost than to find what they were looking for.

The only other security is a multitude of locked doors at the Hive's entrance, painted different colors every week, and small bells strung across the entire interior. Kraven didn't want to draw attention to the place by setting up an elaborate security system. So recently, the humans strung bells, and now a half-dozen humans called walkers stroll the interior night and day, keeping an eye out for our enemies. These humans have previous fighting experience. Most are retired military from various countries that have nowhere else to go. I don't think it's a fluke that Kraven hired them when he was setting up staff at the Hive, because now if anyone breaks in, we have trained humans to ring the bells and be our first line of defense. I don't hear the chimes now, but maybe that's because we're the first to spot this intruder.

Kraven and I move swiftly, with knees bent. When we get to the end of the hall, we pause and meet each other's gazes. I'll tell you one thing, whoever's around this corner has it coming. Homeboy's about to face an ex-demon packaged as the Hulk, and a liberator who's as unpredictable as a grenade.

I grin at Kraven, because even though I don't know what we're chasing, my heart is thumping, and my blood is coursing, and I feel manically *good*. Better than sitting still. Better than waiting.

We turn the corner.

Nothing.

Like Marines, we break apart and plunge forward, exploding into the branching rooms and exploring them with only our bodies as weapons. After we've searched the entire hallway, we move to the next, and the next. They're all empty, save for one. In one room, I find Blue. He flips me off. I return the favor and keep trucking.

"Where do these hallways lead?" I ask. I haven't been on this side of the house much. Our bedrooms—the ones that Annabelle, Blue, Charlie and me share—are on the other side and… My pulse races. "Which direction are we moving in? Away from Charlie's bedroom or toward?"

Kraven's gaze falls to the ground and then his eyes widen.

Crap.

We lurch at once, racing toward the other side of the house like a tidal wave of fury. If someone got her, I'll never forgive myself. Will it be over then? The liberators have Charlie's soul, and they have Aspen, body *and* soul. The savior and the soldier. In a war between heaven and hell, what happens if hell has all the artillery?

Demons on Earth, that's what.

As we run, I pull on my shadow, and Kraven follows suit. Now we're invisible forces barreling forward, using our cuffs as the ultimate camouflage.

My mind fires through the five liberator names as I run—Patrick, Kincaid, Zack, Anthony, and...

Rector.

If a siren broke into the Hive, these are the guys they report to. And though not much worries me, that does.

As we near our bedrooms, we slow to a stop. Annabelle and Charlie are standing like startled cats at the end of a hall. A bulb over-head buzzes, and the sound drives me mad. The shadow—a person—is closing in on them.

The guy is shorter than I am, but is built like a boulder. He has wet, matted hair, and I know instantly that it's a siren. He was probably bathing in the ocean, and when he heard the trumpet, he thought to himself, *Yeah, me first.*

I want to call out to Charlie. To tell her to stay still and let me surprise him. But when she spots me over his shoulder, she springs into action, as if *she* needs to protect *me.* She races toward the siren with a cry ripping from her throat. Her hands land on his chest, and she growls like an earthquake.

Nothing happens beneath her palms. No blue light.

Shock widens her eyes, and she leaps back.

Not quick enough.

The siren grabs her wrists and yanks her against him. I'm there in an instant, on him like a second skin. I drop my shadow and tear him away from my girl as Annabelle rushes forward to help in the fight.

Kraven's white-feathered wings break open from his back, slamming into the walls, and his shadow falls away. He grabs Annabelle and tosses her away from the siren as if she weighs nothing, which is pretty boss since the girl's built like a brick house.

As soon as Kraven puts distance between Annabelle and the siren, he's beside me, fighting against the siren. Though it's two against one, the siren fights with gusto. He breaks one arm away and slams me hard across the face. Pain bursts through my left cheekbone.

Oh, *hell* no.

I pop him a good one in the nose, and Kraven tackles him to the ground.

Everything happens like a flipbook. I see each scene as the page is turned, but nothing in detail. The siren is struggling against Kraven, and Kraven is getting all kinds of pissed off. Knowing Kraven won't hesitate to kill one of the liberators' soldiers, I struggle to get the siren to stop flailing. We could use this guy for questioning, and who knows what Kraven will do to him.

I reach down and grab the siren's bicep and tell Kraven to let me have him. At first, he fumbles to keep hold of the intruder in his hands, but when I see the wild gleam in Kraven's eyes, I bark for him to let the siren go. He does.

I stand tall on my feet and pull the siren up.

He stops fighting, and our eyes meet.

"Holy hell," I mutter.

I recognize the guy in my grasp. It isn't a siren.

It's a collector.

"Zack," I breathe.

Using my bewilderment to his advantage, Zack breaks away and takes three quick strides down the hallway. Annabelle and Charlie press themselves against the wall, but he isn't moving toward them. He turns and meets my gaze. He grins. It's a long smile on a wide, thin-lipped mouth. Hair hangs over his forehead so that a thick strand of it sticks to his eyeball.

"*Semunla Katra*," he says.

I have no idea what gibberish he's spewing, but I lunge toward him.

Then I stop cold.

A black hole opens in the ground like a gaping wound. He waves at me like he's a freaking pageant queen, then takes a small step and drops through it and out of sight.

The hole closes over his head, and he's gone.

⊰4⊱

TALK AMONG BOOKS

I'm frozen like an icicle in the ninth ring of hell.

"Who was that?" Kraven asks in a wary tone.

"A collector." I silently curse myself for not opening my mind to sense another cuff. Because once I realized who it was, I sensed that cuff with screaming clarity. It was a careless mistake.

Turning around, I spot someone I don't know standing near the girls. My legs move before my brain even processes what I'm doing. Then I'm standing between New Guy and Charlie. I grab the guy by his plaid shirt and shuffle him back and into a wall. "Who are you?"

"Whoa, calm down, steroids," he says in a slight, British accent. "Name's Paine, and I'm going to give you some if you don't ease up on the death grip, *capiche*?"

His words hint at smooth confidence, but he speaks in a submissive voice. It's the voice of someone desperate to please others.

I barely recognize it.

Kraven speaks up. "He's one of us, Dante."

Paine nods at his ankle where I imagine a gold cuff must lie hidden.

"A liberator?" I ask. Paine grins sheepishly, and I let go of his shirt. "Don't be sneaking up on us like that again or you'll be taking a dirt nap."

"Sorry," he says, and seems to mean it. He offers his hand. It's wide and calloused, and I respect that it appears he's done real work in his short life. I shake it, feeling like an arse.

The guy looks to be in his early twenties and has a shaved head, though I can still spot the reddish-blond color he's trying to hide. Paine's eyes are set a bit too far apart, and he has long, chick-like lashes. His forehead protrudes, giving him a slight caveman appearance, and his body is that of a wrestler's, like he's itching to take someone to the mat. Overall, Paine kind of looks like a model, someone girls would dig because he's strangely attractive. That's not me. I'm hot like a bucket of fried chicken, baby.

"Didn't mean to surprise you guys," Paine says. But he isn't looking at me. He's looking at Annabelle. "Are you okay?"

"Me?" Annabelle's voice cracks as she points toward herself.

"Yeah, you." Paine steps away from me and toward Anna. "You almost took a fall there." Paine breaks eye contact with her to glare at Kraven. I'd almost forgotten Kraven had tossed Annabelle away like a dirty diaper.

Annabelle runs a hand over her short, ink-black hair. Her quirked eyebrow is barely visible above hard-cut bangs. "I'm okay."

I can practically hear Kraven growling low in his chest. "Stop talking. All of you. A collector infiltrated the Hive." He looks pointedly at Charlie. "Everyone will meet in the library in ten minutes."

"And disappeared through a hole in the floor," I add.

"What?" Kraven says.

"A collector infiltrated the Hive *and disappeared through a goddamn hole in the floor*. You forgot the last part."

"Don't take His name in vain, Dante Walker. Not here." Kraven glances at Annabelle like he wants to add something else. Then he strides away, his wings folding back into his body.

He wasn't surprised, I realize. Kraven didn't even flinch when that collector used a freaking *portal* or whatever to disappear. Me, on the other hand, I'm freaking out, which roughly equates to a long sigh.

I'm not into overreaction.

Charlie presses herself against my chest as Paine and Annabelle walk away together, chatting awkwardly.

"Charlie," I mutter into her hair. "Why did you do that? Why did you lunge at him?"

"I thought I could do that thing with my hands." Charlie inspects her palms, and I inspect her purple skirt. Nothing gets me going like a skirt. Or bacon. Or any sliver of skin on any part of Charlie's body. Jaysus, she's just so innocent. Makes me want to ravage her with my darkness, and I know just how disturbing that sounds.

"Dante?"

"Hmm?"

"We should head to the library." Something tells me this isn't the first time she's said this, but it's all good. Everyone needs to take a mental fantasy break now and then. That's what Kit Kat's really selling.

Charlie hooks her arm in mine, and we stroll like royalty toward dusty ass books that I have no interest in whatsoever. Charlie's into them, though. Says it helps to escape her head, to forget about Grams and Aspen and be somewhere else for a while. I say give me a cigarette, a neat scotch like hustlers drink, and Charlie in my bed. I may have died at seventeen, but I have the heart of a thirty-year-old Viking.

When we spill into the library, a small smile touches Charlie's mouth. I'm not sure why. There's enough dust in here to make Oklahoma farmers extremely nervous. Books clutter the shelves, floor to ceiling, but they aren't organized in any fashion. Some spines face in and others out. Some books teeter in big stacks out of reach, while smaller stacks litter the floor.

The library is similar to the rest of the Hive: chaos. It's like someone came in with a wheelbarrow of books, then starting fly-balling them across the room one at a time, which sounds like my kind of fun with literature. A dozen or more light bulbs on strings drip down, creating the world's tackiest chandelier. It looks like the multicolored bulbs decided to off themselves—death by hanging. I don't blame them, considering their location.

Valery and Max are already in the room, sitting on a brown leather couch that's seen better days. I nod what's up to Max, and he returns the gesture with questionable enthusiasm. If before he was sad about being unable to commit to Valery, now he seems angry. It makes me angry, too. Why shouldn't they be able to wed? Max has more than proven that he doesn't work for Lucifer—err, Lucille— anymore.

The Quiet Ones, two women who sport hideous brown dresses, stride in. Actually, they don't so much stride as they do float. They're liberators, but from what I overheard, they made a choice to serve the soldier and savior versus fighting in the war. I call bullcrap.

Because there are few liberators, eight including Paine, they'll be needed, and saying you'd rather wash dishes and sew clothing isn't right. Then again, I remember the way they cared for Charlie and me after we were hurt following our stint in hell. So it's hard to be too upset.

Paine walks in, all shoulders and thighs, and glances around the room, not finding what he's searching for. When Annabelle enters the room a moment later, the disappointed look on his face vanishes. Blue is by Annabelle's side. He sneers at me, but I only turn away. I don't feel like dealing with his resentment right now, not after what I saw that collector do.

When Kraven comes in, he's walking with someone I've seen only a few times around the Hive. His name is Neco, and he's got a buzz cut and forearms that make me think of old Popeye cartoons. He and two walkers administered our test a couple of weeks ago to demonstrate whether Blue and I had passed the self-defense sector of training. Neco is the eighth and final liberator in the Hive. Outside of him, there's Blue, Valery, Kraven, the Quiet Ones, Paine, and yours truly.

Kraven stands in the center of the room, his back straight, chin tilted. The man of few words looks like he has a handful of them now.

"We'll resume training first thing in the morning," he states.

"Come again?" I say.

His gaze meets mine. *You heard what I said* is what he replies without speaking.

"Yeah, Cyborg, listen." I dig my fists into my pockets to keep from throwing one across his face. Him and his damn training. "A collector just appeared and then vanished through an anus in the floor. We can't sit around learning how to fight. We need to take action."

Everyone who wasn't there to see the collector gasps. Kraven fills them in on what happened in a calm tone, and though I can't believe my eyes, everyone seems comforted after he's finished speaking.

"There will be six sectors of training and an additional course if you pass the others strongly enough." He continues with his spiel as if the collector's ability to pop into our joint at any time is simply a minute obstacle to overcome. Nothing we can't handle. I'll give him props for confidence. "In the past, we've undergone training separately. Starting tomorrow, we proceed through each sector together. We'll need to learn how to battle as one. We need to understand each other's strengths, as well as our weaknesses."

Valery steps forward. "So if we've already completed a sector—"

"Then you'll be repeating it."

Valery nods and steps back. What is up with this guy? Why doesn't anyone question him? I raise my hand like I'm back in high school. *Gag me.* "So we're going to stay here in this easily infiltrated crap hole? And we're going to train? These are the orders you've been waiting for from Big Guy? The man upstairs is telling us to stick around while collectors are popping up like moles? What about launching a counter attack? What about making a plan for war?"

For once, Kraven appears nervous. He shifts inside his white jacket. "There is a reason we must remain here, Dante, especially now that war has been signaled. We have two weeks to prepare before the day our king ordained takes place."

The liberators grow silent at Kraven's confirmation that the trumpet we heard was the signal we'd waited for. And that in two weeks' time, the war between heaven and hell will begin.

"We remain here because we know the Hive's layout better than our enemy, and that provides protection. And we don't launch an attack because we are working on our king's timetable. But trust me, our day will come. Until then, there will be additional patrol as you sleep. As always, the bells will ring if there's a break-in."

I accept his answer, but it seems to me Kraven is auditing his answers. If he insists we remain inside and train, there must be more to the Hive than he lets on. Out of all the places in the world for us to prepare for battle, why here?

Kraven pulls himself up taller and looks to the arched doorway. "Oh, good, you've arrived."

All heads turn to see who's entering the room.

My eyebrows nearly touch my hairline at the sight of him.

✦5✦

OLD DUDE

A dude as old as air shuffles into the room. He's got tufts of white hair sprouting from every part of his body, and his arms are way, *way* too long for his torso. He looks like he's moments from swinging through the Amazon rainforest and biting into a banana. But the most amazing part of this dude is his ears; they're as big as my palms. Many old people are hard of hearing, but I bet this guy could hear a beetle fart from six hundred miles away.

Also, he's wearing a robe. It's red. The moment I spot it, I forget all about him looking like a monkey with semi-sonic hearing and toss him insta-respect for rolling like Hugh Hefner.

"This is Oswald," Kraven announces. "He's a retired professor who taught mythology. He specialized in demon and angel folklore."

Oswald bobs his head as Kraven speaks like, *Dude's not lying.*

"I've let him know about our goal to analyze ancient documents," Kraven continues. "Oswald understands our desire to study here, in privacy, before handing the information over to our investor. I've given him the basement area to work."

So what Kraven's saying is he made up a whole lot of bull crap about some rich MoFo who's into folklore and hired us to research the subject. Glancing at Oswald, at his blue-gray eyes and knowing smile, I doubt he bought a single word of Kraven's cover. I bet, just like the humans working the Hive, he knows something is up. But like I've always said, nothing keeps a secret safe like a mouthful of cash.

"Oswald, would you like to fill us in on what you've learned?" Kraven takes a couple of steps back and waves his arm in front of him, gesturing that the old man can take the floor.

Oswald looks like a kid who got caught with his prick in his hand. His face flushes. "Umm, I—yes, yes," he stutters. "Kraven has asked me to study the scroll you folks found."

He means the twin scrolls; one for the heavens, one for the underworld, each only readable by Charlie and Aspen. I'm all ears waiting to see what the guy has learned and more than a little thrilled that Kraven brought someone in to research it. I wonder if he thinks, like I do, that the answers to winning the war are on there.

"The scroll appears to be blank, but I have located the correct spoken words to uncover the message."

"I'm sorry, what?" I ask as Charlie leans into me. Without thinking, I wrap my arm around her.

Oswald spins around. After he takes me in, he says, "You must be Dante. It's a pleasure to me you."

"It always is," I say. "What is this you're talking about? Saying something out loud to uncover a message on the scroll?"

Soft murmurs erupt around the library. Kraven implies Oswald doesn't know about us, about the freaky stuff we can do as liberators, but what the old man's talking about sounds more like—"

"It sounds a bit like magic, I know." Oswald shows us his open hand as if to admit it seems crazy. To me, it sounds about as crazy as corpses eating and breathing courtesy of gold ankle jewelry.

"How can this be? We would know about this." Valery looks pointedly at Kraven before returning her gaze to Oswald as if remembering the front. "What I mean to say is we've been studying this scroll for a long time."

Oswald wraps his arms around himself. The gesture looks feminine what with his red robe and all. "I've made this my life's work. And I can tell you now, when it comes to things like this, the sacred and historical, you have to keep an open mind. It's said that monks kept messages hidden within the pages of numerous tomes. Revealing them is a mixture of the right words. Some say it isn't magic, that it's the heat from our breath that makes a delicate ink appear. But I disagree. I believe there are a great number of things we don't understand, because we won't allow ourselves to believe." Oswald taps his temple as a closing point.

"So you've seen what the scroll says about the soldier? About how important she is according to the text?" Blue glares at me with vengeance as he asks this.

"I've read about the soldier and the savior, yes," Oswald admits. "And about other things, too. About doorways that can be opened—"

"Let's talk more in the morning," Kraven interrupts. "It's late."

I realize Kraven has basically told us to retire, but I'm barely listening. Instead, I'm concentrating on what Oswald exposed, that there is definitely more on that scroll than Charlie was able to read, because I certainly don't remember anything about doorways. Maybe it could explain how that collector got in here. The back of my neck tingles imagining what else is on there, what else Oswald knows that I don't.

"Meet in the training room at seven o'clock in the morning." Kraven tucks his blond hair behind his ears and pulls in a long breath. "Expect it to be a long day."

Everyone begins filing out of the room, off to bed like good boys and girls. What the H? I can't believe no one else cares about what else Oswald knows.

I turn to Charlie. "Can you believe this?"

I expect Charlie to agree with me, or to tell me to shut my trap and follow someone else's lead for once in my life. Instead, she kisses me. We're alone in the library, and her hands are crawling up my spine, and my heart is slamming inside my ribs.

The past few minutes expire in a rush as Charlie replaces every last thing in my mind. My fingers trace the curve of her hips, the dip of her waistline. Then I run my hands back down and grasp her thighs. She moans softly into my mouth.

"I'm starting to like libraries," I mumble against her.

She giggles and reaches up on tiptoes.

"Let's go to bed," she says low in her throat. I like to imagine she's saying it like an older, experienced woman, because technically, she is older. She and Aspen turned eighteen not long ago.

I don't even reply. I scoop her into my arms and carry her toward our bedroom suite. She laughs, and the sound makes me feel like superman. Even though our destination is some distance from the library, with her lips nibbling at my ear, the journey is over too quickly.

I all but kick the door down, and thankfully, Blue and Annabelle are already in their separate rooms. There's a small lounge area in the center with dilapidated, mismatched furniture, and branching off from there are four smaller rooms. Each one has a rustic dresser, a single nightstand, and a bed. The dresser and nightstand could burn to the ground for all I care.

Charlie and I fumble into the room we've claimed as ours. My chest feels like it's engulfed in flames, and other parts of my body do, too. Ever since Aspen stayed in hell, Charlie has slept in Annabelle's room. She said it wasn't right that we enjoyed each other while our friend was in such a terrible place. I understood what she was saying, but I'm not sure I believed her reasoning. Maybe what she said is true. Or maybe it's that she blames me for Aspen remaining in hell.

Charlie stops before the bed, and for a moment, I miss the flush of her cheeks. The color that bloomed in them before the soul contract made her perfect. If she was her old self, I'd be able to see the excitement written across her face.

We're both breathing hard, and our eyes never leave each other's faces. She reaches out, and my body shudders in anticipation. Her palm comes to a rest over the center of my chest. It's like she's feeling for my soul, like if she concentrates hard enough, she can cradle it in her hands. The dead aren't supposed to have souls, not even liberators, and I sometimes wonder what it means that I've been allowed to keep mine.

But right now, all I can think about is Charlie standing before me. I groan against the feather-light feel of her touch. And before I can stop myself, before I even know what I'm doing, a slight burning smell wraps its arms around us.

Long, black wings slide from my back. I arch them over Charlie and use them to pull her closer. She curls into herself and lays her head over my heart. My arms wrap around her waist, and I feel inky feathers brush against my own skin.

I nudge her cheek until she lifts her face, and then I close my mouth over hers. Something changes in our kiss. Before, leading up until this moment, our kisses were hungry. Now they are tender. I pull my arms out from around her and use them to clasp her face, my thumbs brushing the smooth skin beneath her eyes. Charlie's hips press against me, and I almost lose my grip on this gentle moment, almost allow the monster inside of me to devour her whole.

She pulls back suddenly. "I should go to bed."

Her words blast like shrapnel inside my head. I don't want her to leave this room, don't want to sleep another night without her. But I won't push her to stay.

She runs a hand through my hair, and I close my eyes against the sensation. Then she touches a place on my outer arm. She fingers the tattoo there, the one of a tree rising from my elbow and branching over my shoulder. Her hand lingers there too long, and it's as if she's telling me something. "You're worthy of the cuff you're wearing,

Dante. He believes in you, even if you don't."

My wings open on impulse, and I step back as if stricken.

I don't know where that came from, and I'm not sure I understand what she means. We talk about a lot of things, but my lack of heavenly dedication isn't one of them. She's always known that everything I do is for her and not because of a higher calling. And she's never once brought up my nonexistent relationship with Big Guy.

Charlie kisses her fingers and touches them to my lips. I watch her as I would a lion in tall grass, with a mixture of intrigue and fear. How can her words affect me so much?

She leaves through the bathroom that connects this room with Annabelle's room. I don't understand why she went from sexy time to *that*. Charlie still dwells on Aspen being gone, that I know. I dwell on it, too. But what was that about him believing in me?

What a bunch of crap. I mean, I love the girl, but that's manure of the smelliest kind.

I consider taking a cold shower or maybe plunging myself in a tub of ice, but opt instead to try and sleep off my craving for Charlie. With the smallest of smiles, I decide there's enough pent-up desire in this house to set off an atom bomb.

Once I'm in bed, and I've calmed myself down, I turn over her words again. Big Guy believing in me—what bull. I mean, next she'll be telling me he actually cares. Like, that Big Guy *loves* me and crap. I'll tell you one thing right now, I don't care how merciful they say he is, or how loving he can be, I know the truth. No one forgives that easily, especially someone they say is all-knowing. I've done enough rebellious things that can be seen with the naked eye to make a prison warden blush. And this guy is supposed to know our thoughts, too? Charlie says he believes in me. Thinks I'm worthy of a liberator cuff.

False.

I wipe a hand across my brow and then tug at my hair. I toss onto my right side and throw my fist into the pillow beneath my head. Then

I flip onto my left side and grit my teeth.

Nothing helps.

I can't get the damn thought out of my head.

That Big Guy could care about me after the life I've led.

Somewhere late into the night, I finally succumb to sleep. When I open my eyes again, Aspen is waiting for me.

⇥6⇤

YOU'RE ALREADY DEAD

"What took you so long?" Aspen takes a drag on a cigarette. When she exhales, smoke drifts out of her mouth like fingers.

"Had trouble falling asleep," I answer.

Aspen is sitting on a boulder. Her knees are pulled against her chest, and she's gazing out over a dark chasm. I walk to the ledge and glance down. The expanse goes on forever, and gray spikes line the floor of the crater. Along the chasm's teeth, bluish-black fog swirls. The effect is like staring into the mouth of a great white shark.

I've been seeing Aspen every night since I left her in hell. Though the last couple of nights, the dreams have felt more real and have lasted longer. I haven't spilled to anyone about my seeing Aspen in my sleep, and I don't intend to. But truth be told, she's the real reason I believe the key to our success lies in the scroll.

"Why are we always somewhere like this?" I ask.

"You tell me," she says with a wry smile. "We're in your head."

"It doesn't feel that way, Aspen," I say. "It feels like we're in yours."

Her smile grows, and suddenly the world around us changes. Now the sky is so blue it feels like we're swimming in it. There are no clouds, not even a sun. Just a canvas of blue so bright it sings. Though Aspen is grinning, I can see the intense concentration in the fold between her eyes. Her shoulders fall like she's tired of holding the ruse, and a long, jagged line forms across the sky. It shatters without a sound, and pieces of blue fall to the earth like shards of glass. The sky is dark again; the chasm has swallowed all the blue and buried it beneath its belly.

"I miss you, Aspen." I sit down next to her on the boulder. Aspen hands over her cigarette, and I take a drag. Her hair, black as death, falls over her shoulders and stretches toward her hips. The diamond stud glitters in her nose, and her hands are embraced by green, fingerless gloves.

"Let's not talk about that." Aspen takes her cigarette back and pulls on it. She exhales, and as smoke streams from her nostrils, she says. "Tell me about Charlie. How is she?"

"She pretends everything will work out, but I know better. She can't stop thinking about you." My stomach clenches. "I can't, either."

Aspen points at me with her cigarette. "You know the drill. If you start that again, I'll leave. What's done is done. It was my decision."

"You mean *I'll* leave," I say. "It's my dream, right? My head?"

Aspen smiles again. "You wouldn't ever know, would you?"

I shake my head. "'Spose not."

When I glance at Aspen's hair again, there are tiny black spiders crawling up and down the length of it. It looks a little like she's underwater, her hair rippling with the tide. One scurries across her cheek. I try to brush it away, but it disappears inside her ear before I can. Aspen never even flinches.

"Aspen there are fucking spiders in your hair," I say. But even as I say it, I'm not that concerned. It's only a dream. She's told me time and again.

I never quite believe her.

"Have you learned the words?" she asks.

"You mean on the scroll?"

She doesn't answer. She never answers that question. In a blast of movement, Aspen's head snaps in my direction. She opens her mouth and speaks a phrase I've long memorized. "You're already dead. Go back to sleep."

I don't bolt upright in bed. I don't even open my eyes. I just wake up and lay there in my bed, alone, imagining I feel a spider crawling across my knee.

• • •

When I can't fall back asleep, I get up from bed and pull on a t-shirt. Then I wake Charlie and tell her about the dream. I'm not sure why I decide to now after keeping it to myself for so many nights. But the war has been signaled, and she's a part of this war. Also, she's my girlfriend. The last time I tried to shield her from harm, she ended up in Zack's brutal grasp.

She listens quietly until I reach the end of the story. "So you think she's talking about the scroll?"

I nod.

"It makes sense. Kraven wouldn't be bringing in that guy if he didn't believe the same thing. I wish you'd told me sooner, though, Dante."

"So you don't think I'm crazy?"

Charlie holds up her hands. "I stopped believing in crazy when blue lights shot from my hands." She laughs. "Or maybe when a boy crawled through my window at night and showed me how his cuff could turn him invisible."

I do it now to hear her laugh again, then I snake my invisible arms around her.

"Hey, not fair."

I shake off my shadow and stand up. "I want to talk to Oswald while everyone is asleep. See what he knows. You up for it?"

"Oh, we really shouldn't." She says this, but she's also smiling and pulling on a hoodie the Quiet Ones gave me.

Looking at Charlie, it's hard to breathe. Because as much as we smile and joke, we both know time together is precious. We don't know how much longer we'll be safe, especially with collectors popping up unexpectedly. Or with sirens hovering outside. Or with war only two weeks away.

I hug her once, quickly, to mask my fear and satiate my hunger to keep her against me forever, and then we leave the room. Kraven said he gave Oswald the basement area to study the scroll, so that's where we go. We run into several humans on the way there, all who look like zombies walking the crude mansion. Their eyes are blurry from lack of sleep, and I wonder if I gave them a bowl of brains, if that wouldn't perk them right up.

I knock once on a door that's half off its hinges. The Hive is nothing if not built to last. When no one answers, I push the door open, half expecting Playboy bunnies to be hopping around Oswald's silk robe collection. Since it's the middle of the night, Oswald might be sleeping, and if he is, we're going to seem really unstable tiptoeing around his bed while he slumbers.

There are more lamps in the room than I have ever seen in my short, mind-blowing life. Some are floor lamps and others lounge on desks and shelves and boxes. A few stand without shades, naked for the world to see. Others have shades that are too big, or too small, and some that are *just* right. The bases color the room in different hues, and the bulbs cast a maddening light across the entire area. I change my mind on the whole sleeping thing. There's no way someone can get shut eye up in here.

"Whoa," Charlie says from beside me. "That's a lot of light bulbs."

"I expected you two would come," someone says.

I spin on bare feet and spot Oswald standing near one of two desks. There's a mischievous glint in his eyes.

"And so we have," I respond. "We've got questions for you."

Oswald motions to mismatched chairs, and Charlie and I sit down. The old man sits across from us and tucks his robe around his frail frame so his junk doesn't fall out.

No sense in beating around the proverbial bush. "What else have you found on the scroll?"

"Why?" Oswald picks up a book from a table near his left arm. He flips it open and pretends to peruse the pages. The action tells me he's unaffected I'm here. In actuality, though, I think he's anxious. "Is it important?"

I narrow my gaze. "No, it's just I'd like to know."

"Kraven says you're one of his best pupils," Oswald says to me without looking up, his voice shaky.

I bounce between feeling prideful that Kraven said *best*, and anger that he thinks of me as a *pupil*. "Doesn't surprise me. I'm pretty gangster."

Oswald finally glances up. "Dante Walker, you're about as gangster as Will Smith."

"What's on that scroll?" I demand.

"Why?" he counters, his confidence blooming. "It's just a piece of paper."

"Nice robe, Hefner. Where's your Viagra?"

"Nice attitude, tough guy. Mommy issues?"

I stand up.

So does Oswald.

"Who are you really?" I growl.

"Just an old man with a flair for fashion."

"Covering your wrinkly ass in a bed sheet isn't fashion," I say. "It's called giving up."

"Who are *you*, Dante?" Oswald says.

"I'm whatever Kraven says I am."

"No," Oswald says carefully. "You're a collector turned liberator. You're a demon with wings who's in love with a savior."

"Oh, damn," Charlie says from her seat. "Pow, pow!"

❖ 7 ❖

LANGUAGE OF THE DEAD

Oswald sets down his book and appears nervous again. It's like he had a streak of confidence and now it's extinct.

"Did I get that about right?" he asks, his gaze averted.

I struggle to catch my breath, my jaw grazing the dust-covered floor. I suspected the old dude knew more than Kraven thought he did. But now I *know*, know. I glance at Charlie to gauge her reaction, but she doesn't seem all that surprised. "That was pretty baller, Oswald."

He smiles to himself but still doesn't meet my gaze. The old man shuffles across the room to one of the desks and straightens a stack of papers.

"Do you know everything?" I ask. His back is to me, but I see the way his head bobs. "You know who we work for and what we're trying to do?" He nods. "You know about Aspen and where I went with her?"

"I know everything," he confirms.

Charlie stands up. "Do you know about my ability?"

"Yep," he answers. "That, too."

"Who told you?" I ask.

Oswald checks the door like he's ensuring no one is there. He should try listening instead. Those honking ears of his couldn't possibly miss anything. "Kraven told me."

My brow furrows. "Why did he lie to us then?"

Oswald shrugs.

I step closer, and he fidgets with the papers even more. They're about as straight as they're going to get is what I want to tell him. "So why did you tell us?"

The old guy turns his body so that he faces us head on. "What you did to try and save her soul…that was very brave." He motions toward Charlie. "I told Kraven that he should make you both aware of who I really was."

"And who are you really?" Charlie asks.

"I'm a scholar. That part is true. He just didn't tell you that I already believed in all of this, in all of you, before he found me."

My stomach twists thinking about the collector who nearly attacked Charlie earlier tonight. "You spoke about unlocking words on the scroll. Something about doorways."

Oswald chews his nails. "They're called vultrips. They act as portals between hell and earth. As I understand it, there is only one entrance to hell that you are familiar with."

I nod, remembering Aspen and me spilling our blood onto the roots of a spruce tree, and then watching as a black hole stretched open.

"There have been times in the past where those of your kind, those who wear the dargon and call themselves collectors, were able to step onto earth from any point." Oswald pulls on one of his monstrously big earlobes with his monstrously long arm. "You may remember some of these times from your history lessons: The Bubonic Plague, the Great Depression, the rise of the Third Reich."

A cold sweat breaks across my chest. "How does it happen?" I ask. Oswald's gaze flicks across the room wildly. He doesn't want to tell us. "Answer me, old man."

The guy shuffles his feet and avoids my eyes and then... And then he starts turning in a circle.

"What are you doing?" Charlie asks.

Oswald turns a little faster. "Oh. Oh, I don't know if I'm supposed to say anything."

I've seen nervous tics before—Charlie's cheeks turning red is one of them—but this is something else.

I grab the guy's shoulders and stop him in place. "First off, don't do that again. The turning in circles thing? Super weird. Second, tell us what you know. The answer is obviously weighing on you."

Oswald shivers in my grasp, and I let go, giving him space to breathe. I can't believe this is the same dude who told me to my face that I have mommy issues.

"There's a traitor among you," he whispers.

My legs go numb. "What?"

"Who?" Charlie asks at the same time.

"In order for the vultrips to be opened, someone from the other side must speak the words. I don't know who."

"A liberator?" I ask.

He shakes his head. "It can be anyone, but the words must be spoken with treachery in their heart. Scholars believe there are a great many things these words can do that we don't know about, but this we do."

Traitor. The word bounces around my head like a bullet ricocheting inside a steel room. "What are these words? What do they say?"

Oswald strides toward the second desk. He touches a glass box and gazes inside to what must be the scroll. "There's a dead language demons and angels speak. Some of what is hidden on this scroll requires those words to be revealed." He turns to me and Charlie. "It's the same language used to open vultrips."

Charlie takes a step in his direction. "How do we stop it from happening?"

"Find the one whispering them open," he replies.

"What will you do?" I ask.

"Me?" He touches a finger to his saggy man boob. "I'll try to reveal the rest of what remains on this scroll. I've unlocked some— the part about the vultrips—but there's more here, and I need that in order to help in your impending war."

I pace the basement, dodging lamps and stacks of books as I walk. "How will you find the words that unlock the scroll?"

"There are bits and pieces in old books, most of which are in the Hive's library. That's why I came here, to sort through them."

I'm exhausted by our conversation, by learning that there's a traitor among us, that the doorways to hell aren't going anywhere until we find out who's opening them, and that the way to unlock the scroll's message resides inside the Hive.

I slap Oswald on the shoulder, and he shows every last faux tooth in his mouth. "That's some pretty scary shit you just told me. But I'm glad you did. I won't tell Kraven I know." I run a hand along my jaw. "Let's hit the sack, huh? Charlie and I've got training tomorrow, and you've got to work on that scroll."

Charlie glances at the scroll once more, perhaps wondering why it is she could read one part, but not the others. She sighs and comes to stand by my side. I run my thumb over the back of her neck, and we head toward the door. As we're leaving, I see a book on an iron table. I pick it up. It's the same book Blue had in his hand when he confronted me in the hallway. An old western novel that Oswald can't possibly need.

"Did Blue lend this to you?" I ask. "He was reading it, I think."

The old guy's shoulders tighten. He mutters something.

"Oswald?"

Oswald starts turning in circles.

8

KICK OF CONFIDENCE

After I wake, I find Annabelle sitting in the lounge area. She's the only one up.

"What up?" she says around a mouthful of egg.

The Quiet Ones are standing nearby. I thank them for the grub and then grab a bagel and seventy-three pieces of bacon, give or take. The orange juice is good, and the bacon is better, but my stomach won't take it without complaint. Not after what Oswald told Charlie and me last night.

Traitor.

Annabelle looks chipper this morning. She's wrangled her dark hair into a stubby ponytail with the help of bobby pins galore, and she's wearing black yoga wear. And black tennis shoes. And black wristbands. She looks like a ninja.

"You think Kraven's going to let you train?" I flick my fingers toward her get up.

She leans back, eyeing me over her juice. "It's happening."

"He wouldn't let you train before. What's changed?"

"It's happening," she repeats.

I laugh. "Annabelle, you're my kind of awesome."

Annabelle beams. She pushes herself forward and offers her closed fist. I bump it. We don't often express how we feel about one another, but I know Annabelle respects me. And I've got mad love for the girl. She cares for Charlie, and I care for her.

I take a bite of my bagel, chew, swallow. "Are you scared, Anna?"

Her face rises from her plate, her eyes wide with surprise. She considers me for a long moment. "Yeah, I am. That collector appeared out of nowhere. Do you think it'll happen again?"

I bite the inside of my cheek and glance away.

Annabelle sighs. "They're after Charlie, huh? I barely slept last night. Just watched Charlie. Girl slept like the dead, like there aren't demons popping up out of thin air searching for her."

I think how Annabelle may have slept more than she realizes since she doesn't know Charlie left the room. "I'll sit in tonight after Charlie falls asleep."

Annabelle looks like she's arguing with herself. Like on one hand she wants to say she can take care of Charlie, and on the other she's dog tired and wouldn't mind the help. "Okay," she finally relents. "That'd be cool. For Charlie's sake."

I roll up my napkin and chunk it at her. She swats it out of the air like she's blocking a shot. "Still got your touch."

"Napkinball or basketball, these hands will always throw your crap away." She crosses her arms and purses her lips like she's a thug and this is her house, her court.

I laugh and head toward her room where Charlie still slumbers. For whatever reason, I can't think of it as Charlie's room, even if she has spent the last ten nights there. I shut the door behind me and sit beside her on the bed. She's asleep on her stomach, her head tilted to the side. Blond hair kisses her cheek and sticks to her forehead. I brush it away and lay my lips there instead.

"Angel," I whisper. "It's time to get up."

Charlie groans.

I chuckle and lay down beside her, wrapping my arms around her waist. My body reacts immediately. It's almost embarrassing how much I ache for her.

I'm waiting for her to scold me, but she just laughs into her pillow. "I'd ask if you're happy to see me, but…"

I pull the pillow from beneath my head and hit her with it. She explodes with laughter and rolls over. I drop back down beside her and the smile leaves her beautiful face. When I run my thumb over her full, pink lips, she closes her eyes.

"I wish I could stay in bed with you all day like this," she says.

Her words are like a hand around my heart, squeezing. It feels almost euphoric hearing her talk like that. When she does, it's like we're back in her pink bedroom, seconds from jumping on the bed and raiding Gram's kitchen.

"Did you sleep okay last night?" Her eyes flutter open.

I gaze at those beautiful eyes. I can't help thinking how they looked behind her glasses before the soul contract corrected her vision. They were atrocious frames, but with the right style, she could have looked emo-awesome.

Charlie pulls herself close and kisses me. Her fingers trail up my neck and into my hair. A deep rumble emanates from my throat, and I tug her closer. My hands are everywhere at once, running over her back, grasping her hips, cupping her rear, and using it to draw her near. She ends our kiss too soon and lays her head against my shoulder.

"We're safe because you're here," she says.

It's the absolute best thing she could have said. It kicks confidence into my entire body and gifts me this sense of calm. She's right. I will never let anything bad happen to her. Not again.

I raise her chin and ensure she sees I'm serious. "I will protect you with my last dying breath."

"Again," she says.

My face pulls together with confusion.

"You died fighting for me once before, Dante Walker."

She's right, I suppose. I broke my collector cuff off to save her from Rector and the other collectors. It's the biggest sacrifice I've ever made, considering collectors without dargon die a final death. No afterlife. No hell. Just an eternity of silence. Being a liberator is different, though. It's something about the dargon, Kraven says. Big Guy blesses it so that if it's removed, he can make a choice about our bodies. He can bring us straight to the heavens, send us to Judgment, or damn us to eternal silence. I've heard he's never damned a past liberator, but hey, there's a first time for everything.

"You think Oswald made anymore headway on the scroll after we left last night?"

I hear her question, but I don't want to think about it. I want to pretend war is make-believe, and the only thing that's real is Charlie. I hug her close and breathe in the smell of her skin. Then I pull her head beneath me and rest my chin on her head. We're still embracing each other when Annabelle snorts at the end of the bed. "What should I call this, *Demon Porn*? Wait, Charlie does freaky stuff with her hands. I should work that in the title somehow."

This time it's Charlie who tosses the pillow. She gets up after Annabelle smacks it away the same way she did my napkin.

"Why are you dressed all in black?" Charlie asks Annabelle.

"Don't get her started," I say.

Fifteen minutes later, the Quiet Ones are leading us toward the training room. Annabelle and Blue trail behind, and Charlie walks next to me, still knuckling her eyes from sleep.

I hear voices up ahead, and as we close in on our destination, my blood spikes. Every muscle in my body twitches anticipating physical exertion. There are a few things I don't excel at, things like looking fugly, but I'm a champ at anything that includes the word *training*. My hands curl and uncurl, and my focus ripens like a snoozing cat sensing movement.

There's music. It throbs and pounds, and the sound is delicious to my ears. Maybe this idea isn't the worst Kraven's had. Maybe it won't hurt to take a day or two to sharpen my skills.

I bounce on the balls of my feet and crack my neck. Bring it on, liberators. Let's see what you've got.

I walk through the doorway.

And I'm on my back.

⇥9⇤

LET'S DANCE

Without thinking, I spring to my feet and face my attacker. The guy is my height but has twenty extra pounds around his middle. It won't do much for him.

I spot Charlie coming up beside me, and I step in front of her. My brain says this is a training drill, but I can't be certain since I've never seen this dude a day in my life. The guy opens his arms like he wants to give me a bear hug and bends his knees. We circle each other, and as we do, I step toward the back wall and away from Charlie. I'm like an owner tempting a dog with a tasty treat. *Follow me. This way.*

I stumble when my heel hits a training mat, and the guy springs. He takes me to the ground, and I scramble to escape his grasp. The guy climbs on my back and presses my face to the floor. I growl and buck like I'm the main attraction at a rodeo.

Behind me, I hear the sounds of other people struggling. When I imagine one of them is Charlie, I blast like a shotgun. My elbow finds his side with a dull thud, and I roll away when his grip lessens. Then I jump to my feet. My boot finds his rib cage, and he howls in pain.

Now he's up, too, coming at me again. I'm not sure what else to do when I remember something Kraven said during the training Blue and I went through. *Self-defense can not only save your life, it can tire their spirit so that they flee.*

When he comes at me again, I'm ready. I dodge his punch and then throw my own fist into his kidney. He doubles over and then goes for my legs. I spring away and shove him down as he passes me. He's up quickly, and this time his hands find my throat. I shove my arms inside his grasp and circle outward. His hold breaks enough for me to spin away.

Kraven's voice booms. "Enough."

My gaze dances around the room, searching for Charlie. She's near the room's entrance. She appears fine, but her face is red from fighting Valery. It looks as though Valery has been working with another woman to hold Annabelle in place, while Blue was fighting a man twice his size.

Kraven approaches Blue. "You're category three. You'll work with those two over there for the remainder of the day." I follow Kraven's gaze and see a man in his early forties and a girl in her teens motioning for Blue to join them. They don't seem friendly.

Kraven strides up to me next. "Dante, you're a two. You're over there." He motions me toward a cluster of people. Among them is Paine, his eyes glued to Annabelle.

The head liberator leaves my side and crosses the room to where Annabelle and Charlie stand. He waves Valery away, and she goes to join a group that includes Neco—Kraven's buddy ol' pal.

"Thank you for participating in that exercise." Kraven says to Charlie next. "I do wish for you to learn basic self-defense, but for today, you'll be working with Oswald."

Charlie glances in my direction and then heads toward the basement. I don't want her out of my sight, but after learning what Oswald knows, I decide that maybe he can help her harness that blue energy or that she can help him with the scroll.

I resolve to make a point of asking Oswald about Charlie's ability after we're done here. Over the last few days, I've spent a lot of time thinking about Aspen in hell and about how to win a war where we're largely outnumbered. But I've ignored the fact that Charlie shot a bolt of power through her hands in hell.

Maybe I don't dwell on it because it scares me. Because it rattles me to the core that I could love a girl I don't fully understand.

Kraven turns his attention on Annabelle. "Leave."

"I'm not going to," she says, pretending not to see him. "Not this time."

"I don't need you in the way," Kraven responds, though I can tell some of the bite has left him.

"I want to learn how to protect myself. It doesn't take dargon to know how to fight." Annabelle motions toward the humans in the room, the ones I guess are here to help us train. Her voice drops. "If a siren puts his hands on me again, I won't take it quietly."

It was the wrong thing to say.

Kraven shoots forward. Annabelle stumbles back until her shoulder blades are pressed against the wall. Kraven's arms are on either side of her shoulders, blocking her in. His face is dangerously close to hers, and he growls like a diesel engine. I start toward Annabelle, anger flooding my vision. I stop when Kraven bends his head to her neck. He whispers something in her ear, and Annabelle's face falls. The frustration leaves her in an instant and is replaced by disbelief.

No one says a word as Kraven's chest heaves.

Annabelle places a hand flat against his abs, and without looking at him, she gently pushes him away and leaves the room.

Kraven has barely turned around when he's on the floor. Paine stands over him, his face painted red. "If you ever treat a girl like that again," Paine says. "I'll stop your heart." He moves to go after Annabelle, like he didn't want her to see him attack Kraven, but now he wants to check that she's okay.

Kraven grabs Paine's ankle and drags him to the ground. They claw and kick at one another as I head to the glass wall that overlooks the water. Ocean sprays into the air and then glitters back to earth. Over and over again. It's eerily beautiful and a strange contrast to the crass grunting sounds coming from behind me.

"Remember your defense, Kray-Kray," I say, inspecting my nails. I knew this dude once who used to get manicures. He argued it wasn't feminine. 'They're called *man*icures.' Please. I enjoy sporting fashion labels, but nail files are way too chick for me.

At some point, Kraven whips his wings out, and that's when Neco steps in. "All right, boss," he says. "That's not really playing fair, huh?"

Neco drags Kraven back, and I have no doubt that Kraven lets him do it. It's like he's finally realizing how uncool it is that the guy who doesn't lose his composure just lost his mind, his self-control, *and* his dignity.

He turns his back on Paine and straightens his clothes. In typical Kraven fashion, he says as if nothing happened, "Before we start training, I'd like to go over something. As I stated last night, we've asked for additional help monitoring the Hive at night while we sleep. But that doesn't change what happened. A collector breached our residence quite suddenly and vanished as quickly. We must be on alert at all times. I'm not certain whether this will happen again, but we must plan for it. Going forward, I'll ask all of you wearing a cuff to be on alert at all times. That means if you are alone in the Hive, you need to be sensing if another cuff is nearby. When you do sense something, check it out. Once we finish training, I'll unveil what's next in our plan of action in the impending war. For now, those are the orders." He clears his throat. "The day of reckoning will take place in two weeks, on January twenty-one."

A chill rushes through my body hearing the date we will fight. It makes it tangible, and it makes me that much more eager to ensure we have a plan to win.

I raise my hand.

He ignores me.

I sigh and say, "First off, nice wrestling match with Paine. Solid entertainment. Second, this sensing plan of yours, won't we just sense each other's cuffs over and over again?"

He doesn't reply, which means this is the best idea he has so far. Extra eyes and sensing each other's cuffs all day long for two weeks.

Good times.

"Please go through the basic self-defense techniques for the next twenty minutes," Kraven continues. "We won't stay on this sector too long since you've all been through it. Still, it is essential." Then he is quiet again, standing near the wall, watching as we look at each other like *dude's crazy* and start training.

Max is in my group of trainees, but he hardly speaks. He just glares at Kraven like he's the villain in an action movie. I slap him on the back a couple of times, and he seems to relax when I do. I decide I need to kick it with him tonight to ensure he's doing okay with the whole Valery thing. I can't imagine how hard this must be on him…

My eyes snap to my best friend, now a bitter fiancé to Valery.

Oswald said there was a traitor among us.

No. There's absolutely no way. I know my friend, and he wouldn't risk losing Red for good. He's been working hard to win a liberator cuff from Big Guy, even though that would mean a current liberator cuff would need to become available. Maybe if Max helps me uncover who's opening vultrips, then he'll win that cuff for sure.

Paine slams me down onto the matt.

"Where's your head?" he asks while offering a hand.

"It's about to be in your gut." I slam my cranium into his bread basket, and he doubles over.

"Defense, not offense," a human—one of the walkers—reminds us. Not sure what all these humans are doing buzzing around, or why Kraven doesn't just tell them the truth about us, (which I'm certain they already know) and let them help our cause in the war. Because if push comes to shove on January twenty-first, and things get particularly ugly, I'll save the savior if I have to carry that girl off the battle field kicking and screaming.

Caveman style.

Great, now I'm fantasizing about Charlie's rack again, and Paine's way too close, and this is getting awkward fast. Paine lunges at me, and I play all kinds of defense to avoid his ass.

"Great," Human exclaims. "Very good, Dante. That's the kind of energy I want to see."

Yeah, the kind where I'm avoiding a dude getting anywhere near my wood.

We're nearing the end of our self-defense training, which, as Kraven promised, only lasted about a half hour, when I lay Paine out. He pulls himself up, and I can't help noticing the smirk on his face. In fact, I've noticed it every time I've shut him down.

"What's so funny?" I ask.

Paine runs a hand over his shorn hair, and that smile of his dies. "Nah, it's nothing."

"If you've got something to say, liberator, spit it out."

Paine bites the inside of his cheek like he's debating speaking his mind. Finally, he says, "It's cool training with you. Before I was assigned, I heard what you did, going into hell and all for the savior."

"For Charlie," I correct him.

He looks away like what he's about to say is particularly embarrassing. "I just think it's awesome, man. And I was looking forward to meeting you."

I eyeball the guy for a long time, still thinking about that word—*traitor*. But I can't deny that it feels good to have a bro looking forward to meeting me. Max and I are friends, but we became friends out of circumstances, because we started collecting around the same time. But this guy is all *I've heard about you, and I think you're bomb*.

It's nice, I guess.

Not that I give a crap.

Paine's puffing his chest out, trying to squash some of the vulnerability he displayed. I offer my hand. He takes it immediately, and the grin that sweeps across his face is infectious. I laugh and slap him on the back like I did Max. Except when I do it, Paine slaps me back.

"That was pretty cool how you tumbled with Kraven. And you really don't have to treat me like I'm some supreme being," I say. "But you can call me Jesus if you want."

"Dante!" Kraven yells.

Paine laughs.

I do, too.

Kraven steps in front of me. He's so close I can smell what he had for breakfast, which in his defense, smells like shooting stars and summer roses. And glitter. Maybe glitter, too.

The head liberator is built like a brick wall. He opens his brick wall mouth and says, "You against Neco. No use of wings. This is your final exam for self-defense. Remember what happens if you flunk."

If he's expecting me to panic, he's off base. "Yeah, I remember. If I fail, I flunk angel school, and you take my cuff. My question is what are these groups? Is Neco in a group higher than I am? If so, that's not a real fair matchup is it? Also, if there's a group higher than this one—" I point to the crew behind me, the one that includes Max and Paine, "—then I should be in it."

Kraven's face doesn't change. He's stoic as usual, and I decide his nickname should never have wavered from Cyborg.

Cyborg waves a hand, and Neco comes forward. Everyone else moves back. Blue, in particular, seems excited to see this.

I roll my shoulders, size up Neco's solid frame, and say, "Screw it. Let's dance."

⇥ 10 ⇤

WHISPERS

Neco doesn't waste time. He drives across the mat like a bulldozer and takes me down.

That's fine.

I let him do it.

Right now, this is a game. I'm going to play it like a pro. I fight back some, but I hold back most of what I have and let him imagine I'm an easy victory. Neco takes hold of my left arm and pulls it behind my back. I squeal like a pig, and it might be my imagination, but I think I see the corner of Paine's mouth twitch across the room. He knows I'm half-assing, and I like him a touch more for realizing this.

For about five minutes, I let Neco have his fun. But I don't want to wait too long. After all, what if Kraven calls it before I've had my chance to rumble?

Neco has me pinned on the training mat, his stomach on my back and his hands reaching for my throat. I give Paine a nice, big smile, and then I throw my head back into Neco's nose. It crunches. His hands jerk away from my neck, and I leap up.

Even though his nose is gushing, painting his lips red, Neco pummels toward me. I step to the left and then sweep the legs out from beneath him. He's back up quickly, and this time he waits for me to make the first move. He'll be waiting a long time if that's his ploy.

After tiring of our circling, Neco spins around and throws his leg out in a roundhouse kick. It's some kung fu shit, and I know just what to do with it. I grab his ankle and spin against his momentum, tearing the muscles in his hip. I drop his leg and bounce back, light on my feet. Look at me, I'm a cat. I got nine lives!

Neco's eyes widen, and when I flash him the same smile I did Paine, he realizes I played him. I'll be honest, I feel conflicted over the physical pain I've caused him. Not that he spared me any discomfort when I gave him his turn.

The liberator laughs like he's about to show me what he's really got.

Then he roars like a chainsaw and barrels forward.

Neco fakes like he's going to grab me on the left, but at the last second, he goes for my right arm. He pulls it over his shoulder and—oh, damn!—I'm airborne. My back slams into the ground, and the breath is ripped from my lungs. He pins me, and across the room, I spot Kraven's mouth move like he's going to call the match. I struggle against him, trying to recall defense moves that'll get this dude off me. But he's got his arm beneath my knee and the other around my neck, pinning my arms beside my ears. I don't know how this happened, and I don't know what to do.

My heart pounds, and my face drips with sweat, and Kraven is going to call it. *He's going to call it! My cuff!*

I've passed this test before. It was Blue and me against Neco and two humans. How could I do it then and not now?

And I realize why at the same moment that Neco whispers her name.

"Those collectors are going to slaughter your Charlie," he says into my ear, his Australian accent thicker than I've heard it in the past. "And then there will be *two* girls you've let die."

I hear what he just said.

I hear it.

His words are a bloated corpse floating to the bottom of a swimming pool.

My entire body pulls in. It's like every muscle, every tissue, every last tendon that weaves itself together to create *me*, wants to be as small as possible.

Then they are bigger than life.

They are too big, stretching me out until I am swollen version of myself. I take up every last bit of space. It is mine. Everything I've ever wanted is mine. It always has been, but now it's solid, and I can touch it.

A light flashes behind my eyes, and I erupt like a thousand soldiers cresting a trench. Neco shoots across the room like he's an iron ball blasting from the throat of a cannon.

Everything stops.

Neco lies still.

I'm on my feet, my arms thrown out by my side. My wings are spread out in a great black sky about my body, but that's not what helped me. I don't know *what* happened. I don't know what that sensation was or where it came from.

Valery rushes to Neco's side, and he groans. Within a few seconds, she's got him to his feet. Neco points a shaky arm at me. "Kraven said no use of wings. Are you deaf?"

I regain my composure, forget what just happened inside me, and instead remember what he said right before my body turned into a weapon. I cross the space between us and grab him by the jugular. "Want to repeat what you said about Charlie and Aspen?"

"Dante, let him go," Valery says.

Someone pulls me off Neco and attempts to hold me back, but I'm a bull hoofing the dirt, ready to charge. For a moment, I thought Neco might have been dead, and now I'm almost disappointed he isn't. "I know what you are," I growl. And my head chants *traitor, traitor*.

Neco tears away from Valery. "I don't know what you're talking about."

"I heard what you said!" I lunge at him again and another pair of arms pin me in place.

"Kraven told us to get you guys riled up, to say and do whatever we needed to in order to push you to your limits." Neco glances at Kraven, and I follow his gaze. Kraven nods, but he's hiding something.

I realize Max and Paine are the ones holding me, and I bark at them to let me go. They exchange glances before doing so. I take a step toward Neco and hold up my hands like I'm not going to do anything to keep Max and Paine from grabbing me again. Then I stare into Neco's face. His jaw is clenched, and his eyes are storming, but I can't be certain he's lying about what he said being for training purposes.

"Even if Kraven told you to provoke me," I mutter, my voice low, "what you said was poison. It was disgusting."

Everyone is quiet as I stride toward the exit.

Kraven speaks as I pass him. "Come back after you've cooled off. We have more training." And then he adds quietly, "You and I need to talk about what you did to Neco."

He means when Neco flew across the freaking room. To anyone else, it might have seemed like I tossed him with my wings. Kraven and I are the only ones who can call them, so they have no idea what they can do. But this was something much bigger, something I don't understand at all.

So I'm relieved Kraven says something about it. It suggests he may have answers.

My mind whirls as I leave the training room and pace the hallway outside. I can't stop thinking about what my body did back there and where it came from. I can't stop thinking about Neco and if he's the traitor Oswald spoke of. But mostly, I can't stop thinking about what he said. Not only about Charlie dying, because that's a fear that's haunted me for weeks. But about Aspen. What if what Neco said about her is true?

What if Aspen is already dead?

⊰ 11 ⊱

SOUL TOUCHING

I return to training a few minutes later, but my brain is stuck on
Aspen. Why is it that I've always assumed she was alive? Maybe
it's because I could never allow myself to believe the opposite. That
she could truly be gone, burning in hell for eternity. I always imagined
that Rector and Lucille had a plan for Charlie and Aspen both, that
they wanted to collect their bodies and souls and somehow use them
for their benefit. But what if that's not it at all? What if they just want
them gone so *we* can't use them? Collect the savior and soldier's souls
first—

Then stop their beating hearts.

I can barely concentrate as Kraven introduces us to the second
sector of training—using shadow in battle. The whole time I practice
becoming invisible at key moments, I keep one eye trained on Neco.
He doesn't notice I'm staring, but maybe it's because he's avoiding
looking in my direction. Any other attention I have is focused on
keeping my legs beneath me as I think about Aspen.

Aspen with blue lips and vacant eyes.

Aspen, dead.

The dreams I've had don't help matters. What if somehow, someway, I'm seeing Aspen in death?

Max pins me for the last time, and finally, as the sun dives into the ocean, Kraven says we're done for the day. "We'll begin tomorrow morning at 7:00."

Everyone files from the room, and Kraven takes hold of my shoulder. He leans in and says in a low voice. "I'd like to see you tomorrow morning before training. Report to my room at 6:30."

I'm too exhausted to argue, which is perhaps the reason he trains us so hard. I nod and leave. Even though I'm too drained to banter with Kraven, I'm never too tired to seek out Charlie. So I head to the basement.

I hear Annabelle and Charlie talking over each other as I approach the open doorway. As I get closer, I notice Annabelle has a lamp shade on her head, and Oswald is chuckling to himself. Charlie is walking like a zombie and making grunting sounds. I stop and watch them, smiling to myself. My girl appears so happy. I wish there was something I could do to make this moment last longer. But the second they see me, Annabelle removes the lamp shade and walks over. Charlie follows her.

"How was training?" Annabelle asks. "Can you show us what you learned?"

Charlie wraps her arms around my neck. "I missed you."

"I missed you, too," I whisper against her neck.

Behind Charlie, I spot Annabelle pouting from being ignored. She cocks a hand on her hip and purses her lips. I pull Charlie closer and say to Annabelle, "I'll teach you a thing or two tonight before we crash out."

Charlie's friend perks. "More like, you'll try and teach me, but then…but then I'll be the one teaching you how to be…a liberator… the awesome skills…."

"Good one," I say.

"They can't all be winners." Annabelle sobers. "I just want to help. I want to do something besides take up space. Maybe if I learned how to fight…"

"Annabelle, you are helping," Charlie says. "Look at you. You have a smile on your face and a can-do attitude. It's hard to imagine we can't win this war when you're around. You make people believe in goodness and fun and all the stuff that's worth fighting for."

Tears spring to Annabelle's eyes, and she grins. Then she points a finger at Charlie and me and says, "I am not crying. I don't cry. I'm hard as steel."

"Jaysus, Annabelle," I groan. "You've been hanging around me too long."

"Hey," she says, directing her next question to me. "Did you see Kraven get all wild over me? He's kind of hot, right? I mean, he's completely unstable. But he's unstable in that 'I want you to kidnap me and take me to the middle of nowhere and show me just how volatile you are' kind of unstable, am I right?"

"This again," Charlie says through a laugh.

Annabelle can't stop herself now that she's on a roll. "Dude's built like a tank and with that blond hair and crazy eyes? Yes. That."

I can't believe what I'm hearing. Everyone knows Kraven has lost his head to her, or that he hates her in his profoundly twisted way, but Annabelle reciprocating the feelings? "So you like him?" I ask.

"Whaaaat?" Charlie looks like I said a man in woman's underwear isn't that strange.

At the same time, Annabelle says-slash-screeches, "Are you serious? No, I don't like him. Gross."

"But you just said—"

Annabelle rolls her eyes and punches me in the shoulder on her way out the door. "Dante, sometimes you really are dense."

After she's gone, I hold my palms out in silent plea for Charlie to explain what just happened. She just wraps herself around me again. "Don't try to understand us. It's impossible, like staring into the sun."

Oswald clears his throat. I glance at him and take in his shamrock green robe. It ends at the knee, which adds insult to injury. I imagine in the department store, all the other robes made fun of this one. There may have been a yellow one that was nice to its face, but that's the one that was really behind all the name calling.

"Oswald," I say. "Your robe is the color of testosterone."

The old guy touches his hands to his robe and Charlie elbows me in the ribs. "Be nice."

"Did you two work together?" I ask them.

Charlie practically skips in place, and Oswald shuffles his feet. I narrow my eyes at him. He acts the part of a shy, awkward, old man, but he showed streaks of boldness last night. I don't forget that.

"She's a quick learner," he says.

"I felt some tingling in my hands." Charlie glows like a polished apple. "It's a start."

"That's amazing." And it is. I turn to Oswald. "Wait, doesn't Kraven want you to lie low about this, keep us thinking you don't know about us?"

He grins. "I just told the girls. They won't tell anyone."

Charlie shakes her head like the secret is as good as dead. When she leans back, she says, "And that's not all. We uncovered another part of the scroll."

My brows shoot to my hairline. "Tell me."

Oswald is smiling so big I notice one of his molars is missing. Might not be such a bad thing since the last time his teeth were white was circa 1960. "It's all about utilizing the books in the library to work it out." Oswald takes a few quiet steps and retrieves a book from one of the two desks. It's covered in blue cloth and is worn at the edges. A gold clasp cinches the middle. Oswald opens it and points to the introduction. "Read this."

I start to read it to myself, but Oswald tells me *out loud*.

I begin again.

"The purpose of this work is to define the relationship between the demon, Mongo, and the angel, Hidalgi. It explores the dynamic the pair shares in an evolving environment in which humans walk alongside demons and angels without seeing. Mongo, the *criuttel,* is said to be…"

"Stop." Oswald holds up a hand and points to the word *cruittel.* "Now, what do you imagine that means?"

I think about it. "Demon? That's what they said he was in the first line."

Oswald shows me his old man grill. "Very good. He sets the book down and picks up a notebook overflowing with yellowed paper. "There are common phrases used to unlock ancient documents like your scroll. Unfortunately, we don't know the translation for all the words. See here? See this one?"

He opens the notebook and points to a short phrase. Charlie looks over my shoulder at it, too.

Fa windows *ri giovunkrol* wicked will fall *bftello piv*.

"This could very well be the phrase that unlocks the next part of the scroll, but I'm missing the translation for certain words," Oswald says. "Do you understand?"

I lean closer to the parchment. "I think so. You want me and Charlie to spend hours of our life digging through books to find a handful of funktified words and use context clues to translate what they mean?"

Oswald beams. "Yes, yes exactly." He digs through his notebook and offers me a sheet of paper. "Charlie and I used a few of them here to translate a line today."

Charlie comes to stand beside me. "The words suddenly appeared when we read the old language aloud. Look." She points to the scroll on Oswald's desk, and sure as hell, there's a line there even I can read.

The room unburned holds a sparrow among crows.

"What does it mean?" I ask Oswald.

He shrugs. "Could be anything, but it's a starting place."

I check out the list he shoved into my hand. "We're missing a lot of words. What if we're wasting time doing this?" Even as I ask this, I remember what Aspen said in my dream last night, about learning the words. This has to be the key.

"I don't think we are," Charlie whispers.

I run a hand through my hair. "No, I guess I don't, either."

"It'll go faster with two of us working," Charlie says.

Oswald flips on a lamp, as if there isn't enough light from the forty currently lit. "When you two are searching, look for words that are italicized or in a heavier handwriting. Essentially, a word that's offset from the rest of the text. Once you find a book that has one, dig deeper. Many of the books won't have any at all." He raises a finger and smiles. "But where you find one, you'll find more."

"Why don't more people know about this dead language?" I ask.

He waves the statement away. "They do. They just don't know what it can do. That is something only I know. A lifetime of work."

"Except for the person whispering the vultrips open," Charlie adds.

He pulls at the collar of his robe, and I notice something I didn't before. There's a silver necklace around his neck that's mostly tucked into his robe, but not quite enough.

"Oswald. That's Annabelle's necklace, isn't it?"

He looks everywhere but at me. I'll give him this, at least he doesn't start turning in circles.

I shake my head, but I can't help the laughter that builds in my throat. It dies when I remember there's one more thing I wanted to ask Oswald. "Hey, Hef?"

"What's that, son?" he says, covering the necklace with his palm.

The word *son* strikes through me. I miss my dad. I killed my dad. Killed him driving a car on our way to get brownies. Maybe this is why I can't envision Aspen being dead. I can't be the person who kills another innocent person. It would destroy me.

I bite my lip and hesitate. Then, because I can no longer keep it to myself, I say, "I'm seeing Aspen in my dreams."

Charlie glances up at me, surprised I told him.

The old man's eyes widen. "What happens in them? Do you speak? Are they clear dreams?"

My breath quickens at Oswald's reaction. "We're in a dark place. Not hell, but somewhere else. Purgatory, maybe? If that exists. And yeah, we speak. The dreams are clear. I remember every detail when I wake up. It's like she's really there with me."

Oswald comes close. Too close. *Way* too close. "Dude."

"I've heard of things like this," he drawls.

I step back. "Care to elaborate?"

"It's called soul touching," he says. "It can happen when two souls experience something extraordinary under duress."

Charlie doesn't sound exactly thrilled at the term.

"Not to poke holes in this soul touching theory," I say. "But I've been through a lot of extraordinary stuff with people lately. And there's certainly lots of duress going around. Why would what Aspen and I went through be any different?"

"You went to hell together, right?" His eyes urge me to understand. "You experience trials like that with others every day?"

No. Even when I fought off Rector that night in the woods to save Charlie...no.

Oswald fingers the tie around his robe. It makes me nervous. I don't want any slippage happening. "After you'd slid your own soul back into your body, did the two of you embrace?"

"How did you know I have my soul? Jaysus, Kraven told you everything, didn't he?"

Oswald waits while I answer the question.

Did Aspen and I embrace?

I think back.

And I remember.

"I understand now that we must all make sacrifices," I whisper to her. "But I will be back for you, Aspen. I will return, and I will blow this entire place apart with the strength of God himself to save you."

Aspen collapses against me.

I hold her as she cries.

"We hugged," I whisper, my stomach rolling.

Charlie takes my hand, and Oswald pulls in a long breath. "It could be her you're seeing," he says. "Soul touching is largely unexplored."

I stare down at my feet, avoiding his gaze. "Thanks, Oswald. We'll help you find the words you're missing."

I spin around and stride toward the door with Charlie by my side, wanting to leave this conversation behind. But before I can go, Oswald says, "Dante, I don't want to mislead you. The Aspen you're seeing, it may not be her. I've heard of soul touching, but that doesn't mean I believe in it."

I bite down and grip Charlie's palm tighter.

Charlie is real.

I can touch her, and she's here, and she's real.

That I know.

⇥ 12 ⇤

WHAT SHE SAID

As soon as we exit the basement, I tell Charlie what happened in the training room. Her face tells me she's every bit as confused as I am.

"You think it's because you have your soul?"

It's the same thing I thought, but I tell her I'm not sure. "That's cool that you guys uncovered another part of the scroll."

She does a little jump, and color rises on her neck. "It was so awesome. It just appeared out of thin air."

"To bad we don't know what it means."

Charlie is about to respond when I see a dude stumbling around. My heart high-vaults into my throat. My body swallows Charlie as it would oxygen at the bottom of the sea. There's a kind of desperation about protecting her. Not saying this reaction is healthy, but there it is.

"Dante, calm down." Charlie edges away, and I recognize that it's Blue who's staggering toward us. Instinctually, Charlie steps between me and him. When I see the red in his eyes, I realize what's happening.

Blue is wasted.

"Hey there, Vodka," I say.

A growl rips from Blue's throat, and he lunges past Charlie to take me down. Color me surprised when the stumbling, slurring, red-eyed liberator is successful. My back hits the hardwood floor, and I gasp as the air leaves my lungs. I'm already sore from today's training, and this is the last thing I need before tomorrow's session.

Charlie tries to pull Blue back, but he's all over me, throwing punches into my side and kneeing me anywhere he can. I grab hold of his shoulders and roll him onto his back. His head slams into the wood, and for a moment, he seems dazed. Then he yells something incoherent and half-slap, half-punches my left cheekbone.

Even though I know Blue doesn't really want to hurt me, blood pounds behind my temples and adrenaline sharpens my senses. He's drunk and heartbroken and desperate, and that makes him dangerous. Not because his aim is true, but because he's feeling no pain and isn't likely to stop until I'm unconscious.

I hook him into a headlock and try to calm him down, but he's like a crocodile, spinning in an effort to drown and rip me to pieces at once. He mumbles something and throws his fist into my stomach. I double over and groan. Charlie lays her palms on our twisting torsos, and I ask her to please stop trying to do the Blue Hand Thingy on us.

Blue slams his heel down on my boot. I pick up my foot and dance on the other. "Damn it, Blue, stop." I shove him away and prepare for him to charge me again. He doesn't.

Instead, he does something worse.

"You said today that Neco's words were poison," Blue slurs. "But you know what, Dante? You're poison."

"Blue," Charlie pleads.

Blue narrows one eye at me and points a sharp finger like he's piercing my heart. "You may wear a liberator cuff, but you're still worthless." He's drunk, but each word he spews is a round, solid marble. "You're the reason Charlie's soul is gone. You're the reason Aspen is in hell. Everything you touch turns to crap. There is one savior and one soldier. And you've screwed them both."

He opens both his arms and stumbles. "Congratulations."

Guilt courses through my veins. My throat tightens, and my vision blurs. I don't think I can stand. I can't possibly carry what I'm feeling inside. Because what he said are the same things I've told myself. But to hear him voice those same thoughts, to know everyone blames me… It's too much. And why shouldn't they blame me? What he says is true. It's my fault. I'm selfish. I'm a coward. If I could, I'd put my ankle to the guillotine and let Blue swing the axe, let him sever my dargon. At least then the pain would stop. At least then I could stop hurting people.

Blue sighs like some of the fight has left him. He shakes his head and says, "You know He doesn't want you, right? He just needed a strong, mindless body to fight. After this war is over, He'll retrieve his dargon and let you rot." Blue turns his head, but I hear him clearly. "He should have let you die."

Charlie shoves Blue and screams for him to take it back.

But he's not going to.

He shouldn't.

I don't know what to do, except this… There's something I've hidden from Blue. Something I knew would hurt him even worse and destroy any chance of me and him being friends. But I owe him this. Aspen told me not to tell him, but I have to. He deserves to know.

I keep my eyes on the floor when I speak, my voice shaking ever so slightly. "There was this room in hell, this place where the ceiling comes down on you. It's an illusion. But if you allow yourself to imagine it's happening, that this wall is really descending, then the pain and torment become real."

Blue doesn't respond, but I can tell he's listening.

"I'd been through this room before, so I knew how to handle it. But Aspen was having trouble. She couldn't get outside of her head no matter what I said." I swallow and take a deep breath. "The only thing that got her through was you."

His eyes snap to me, and I can feel them burning my flesh.

"When she started panicking, she said that she didn't want to die without…without kissing you. Thinking about you, Blue, it's the only thing that got her through. When I was leaving hell, she was about to ask me to tell you something. But then she took it back. In the end, she didn't want you to know that she'd started to care. I don't think she wanted you to suffer thinking about her."

Blue's chest rises and falls quickly. "Is that it?"

I say it is.

He hits me. It's the kind of clean blow that says there won't be any more to follow. The pain is so overwhelming that it numbs the entirety of my face. I don't even realize I'm on the ground until I see Charlie kneeling beside me.

Blue weaves his fingers together and places them atop his curly hair. He groans like a wounded animal and stares up at the ceiling. Then he turns and strides away, stumbling down the dark hall in search of his bed.

Charlie helps me up and asks a dozen questions about how I'm feeling. I hardly hear her. All I'm thinking about is how I'd feel better if Blue had hit me a hundred more times the way he had at the end. The one time doesn't feel like enough. I was the guy who guided Aspen down into hell. It was up to me to bring her out again. And I didn't. People can rationalize the situation all they want, but in the end, I left her.

Charlie and I linger in hopes that Blue is asleep by the time we get to our rooms. When we finally arrive, Max is in the lounge area outside our bedrooms. He has his elbows on his knees and his head in his hands.

My girl doesn't ask if I need time alone with him or what she can do, she just reacts. She moves toward him without a word and places a hand on his neck. "All this will be over soon. And you'll be with Valery again."

Max looks up. His face is red, and tears swim in his eyes. He's not crying, but he's damn close. "I can't do it much longer. She won't even let me touch her. She says she loves me, but she won't go against Big Guy and—"

He breaks off and pinches the bridge of his nose to stop the flow of emotion.

"Charlie's right." I sit down beside him. "This thing is going to come to a head. The sirens are growing in numbers, a collector broke in, and we're training. Shit's about to get real. And when it's over, we'll be able to focus on the people who matter."

Max shakes his head. "Every day, I wake up thinking about that scroll. About Aspen and Charlie."

A ball of ice forms between my shoulder blades.

"But at night, it's hard not to miss her," he says. "It's hard to see her during training and only exchange a smile."

"Max—" I begin.

"It's fine." His mouth pulls into an unconvincing smile. "I get like this sometimes, that's all. I'll be cool in the morning." Max bolts up and heads toward the door. I try to stop him from leaving, but he only says, "I'm just so angry with Him."

Max leaves at the same time as Annabelle steps out of her room. "Oh, good," she says to me. "You can show me those moves now."

I start to go after Max, but Charlie grabs my arm. "Give him some time to be alone right now. But tomorrow, let's make a point of talking to Kraven. Maybe he can change something for the two of them."

I nod, because she's right, and also because my body feels broken in ten different ways, and I'm fairly sure Blue broke my nose. The Quiet Ones come in bearing beef and shallot stew, and after I eat, they immediately go to work healing my wounds with their pastes and creamy concoctions in blue glass jars. Annabelle gives me approximately seventeen minutes to rest and gorge myself before she pulls me up and begins acting out karate moves and asking me to *come at her and see what happens.*

As I train her, my mind trails back to my conversation with Max. Something he said at the end unnerves me. It was the thing about Max being angry with Big Guy. That little confession burrows, but every time I start to dwell on it, Annabelle demands my attention. Soon, I forget all about it, and focus on Annabelle.

For every move she masters, she asks Charlie her thoughts about Kraven.

And Paine.

It feels like old times, like maybe we just got done playing basketball and now there's pizza to be had. Grams is sleeping upstairs in Charlie's house, and Annabelle is busting out black and white movies and asking which we'd like to watch.

As we laugh and work late into the night, it's hard not to imagine that Max will be just fine.

⊰ 13 ⊱

STONE ANGEL

After Annabelle is asleep, and I'm stationed outside her door, I hear a soft rap.

My heart leaps with hope.

Charlie steps through the bathroom door that connects our rooms and finds me sitting on the tile. She squats down and takes my face into her hands. Then she stands and draws me silently along with her. I follow the lead of her body like a horse steered to water. Her hand slides into mine, and she guides me into my bedroom. *Our* bedroom.

There's a low light burning in the lounge area outside our room. It stretches beneath my door and casts shadows over Charlie's face. Her lips are full and parted. Her breasts are pressed against me, demanding a fierce reaction in my body. I take her in my arms as if on impulse and decide that this time, I won't let her go. I'll shatter her reservations and ask her to realize that us being together, regardless of the situation, is always right.

I open my mouth to say something, but Charlie lays her fingers to my lips. She breaks away from me so easily that I nearly gasp. Charlie moves toward the bed. Her body slides backward on it, and she opens her arms.

It's an invitation.

Blood pounds through my veins, wakes me up, makes every last nerve in my body electric. I reach the edge of the bed, and now I'm crawling, moving over her body like a blanket. I lower my pelvis, and her legs ease open. She's wearing a long T-shirt, but not much else. When my hips meet hers, I groan. My body throbs. The desire I feel for Charlie is a living, breathing thing, thrashing its anxious head.

I'm holding myself up with my arms, and Charlie is beneath me, her blue eyes wide open with life and lust and love. I want to swallow them so I can see what she sees. Her hands move up my back, tracing the hard muscles there. Then she grips the arch of my neck. I greet her skin willingly, my lips trailing warm kisses up her throat. I kiss her chin, the small, fleshy part directly beneath her lower lip.

And then my mouth touches hers.

My tongue slides into her mouth and greets the tip of hers. I growl like a monster and kiss her deeper. Something wild claps through me, a lust so bottomless it scares me. I want to make love to her, to touch her as gently as a falling leaf. But I also want to ravage her, to drive and dominate and howl like a dog. I want all of her and so much more. We've been together before, completely, but I need to feel that perfect closeness to her again, now.

Charlie widens herself to me, and her lips move to my ear. Her breath is warm, and her teeth push me over the edge as she nibbles and bites. We haven't spoken a word, and there's this sort of quiet intimacy about that. I lose myself in her, forget where I am and what I am.

It's so quiet. So quiet until she whispers, sweet as warm sand, "I want you, Dante."

My head drops, because it's all I've wanted to hear the last few days. Late at night, Charlie has denied me time and again. And even though she had her reasons—it's unfair to celebrate each other when

Aspen was gone—I secretly wondered if there was more to it than that. If maybe she didn't resent me for leaving Aspen in hell.

But now. Now she wants me, which means even if she was upset, she forgives me. I dip my head and kiss her, the heat in my body pulsing. I reach down and inch her shirt up until it's bunched around her hips. When my hands crawl back down, feeling her, she exhales.

Charlie wants me.

She loves me.

But if all that is true, then why is this uneasiness spreading through me like arsenic? I try to ignore it, to push it away. But it stays all the same. I bite the inside of my lip and turn my head in the direction of the pain. I want to shake these doubts loose, this thought that something is off. I only want to be with Charlie right now and damn anything else.

Charlie must sense my hesitation, because she wraps her hands around my cheeks, grazing the slight five o'clock shadow there.

"Tell me," she says, as if she already knows without question that something is wrong.

"It's nothing," I mumble before bending to kiss her again. She moves against me for a moment, trying to recapture the moment, but we both seem to stop at once. I grunt with dissatisfaction and pull away a fraction. "Just tell me why now," I ask, feeling like I'm losing my man card for questioning this at all.

I want her to say she's missed me, that she can't stay away a second longer. Instead, she pushes me gently to the side and sits up. She stares at the wall as if there's a window there, as if the moonlight is shining down on her. "I missed you."

Sweet relief.

She wraps her arms around her knees and pulls them against herself. Charlie becomes a tight ball of curiosity. "And…" she says, drawing the word out, "And I have this feeling."

"What feeling?" I don't move closer, I just let her be. As I watch, she becomes this statue of beauty, hair draping her back and shoulders.

Charlie doesn't answer, and no matter how much I press, she doesn't say another word. She just sits, immobile. So I remind her of my own burden, the one that says something big happened to me in that training room, and that I'm worried there's something wrong with me.

"Is that what you feel like, Charlie?" I say. "Do you feel like something is happening that you don't understand?"

She shakes her head. Her velvet hair and the curve of her skull goes right and then left. *No.*

I remain quiet and hope she speaks without prompting.

She does.

"I have a sense of foreboding I can't explain," she whispers. "Like I know what's going to happen in the end."

I can't help it. I'm off the bed and standing in front of her. I take her face in my hands, and I bend down so that she looks at me. "Tell me what you think is going to happen."

Charlie pulls away and tucks herself into bed. I want to push her to tell me, but I know she's done talking. And right now, what I want more than anything is to have her close. I want to know in this small moment that she's here and I'm here and the future is so far away.

So I get into bed without a word. I hold her as if I'm critically ill and she's the cure. Sometimes I think about how quickly we fell for each other. We didn't know one another but for a few days when I spoke the words. Even now, I feel like I don't know half of what I'd like to know about Charlie. But maybe love is like that. Like two souls greet each other and say, *it's you*, and then they wait while the bodies and brains catch up. Maybe sometimes, that's all it takes. A few moments, and then you know.

I fall asleep with Charlie in my arms.

When I'm conscious again, Aspen is standing before me, wearing a grey dress that's torn in too many places to count. I open my mouth to ask if she's still alive, if she believes our souls have touched and now we can communicate with one another. My body aches for her to admit it's true.

But my lips can't find my tongue, and all that comes out is a dry, hissing sound.

"Find the sparrow," Aspen says. Her green eyes widen, and then they begin to fill with blood until the entirety of her eye is a sticky, crimson ball. She covers her face, and I think maybe she's ashamed. But when she pulls her hands away, there are only empty, black sockets. Aspen opens her palms. Inside are her eyes. The tendons that once stretched into her brain are still attached.

She smiles as if she's proud of what she's done.

I take the eyes from her and place them one by one into my mouth.

When I wake up, Charlie is gone. I move to sleep outside of Annabelle's door, and after I ensure they're both breathing deeply, I fall asleep again.

This time, Aspen doesn't return.

⊰ 14 ⊱

PURGE YOUR DEMONS

Valery rouses me from the floor the next morning. "Get dressed, Dante," she says in the softest tone I've ever heard her use. "Kraven has asked me to bring you to his room."

I'm so exhausted that I get up without complaint, grab a cranberry-orange scone, and follow after her. I stop outside of Annabelle's room and listen. Valery tilts her head. "Charlie will be fine. She's going to work with Oswald again while we train. She'll figure out how to harness her ability eventually. Maybe today."

I shake my head. "Oswald told you he knows everything about us?"

Valery grins.

"That little dude does not know how to keep a secret," I say.

Valery clicks down the hallway in piss yellow pumps and a black, knee-length dress. She looks like she's ready for a dinner party with the Obamas. I've seen Red kick off her heels for training. But that's the extent of her break from formality.

"You think it's crazy what Charlie can do with her hands?" I fall in step beside Valery even though I know she likes to be a few paces in front.

"Oswald said there have been humans in the past who—" she begins.

"Yeah, yeah, Big Guy's will and all that," I finish for her. "But it's still crazy, right?"

Red smiles. "It's crazy."

We continue walking through rooms until we arrive at a final hallway that's brighter than the rest. Bulbs hang from the ceiling in a stiff line down the stretch. It's almost like they're pointing to Kraven's chambers.

I stop Valery from going any farther. "Hey, Red, have you talked to Max lately?"

Her shoulders slump. "We're not allowed to be together right now. You know that."

"Haven't you ever thought about breaking the rules?"

Her brow furrows, and she shakes her head. "When this is all over, and Max has helped His cause, we'll be together. The right way. Until then, it'll be hard, but Max knows I love him."

"Well, you might want to do a better job of communicating that. Dude's losing it."

"Don't say that," Valery scolds. "The last thing we need is for Kraven to think Max isn't doing well here. He's unsettled enough that a collector is among us, but he's letting him stay for me."

I raise my hands. "All right, Max is fine. And what about you, Red? How are you doing?"

She turns her face away. "It's unbearable. But I have to believe in His plan. We must focus on the war that's coming."

I do something I don't normally do. I hug Red. It's about as awkward as getting caught masturbating. But I persist with my Hug Nation until she sighs and hugs me back.

"There now, we're all better, huh?" I slap her on the arm. "Charlie taught me that crap."

I leave her standing there, adjusting her formfitting dress, and stride toward Kraven's door. He must be waiting for me to knock. So I go right on in with a grin on my face. He's standing near a fireplace that's large enough to toss full-grown adults into. His dark eyes rage with surprise.

"What up, Cyborg." I take in his room. It's a circular design with a single window at the top of a domed ceiling. The walls are coated in dark maroon paint that's lighter in places where hands have touched too often. There's a lamp every five feet around the perimeter and a half-moon table with meticulously labeled books and a map atop it. On the corner of his desk is a silver picture frame. There's isn't a photo in it. Also, his bed is round.

Freak.

Kraven crosses his arms over his broad chest. I decide my chest is bigger. It may be wishful thinking. "We need to discuss what happened yesterday at training," he says.

"When I hulked out?" I wonder if he likes the term, considering how hulkish he is.

Kraven doesn't even pretend to smile. "What did you experience?"

I consider lying, but I want to know what happened in there, too. "I felt this boiling inside. Then it's like everything just…" I touch all ten fingers together and then spray them out like I'm imitating an explosion.

"Have you felt something like that before?"

I shake my head.

Kraven moves toward me and studies my face, my body. I'd be a little weirded out if I wasn't so accustomed to Kraven's peculiarity. "I believe you're experiencing heightened abilities because you harbor your soul." He watches my reaction carefully. "Liberators and collectors are not supposed to have their own souls. Not after they expire."

"Well, I do." I wish I had an apple so I could crunch into it, display my astounding composure.

Kraven strolls back toward his fireplace. "You may be able to do other things."

Hells, yeah! Now he has my attention. "What kind of stuff?"

"Things above and beyond what liberators are capable of."

"Well, we don't even know what those things are since we're only focused on training."

He ignores my last comment. Nothing new there. "I want you to pay attention to your body's signals, Dante. Listen to what it's trying to tell you." Kraven bows his head and pauses. He seems to be contemplating how to position what's on his mind. "I asked if you should return your soul," he says evenly, like he's weighing his words. "I was told you are to keep it. For now. For fighting."

I could be mistaken, but Kraven sounds a touch envious.

Kraven turns around. His gaze is like an axe in the hand. "In order for you to use your soul in this war, you must submit to His will."

"I'm here, aren't I?" I'm pretending to be cool about this, but inside my lungs shrivel, and my blood drags its feet. Big Guy wants me to keep my soul? Not that I was planning on giving it up. But Kraven asked, and He said I'm to have it?

Kraven reaches his hand toward the fire, warming it. Or burning it. Not sure which. "What I mean is you need to become His soldier. You need to wash the demons from your mind and body and open yourself to Him."

"Yeah, Mr. Clean? We already tried that. It pissed my personal demons right off."

"The sirens are planning an attack," Kraven exclaims, surprising me.

My voice lowers. It seems as if this admission is an invitation to discuss strategy. I tread carefully. "That doesn't surprise me. We need to prepare to fight logistically. War is less than two weeks away, right?"

Kraven nods. He thinks I'm referencing training.

"I don't just mean awakening our liberator skills and practicing defense. I mean creating a strategy." I lick my lips, take a chance, go for the kill. "We need weapons. We need to rally our warriors so that they're enraged at what's happened to their soldier and savior. And we need to get Charlie out of here before the worst of it begins."

"Weapons," Kraven growls.

"Yes, Kraven, weapons. You think the collectors will hesitate to put a bullet in one of our own? In Charlie?"

"The war between heaven and hell won't be fought with modern weapons."

"Did you know I've been seeing Aspen in my dreams? Did you know Charlie and Oswald uncovered a new passage on the scroll? Something about finding a sparrow among the crows in an unburned room. If you sent this guy in to research the scroll, you have to believe it could help us in our battle against the collectors and sirens. Why aren't we all working on it?"

"It could be a waste of precious time in the grand scheme of things," he says. "Better that we have one dedicated professional who's used to working on this kind of thing rather than eight liberators arguing over it." Kraven's face softens. "You really have been seeing the girl in your dreams?"

"Yep. And last night she told me to find the sparrow. Super weird."

"Probably your mind rehashing the newest part of the scroll." Kraven glances at the oversized fireplace for whatever reason. "Still, I will look into it."

I roll my eyes. "Just think about what I said. We need a strategy. We need a plan before we're infiltrated again and there's chaos. Just because we're watching for them, Kraven, doesn't mean we're prepared for what will happen." The liberator remains silent, so I take the opportunity to add, "And your little protégé, Neco? Something's off about that guy. He told me Aspen was dead. And that Charlie would die, too."

"He was triggering your combat skills. That's all."

I grasp his shoulder. It might be the first time I've ever touched him without using my fist. "All I'm saying is think about it. Think about an offensive strategy. And think about Neco, too. Can you be sure he's on our side?"

Kraven's head whips around, and a shadow crosses his face.

It looks a lot like doubt.

• • •

We train most of the day, picking up where we left off and learning how to use our shadow in war. This is Sector 2 in our training regiment, and I'll be the first to admit it's pretty damn cool. Paine and I fight across from each other, and sometimes Max and I do, too. We practice bleeping out from view as a fist flies in our direction or as a heel is about to slam down on us. We can sense one another's cuffs, but when we wink in and out of view, it's jarring. It gives you a moment, a nanosecond, to avoid being wounded.

I hate the thought of training. It's like we're testing our luck, seeing how much we can learn while the walls cave in around us. The sirens are out there, a collector could reappear at any moment if another vultrip is whispered open. But I'll admit that every time I learn something new, I gain a morsel of confidence.

The entire time we train—and even after as I'm eating dinner, one hand on Charlie's thigh—I think about what Kraven said. That I need to purge my demons to see what I'm fully capable of, a liberator with a soul. It seems like there are too many things I need to do: find a way to protect Charlie from the encroaching sirens, save Aspen, translate a dead language to unlock the scroll, uncover a traitor, and embrace the angel inside me.

The last thought makes me laugh.

Me. Dante. An angel.

Get the hell outta' here.

15

FLESH

After everyone has fallen asleep, I wake Charlie. I hate the thought of her missing out on much needed rest, but I also know she'll want to come along to where I'm headed. She slips out of Annabelle's room, and together, we leave the suite.

On our way to the library, we pass the humans—the *walkers*—Kraven has stationed outside our rooms to protect Charlie. It's dark when we arrive. And I have absolutely no idea where to start. Charlie flips a switch, and the multi-colored bulbs buzz to life overhead.

"It's eerie in here at night," she says.

I shiver. "When is being surrounded by books not eerie? Or wrong? Or painful?"

Charlie shakes her head, but I don't miss the smile on her face.

I retrieve the list of words from my back pocket and grab the first book I spot. Charlie grabs one, too. Then we sit side by side and flip through them. After twenty minutes, we haven't found a single word that's italicized or in heavier handwriting. I grab a few more and browse their pages. No luck there, either.

On the ninth book, however, my eyes spy something. I'm breezing past the pages when I see it. A word, different from the rest.

The twelfth star on the seventh moon grows wings. It flies. The farah burns brighter than the rest, and soars higher.

Farah means star.

I think?

"Charlie, check it out."

She leans over for a look. "That's got to be one."

"I think so, too."

She takes the list and checks. That word isn't on there. Though Oswald said where there was one, there'd be more. We search the rest of the tome and find several others, some we need, others we don't. So we surge onward. For another hour, we dig through books, making good progress, all things considered.

I can't help but question why Charlie and Aspen were able to read parts of the scroll and not others. Perhaps Big Guy wants to reveal things slowly. Perhaps Big Guy doesn't know what he's doing. Perhaps Big Guy is a sadist.

I frown at this last thought. I'm supposed to be all *Oh, Big Guy, you and I are cool now. We're cool. Even though my dad died in my arms. Even though you put that fucking deer in the road that night. Even though you're supposed to be able to control everything, but you didn't control that.*

The next book lies heavy in my hands. So do the next dozen. But I continue to probe their guts, hoping one of Oswald's miraculous words will make an appearance. At some point, I find myself staring at Charlie. Her tongue touches her top lip, and she furiously turns pages. A desperate tugs pulls inside my chest. We have so little time left. And every moment I have with her now feels stolen and impossibly perfect. I want to touch her hand, to kiss those gentle lips. But I don't. For once, I only watch her in the soft light. Take my girlfriend in without her noticing me staring.

It's late into the night when I tear my eyes away from Charlie and flip more pages. Charlie stands to stretch her legs, and I reach out and rub my hand against her calf. She smiles down at me and then gathers a few of the books into her arms. "These are the best books so far. The ones with the most outlying words. I'm going to take them down to Oswald's and drop them off. Be right back."

"I'll come with you." I start to get up, and then yawn so fiercely that Charlie laughs.

"Dante, the walkers are everywhere. I'll be back in five minutes. Stop treating me like an invalid."

"I wasn't treating you like an invalid. I was treating you like a piece of womanly meat I want to ogle. I was going to watch your booty shake as you walked with all those books."

"You're impossible." She leans down and kisses me, hardly able to keep the books in her arms.

After she leaves, I discover another book with the dead language buried inside. I toil to translate the first four words it holds, but when I come to the fifth, something happens. Maybe it's because I'm delirious from loss of sleep. Maybe it's because I feel like a human wrecking ball, and I'm hallucinating from the full body ache.

But when my eyes see that fifth word, I know what it means. I know what it means before I use the context clues. I know what it means, and it's like my mind has always known.

The word is *gregari*.

It means grace.

It's as simple as that.

I speak the foreign word out loud, and my tongue wraps around it like an old friend. The book tumbles from my grasp, and my heart clutches at the bones surrounding it. My eyes search the library. For what, I don't know. The hair on the back of my neck rises, and I feel like I could run the width of the world and it wouldn't be enough. I'm royally freaked out from discovering all these things I can do that I shouldn't be able to do.

My ears ring.

And I stop breathing.

Not because I understood a word I wasn't supposed to, but because I sense someone moving outside the hallway. At first I think it's Charlie, returning after dropping off the books to Oswald. But the way the shadow darts by, I know better. It could be a liberator, but even if it is, what are they doing out of bed? Kraven was firm when he said we needed to sleep between training sessions. And I'm the only one who goes against Papa K's direction.

I move toward the door, muscles burning with anticipation. When I get close to the entryway, the heavy, oak door slams shut from the outside. I grab for the handle, but it won't budge.

Charlie.

They've locked me in here, and she's walking the hallways.

I lose my mind with fear. I slam myself against the door again. Over and over until I'm certain my shoulder jerks out of socket. When I breathe in, the heavy scent of a fire blazing hits me. I spin around and see that a corner of the library is ablaze. I've had my back to that part of the room this entire time, but I don't now. The certainty of what's happening is unmistakable: the heat of the flame, the sound of the books crackling, the door locked shut.

Someone has started a fire in the library and trapped me in here.

My wings burst from my back, and I take myself high into the air to escape the licking orange and red. But there's too much smoke up here, and now I'm dropping down, hitting the ground with a *thud*. The fire spreads quickly, and my body warms even faster.

I have to get out of here!

I return to the door and throw myself into it once again. This time I yell. I remember the bells, the ones I thought where so useless, and charge toward where I see a string. I yank, but nothing happens. The blaze has burned through the strings that connect around the house, eaten it alive.

I'm going to burn to death. But I have dargon on my ankle. Liberators can only die if their cuff is removed, but how can my body heal if it melts into ash and that ash scatters? And what of the fire? Will it reach the rest of the house and consume the others?

I'm not one to ask for help, but just this once, I scream. I yell so loud the sound rattles me to my core. It unnerves me more than the fire does. Even more than feeling the heat grow into an unbearable pain.

I search for something to break the door down with. The table, a chair. I can hardly see either through the dense blue-black smoke. I grab the chair and, holding my breath, I ram it into the door. The heavy wood doesn't budge. Everything in the room is getting eaten alive by the fire, but the door is still standing. I grab the table next and slide it across the floor until it rams the door. Nothing.

My lungs begin to spasm. I've never felt them before, and to feel them now—burning for air, burning to escape my body—it almost takes me out of my own head. I cough until I'm sure I'll never inhale again. Smoke fills my nose, my ears, my mouth. A heat more intense than I've ever experienced in my life slithers up my left leg. I glance down.

I'm on fire.

This time when I yell, I'm sure the sirens outside must hear my cry.

I don't want to go out like this. Not screaming. Not crying for someone to rescue me. And then a strange thing happens. A peace crawls over me. I think to myself, if I were ever going to ask for His help, to reach out to Him, now would be a good time. I'm not sure why I've never thought about this before this moment, or why I do now. But once it's in my head, I can't help it. I can't help imagining what might happen if I asked.

And yet, I remain quiet.

My mind screams with agony as I try to escape the crackling

flames on my legs. But I won't ask Him for anything. He left me before, on that dark road with my father. Why would anything be different now?

The pain is all consuming.

I forget everything.

I forget Charlie.

My senses all call for my attention at once. They all hurt in torturous ways, and the cacophony of anguish is unbearable. I crumble to the ground.

I raise my head once more. I want to see how this all ends. I want to watch as I burn.

Someone is standing an arm's length away.

Their body dances behind the flames.

⊰ 16 ⊱

EYES THAT BURN

Soon there are two bodies I see amid the flames.

The one I first saw rushes forward, and the second dashes right behind him. They grab me and drag my body outside the library. The guy holding my right arm, Neco, rips off his shirt and orders me to roll back and forth.

"Listen to my voice," he roars. "Do it!"

My mind drowns in pain. It can't comprehend what he's saying. But somehow, my body understands. It rolls back and forth, and Neco smothers the flames that suckle my flesh. The other guy—Max, I think—barks instructions at humans nearby, though his voice quakes with uncertainty.

"Go to the kitchen and get buckets of water," he says. "Ring the bells. Get everyone. Do something!"

It sounds like Christmas as the bells chime their tune. It's like the whole house is laughing.

Smoke pours from the open doorway and into the hallway. There's so much, great, thick pillows of it. I can actually hear it rushing out like a flock of crows in flight. Neco drags me back farther and manages to kill the fire on my legs.

Soon Valery and the Quiet Ones are there. Everyone jumps into action by helping bring water from the kitchen, but they're all terrified, and it makes them clumsy. The fire's thirst isn't being quenched, and I'm afraid the whole house will fall victim to its greed.

My legs feel like they have a heartbeat, and that can't be a good sign. I get to my feet and howl. At least I can stand. My jeans are now '80s-looking blue jean shorts, shredded at the knee. As smoke continues to billow from the library doorway, and the fire eats away the last of our books, I experience a sharp clap of fury. This is Kraven's fault. He's the one who made us stay here when we should have left. He's the one who told us to train when he should have been planning a way to rescue Aspen and hide Charlie.

Where is he?!

Annabelle rounds the corner, her face filled with fear.

Something else dawns on me the moment I see her. Something I can't believe I haven't thought of before now. If a siren or collector locked me in the library, where are they now?

I run to Annabelle, limping from the pain. "Did you see Charlie?"

Annabelle shakes her head, crying. "I…I don't know. I left the room a while ago."

Kraven rounds the corner. Charlie is behind him accompanied by Paine and, farther behind, Blue. She's safe. I want to go to her. But what I want more is an outlet for this anger.

I fly at Kraven.

"This is your fault!" My hands grab his shirt, and I throw him into the wall as if he's a play toy. Kraven sees the blaze and begins to yell commands, but I'm not having it. I don't want to hear the sound of his voice.

I slam him back into the wall and am overcome by an irrational desire to end Kraven. If he's gone, I can create a strategy. I can lead these liberators to war, and I can save Aspen and Charlie both. "I'm going to kill you, Kraven. This is your fault!"

"Get off me, Dante," he clips. "We must stop the fire from spreading."

I grab his head in my hands and knock it once, twice, three times against the wall before he can react. "You let me take her there. You knew what would happen!"

I'm not making any sense. I've lost my freaking mind.

All I know is I want to hurt someone.

My fist crashes into Kraven's face. Then I grab his head again. I want to smash his skull until it spills open. But once I have it in my hands, once I really look at him—

Everything stops.

As I watch, Kraven's eyes fill with green so that there's no white, no black. Just dragon scale green. It looks like the liberator inside him has vanished, and all that's left is the shadow of a monster inhabiting his body. His face is every horror movie I've ever seen, every nightmare I've suffered. The bones in his cheeks protrude farther than they should, and his chin elongates. His ears lengthen into a pointed tip, and his nose flattens. I scramble to get away from him, but now he's the one holding me fast. I can't look at him. I can't. Because when I do, it's like I'm seeing the face of the devil himself. Or perhaps it's the face of God I'm seeing. Maybe this is what God's wrath looks like.

He opens his mouth and says, "Stand down." Except when he says it, it's more of a guttural growl that's hard to understand. His whole body is shaking as if he's about to emit fire of his own.

I escape his grasp and slam into the wall opposite us.

He blinks, and his eyes and face return to normal. Then he turns away and calls out orders in a calm tone. "Max and Blue, help the humans put out the flames. Valery, go and find anything else that can hold water. Annabelle and Charlie, go with the Quiet Ones and bring back blankets. Thick ones. Paine and Neco, pull doors from their hinges. We'll use them to seal off any entrance into the Hive the fire might have created."

Kraven turns to me. "Go and find Oswald. Ensure he's safe and then return to help."

Everything and everyone was in a state of chaos before Kraven arrived. And now, even though their faces are smeared with fear, they have a job to do. It comforts them. Kraven is here, and he's going to take care of everything.

"Dante," Kraven says, his voice a warning. "I said go."

I glance around one more time, at the smoke heaving into the Hive, at the liberators and humans thankful for their leader. Then I glance down at my own hands. "I'm sorry, Kraven. I don't know what came over me."

"It doesn't matter. Look in on Oswald."

I check to make sure Charlie is really okay, and then race down the hallway.

If I were being honest, I'd say I want to question Kraven about who locked me in the library and set it ablaze. I'd want to ask him where that person is now, and whether it was a coincidence that Neco was the first to find me.

But I don't do any of those things. I just run as fast as my charred legs will carry me. Pain shoots through my body with every step, and my lungs *burn, burn, burn*. I'll do as Kraven asked without question. Because for the first time tonight, I saw the leader in him. Even if his eyes and face did freaky shit there at the end, I trust his decisions. He doesn't have all the answers, I know that. I've seen the doubt in his features before. But he's doing what he can, and he's doing it with concern for each of us.

If I were being honest, I'd say that tonight I was scared.

And that Kraven being there made it better.

• • •

Two days after the fire, the flames are gone, and the library is boarded over. All but a handful of books remain, namely the ones Charlie took to Oswald. The old dude is beside himself that the library is destroyed, and I don't tell him how last night I could interpret that one word without using context clues. I don't want to get his hopes up before I'm sure I can be of any help.

One good thing comes out of last night: Oswald was able to unlock a new part of the scroll with our new translations.

Those with hardened hands shall pave the way to victory.

Today, everyone in the house is assembled in the training room. It's a tight squeeze. I'm not sure I ever realized how many humans resided at the Hive. There are a small handful, the walkers, who know how to fight like we do. They help secure the corridors as we sleep and help us train in shifts during the day. They're also the only humans who know exactly what we are.

But the rest are cooks and maids and repair men who buzz around the house and keep things running. They wouldn't know fighting if Chuck Norris walked in the room. I wonder why they are here.

Kraven stands in the center of the room. "I called you all here today because I wanted to address what happened last night. As many of you know, the library was lit on fire, and we believe the person who did it also locked Dante Walker in the room with the intent of killing him."

Charlie stands beside me, and when she hears this last part she clutches my hand. I kiss the top of her head to ensure her I'm okay. The Quiet Ones may have had to knock me out last night and work miracles on my calves and lungs, but I'm okay.

Kraven addresses the humans now. "What some of you may not know is that Dante Walker cannot be killed."

Kraven may expect the humans to gasp.

They don't.

He then proceeds to tell them everything about us, about how they may be in danger if they choose to stay. And yet they still don't gasp or scream or point fingers or grab pitch forks. Their faces are more like, *Yeah. And?*

A woman wearing a gold shawl and a pale blue blouse steps forward. "Kraven, if I may?"

He motions for her to speak.

"We all know what you are," she says. "But we're happy to stay. We came here to work because the pay is good, and we don't have anywhere else to go. You didn't ask questions about us when we arrived, and so we don't ask questions about you."

Kraven doesn't seem shocked. Not that he'd show it if he did. He seems more relieved. "I wondered if you knew."

A guy on the other side of the room, hidden by a row of bodies in front of him, calls out, "You guys have yelled about wings and saviors and demons right in front of us. Did you think we believed you were writing movies or something?"

The humans laugh, and surprisingly, so does Kraven. "So you'll stay?"

They nod eagerly, like they can't wait to be a part of something bigger than themselves. What I want to know is how Kraven planned on getting them out of here if they'd insisted on leaving.

"You won't be asked to do more than you already are," Kraven adds. "And you should know that He is thankful for each of you. You will be written in His heart for eternity for your work here."

The woman in the gold shawl is moved to tears at this. I gaze at her and the others. Were these bad people? Did Kraven give them a second chance at life and salary and camaraderie by asking them to work here? I've never questioned these people's choice to work at the Hive, but today I do.

Kraven thanks the humans for joining us and reminds them that if they change their mind about staying, to please find him. That he won't be upset. Though seeing the determined looks on their faces, I doubt that'll happen. Together, these people seem like a family, and what's more, I think they've come to consider the Hive as their home, a place they will stay aboard even if it pulls a Titanic.

Once the humans have gone, and only the liberators and walkers remain, Kraven speaks again. "Some of you may be nervous about what happened last night. Please know, things like this will continue to happen. As the rest of the world sleeps, we alone will face these battles. We will not fail in our trials. I have a plan in place. And a crucial part of that plan is preparing you for battle. I will be accelerating the pace of your training, and some of you will be surprised at what your liberator body is able to do with war approaching."

Kraven stops and shoots a pointed look at me.

I'm guessing he's referencing his trippy face transplant from last night. Or maybe to what I was able to do in practice against Neco. Either way, his words are unsettling.

• • •

The liberator isn't kidding when he says we'll train harder than ever before. Over the next several days, we complete Sector 2, Shadow in Combat, and move on to Sector 3, Incapacitation. In this sector, we learn how to be the aggressor in a fight. Half way through the session, I feel as if I could take on a professional cage fighter. We're taught how to step into our enemy's body and to take another step for each punch we throw.

"Accommodate for your enemy's head kicking backward," a walker says. "Step into him. Again. Again."

We learn where to kick and where to debilitate the human body, collector or not, and with what part of our hands. And we learn when to take a fight to the ground and when to stay on our feet. This sector is so different from the first, Basic Defense, it blows my mind. I'm freaking loving it. In Sector 1, they told us to avoid being hit. In Sector 3, they urge us to avoid being hit by never giving them the chance.

"The key," Kraven says, "is to know when to use defense and when to use aggression. When in doubt, be the aggressor."

Hell yeah.

I never experience a burst of power like I did with Neco, but that may be because I have a sense of calm today. War is coming in one week. Kraven is preparing us. It will be tragic, but in the end, everything will be okay. We'll have our day to fight, and we'll bring Aspen home.

She's alive. She has *to be alive.*

But for now, we'll stay near the Hive because the war is unavoidable, and at least here we know the lay of the land. Or at least that's what Kraven says. I decided something last night in the fire and that's this: I'm committed to learning this defense stuff. But even though I've stopped fighting Kraven on this one point, I still keep an eye on Neco at all times. Because I won't forget there's a traitor among us. I won't forget who the first person was at that fire last night.

Neco. Hey, Neco. I'm watching you, asshole.

⊰ 17 ⊱

CIRCLE OF FRIENDS

Tonight we take dinner in the only room made entirely of windows. It's on the third floor of the house and overlooks the ocean. It reminds me of the training room without the red, spongy mats or the stank of eight liberators attempting to hurt each other.

The Quiet Ones don't serve us the food. In fact, I haven't seen them all day. Not after they put some sweet healing balm on my burns last night and massaged it in with hands of awesome. I wonder what the H those mute broads are up to.

I'm sitting on a shoddy bench that circles the perimeter of the room, and Charlie is on the ground, leaning back between my legs. I work my hand over her hair, and she leans into my touch. She likes it when I braid and unbraid her hair, even though my version of this braiding business is twisting two big chunks around each other and trying to pretend I'm still a man.

Annabelle lounges on a yellow slip chair that used to be white. "Do you think my dark hair makes me look seductive?" she asks.

I snort.

Charlie elbows me and gets way too close to my junk. "Yes,"

Charlie says. "Totally."

My eyes narrow. "Did someone tell you that?"

Annabelle's cheeks redden like Charlie's did before the soul contract.

"Oh, man," I say. "What a line. Who was it?"

Annabelle's blush deepens. "Paine."

"You're really considering all your options, aren't you?" I rub my thumbs in circles over Charlie's scalp. I don't have to check to see if her eyes are closed. I know my touch is magically delicious.

"I like him." Charlie's voice is groggy from pleasure.

I stop rubbing. "What?"

She giggles and turns to face me. "He's nice. And he helped me last night when the fire broke out."

"He did?"

"Yeah. He saw me in the hallway and asked me what I wanted to do, if I wanted to find you or move to the opposite end of the house. Everyone treats me like I'm breakable, but he asked me what *I* wanted to do. It was nice."

My brow furrows. "He didn't say anything about it during training today."

"'Course he didn't," Annabelle says. "He thinks you're the bee's knees. Probably figures what he did is nothing compared to his beloved Dante Walker, the all-powerful."

It's weird, but I allow myself to imagine Paine as my friend. I want to be wary of him, to believe he and everyone else has an ulterior motive. But he hasn't given me a reason to suspect him of being anything other than chill, so why am I so hesitant?

"Hey, Charlie," I say. "Have you had any more luck with your hands?"

She stares down at them. "I'm getting better at it. Still nothing like that one time."

"Why does everyone have something cool but me?" Annabelle

says.

I straighten. "Well, you do have seductive hair. That's a weapon if I've ever seen one."

Annabelle roars with laughter and then makes a pose like she's hot stuff, one hand on her hip and lips pursed.

There's a knock, and we all turn and see who it is. Paine stands in the doorway, an awkward smile on his face. He takes us all in, but stops when his eyes fall on Annabelle. "Nice pose," he says in his British accent.

If her cheeks were red before, now they're nearly purple with embarrassment. "I've got other moves."

Paine nods and smiles wider, but doesn't move to come inside.

It's Charlie who invites him in. Of course. "Come hang out with us," she says. "We haven't been able to just lounge in a long time."

Paine glances at me as if waiting for my approval. I nod for him to come in. He grins like his world is complete and strides toward us. He's wearing an orange plaid shirt that picks up the red in his hair he tries so hard to hide. I want to suggest he try another color, but that'd make me a dick, right? Yeah. Dick.

"You always wear plaid?" I say.

He laughs. It's too loud for what I said, and he seems to realize it. He coughs into his closed fist. "I love the stuff."

"Why?" I ask.

Charlie elbows me again.

"Woman," I say. "You are getting way to close to my precious."

"I always wanted to be a farm kind of guy," Paine says.

"Jaysus," I say. "Hang out with cows and hay bales all day? Pass."

Paine isn't listening to me, though. He's focused on Annabelle, who I'm pretty sure said *hot* right after he said *farm kind of guy*.

He sits down next to her. Not too close, but close enough. Paine narrows his eyes at the ocean as if there's something out there he's searching for. But I know what's happening here. Home boy wants to strike up a conversation with Annabelle and has no way to start it.

"So…you like Oswald?" he asks Annabelle.

I roll my eyes.

Annabelle, however, has much to say on the subject.

"This is fun," Charlie says. "It feels like old times. Kicking it with friends and stuff."

Annabelle agrees, and so do I, even though my old friends were rat bastards who used me for cash. I notice Paine doesn't agree. In fact, he sort of diverts his gaze like he wants to avoid the subject.

"You miss your life before being a liberator?" I ask Paine directly.

He smiles. "Yeah, I do," he says. But then his smile falters. Paine eyes Annabelle. "Actually, I don't. My family moved around a lot. Made meeting people hard. I had this one girl friend. Not a girlfriend. Just a girl who was a friend. I miss her especially."

"What was she like?" Annabelle whispers.

Paine looks at her without speaking until we all understand that Annabelle must remind him of her. She blushes.

Listening to his sob story, my heart does this damn clench thing. Totally Charlie's fault. I didn't used to care when I heard this sort of crap. Now I do, apparently. I groan inwardly and say, "Well, today you're a liberator. And we're all here for the same reason. So, you got friends now."

I want to puke at how disgustingly emotional what I just said was.

But Paine, he's looking at me like he wants to call me brother and exchange friendship bracelets. I decide, maybe, that I do like the kid all right. Perhaps it's hard to admit that another dude could think of me as a true friend. That I could have that kind of relationship outside of Max, a partnership that began in hell. Max is still my No. 1 bro. Always will be. But I guess that doesn't mean I can't be nice to Paine.

"Thanks for watching out for Charlie last night," I tell him.

He waves me off like it isn't a big deal, and I respect him even more.

The four of us hang out for more than an hour, and Charlie's right, it feels good. Even if we are surrounded by reinforced glass. And even if there is less than a week until we are forced to fight. Or that we don't know how long we have until the sirens eat through the walls like termites or before the collectors pop up through the floors.

Or how many hours until Rector steps foot inside the Hive.

Someone clears his throat near the doorway, and I wonder who it is this time. When I glance up, the tendons in my body ache with anticipation.

Blue stares me down.

Then he sighs like he's been holding that breath for almost two weeks. He shoves his hands into his pockets, and his eyes fall to the floor. "Can I hang out with you guys?"

When his gaze lifts, it's me he's looking at. I can't help the skip my heart performs. I'm mortified by how happy I am that he's here. I mean, he's practically apologizing in man speak.

I swing my leg over Charlie's head and walk over to Blue.

No one says a word.

I stand in front of him, and when his mouth cracks into a smile, mine does, too. And suddenly, his arms are around me, and mine are around him, and we're slapping each other on the back so that everyone knows we don't swing that way, but man, it's awesome to be hugging. I mutter that I'm so damn sorry, and he mumbles that it's not my fault and he wanted someone to blame, and I say I'm to blame, and he says to go fuck myself.

And just like that, Blue and I are Blue and I again.

I drag the curly-headed dude over to my bench and practically pull him into my lap. I want to do all the crap dude's do when they're happy to see each other. I want to punch him in the arm and call him names and tease him mercilessly. And so I do. Blue returns the favor, and each time he does, his smile broadens. Paine does a good job hanging with us. He's shy, except when he's defending Annabelle, but he wants to fit in this time. And it just so happens that I'm accepting applications for new bromances.

What's weird, though, is that each time we laugh—each time we grab our stomachs and roll from delirium or from the fact that Blue clearly said the word panties even though he insists the word was *pansy*—I miss Max. Here are new, shiny friends.

But I miss Max.

A heavy sensation rolls through the room like a hot breath. When I turn, I spot Kraven standing just outside the doorway. We must be making a lot of noise. But Kraven's eyes aren't on us. They're on Annabelle.

Maybe her hair is seductive, because the liberator is wearing the same expression Paine is. But that's not true, exactly. Because Paine appears more enamored with Annabelle, like she's a girl he'd like to make cupcakes for even though he hates cupcakes. The kind of girl he wants to kiss like he means it, and the kind of girl he'd like to introduce to Mom. That is, if Paine could do those things. If he wasn't wearing a liberator cuff.

Kraven, on the other hand, looks at Annabelle with unadulterated passion. He looks at her like she's his heart, and if she moves too far away, he may drop dead. Kraven's eyes take her in like he would a love he believed forever lost. Like he would his own soul.

He looks at her like I look at Charlie.

The liberator grinds his teeth, his hands balled into fists at his sides. It's the only sign that announces he's upset. When Annabelle sees him, she leans toward Paine to finish their conversation. She didn't need to be so close to Paine to hear his words a moment ago, but now she does. Her jaw tightens, and her eyes storm with defiance.

"Annabelle," Kraven says.

Paine stops speaking and turns to see Kraven. He doesn't seem pleased at our newest guest.

"May I speak with you?" Kraven asks.

"No," she answers. There's no room for argument. That single word is like a bullet, and Kraven flinches from the impact. I wonder if his face will trip out again, and I also wonder when he'll tell us what we're really capable of, and whether one day my face will do the same thing.

I seriously hope not.

I can see what Kraven is considering. He's thinking about begging. But he won't. Not in front of us, and maybe not in private, either. Perhaps that's the problem. Because for Charlie, I'd get on bended knee and kiss her painted toes if it meant making amends.

Then I'd ravage her, obviously. That's the only way to argue: bend to your woman's will, then show her you're a man.

But Kraven only watches as Annabelle touches Paine's arm and says, "I'm busy."

He studies her so long that Blue clears his throat. I almost make a joke about the awkwardness, but I'm afraid Kraven will Unabomb us for real. Finally, he turns and leaves. I almost feel bad for the dude.

Almost.

Paine examines Annabelle's face. There's no way he doesn't know she used him to make Kraven jealous. But he covers her hand with his anyway. I've known dudes like that. They realize they're second choice, but they're willing to wait until they're first. Because in the end, they win. And sometimes, if it's the right girl, that's all that matters. Me? I don't play that game. I'm your first choice, or I'm outtie. But it's cool if Paine's down with that strategy.

The five of us hang out a while longer before Blue heads to bed and Paine offers to walk Annabelle to her room. I shoot the dude a look like *don't even think about it,* and he shows me his hands in surrender. He'll walk her to her room, that's fine, but I don't want him getting funny ideas about getting some from Annabelle. Me being with Charlie is one thing. But Anna?

I'll murder someone.

I offer Charlie my hand and pull her up. "Let's go to bed, too, huh?" I try to say it casually. If it's casual, then maybe she'll oblige.

She glances out across the ocean like she's thinking. Her brows pull together, and she looks a lot like she did two nights ago. The night she said she envisioned how this would all end. "Okay," Charlie says.

She takes my hand.

We walk in silence back to our suite of bedrooms. There's this hush about the Hive, and once again, I can't help wondering how long this will last. It feels like we're living inside this glass ball. Outside, wasps buzz impatiently, waiting for their chance to strike. And inside, black widows discover crevices in our armor and slip in unnoticed. They're here, and then they're gone. Or maybe they came in the night, and they never left.

When we turn the corner, Oswald is there waiting for us. His drooping cheeks are pale, and his mouth is downturned. The old man moves quickly toward us, gray robe swishing around him, long arms brushing his sides.

His small, alert eyes speak volumes.

He has come to tell us something important.

⇌ 18 ⇌

ROOTED

Oswald comes to a stop and pulls on his earlobe. His eyes dart around, ensuring we're alone.

"Spill it, Hefner. What's going on?"

"Kraven said I shouldn't say anything until we were sure," Oswald squeaks.

"But you're here. So you must think differently. What's up?"

Charlie's grip on my hand tightens.

Oswald drops his arm to his side. "I was able to translate another portion of the scroll using the books you found in the library. How I'll translate the rest of the document is beyond me, but at least we have this one part. It's quite fascinating, really. How the collectors, or whoever it was, knew to target the library and burn—"

"Oswald," I interrupt. "Tell us what you found."

He wraps his arms around his stomach and inspects each of us in turn. Then he says, "The scroll spoke of a pair of hearts that…" Oswald clears his throat. "It said… *Two hearts that beat as one will make a great sacrifice.*"

I wait for him to reveal more.

He doesn't.

"That's kind of encrypted," Charlie says.

"They're *all* encrypted." I press the heel of my hands to my forehead. "What you're saying is English, but it's still in code. What's the point of finding the translations if what we read doesn't make sense? We've got find the sparrow among the crows in some unburned room, something about people with calloused hands leading to victory, and now this."

Oswald's bushy eyebrows rise. "Perhaps it will make sense when the time is right."

I roll my eyes. "What does Kraven think it means?"

"I'm not sure he knows," Oswald says.

"Have you been able to work out other parts?"

"I believe there are only two other part," he admits.

"Well?" I say. "Any ideas on what those will say?"

A shadow falls over his face. "N-no."

I cock my head. "Oswald."

"What is it?" Charlie asks him.

The old guy cinches his robe belt and meets my eyes. His entire body seems to quake like he wants to disappear from sight. And slowly, Oswald begins turning in a circle.

"Aw, Oswald," Charlie says. The lack of surprise in her voice says she's seen this from him many times. She touches his shoulder, and he stops turning. His eyes take her in, and his breath catches.

And in that moment, I know. One of the last parts of the scroll is about Charlie.

• • •

Charlie falls asleep in my arms, my black wing wrapped around her small frame. I know she won't stay through the night regardless of how close I hold her. But I wish she would.

I stay awake as long as I can and watch her breathing deeply, her chest rising and falling. Her skin is flawless during the day, a side effect of the soul contract, but at night it seems to glow. I can't help running a thumb over her porcelain cheek. There used to be small, pink bumps here and a flush that I could bring out at any time. Now she is a mirage of the girl I met in Peachville, Alabama.

My head hangs heavy on the pillow, and though I don't want to miss a single breath she takes—I tumble into sleep.

I open my eyes, and my stomach dives into my throat. I'm in a room that's smeared with soot and decorated with furniture still smoldering from a forgotten fire.

And I am lying on the ceiling.

At first I lie perfectly still, afraid if I move I'll come crashing down. I'm not so high up. Maybe only twelve feet above the floor. But it's more than enough.

Carefully, my hands explore the space around me. And when I discover that I don't fall, I push up onto my hands. Then to my feet. Blood doesn't rush to my head like I expect it to. Because even though I'm hanging upside down, it feels completely natural.

I take one wobbly step, and then another, and walk toward the closest wall. When I reach it, my hands pass through to the other side. I contemplate what to do next as my heart dances in my chest. This is a dream, I remind myself.

But I know that may not be true.

I've never dreamt like this before.

I close my eyes and walk through the wall. My body free falls, and I crash to the ground. Small pebbles dig into my skin, but I'm too relieved to be right side up to care. When I raise my head, I spot Aspen.

She's wearing a dress of scarlet and plum. It cascades down her body like ripples in the desert heat. The folds of the dress appear to move though her body is still. She holds her arms out to me, and her mouth opens in a perfect circle of black. The teeth and tongue are gone from her mouth, and all that remains is a deep, empty cavern.

Though her lips move, no sound greets my ears.

"Aspen." I move closer, but something stops me. It's her skin. Something is wrong with her skin. It has an odd sort of rise and valley to it like wind trails left in sand. Aspen is standing on a podium of sorts, surrounded by a moat of inky water. The moat isn't wide, maybe five feet across, and it certainly won't stop me from getting to her.

"Jump across," I tell her, my body heating with a sort of mad fever. "I'll take you back."

I don't know why I say it, but once it's out there, I can't unthink it. Maybe I could wrap Aspen in my arms and scream myself awake. Perhaps if I hold on tightly enough, she'll be there when I wake. Charlie will call for the Quiet Ones, Blue will race in and drop to her side, and Aspen will be back, safe. Simple as that.

The podium is large enough for two people to stand on, so I make a motion for Aspen to move back. She seems afraid to leap, so I'm going to jump across the empty space, over the water that runs quick like an open vein, and take Aspen into the waking world.

She opens her mouth again, and her throat works, but again there is no sound.

"It's okay, Aspen. I'll come to you. Just step back so there's room for me."

The podium projects from the water like a perfectly square island. An island for two.

Aspen tips her head back and screams a silent cry for help. Black tears escape her eyes and run down her milk-white neck. A thick lump forms in my throat at the sight.

"Just move back a step, *please*." But she won't move, she can't speak, and something tells me that this is all part of a plan. That I'm supposed to be driven into insanity. I'm supposed to be so filled with angst that I jump and risk tipping into the water.

I judge the space around Aspen. If I leap, and grab onto her, perhaps it could work. It's a chance I'll take.

My legs itch to run, my body fires with eagerness. I back up a few steps and ready myself. Three…two…

I stop.

A watery figure rises up from behind Aspen like a liquid moon. The figure takes her in his arms. Water races down the human form, and slowly, I begin to see that this is not a body made of water, but someone I recognize. A collector, flesh and blood.

The man—tall, cropped hair, knowing smile—bends his head so that his cheek touches Aspen's cheek.

Rector.

His hands explore the length of her body, and she gasps in silent protest. He raises her dress, inch by inch, his smile widening. I begin to see her legs, her knees.

And I wretch at the sight of her.

Her extremities have fused together to resemble a tree trunk, and her toes have grown deep into the platform like roots, searching for water. She is literally planted in place.

I right myself, feel anger rupture any rational thought I may have had, and I run.

Aspen shakes her head.

No, no, no.

I run.

I leap.

My feet touch the platform for an instant. My fingers brush her bark-like skin for a moment. And then I am falling. My body hits the water, and a cold like I've never experienced before sucks me down, down. The cold is a dead thing, but it wants to live. And here I am with life to give.

As I drown, sinking deeper into the water, Aspen finally finds her voice.

"You-You-You…" she stutters.

Rector kisses her cheek and keeps his eyes on me. *Mine* he seems to say.

"You-You-You're already…" Aspens swallows, sees that my ears are almost fully submerged. She opens her mouth, she fists her hands with a crackling sound, and she says in a hiss, "You're already dead. Go back to sleep."

I wake up.

I wake up, and the bells in the house are ringing.

PURGATORY

"Heaven wheels above you, displaying to you her eternal glories, and still your eyes are on the ground."

—Dante's Inferno

19

THE SIRENS SLITHER

I leap from my bed and search for Charlie. She isn't in the room with me.

Racing through the bathroom, I find her and Annabelle sitting up in bed, their eyes wide with fright.

"What it is?" Charlie's spine is as straight as a pencil. "What's happening?"

Blue barrels into the room, breathing hard. "Do you know anything?"

I shake my head and think. I can either see what's happening, or I can stay and protect Charlie and Annabelle. My heart says to stay, but my brain says I'm more equipped for fighting than Blue since I can summon my wings and who knows what else. I make my decision.

"Blue, can you stay with the girls?"

Charlie starts to argue, but I stop her. "I know you want to help. But you're the savior, Charlie. We can't risk you until it's necessary."

I don't know when it will be necessary, or if I could watch her be in harm's way even then, but it pacifies her for now. She nods and stands at the foot of the bed, like if she's the last line of defense, she'll defend Annabelle to the death. I love her so much in this moment I can actually *feel* it in the beat of my heart.

I glance at Blue and then rush out the door. The first person I find is Valery. Her lips are parted, and she looks close to tears. Valery. Strong and fearless.

Battle makes cowards of us all.

My legs burn beneath me as I race through the Hive, searching for the source of the alarm. For once, Valery is on my heel instead of the other way around. I spot Kraven and race faster. I call out to him, but he plunges forward without looking back.

The three of us spill into the great room.

My blood stops.

My heart stops.

The truth of what's happening is too much.

Sirens pour through the roof like bats from a cave. They drop down on ropes strung from the ocean's guts and they scatter across the floor. Standing in the center of it all is Anthony, the largest of all the collectors. He's built like a vending machine with a head that's way too small for his body. He is all muscle, small brain. But tonight, he's using what little brain power he has to direct the sirens.

I imagine Kraven will immediately summon his wings and begin fighting. Instead, he barks orders as humans and liberators spill into the room, their once sleepy faces alert with terror.

We expected this.

Have prepared for this.

Yet as the battle reveals itself, we are aghast. We are immobile. Maybe because we believed we had another few days to ready ourselves. Kraven jerks us out of our stupor with sharp words.

"Max, go and find the Quiet Ones. Tell them what's happening and get them to my chambers. Valery, find the humans and do the same."

Kraven turns to me. "Go and find Oswald. Bring him here."

"But—" I start to protest, to yell that we have to get Charlie out of here first and foremost. But two days ago, I said I was going to trust Kraven. And though I've never relied on anyone but myself, this time I do.

I race to the basement, and as I do I set my mind on Blue. I hope for him to be strong and smart. I hope for him to hide Charlie and Annabelle and for something *bigger* to be with them all, protecting them.

What I'm doing in my head…it feels a lot like praying.

But it's not.

I crash into Oswald's personal dungeon and blink at the horde of lamps lighting the area. *What is his deal with lamps?* It's the only thought I have before grabbing his arm and telling him what's happened.

"Kraven wants me to come *there?*" Oswald's voice is wobbly, his fingers curled in horror.

I shake my head. "I don't know why, either. But that's what I was told."

Oswald stumbles after me like it's the last thing he wants to do. Twice I have to grab his elbow and force him to move faster. The old man seems as if he's two seconds from fleeing the Hive entirely.

As we near our destination, my body feels like it's electric. Every hair stands on end. Every nerve ending crackles with anticipation. The sirens are inside. A collector is among us. A traitor has struck again.

This is the beginning of something terrible.

Kraven sees us coming. He's yelling something I can't hear. The sirens are too loud with their stomping feet and the bells are too suffocating with their insistent ringing. He's like Aspen on the platform, his mouth is moving, but nothing is heard.

I grab Oswald once more and he fights against me. "No way, old man," I say. "Come *on.*" I don't like dragging him toward danger, but I'm doing this thing. I'm *trusting.* I'm trusting and it's scaring the ever loving crap out of me.

I jerk to a stop beside Kraven and my eyes take in the great room. The sirens have stilled. Anthony stands at the front of them. Six sirens are holding six of our own.

The walkers. The humans who know how to fight, who have trained us for the last several days, have been overcome by the sirens. Strength in numbers and all that. One walker near the middle meets my gaze. Her eyes sparkle like two stars set in the folds of her skin. The siren behind her holds a knife made of the ocean's stone to her neck. Around the woman, five other walkers stand still as death, a blade touching each of their throats.

We need these people alive if we are to stand a chance. Kraven doesn't believe in using humans in the war between heaven and hell. But here they are, hostages, lambs at the slaughter.

Anthony raises his arm into the air.

The woman with the knife at her neck screams.

Kraven pleads with the collector, who grins like this is funny.

Oswald begins turning in circles.

I breathe. I close my eyes. I open them.

I run.

My body charges toward the siren grasping the woman. If I can just save her. If I can just save one person, it'll be okay. Kraven may believe he can reason with Anthony, but I know better. I trained this guy. I taught this monster how to eat, to never leave gristle on the bone. And now here he is, showing me he's all grown up.

I'm almost to her, can almost spot the relief on her face when the siren pulls the knife across her neck. The skin opens so easily, like pulling a crisp white sheet of paper in half. And then the blood comes. It gushes from the open wound and spills down her chest like a strawberry bib.

Her eyes roll back in her head.

And her body slumps to the ground.

Across the room, the sound of five more bodies hit the floor.

These people are dead. They chose to help creatures most would consider detestable, creatures that shouldn't be alive. And now they are dead. I think about what Kraven said to them just yesterday; that they would be written in His heart for eternity for their work. They are in the heavens now. They are safe.

I don't believe in much, but I have to believe that. Just this once.

I look to Anthony.

He smiles.

The room holds its breath.

And then he releases the sirens. They charge toward us, stepping over six human carcasses in their flight. The sirens look like a swarm of flies, buzzing, swaying as they race toward us.

Anthony finally speaks. It's the first time I've heard his voice in months. "Find the girl!"

Hearing what he says, my mind snaps to attention. We must fight. No, we must flee. There are too many. There's nothing to be done. Kraven should have planned for this. I trusted him to take care of us, and what did he do? He told us to train. He told me to bring an old man.

He failed us all.

And I failed Charlie.

Kraven's wings burst from his back and he staggers, nearly falls to the floor. I grab his arm to steady him. Then I remember he's done us no favors and I throw his arm away. Oswald remains rooted in place, shaking, crying. The sirens are a sigh away and Oswald is frozen with fear.

"Oswald!" I yell. I don't know why I call out to him. There's nothing to be done for any of us. But I don't want to watch him die. I have to save him and find Charlie and spend my last few moments holding her against me.

Oswald is overcome with terror. And the old man only knows one thing to do when he's nervous.

He starts turning in circles.

I rush toward him. "Oswald, run!"

But it's too late. A siren is one step away from him, and I am three.

Oswald spins and spins. The siren reaches him and raises his blade into the air.

Oswald spins and spins and spins and spins and something is happening—

An orange light begins to radiate from his body. The siren nearby falls back but it's too late.

The.

World.

Explodes.

Orange light blasts over the entire room like a nuclear bomb and I'm thrown twenty feet. My head hits the wall and I see black. I see black, and I see Charlie jumping on her bed in Peachville. I see her feeding raccoons and I see how beautiful she was the first time we made love.

When the light recedes, Oswald is hunched over as if he's in pain. Half the sirens are dead, and Anthony is gone, probably gone back to hell through a vultrip. The sirens that remain scramble to their ropes and they clamor up, leaving their brothers and sisters behind.

Kraven rushes forward to help Oswald.

And I run to Charlie.

⇥ 20 ⇤

A ROOM UNBURNED

Hours later, after we'd removed the bodies from the great room, I still couldn't stop thinking about Oswald. Never did I think the old man had it in him. But why not? Charlie is able to do a similar kind of thing with her hands. Oswald's ability just takes turning in circles. I wonder if I should rename him Tornado.

As I think about Oswald, I also think about the humans who died. The walkers.

Dead.

Like Aspen, maybe.

Dead.

After Charlie has assured me for the hundredth time that she's okay, I head to Kraven's room, glancing up every few seconds as I walk. The ceiling above the great room has been patched, even though the thought of the sirens having spent days up there—chipping away at the tiled roof unheard—still disturbs the hell out of me.

I knock once on Kraven's door before letting myself in.

He's sitting on the edge of his bed, blond hair tucked behind his ears. The features of his face seem sharper somehow, like he's changing as war grows closer. Because war is growing closer. At first

I thought it was upon us, but now I know that was merely a strike before January twenty-first arrived.

"We need to consider leaving the Hive," I tell Kraven. "And you need to let me in on your strategy. You ask everyone to trust you, but you don't trust us."

Kraven turns his face away. "I didn't ask anyone to trust me."

I don't respond.

The liberator sighs. "There's a traitor who's whispering the doors open."

"I know."

Kraven's head snaps in my direction. Then he shakes it. "Oswald."

"Old man can't keep a secret to save his life," I say.

Kraven holds up a finger and smiles an unconvincing smile. "Except one."

I nod, remembering Oswald's ability. "Except one."

Kraven stands and walks to the center of the room. He gazes up at the circular window at the top of his room. I take his place at the foot of the bed. "Tell me why you want to stay here," I say.

Kraven's shoulders tense and then relax. He crosses the distance between us in a flash and grabs my face in his hands.

"What the fu—?"

"Can I trust you, Dante?" His eyes flick across my features. "Because I believe He trusts you. Why else would He have brought you back?"

I shove him away. "Tell me what it is you're hiding!"

Kraven's eyes storm. "Tell me exactly what it is the scroll said."

"Which part? The first part talked about a sparrow among crows or some crap, the second thing—"

"Stop. What exactly did the first part say?"

I think back, clear my throat. "It said, 'The room unburned holds a sparrow among crows.' What does it matter? It's all gibberish. I thought the scroll could somehow help us win, but we need to focus on more tactile assaults."

Kraven grabs a white coat from a single rusted hook and pulls it on. "Follow me." The liberator strides toward his fireplace and I'm about to ask what the H he's doing when he ducks inside of it and disappears.

I move toward where I last saw him. No flames dance in the hearth, and when I inch closer, I see that there's a wall stopping any entry. But Kraven is gone. I take a cautious step forward and my eyes reveal the truth: the back of the fireplace is a mirage, one that easily fools any onlooker when a flame is lit within. But with the embers hushed, I make out that it's a tunnel.

I swallow any doubt and stride after Kraven.

Following the sound of his footsteps, I walk on, feeling as if we're being swallowed by the earth. After only a couple of minutes, I spot a light up ahead, and a few paces later I come to a stop beside Kraven. We're standing outside a door that's perhaps three feet tall and is more a crawl space than an entrance. There isn't even a knob, but light seeps through the bottom and sides enough so that I can tell it's some sort of opening to another room.

Kraven rears back and kicks the door in. A plume of dust tickles my nose and then we're on our hands and knees, ducking through the entry way and coming to a stand again.

The liberator spreads his arms. "The reason we mustn't leave the Hive."

My eyes take in the room and my ears ring.

Weapons.

Hundreds of them.

There are shields crested with horses of fire, and swords hilted in glittering silver. There are daggers paired like twin brothers, and throwing stars with vengeful, serrated edges. Near the back wall hang axes with lethal heads, and stacked on the floor are helmets and body armor. The room is enormous, and there are enough weapons here to equip a small army. Everywhere I look—weapons. Everywhere I look—a fresh way to murder someone.

And then there is this: a sword blending seamlessly against the rest. It has a yellow gemstone in the hilt, and a glittering tip I can't ignore. It's like it's calling to me, but that might be the jewel talking. I once rocked half-carat diamonds in my ears. Not saying I'm proud of that fashion statement, but precious jewels and I have a deep-rooted relationship that's withstood the test of time.

For a long time, I run my hands over the smooth finely made artillery, keeping an eye trained on the bedazzled blade. Finally, I find my tongue. "I thought you said the war between heaven and hell wouldn't be fought with weapons."

Kraven shakes his head, but doesn't reveal any real emotion. "No, I said it wouldn't be fought with modern weapons. These are not modern. These were made hundreds of years ago by a woman named Beatrice Patrelli. She was graced by Him to create these weapons in anticipation of this war. And they have been buried here ever since."

"Wouldn't they be, I don't know, rusted by now?" I ask.

Kraven picks up a knife the length of my forearm and holds it to the light. "Before there was the Hive, a small cottage sat here. This was the basement." Kraven touches the tip of his blade to the stone wall, stained green from lime deposit. "Generations of Patrelli lived here, devoting their lives to the upkeep of these weapons."

"Where are they now? The Patrelli?"

Kraven meets my gaze. "All that remained were two sisters. But they died about a year ago, before the Hive was constructed."

I run my calloused palm over a shield, taking in the smooth metal. "How did they die?"

"They killed themselves."

The blood freezes in my veins. I suddenly don't want to be in the room anymore. Who knows where the girls' bodies were buried. Even though I'm technically dead, there's a big difference between me and a decomposing corpse.

Corpse.

Aspen.

The walkers.

I want to move forward with this conversation, to do something that will get me closer to rescuing Aspen and hiding Charlie. So I say, "Why can't we take the weapons with us somewhere else?"

"And carry them on trains and ships and airplanes?" he asks. "Or in a car where we can get pulled over by American authorities?"

"What are we going to get arrested for? Unlawful use of swag?" I'm making a joke, but I know he's right. We can't carry all this stuff discretely. "Why is there so much when there's so few of us."

Kraven doesn't answer.

Kraven doesn't know.

"You think we'll really need them?" I can't believe the words leave my mouth after I've pushed for weapons for so long.

Kraven pulls himself taller. I do, too. Just in case this is a contest.

"These weapons were meant to be used in the war," he says. "They were meant for us."

"Oh, right. You got that faith thing going on."

The liberator sighs. "Dante, the eight of us can't win against the collectors and a hoard of sirens if you don't believe in something."

"I believe you got it bad for Annabelle, that's what I believe."

He turns away so that I can't see his face. "You're deflecting. But there will come a time when you'll realize how you are on the inside."

"How's that, Cyborg?"

He meets my eyes. "Empty."

I pull back like he landed a solid one on my chin. "I don't feel empty. I'm all filled up. There's nothing but magnificence inside in this body."

Kraven's jaw tightens.

"What's the plan, Kraven?" I ask, being serious. "You must have one."

"We *must* finish training."

I begin to say something, but he cuts me off.

"And *you*," he snaps. "You have to understand how important it is that the liberators are prepared to fight this war. Battles will come and lives will be lost. But when the sun rises in six days, we must be ready. Training, Dante. That is what will ready us. Remember, the day of war was determined long ago. Both sides know about it. Anything that happens between now and then is merely a tactic to gain an advantage on the day war has been fated."

"Why are you showing me this now?" I ask.

"Because of what you and Charlie found on that scroll. 'A room unburned.'"

Understanding dawns on me. "You believe one of these weapons is different than the others? A sparrow among crows?"

"I'm not sure. Do you feel a pull toward any particular sword?"

On reflex, my eyes dart to the sword I saw earlier. The one with the yellow jewel buried in its hilt. It seems too wimpy to be special compared to these gangster axes. And throwing stars? Hook a brother up.

"Let your heart speak to you."

"Give it a rest, Oprah." I step toward the knife and crouch down. My heart beats wildly against my chest and sweat breaks out across my forehead. I don't reach for it, or ask Kraven if I can take it back to my room. But I do whisper inside my head, *Hello, sparrow*. I stand up. "I can't be sure."

The same reason that Kraven neglected to show me this room for weeks, is the same reason I don't tell him the driving impulse I have to pick up that blade. I've accepted his leadership, but during these dangerous times I don't trust anyone but my Charlie.

Kraven inspects me closely, like he's trying to find something that's lost to him. "They would listen to you. If you tried leading the people in this Hive, they would listen."

"Of course they would," I bark, even though he's changing the subject. I've led collectors before. And I could lead liberators and humans alike.

But do I *want* to?

And do I truly believe I'd know what to do? Enough to rescue Aspen? To save Charlie?

"We can't leave the weapons unguarded like this," I say.

"The Quiet Ones guard them." Kraven ducks down and clamors his dump-truck-sized ass through the opening. Watching him pull himself through, I wonder if the Patrelli were midgets. It'd be kick ass to be a midget. If I were a midget, the first thing I'd do is get it on with Charlie. As a midget.

I crawl out after Kraven and we make our way back to his chambers in silence. On the way, I decide I want to call my room *chambers* also, because it sounds much more official. Contemplating this is much easier than thinking about that woman's neck split open like a clam, pink flesh bubbling out.

When we land inside Kraven's chambers, neither one of us is prepared for what we see.

⚔ 21 ⚔

HARDENED HANDS

Humans take up every available space in the chambers. When Kraven and I try to move farther into the room, the tide of bodies has to spill into the hallway outside in order to accommodate us.

My mind races and I listen for the bells. But I don't hear anything. My heart slows when I see Charlie at the doorway. People move aside as she makes her way toward me. I wrap my arm around her, kiss her temple, and face the gathering.

Kraven addresses the people who work the Hive. He doesn't ask what they are here for. He doesn't tell them to return to their duties. "I'm deeply sorry for the loss of your fellow humans."

The crowd parts and a man in his fifties steps forward. He has liver spots on his forehead and hands though he seems too young for such a thing. Silver whiskers grow along his jaw, which makes him look James Bondish. I vow right then and there that as soon as I'm ancient, I'll do the same—sport silver stubble. Then I remember with a pang that I'll always be seventeen.

James Bond speaks. His voice is higher than I expected. "We don't want your condolences."

"You're angry," Kraven responds. The crowd mutters their agreement. Kraven lowers his head. "I'll make plans for you to leave at once."

The man looks behind him at a woman. It's the same woman who spoke in the training room. She still wears the gold shawl around her shoulders. Maybe it's his wife. Did these two know each other before they came here, or did they meet inside the Hive? James Bond returns his gaze to Kraven. He squares his shoulders. "We want to fight."

"No." Kraven looks down and shakes his head. *This isn't up for negotiation*, he seems to add.

But I study these people closer. I see the anger painted on their faces and their need to help. They've washed our dishes and cleaned our sheets and replaced old light bulbs. But now they wish to do more. Now they want retribution.

"Did you know the ones that died?" I ask James Bond.

The man turns to me. "One of them, Edward, he was my cousin."

Someone near the back adds, "Sara was my friend."

I don't know who Sara was—a walker, sure—but was it the woman who watched me as she died? Other humans in the room call out how they knew one of the walkers.

"Tom helped me get over my nightmares."

"Joshua walked by my door each night so I'd feel safe."

"Sara and Jolene loved my blackberry cobbler."

Every last walker is gone. Every human who knew how to fight, dead. But these people are here, and they want to take action. I step in front of Kraven. "We can teach you how to fight like they did."

"I said *no*," Kraven growls.

"And I'm saying yes," I challenge. "You said it yourself these people are in His favor. They know what's happening. They know they'll be risking their lives. You can't make this choice for them. It's called free will, right? Isn't that what He's all about?"

Kraven's scowl says he's not convinced, but I catch the confliction in his eyes. "It's wrong. This isn't how it's supposed to be. I never should have allowed humans to work here."

"But you did," I say. "And the sirens are humans, too. If they can choose to fight alongside collectors, why can't these people fight alongside us? With them by our side, we could stand a chance. You saw how many sirens Oswald took out." My heart is racing because what I'm saying makes sense. There are countless sirens, and even more the collectors are probably recruiting. Maybe with the weapons, and with these people, we could win. But then I remember the way that walker's neck opened, and my certainty wavers.

It's Charlie who ultimately seals the deal. "Did you read the passages we revealed on the scroll?" When Kraven doesn't respond, she continues. "Remember this line? *Those with hardened hands shall pave the way to victory*." Charlie motions toward James Bond. "Please, sir. Your name is Harold, correct?"

The man raises his head.

"Could you show Kraven your hands?"

Harold looks as confused as I feel, but he offers them to Kraven to inspect. Charlie runs her fingers over his palms. "Hardened hands," she says to the head liberator. "See these callouses? These people have worked the Hive in every way. And my guess is they didn't do easy work before they arrived. What if these are the people the scroll is referring to."

My girlfriend, The Genius.

"It makes sense, Kraven," I add. "You know it does."

Kraven runs his hands through his hair and squeezes his eyes shut. "Even if we wanted to, we can't train them. We must train ourselves."

"Surely we could spare some time," I argue, my excitement growing. But I know he's right. As much as I question his tactic to spend our time training, we must be at our best to take on the collectors.

The liberator shakes his head and the humans voice their

complaint. *We'll fight without training*, they say. *We are not afraid*, they say.

An idea flicks to life and suddenly I'm invigorated. "Kraven," I say. "I know someone who can train these people."

He raises an eyebrow.

The humans quiet.

"Who?" he asks.

I grin like a fox and say, "A crazy-ass dude named Lincoln."

⊰ 22 ⊱

UNAFRAID

I don't know how, but eventually the humans convince Kraven that they won't be turned away. And Charlie convinces Kraven that she's right about the message on the scroll. His hands are tied, so he tells me I can go find this Lincoln, whose dad is in the CIA and knows a thing or two about military tactics, as does his son. Who dresses all in black and has a plethora of face piercings but was always loyal as a friend to Aspen.

"If he exposes us to anyone…" Kraven warns.

"Chillax," I tell him. "Lincoln's a crazy MoFo, but he isn't a nark."

"I think you misunderstand the word *nark*," Kraven replies.

"And I think you misunderstand how amazing I look under fluorescent lighting." I reference my spectacular build. "Most people hate those things, but this was meant to be seen in Hi-Def."

"You'll take Max with you," he says. "Better that he's not here."

"Why you always got to hate on Max?"

Kraven rolls his shoulders. "He's still a collector."

"Why? Because he wears dargon given to him by Lucille? I did, too."

Kraven gives me a look like that doesn't help my argument.

"You'll take Paine as well."

So the liberator wants his competition out of the house? Guess he's not the saint I thought he was. Still, I don't fight him on it. I'm in too good a mood. First we found the sparrow among the crows, and then those with calloused hands who really need a good lotion but will also help us win the war. If we keep going at this rate, we might have this thing in the bag. Eight liberators against five collectors and hundreds upon hundreds of sirens?

It ain't no thing.

"And Annabelle," I say. "She goes, too, right?"

The liberator's head whips in my direction so fast I imagine he must give himself a concussion. I laugh until my side aches. "Calm down, Casanova. I'm just busting your balls." But then I really think about Annabelle. And Charlie, too. The smile evaporates from my face. I glance down and clench my hands into fists. "You have to swear to protect them."

"I already swore my allegiance to Him. Part of that is protecting humans and the savior. I wouldn't — "

"Swear to *me*," I say.

Kraven meets my gaze. "I swear."

It's not enough. I want it in writing. I want a blood oath. I want his mother as collateral.

I turn away and say before I leave, "I'll be ready to go at 6:00 a.m., before the sun is up."

As I walk back to my room, I contemplate how Kraven will get the three of us out of the Hive. But mostly I think about Charlie. She was doing okay when I left her to talk with Kraven, but every second I've been away has been a different kind of war.

Blue is awake in the lounge area when I come in. He gets to his feet. It's the first time I've seen him since the sirens broke in and the walkers died. We look at each other for a moment, not saying a word, and then we embrace. There's no back slapping or amusing words exchanged. We just hug. For real. Like chicks do.

I let go of him. "Where are the girls?"

He motions toward Annabelle's room. "Annabelle's in there."

"And Charlie?" I ask.

His mouth lifts a touch. "In your room."

I touch the outside of his bicep and head toward my room. But then I stop. "Blue?"

"Hmm?"

"I'm going to get Aspen back. I know it's been several days, but she's a strong girl. We'll win this war, and after we do, we'll storm into hell and save her." My voice lowers. "I miss her, too."

Blue's eyes are downcast. He nods.

When I go inside my room, Charlie is sitting up in bed, knees pulled to her chest. I hate seeing her tense. I miss the Charlie that stretched out like a sunny day. She used to take up space, all of it, but now she curls into herself. It's like she wants to disappear, and I want nothing more than to wake her up.

"Did you miss me?" I ask.

She glances up. Her eyes are wet with tears.

"Charlie." I rush forward and take her in my arms. I stroke her hair and I tell her everything will be okay.

She cries as she says, "They killed them all."

"I know," I mutter into the crown of her head. But I'm not sure I *do* know. Charlie seems to connect to other people in a way I don't. It's like their happiness is something to be shared, and their pain, something to be felt. Earlier she seemed okay. I should have known.

She wipes at her eyes. "I want to go to the sunroom."

I don't question her for a moment, I just help her to her feet, and we cross the Hive to where we hung out earlier today. It seems an eternity ago that we were laughing and messing around and acting like children. Because now we are adults, facing adult problems no one should have to face.

As we walk, I tell her about the knife I saw in the *unburned room*. She nods at this, but doesn't say much else. When we get to the sunroom, Charlie presses her hands to the glass and stares out at the ocean. The moon is a silver yo-yo in the sky, coiled by an invisible string, poised to unroll into dark waters. She turns and faces me. She's smiling. The sight is so beautiful; it reaches inside my chest like a hand and grabs hold.

"You see how wonderful this world is?" she says. "Look at all that water. Look at that sky. We think we're so big..." She opens her hands to show me just how big. "But on earth, we're small. We have to remember that we're part of something historic."

"Historic?" I move closer to her.

She steps back and grins playfully. "The world has turned for over four billion years. Maybe we help it turn. Laughing with a best friend and spinning an umbrella in the rain and swimming without bathing suits. Maybe that's the stuff that keeps earth clunking along in space."

I smile and step nearer, but she leaps back with a small laugh. "Maybe we're all a part of each other, and a part of the ground we walk on, too."

Charlie continues stepping backward and I continue pursuing her. Finally, I can't take it any longer. I reach out and snatch her and make her mine. She's my moon, and I've plucked her from the sky.

She giggles and fights against me until I kiss her. Then she relaxes in my arms.

"What's all this talk about, Charlie?"

Her smile falls away. She turns her head to the sea. "It doesn't seem so scary anymore."

"What doesn't?" I ask.

"Dying."

• • •

That night, Charlie doesn't leave my bed. But when I wake the next morning, I still can't shake what she said. I assured her a dozen times that I'd never let anything happen to her. But that's not true, is it? Because I couldn't protect her soul from Rector. And I couldn't protect Aspen from him, either.

Charlie tells me she's been afraid for a long time. But that now she understands what we're facing, and she's accepted it. I am far from that place. I could never accept the thought of Charlie being physically hurt.

I shake my head and finish getting ready, and when Kraven knocks on my door a moment later, I'm ready. My sweet girl grabs hold of my middle and pins me in place. She understands what's happening, agrees with why I need to go, but that doesn't means she's happy about it. I myself can't believe I'm doing this. With collectors popping up through the floor and sirens falling from the ceiling and a traitor walking among us, it doesn't seem like a good time to leave. But Kraven assures me he's going to question every single person in the hive to try and find the traitor while I'm away. And I don't think Lincoln will believe anyone else. Without his help, we won't be ready for war. So, what choice do I have?

"Kraven says there's still almost a full week before the war. And I'll be back tonight." I kiss her. My arms link around her waist and I pull her against me and I drink her in. I wish I could swallow her down and keep her inside of me. This isn't a healthy thought, I know that. But I don't want healthy. I want this. I want to *want* this girl more than breath and more than my own bloody, beating heart.

She breaks our kiss and bows her head. "I'll see you soon."

We don't say I love you. It seems like if we do, we're admitting something bad may happen while I'm gone. I kiss her forehead once more. Then I follow Kraven out the door. My mind stays with Charlie, though. Always.

Once we have Max and Paine in tow, Kraven leads the three of us to the great room. Though the sirens' bodies have been removed, but their blood still stains the floor. Kraven marches over the darker parts in the wood and peels up the loose floorboards that I discovered weeks ago when I was hunting for the scroll. At first I found a fugazi scroll, and then I found the real one.

Kraven begins to explain about the secret room.

"Can it, Cyborg," I say. "I already know about your masturbation den."

Kraven closes his eyes but doesn't react. Max, Paine, and I step down into the room, and I'm feeling pretty proud of myself for already knowing about this part of the house until Kraven uncovers a second doorway.

"What the hizzle is that?" I say.

This time, Kraven does grin. "When people discover a hidden room, they usually don't think to look for another one beyond the first."

Point taken.

"So, we're going even lower?" This room, though it feels like it's basement level, is actually on the first floor. "Is this just another route to Oswald's pad?"

Kraven moves some crates that weren't there before and sweeps away dirt. Then he lifts a hatch in the floor and hands us a flashlight. "This tunnel descends beneath the basement. In one direction, it leads to the ocean, in the other, a waiting car."

"Yeah, 'cause that seems natural," Max says.

I'm so happy to hear Max make a joke that I slap him on the shoulder and laugh harder than needed. "So you want us to go in the direction of the ocean, am I right?" I say to Kraven.

Kraven sighs. "You'll go west for three miles and there will be a car waiting for you."

Paine lowers himself into the dim tunnel first. "So, head toward the ocean. Check."

"Man, I can't *wait* to see the ocean," Max adds.

Kraven covers his eyes with his hand like he can't handle us. "Do *not* go toward the ocean. The sirens are there and—"

I bump Kraven with my shoulder. "Relax, holmes. They're messing with you. We'll be back tonight with Lincoln in tow."

Kraven's brows pinch together. "You really think this man can help?"

Man?

"Yeah, this *man* can totally help," I say.

"Why did you just do that?" Kraven asks.

"Do what?"

"Say *man* that way?"

"All right, see ya later!" I take the flash light from Kraven's hand and dive into the tunnel.

"Dante!" he yells.

But Max, Paine, and I are already moving west through the tunnel at a quick pace. As we walk in silence, our jokes forgotten, I wonder how long ago this tunnel was built and if the roof ever caves in. I'm not claustrophobic or anything. Nail me in a pine box, and I'll just ask for a fattie so I can take a nap.

Still, I don't want to run into any unforeseen obstacles.

The flashlight skips along the ground as we march. The dirt is wet beneath our heels. The air is muggy and I can taste salt in the air. It's dark in the tunnel and the walls are packed with black clay. I run my hand along one wall and my fingers come away slick with moisture.

"It's like we're walking down a vagina," Max says.

I shine the flashlight at his face, and he's grinning like a kid who just got his first handie.

Paine's giggling so hard I think he's going to wet himself, and I'm laughing, too. It's good to have Max in good spirits.

Even if he is faking it.

⊰ 23 ⊱

FANNY PACK FANTASY

True to Kraven's word, as soon as we climb up a steel ladder at the end of the tunnel, a navy blue car is waiting. A guy who doesn't speak a word opens the door for us and we climb in. And for the next sixty miles the three of us glance at one another, red in the face from trying not to laugh. Because the driver, he may be quiet. And serious. And perhaps someone important.

But sure as shit, that dude is rocking a mullet.

We pay the guy with some cash from the envelope Kraven gave us, and then die laughing all the way to the tarmac. Because the mullet was funny, but now that we've gotten each other started, we can't stop.

Inside an airport gift shop, Max bought a rubber strap for his sunglasses, the kind old geezers wear at waterparks. My best friend looks like a complete douche.

And Paine, that dude… That dude is now wearing a fuchsia fanny pack. And he's sporting that thing without cracking a smile. The fact that he's wearing it without laughing is making Max and me roll even harder. Every once in a while he taps someone on the shoulder and asks them what they think in his British accent, says his Nana got it for him and do they think the color clashes with his shirt?

On the plane, when we're in the air, Max dares us to do random crap. I'm challenged to spring up and run toward the bathroom holding my crotch. Easy enough. Paine, however, has to ask the stewardess why the plane is so *hood rat*.

"Excuse me?" the stewardess says.

Paine adjusts his fanny pack so he can really get into character. "I said, 'Why is this plane so hood rat?'"

Her face scrunches. "I don't think I understand what you mean."

"Hood rat," is all Paine says.

"I'm afraid I don't—"

"Hood rat."

"Please stop."

"Hooooooood. Rat."

She walks away.

Paine looks at Max. "What the hell is hood rat?"

Max shrugs. "I have no idea. My uncle used to say it."

"Your uncle is an idiot."

Max nods. "That he was, my friend."

A few minutes later, Paine is drooling on my shoulder and Max is asleep against the window. Idiots. My chest aches from happiness. Max has always been my boy, but with Paine here, it's like we're a group of friends. I image that maybe Blue would want to hang with us, too. Is it too much to hope for? That the four of us could be a crew of sorts?

Initially, I was afraid Max might not like Paine. That maybe he would be threatened by Paine's interest in being my friend. But the opposite happened. Perhaps Max has always wanted another friend, too. The thought triggers a strange stab of jealousy. Maybe I want more dudes to roll with, but I don't want Max to want that. Call me selfish. Call me incredible. You'd be speaking the truth on both accounts.

My mind drifts back to the Hive. I'm curious as to what Charlie is doing. Is she still sleeping? No. Kraven will have her up and working with Oswald. That guy's got a personal vendetta against REM.

I think about Neco, too, and whether Kraven heeded my warning to keep him away from Charlie. There's no way to prove that Neco is the traitor, but I can't get what he said that day in training out of my head. And let's not forget about his sudden appearance in the library when I was almost made into a human S'more.

Max shifts beside me and his bottom lip falls open. He snort-snores, which is awesome. I'm relieved that Kraven sent Max with me on this day trip. We needed to get out of the Hive, and Max seems to be doing better with his mind off Red. I think about telling him about Neco while Paine is sleeping, but reason against it. For once, I decide to keep this thing I know between me, Kraven, Charlie, and Oswald.

As Max's small snort-snore morphs into full blown ripping and tearing, I recall the newest line Oswald found on the scroll. I haven't had much time to dwell on the discovery. But ever since he told me about it, hot coals have burned in the pit of my stomach.

TWO HEARTS THAT BEAT AS ONE WILL MAKE A GREAT SACRIFICE.

A great sacrifice implies a melody of terrible things, which is bad enough. But it's the *two hearts that beat as one* that really gets me. Because I can't help thinking, no matter how much I try and convince myself otherwise, that the scroll is talking about Charlie and me.

• • •

When the plane touches down, I'm startled awake. Paine's head pops up from my shoulder and Max is wiping the corner of his mouth. All in all, we come off as anything but manly.

Max glances at me. "I was dreaming about you."

I shake my head.

"I was dreaming about *you*," Paine says to Max.

A deep line forms between Max's eyes like he's thinking. "Come to think of it, I was dreaming about you, too."

Paine stretches his hand across me and Max takes it. They give each other googly eyes without breaking a smile.

"Cut it out," I say.

"Your fanny pack caressed me in the most amazing way," Max tells Paine.

"I tied you up with your sunglasses strap," he replies.

"All right," I say, standing up. Max and Paine laugh like they are, without a doubt, the funniest human beings alive. It's amazing to me that these two can make jokes like this, but ask them to hug longer than three seconds and they'd sooner shank each other.

The three of us disembark and get our bags. Then we hop in the first cab we see and head for Lincoln's place. I'm not certain I know where it is, but I do remember the general area. After that, it's all about trial and error. Gazing out the window—taking in the snow-covered ground and the blue mountains—I can't help thinking of Aspen. Ever since we landed, I've had trouble breathing. It's like there's an elephant sitting on my chest and the only thing that'd remove it is seeing her.

I think about the party she took me to, how she danced on the table like no one else existed. I think about her gloved hands and the shame she hides on her palms where her father burned her. And I think about her sister, Sahara. How she must wonder where her Aspen went.

I feel like I'm going to be sick.

"You thinking about that chick?" Paine asks.

My eyes stay on the landscape zipping by.

"Sorry, dude," he adds. "We'll get her back."

"I left her there." I don't know why I say this out loud. The moment I do, I wish I could swallow the words back down.

Max doesn't respond. Neither does Paine. We guys are good for a laugh. We're good for a joke or an honest question.

But we're not the best at dealing with real emotions.

I miss Charlie already. The look on Max's face says he misses his girl, too. And even Paine seems as if he's somewhere else, with someone else. For a moment, I forget about Aspen and study Paine. He's a good guy. And he really likes Annabelle. Maybe I should root for him to end up with her. He'd be kind to Annabelle. Maybe fall in love with her.

But something tells me Anna's heart belongs to Kraven, even if the liberator does keep her at arm's length.

Eventually, we pass a ten-story glass building and I experience a sense of déjà vu. "There," I tell the cabbie, and he pulls over. I pay the dude from my envelope stuffed with cash. The cab driver stares down at it like he's certain I earned it from selling heroine to infants with a hankering.

"Don't tell anyone you saw us," I add, just to see his face.

24

COBRA

Max, Paine, and I take the elevator to the ninth floor. It's one of the few things I remember. *Tenth floor is for the corporate assholes*, Aspen had said. The floor is the only thing I remember though, so after we turn left out of the elevator, we begin knocking on random doors in the area I feel is right. Surprisingly, no one opens up for three random guys they've never met before pounding on their door.

"Little pig, little pig, let me come in," Paine says.

Max raises his voice into a high pitch. "Not by the hair on my chinny chin chin."

They laugh, but I have no idea what they're talking about.

"Seriously, Dante?" Max says.

I shrug.

"It was a nursery rhyme," Paine states.

"Let's just find this guy, all right?" Max and Paine drop it, and I do my best not to remember the mother I loved; the one who didn't read me nursery rhymes or hide Easter eggs in the grass. Doesn't mean she didn't care about me, I tell myself. She just wasn't that good at loving.

A door cracks open and then slams shut again. I glance at Max and Paine and then creep toward the sound. I push my mouth against the crack. "Lincoln?"

Nothing.

"Lincoln, it's Dante." I have no clue if this is his door or not. The number reads 917. That sounds right. Maybe. I wait for a minute but no one responds. "Let's keep trying doors," I tell the guys.

But then as I'm walking away, I hear the same door open.

"How do I know you're not lying?" a voice says that is clearly Lincoln's paranoid ass.

I roll my eyes and stroll back over to the door. It slams shut right before I reach it. "Lincoln, open up."

"Back away so I can see if it's you," a muffled voice calls out.

I do as he asks.

"You could be someone who looks like Dante," he says.

Max groans. "Dude, no one looks like that Pretty Boy."

Lincoln hesitates. "Is Aspen with you?"

"That's what I came to talk to you about."

The dude swears. "I knew it. I *knew* you took her. What did you do to her?"

"Let us in and I'll explain everything, I swear." I speak gently, even though I'm seconds from kicking the door down. When Lincoln still doesn't budge, I add, "If you really cared where Aspen was, three guys wouldn't stop you from opening up."

The door flies open and a nine millimeter gun is shoved in my face. He comes at me fast and I fly backward until my back hits the wall. The barrel licks the bottom of my chin and tips my head back.

"Oh, *shiiit*," Paine says.

"Real slow like, the three of you are going to step inside my apartment. If either of you makes a sudden movement, I'll put a bullet in your throat. Not your chest. Not your leg. Your *throat*. Understand?"

"We understand." My heart taps a quick rhythm. The cuff around my ankle will keep me alive, bullet or no, but without the Quiet Ones here I'd be on my back for days recovering. Days that will leave Charlie, and Annabelle for that matter, without our protection.

Paine and Max slide into the apartment and I follow them in. Lincoln shoves the gun between my shoulder blades and keeps it plugged there as I move. A blinding magnitude of white washes over me as I step inside: white walls, white furniture, floor-to-ceiling windows facing a city dressed in snow.

"Sit," Lincoln orders.

We do.

He sits across from us and rests the gun on his right thigh like a kitten. "Tell me where Aspen is."

I take a deep breath. If I tell him the truth, he'll freak. He might shoot all three of us, but what choice do I have? So I tell him everything. I tell him what we are, what we believe Aspen is, about Trelvator. I tell him where Aspen is now. And I tell him about the impending war.

Lincoln rises like a length of black ribbon and glides toward the windows. He gazes out.

He reminds me of Charlie when he does this.

But Lincoln isn't Charlie. Not with his black hair and piercings and camo jacket he never removes. This guy is ballin' like Donald Trump, but his appearance definitely doesn't speak to that.

He spins around, one eye narrowed, the other sharp as a crow's beak. "I believe you."

"You do?" I ask.

He nods.

For good measure, because I can't believe anyone is that easy, I tell him I'm going to show him something. "Don't shoot, okay?"

Lincoln points his gun at me.

"Dude, I said don't shoot."

"That's what people say when they're about to do something terrible."

"Just lower the gun, man."

He does, and when I'm confident he's not going to fire off a round, I shadow out of existence. Then I reappear. I nod toward Max and Paine and they do the same. Now you see us, now you don't. Ta-dah!

Lincoln squats down and scratches his head with the tip of the gun. As his eyes are diverted, Max looks at me and shakes his head like, *This guy is effing nuts and what are we doing here?*

"You guys just disappeared," Lincoln deadpans.

"That's right," I reply.

"Am I crazy?"

"As a fucking shithouse rat," I say. "But you're not imagining this."

Lincoln stands and walks into a kitchen area that opens to the living room. He grabs a cell phone and punches in a number. "Hey," he says into the speaker. "Cobra to Chrome. Initiate Operation Jackrabbit. This is not a test."

Lincoln lowers his voice and loses the serious face. "I said it isn't a test, didn't I? Just call everyone." He covers the speaker with his hand. "What airport are we flying to?"

"The one in Medford." I glance at Max and Paine with a look that admits I have no idea what's happening.

"The one in Medford," Lincoln repeats. "Take the earliest flight. I'll be traveling separately and will meet you in the baggage area."

Lincoln hangs up and says, "Let's roll."

"Do you want to pack anything or—"

The guy grabs a shopping bag and tips four boxes of granola bars inside. "Okay, I'm ready."

"You like granola bars, huh?" I follow him out the door. I'm beginning to think this may have been a huge mistake. From the worry etched on Max and Paine's faces, I'd say they agree.

"They're for Aspen," he answers. "She likes them."

I suddenly have an image of Lincoln standing at the mouth of hell waving an unwrapped granola bar. *Come on, girl. Come on. Can't believe you got out of the gate again.*

But the fact is Lincoln cares for Aspen. And that's all I need to know.

Four hours later, we touch down in Oregon. Lincoln sat by himself the entire flight jotting down notes on a napkin. He also ate one of Aspen's granola bars. I want so badly to tease him about this, to tell him there won't be enough for her when she returns. But I stop when I remember with painful clarity the dreams I've been having. Because Aspen may not even be—

No.

Just, *no.*

Before I do anything else, I flip on Lincoln's soul light. He has a sprinkling of tiny black sin seals partially obscuring the light. There are no larger collector seals among the black ones. If his soul was ever completely covered by sin seals, or collector seals, his soul would be collected while his body went on living. I'll never let that happen to Lincoln.

I release a blue seal, shaking my head that my seals are no longer red, and wait until it attaches itself over a handful of the preexisting black ones. Almost immediately, my blue liberator seal begins eating away at the black ones like hydrogen peroxide bubbling inside a wound.

When we disembark, Lincoln leads the way to the baggage area like he's visited the airport a hundred times before. Considering he's a military brat, it may be close to the truth. The four of us gather our bags and find a place to sit.

"Do you know when these friends of your will be here?" I ask Lincoln.

"Just as soon as they can."

As we wait, I wonder how I'm going to deal with this situation. What if Kraven doesn't want this many humans returning to the Hive? The deal was I'd bring back Lincoln and that's it. But then again, we need all the help we can get. I'm certain the collectors are out recruiting more sirens so why shouldn't we do the same?

Something Kraven said nags at me, though. These humans will be risking their lives. At what point does it become too much? Then again, what choice do we have? Turn down help and let Rector and the collectors find Charlie? Let a chance at Trelvator, a hundred years of peace, be ruined? What's more, if hell gets their hands on Charlie, then the scales between heaven and hell could be tipped in their favor, meaning demons on earth permanently without the use of dargon.

"How much longer, you think?" It's been an hour and a half, and I'm eager to return to the Hive. What if a vultrip has been whispered open? What if Neco has hurt Charlie? What if the sirens broke in again?

I stand up and pace the baggage area.

My body halts when I spot Lincoln's friends.

✦⇥ 25 ⇤✦

THE JACKRABBITS

Max stands up and so does Paine. An entire airport of bodies seems to move aside as if Lincoln's friends carry a sack of anthrax in each hand.

There are twelve of them and they walk in a formation that's anything but necessary. Their faces are pierced and their clothes are black and they look like carbon copies of one another. Over their shoulders, they carry camo bags as if to announce to the world that they are the sons and daughters of soldiers.

They stride forward like a closed fist.

Their faces are void of expression.

These are the kids who get picked on in school worse than anyone; the kids who fancy themselves someone special though others disagree. They've got chips on their shoulders the size of Mount Plymouth and they're tired of being laughed at.

They're angry. They're conflicted. They're hostile.

They're *perfect*.

Lincoln stands beside me. "We call ourselves the jackrabbits."

I'm so tempted to laugh, it hurts. But something stops me. Maybe it's remembering the way Aspen fought, and that she taught Lincoln those same moves, which means he probably taught *these* guys the same material. Maybe it's that these kids have been kicked enough. Or maybe…maybe it's because I know what they're facing, and it's not something I can crack a joke at.

What will their parents say if they never return? If there's one thing I know, it's that these kids lied about where they were going.

"The jackrabbits," I say. "Cool."

The kids look at each other and smile back at me. They're crazy as the day is long, but perhaps that's what we need up in here—a touch of Psych Ward. When we get outside, the car that dropped us off is waiting. I have no idea how long he's been sitting there, or how long he would have sat, but I'm glad for it. Kraven didn't want to use cell phones in case our lines got tapped. If you ask me, Lincoln and Kraven are going to get along like a house on fire, what with their paranoia and all.

I tell the driver we're going to need more cars. He and his mullet analyze how many of us there are, and he calls someone with a car phone that looks like it was created in 1987. Twenty minutes later, a limo bus pulls up. I cringe. This can't be the discreet picture we need.

Anyone Kraven hires must know to keep their trap shut, but what about the new guy? "Can we trust the driver?" I ask Mullet Man.

Mullet Man scratches his cheek. "He ain't got no one to talk to."

His voice is void of concern, and I take that as a good sign. There's no telling how many people work for liberators, or collectors even, that we don't know about.

I wave Max and Paine into the car, and Lincoln orders the jackrabbits into the bus before getting into the car himself. The ride back to the Hive seems to take twice as long as it did the first time. But maybe that's because Lincoln and Mullet Man sit in the front seat without speaking a word. They just stare forward like they're comatose. Eventually though, we're dumped outside the tunnel and the vehicles take off, driving away on a nonexistent road.

It takes me a few minutes to find the small boulder that blocks the entrance, and several more to get everyone below ground. I retrieve the flashlight I hid inside the tunnel, flip it on, and we're on our way.

The jackrabbits shuffle behind without questioning what is happening. A couple of times I glance back at their faces and am struck with respect for how loyal they are to a cause they know nothing about. They just know Lincoln said it was time to go, so they came.

I wonder if it wouldn't have been so bad to be an outcast in school. Maybe being a social pariah bonds you to other pariahs in a way no one else can understand. Beautiful, popular people don't have to be loyal. There are always new shiny friends waiting around the corner. But these people know they're few in numbers, so they lock arms and stick together through the crap storm that is life.

I look at Lincoln.

Could we ever be friends?

In one swift moment, I'm blinded by a feeling that can only be described as joy. I'm beginning to understand how Charlie sees a potential friend in everyone. She sees people, accepts their differences, and says, *let's be friends anyway, because you've got good stuff even if we're not the same.*

I dare to imagine that after this war is over, that I'll have a group of friends that care about me, and that I in turn care for. What kind of life would that be? To be a part of a family that nurtures one another and is never too busy?

Before I know it, we're nearing the Hive entrance. The sensation of other liberators nearby is subtle, but it's there. It's only slightly different from the feel of Max and Paine's dargon though theirs is much closer.

I raise my hand and everyone pauses. "When we get inside the Hive," I tell Lincoln. "Let me do the talking. Kraven is going to want explanations, and I need to be the one who gives them."

We walk for another couple of minutes before I spot the ladder that will take us above ground. I wonder just how far below we are. Above sea level? Below?

"What's that noise?" one of the jackrabbits, a girl with a bull-hook nose ring, asks.

I listen and don't hear anything.

"Yeah, what is that?" someone else asks. "It's like a hissing."

Lincoln passes the ladder and heads in the eastern direction, toward the sea. "It's like a tapping."

"Stay here," I say, though the second I move past Lincoln, Max and Paine follow. The flashlight bounds along and the three of us trail after it like a cat with a laser pointer. "Okay, I hear it."

"Me, too," Max says.

"I think the lot of you are nuts," Paine adds. "I don't hear anything except the sound of my life passing me by."

"You're already dead," Max corrects him.

"True that." Paine grins like he's glad for it.

"Stop talking." I run the flashlight in a large circle, covering the ceiling and floor in intervals. I stop when the noise grows louder.

"What *is* that?" Max says.

"We should just go up," I decide.

But then the noise stops. It's almost as if whatever was producing it heard us. I twirl the flashlight and a beam of light lands on a man I've never seen before. He has a wide forehead and ears that stick out. He covers his face and shies away from the light. Then he pulls his arm down and smiles like he's an actor on a stage. He bows, grabs a rope dangling above his head, and scuttles up and out of sight.

"Damn siren," Max says.

I shine the light in the direction of where he went, but don't see anything. "Let's get out of here." I don't have to repeat myself. The three of us turn in unison as if it's choreographed and hurry toward the ladder. "Go up first, Paine. Tell Kraven I'm coming and not to freak."

He grabs hold of the ladder and climbs, his wrestler body swaying awkwardly up and away.

A new sound sizzles through the tunnel. It's a cracking, a hissing. And it's growing louder. "Hurry," I tell the first jackrabbit. "Start climbing. Go as fast as you can." The back of my neck burns with anxiety as Lincoln's friends begin to scurry up.

The sound grows louder.

A pop.

A groan.

The sirens are coming. I know it like I know how to please a chick in bed. "Climb faster!" I try and push Max and Lincoln toward the ladder but they refuse. Lincoln won't go before his comrades and Max won't leave without me.

There are still seven jackrabbits left to begin their ascent. The sounds grow louder, angry that we're not awaiting the finale. My heart pounds so hard in my chest, I can feel it in my neck.

The entirety of the tunnel moans a long, sorrowful sound. It wails. It whimpers.

It releases a noise like a deep sigh.

And then it's explodes.

❧ 26 ❧

SALT VENDETTA

Somewhere along the tunnel, a wall bursts open.

I understand then what the siren was doing. He was chiseling away at the tunnel interior, trying to create a fissure that the sirens could slip through. That's what they do—chip, chip away and then slither in.

I yell for the jackrabbits to hurry and they scramble up. They don't need the urgency in my voice, because they hear the same sound I do. It's growing nearer, louder.

Max paces beside the ladder and Lincoln mumbles to himself.

My mind spins and I frantically search the tunnel for something to fight with. Then I remember. A burning smell fills my nose and my black-feathered wings spring from my back. Lincoln screams and dives away like I'm harboring the Bubonic Plague. Now the jackrabbits are springing up the ladder even faster, trying to get away from this winged nightmare.

Four jackrabbits left.

Three.

Two.

"It doesn't sound like people coming," Max calls out over the roaring noise.

He's right. It doesn't sound like bodies at all.

One jackrabbit left.

The noise comes to a head and understanding dawns on me —

Water rushes down the throat of the tunnel like a horrific vendetta. It swirls and slams into the walls of the tunnel rushing faster and faster. It swallows everything in its path and aches for more.

Max grabs onto the ladder and hoists himself up.

Lincoln and I are left. One of us isn't going to make it. There are still a line of jackrabbits above Max and he can only climb so fast. I shove Lincoln toward the ladder and he shoves me back, trying to act brave even though I see the way he eyes the water and my wings. Growling, I physically pick the hundred and sixty pound guy up and slam him toward the ladder. He doesn't need any more persuading. Lincoln grips the bars like a June bug and shimmies up.

The water is so close. I can't hear anything but it's whooshing. Standing and staring at the mass of dark water, I can't help but be awestruck. People underestimate the power of water, how dangerous it can be. We swim in it, bathe in it, drink it to stay alive. We sunbath at its lip and build castles in its regurgitated sand. Yet here it is — violent, ready to reclaim what it has given.

I won't make it.

I won't.

But my body doesn't accept this. So my hands grab hold of the ladder and my legs push upward and my arms pull with everything they have. My mind, though, laughs at their silly effort.

The water slams into me with the force of a freight train. It clips my bottom half and my legs sweep out from beneath me. Right before the water washes over my head, I glance up. Lincoln is several feet above and climbing fast.

And then my vision is gone.

Water surges over my body and whips me sideways, my legs

trailing behind. My arms ache and salt water forces its way down my throat and into my lungs. I manage to pull myself above the water level and gasp. Then I'm belted back under. My arms shake and my entire body goes numb. The water is colder than the devil's dick. It tears my legs and wings to the right, then to the left. My body crashes into the wall and my skin tears like a wet tissue.

I'm freezing.

I'm losing my grip on the ladder.

But most importantly, I'm drowning.

My mind screams and images of Charlie fill my head. I glance up through the murky water and imagine how close she is. Does she know what's happening? Is she scared? I don't know where this water leads, or if I'll ever be able to pull myself out if I drown. I need to be away from the thing that killed me in order for me to survive. If I'm unconscious under water, how would my body ever heal?

I try once more to pull myself up and fail.

The water growls next to my ears, furious that I won't release my hold. It won't be angry for long, because I can't feel my fingers and they're uncurling from the rung. Salt scours every crevice on my body, ripping the feathers from my wings. Water whips my hair about my head. I can't hold on any longer.

I let go.

My mouth opens and I call out. I don't know why. No one can hear me in this watery grave. But I do it all the same. The water wraps itself around me in an embrace, pleased to have won its prize.

I'm only a sigh away from the ladder when something firm grabs onto me.

An arm.

A hand!

I latch onto the wrist that's holding my own wrist. Then I grab hold with my other hand, too. Fireflies prance before my eyes. But that can't be right. I clutch the wrists as best I can but my brain is shutting down.

I need oxygen! it says.

"No," I tell it.

Then goodnight.

The hand that holds onto me is strong. It jerks my head above water and liquid spews from my mouth like I'm a demon fountain.

"Hold on," a voice yells.

I hold on.

"Grab onto the ladder," it adds.

I grab hold.

The person pulls me higher until my hips are above water. I find my legs and place them onto the rung. Twice, I lose my footing to the current and am nearly pulled back under. But the hand is always there, yanking me up, ensuring I'm safe.

Rung by rung, I manage to climb toward the Hive. My drenched wings feel like apes clinging to my back. I can't pull them back into my body, so I just struggle upward with the added weight.

When I land inside the Hive, I collapse onto the ground. Kraven is there, heaving for breath, falling down beside me. It was him who helped me. Of course it was him.

I cough and more water sprays from my lungs. Max, Paine, and the jackrabbits give me room to breathe. Once I've cleared my airways, I fall onto my back. "That was stupid," I choke out, eyeing Kraven. "You can't risk yourself like that. These people need a leader."

Kraven leans forward, forearms on his knees, still catching his breath. "And I need you."

"Aww," Max coos, making light of the moment. "I feel the love."

But I'm not laughing.

Neither is Kraven.

I pull myself up and the liberator slaps me on the back. "Get some sleep, Dante Walker." He nods toward Lincoln, toward the jack-rabbits. "The Quiet Ones will ensure these people have a place to lay their head."

No questions about Lincoln's age.

No criticizing my decision to bring Goth kid's friends with us.

Just, *get some sleep*.

The room is silent as Kraven gets to his feet. He strides toward the exit that leads to his chambers, dripping water, a slight limp in his step. "Training resumes in the morning," he says without turning around. "Seven o'clock."

✦≈ 27 ≈✦

RAINFALL

The room is dark when I come in. Charlie sits by herself in the lounge area, her face tilted toward the ceiling. I decide she must be asleep, but when I close the door behind me, her head snaps in my direction.

"Dante," she breathes.

She's off the couch and in my arms in a flash. I bury my head in her hair and she squeezes my waist with the eagerness of a pup.

"You're soaking wet," she says, lifting her head to stare into my eyes. "And you're shaking."

"I'm fine." Now that I'm safe, holding Charlie against me, I can't help but relive the fear from that flooded tunnel. I hold her tighter, confiscating her body's warmth. The feel of her hands rubbing my back soothes my worries.

"Did you find Lincoln?" she asks.

I tell her I did.

"Why are you drenched?"

I tell her I'm okay, not to worry.

"Kraven wouldn't let me out of my room all day," she says in a rush. "But I snuck out once. I wanted to know if anyone had heard from you. And maybe one more time to meet Oswald. Dante, we found another phrase on the scroll."

I cup her face in my hands. "What did it say?"

She licks her lips. "Unconscious words spoken on an unpracticed tongue will drive the beast down."

"Wow. That sounds ominous, and predictably confusing."

She bounces on the tips of her toes. "We already solved the two. You found the sparrow in the room unburned, and the humans, those with hardened hands, have agreed to help us fight. If we can figure this out, that leaves only one phrase left."

"A phrase we may never unlock."

She waves her hand like this isn't important now. "Babe, what *happened* to you?"

"I brought something for you." I step closer to Charlie, forgetting the chill in my bones, the water pooling on the floor.

When she tilts her head with curiosity, I pull a bag of dripping Skittles from my pocket. It's a wonder they managed to stay put after what I went through. I guess the ocean isn't one for rainbow-inspired candies.

Charlie laughs though I can tell she's still worried. She presses her lips against my neck. "We need to get you out of those clothes."

My body reacts with the swiftness of an asteroid.

Charlie takes my hand and leads me toward my room. She walks through it and into the bathroom. Charlie reaches out and locks the door that leads to Annabelle's room. She turns toward me, and she grins. In that small smile I see love, but I also see relief. She's glad I'm back, but she's also desperate to be close to me, to reassure herself that I'm close.

I'm desperate for that, too.

Her hands take the bottom of my shirt and time slows down. Her blue eyes connect with mine, and she pulls the shirt from my back.

It falls to the floor.

"You weren't even gone a day," she says. "And it felt like you'd never return."

I sigh, because I know exactly what she means.

"I've been distant with you." Her lips come to rest over my heart. She presses a light kiss there and then kisses me again on the hollow between my collarbones. "It felt wrong to be together when Aspen..."

She trails off and closes her eyes.

She opens them.

"I don't want distance between us anymore," she whispers. "I'm not afraid of what will happen. But that doesn't mean I want anything to change."

Her finger slides along the hem of my jeans and her mouth finds mine. I want to ask what she means. What does she believe will happen? But with her lips pressed against me and her hands moving lower, my mind spins out of control. All I know is that I was cold. And Charlie...Charlie is filling me with comfort. My body warms to her touch and the memory of what happened minutes earlier leaves me in a rush.

My legs threaten to buckle. My arms are weak. But somehow in this moment, I find the strength to stand.

And so much more.

Charlie unbuttons my jeans and my body shakes. This time, it's not from cold or exhaustion. It's from her. This girl I love who's telling me she wants to be together again. It hasn't been that long.

It's been an eternity.

She pushes my jeans over my hips. I step out of them when they slump to the floor. Charlie steps away and the absence of her is a pain I can feel. She turns off the lights. I want to ask her to turn them back on. I want to see every last curve of her. I want to take in her face when she calls out my name.

But when her hands return to my chest, the argument dies on my tongue. With the lights out, and no window to accommodate the moon, we are in complete darkness. When she touches me, I feel absolute. It's like our worries and fears are gone. Our voices—gone.

All that's left is our bodies. To touch, to tell each other how we feel. My hands run up her slender back slowly. I take her thin cotton shirt in my hands and pull it off. When her stomach kisses mine, I lose my mind to her. I can't stop. I can't slow down. My fingers find the button to her shorts and I pull them off.

The rest of our clothes fall away.

Charlie's hand slips into mine and she leads the way. I fumble in the dark, not sure where she intends to take me. Then I know.

The door of the shower slides open and I hear the unmistakable sound of streaming water. She guides me for a couple more steps and then the water is hitting my shoulders, racing down my chest, sliding over my hips and thighs. My hair mats to my head and I brush it back with my hands and tilt my face to the water. She sets the water to hot and already the chill that stretched into my bones has left. Steam fills the small glass space and envelopes our bodies.

I reach up and take Charlie's face. My lips find hers. I kiss her slowly, but with deepness. I want her to know I'm not letting go this time. My hands slide down the length of her body, feeling her breasts and the curve of her hips. Charlie explores my body, too. She slides her fingers over my shoulders, over the dragon tattoo covering my back. She dips lower and grabs hold of my rear, pulls me toward her.

Her lips move to my neck. She walks a trail of kisses toward my ear and when she can't reach the place she wants, she stands on tip toes and wraps her arms around my neck, dipping my head closer. Her tongue flicks over my earlobe and I crumble with desire. The water washing over our bodies, Charlie's soft, sweet body next to mine, the minutes that felt like days while I was gone—these things combine to create this perfect moment.

And nothing will stop the two of us from being together.

"Charlie, are you in there?" Annabelle yells. "Why is the door locked?"

My heads falls back and I groan.

"Oh, man," Annabelle says. "Please, please don't tell me that was Dante."

"Hey, Anna," I say, half frustrated, half amused.

"No," Annabelle says quietly. "No, Charlie isn't in there. You're just taking a shower. That's disgusting enough. But Charlie, my best friend, is *not* in there with you."

Charlie is covering her mouth. I can barely see her, but I absolutely know she is. I pinch her butt and she squeals.

"Oh, gawd," Annabelle moans. "I'll never be able to shower again."

"We're getting out." I leave the water's heat and fumble for two towels.

"Oh, *no*," Annabelle says, though now I'm beginning to detect a note of humor in her words. "By all means, please continue screwing in the shower. Hey, maybe you want to use my bed next."

"Good night, Annabelle," I say.

Charlie finds her voice. "I'm so sorry, Annabelle."

"What are you apologizing for?" I say.

"Because she realizes there's no sex in communal showers," Annabelle calls out from farther away, probably her bed. "It's like common law."

Charlie takes the towel I hand her, dries off, and dives into my bed, mortified. I know there won't be any more sexy times tonight, though that doesn't stop me from trying. She shoos me off and giggles into my chest. And somewhere in the late hour, with Charlie curled close to me, I fall asleep.

My last thought before I nod off is of Aspen. Charlie was right after all; it makes me sick to smile while she's trapped inside hell.

⤙28⤚

POW!

I speak with Kraven briefly before training. He assures me he has a strategy for war, but he won't reveal it. I tell him to try a little trust and see how it tastes. He also tells me that he questioned everyone in the hive, and that no one said anything worrisome. His confidence doesn't soothe my anxiety, but maybe now that the traitor knows we're suspicious, they'll back off. The Quiet Ones are watching the weapon room day and night, he adds, which is good. But now that the tunnel is flooded, there's no way to sneak in or out of the Hive, which is bad.

All in all, it sounds like a typical craptastic situation that is a day in the Hive.

We train for hours, until our muscles lock up and our teeth are set on edge. Every liberator completes Sector 3, Incapacitation. Now we're on to Sector 4. The general sentiment in the room when Kraven announced the title of the fourth sector—Execution—was pretty much, *It's getting real up in here.*

Blue is working with me, Max, and Paine today since there aren't any walkers left to create a third group. As I battle against the three guys, I can't stop thinking about the missing humans. I wish I'd gotten to know them better. I wish I'd thought to ask their names. As I try out a technique that involves snapping someone's neck, Kraven taps me on the shoulder.

"Go and work with Valery and Neco," he says.

I glance at him and then at my crew. "No dice. I like working with my boys."

Kraven steps toward me. One moment he's a friend and confidant, the next he's my freaking big brother gone rage. "Go."

Paine nods toward Red, and I sigh. I snatch a water bottle from the ground and head over to their group of two. "Why are there even groups anymore? Shouldn't we all be working together?"

Cyborg ignores me and demonstrates a new move involving a direct blow to the throat. But as he's talking, all I can think about is Neco. He's eyeing me and I'm eyeing him and I want to open a can of whoop ass so bad I can smell it.

So I punch him.

His head cracks back and I relish the sting in my knuckles.

"What the hell, freak?" he growls, grasping his face. He moans into his hands and then stands up straight. "For the last time, I only said what I did to get you to fight harder."

"Eat a dick."

Neco shakes his head and then Kraven snarls something about *off sides* or *out of bounds* or *foul ball* or some kind of horse crap.

"Go and take a breather, Neco," Kraven orders.

"Why me?" he argues. "He's the one that punched me."

My nose scrunches. "Aw, are you upset with Mommy? Want a snack pack to pacify your feelers?"

"Dante." Max is suddenly beside me. I glance at his face for a moment. He's wearing an unreadable expression, and a subtle nagging twists my stomach. I quickly push it aside and turn back to Neco.

The liberator glares at me and storms toward the exit. For one fleeting moment, I begin to doubt my suspicion. But then Neco stops in the doorway—and as everyone is arguing among themselves about whether it's break time—he shoots me a grin so wicked it lights my britches on fire.

He forms a gun with his hand and fires it off it in my direction. His mouth forms a word I can't hear. But I can read his lips just fine. Neco, that bastard, just said, "Pow!"

That's it.

I'm paying Neco a visit tonight, and I'm going to put the hurt on him until he admits what I already know—he is the traitor.

. . .

Late that evening, after Charlie has fallen asleep and I've had some time to calm down, I decide to chat with the old man in the basement. He was the first one to tell me about a traitor, so maybe he has some tips on how best to deal with this situation. After all, if I'm wrong (which I'm not), I may be ridding ourselves of a liberator we need in the fight against hell. As far as I'm concerned, this is the most pressing matter at hand. If we rid ourselves of the traitor, we can stop the vultrips from opening. Like Kraven said, he doesn't believe they're trying to destroy us. Not yet. They're just trying to weaken us.

So let's get rid of the weak link.

I consider letting Charlie sleep, but I know she'll maim me if I don't wake her. She climbs out of Annabelle's bed quickly, and follows me into the hallway.

"I want to see if I'm right about Neco being the traitor," I tell her when we're a safe distance from our bedrooms.

She rubs her face and yawns. "I don't think it's him. Why would he have said the things he did if he was? It's too obvious."

"Because he's an overconfident turd. I hate guys like him."

Charlie stifles a laugh, but doesn't respond when I ask her what's funny.

Outside the Hive, a storm rages. Thunder rattles the bones of the makeshift mansion and rain pelts the newly patched roof. As we head toward the basement, I think about the sirens outside, clinging to the ocean cliffs. I imagine lightning slicing the sky, illuminating the dozens of rain-drenched bodies. The thought is an unsettling one. It doesn't help that when we get to the basement, Oswald is nowhere in sight.

"Old man?" I call out.

When I don't get an answer, we stroll through the room, dodging his collection of lamps. I pick up shoes laces that I know I've seen Paine wearing and shake my head. Old Man steals stuff like a robin making a nest.

Charlie has stopped in front of Oswald's desk, her back pressed against it.

I stride toward her, and she moves a fraction to the left, almost like she's blocking me from seeing something. I narrow my eyes and step closer.

"Just…don't freak out," she says.

"What is that supposed to mean?" I nudge her away from the desk and spot the scroll lying on the desk. Except part of it is missing. The bottom part, the part that must have held the last and final piece of the scroll, is missing.

I instantly forget about Neco and the vultrips and grind my teeth together. "Where is it?"

Charlie bites her bottom lips. "It vanished when you were gone."

"You didn't tell me." I close my eyes against the sting.

"Oswald looked everywhere. Kraven did, too."

I wince. "Kraven knew about this also?"

She doesn't respond.

I rush to the opposite desk, ripping out drawers and overturning them. Pens and pencils and paperclips clatter to the floor. Note cards and markers and a bronze paperweight. But no missing piece of the scroll. I'm about to turn the entire desk over on its side when I see the list of phrases on the desk's surface.

I'm almost growling when Charlie whispers my name.

My eyes travel over the words.

I relax.

I breathe.

My mind rushes back to the training room incident with Neco, the time I experienced super human strength. And then to the library when I understood a language I shouldn't have. Something is happening to me, and I've had so little time to question it. Now, though, worry twists my stomach. I like to think if there's one thing I know, it's me. But lately I've felt alien inside my body. It's an unsettling feeling, one I enjoy ignoring.

And now the last part of the scroll, the very thing we believed could help us win this war, is gone. Maybe if I can interpret the phrases. Maybe if I spoke them aloud, I could somehow find it.

The house rocks from the storm and I ease my mind back onto the page. Rain beats down, the lights flicker, but still I study a singular word.

Havaga

Charlie crosses the distance between us. "Dante, don't be angry that I didn't tell you."

I roll the word over inside my mind, inside my mouth. I don't know this word. I don't know this word.

Yes, you do.

I shut my eyes and drop the paper. It flutters downward but I don't hear it brush across the floor. The rain is too loud, the sky too wrathful, Charlie is too present. I press my knuckles to my temples and push. What is happening to me? What is happening to all of us? Oswald is deadly, my girlfriend has a buried power, Kraven's face changed the night of the fire, and I can do things I shouldn't be able to. It's as if all these years we harbored secrets, and as the war grows closer, we begin to whisper them awake.

I glance up at the ceiling.

What is wrong with me?

Charlie must see the look on my face, because she grabs hold of my arm. "Are you okay? Talk to me."

I don't know who I'm speaking to in my head. Not Him. Even if I were, it's not like He'd listen to an imp like me. I tilt my head and keep my eyes closed. I listen, I listen, and Charlie stays quiet beside me. But all I hear is the thrumming of my heart and the wind leaning strong shoulders into the Hive.

I chastise myself for even pretending I'd hear a response. Not that I was *really* expecting anything. When Charlie reaches for me, I allow myself to be wrapped up into her arms.

A loud scream rings through the house and my eyes snap open. Charlie meets my gaze, I spot my fear mirrored in her face.

We run.

Pulling on my shadow, I slow to a stop and listen. If someone has broken in, let them believe Charlie is alone. Let them believe I'm not right here, ready to tear them apart with my teeth if they touch her.

When I hear the voice again, I realize it's Annabelle. Anxiety ignites my muscles with renewed energy, and we run faster. But when we hear a second voice, we both stop. Kraven is with Annabelle. The rain is roaring overhead, so we inch closer to hear what's being said. Charlie glances at me like she's wondering whether we should announce ourselves. I raise a finger to my lips.

"Tell me," Annabelle snaps. "Where would you have me go?"

Footsteps, and then Kraven speaking in hushed tones. "Don't twist my words."

"Words." Annabelle laughs. "What words?! You hardly speak. What do you want from me, Kraven? I came for Charlie, and I stay for Charlie."

"That isn't true," Kraven says, finding his voice.

I take a few slow steps and peer around the bend. Charlie follows behind me, though I can tell she's hesitant about eavesdropping. The two of them are standing in a small room outside the kitchen area.

It holds mismatched silver serving utensils, bold green plates, and porcelain coffee cups. A single dim light glimmers overhead, casting long shadows across the area. We watch them in silence, invisible to their eyes. I know Kraven must sense my dargon. Then again, he's probably not being *aware* like he instructed us to be.

"I can't keep doing this," Annabelle says. "I need to focus on my friend."

"Then don't," Kraven growls.

My jaw tightens and the wind howls.

Annabelle turns to him and a new look crosses her face. It's one of silent pain. And it's one that makes me feel as if we're intruding. I mean, we are intruding. But with everything going on in the Hive, I won't risk being in the dark about anything.

"My Belle," he breathes.

"I don't want this anymore," she says. "Not like this. Not this back and forth and indecisiveness."

"I should never have touched you."

Hell, yeah, you shouldn't of. Jaysus, I want to kill Kraven for what I just heard.

"Then why did you?" Annabelle's pained expression is gone, replaced by anger. "If you knew you couldn't be with me, why? Or maybe you *can* be with me; maybe you just don't want to be?"

Kraven spins away from her, his shoulders tightening.

"Coward," she whispers.

"Liar!" she yells.

"I never lied to you," he says.

"Oh, you didn't?" Annabelle is crying now. "You didn't lie when you said you wanted this to work? You did lie! You're giving up because you don't want this."

"I don't want you to get hurt," he responds with defeat.

Annabelle covers her heart. "I'm already hurt."

"Not like that," he says. "I can't protect anyone if my mind is always on you."

Annabelle's hands drop to her sides and she screams, "Your mind is *never* on me!"

Kraven whirls around and crashes across the room. The storm seems to thunder along with his footsteps. His arms land on either side of her and he growls like a monster. I move to run inside, to help Annabelle rid herself of this psycho. But then Kraven's mouth is on Annabelle's and his arms are around her waist.

Charlie is pulling at my shirt, telling me without speaking that we should leave. Now. But I keep watching.

Annabelle kisses Kraven back and then shoves him away. Her hand whips across his face in a stinging slap, and then she's kissing him again. Her bare feet shuffle across the floor as she releases him a second time and starts to hurry away.

Kraven grabs her wrist. "Please."

She slaps him again, harder this time.

He doesn't even flinch. His jaw is set and his brows are furrowed. He appears angry, furious even, but I spot the sorrow easily enough.

Without turning around, Annabelle says, "I came to tell you something tonight." She places a hand on her stomach like she's going to be sick. "But I've decided it's a secret I can keep."

Annabelle turns the corner and Charlie has to press herself against the opposite wall to avoid being seen. As Annabelle walks out of the room and down a short corridor, seeking her bed, she seems older. She's not simply a teen girl anymore, I realize. Annabelle has become a woman in these weeks at the Hive. She's fallen in love, she's carried the fear of war like a soldier, and she's been a true support system for Charlie.

Annabelle always says she wants to take a more active part in our cause.

But look at her go.

The North Star of the Hive.

✤ 29 ✤

THE SCREAMS BENEATH OUR FEET

The next morning, Charlie and I discuss the missing part of the scroll and what we witnessed between Annabelle and Kraven. My girlfriend is mortified that we spied on them. Me, not so much. Eventually, we decide to leave our unanswered questions and go into the shared living space. As soon we do, we're greeted by a young girl bringing breakfast. Her hair is the color of peaches and her eyes are an all-seeing green. She sets down the tray and smiles at Blue with the sweetness of a honeycomb.

He doesn't return the gesture.

Nobody remarks on his coldness as the girl leaves. I understand it. The girl he's fallen for isn't here, and he can't imagine looking at anyone else.

As we eat red potatoes and scrambled eggs mixed with cottage cheese, I try not to stare at Annabelle. She's this new person I don't quite understand. But when she catches me looking and hurls a potato straight at my crotch, I know the old Annabelle is still in there; the girl who likes black and white movies and hates skinny jeans. The girl who loves shooting hoops with Blue.

The girl who must miss her parents.

I wonder for a moment how terrified they must be, and how she must worry about what they think. And what of Blue's parents who lost their son? Or the school that had three students vanish within a few weeks of each other?

If they ever return to their hometowns, there will be a lot of questions to be answered.

"You okay?" Charlie asks, squeezing my thigh.

I lean over my plate and kiss her. She smiles against my mouth.

"Gross," Annabelle says.

"I'm eating," Blue says.

I pull away and laugh. Then I launch a potato at Blue and another at Annabelle. Charlie elbows me when I try to replace my lost potato rockets with two from her own plate.

"Forget it, buster," she says.

• • •

By lunch, we've wrapped up Sector 4 training. Kraven admits we're rock stars at killing people, though not in those words. Fear races through my body realizing how swiftly we're moving through these levels. The war is days away, and we're on borrowed time until the sirens launch another preliminary attack.

Kraven explains what Sector 5 will entail—utilizing wings in combat. A nervousness flutters across the room, but the liberators are also eager. To date, Kraven, Rector, and I have been the only ones capable of summoning our wings.

A faint burning smell touches my nose as Kraven's white wings spring from his back, slicing a path through his cream colored T-shirt. Kraven motions to me and I do the same, though mine are coated in black feathers. Rector's wings weren't like either of ours; his were a black leathery material, frayed at the edges.

Kraven walks to Valery and explains what she must do to

summon. "Reach inside yourself. Push the darkness out, and find something pure you can hold onto."

Valery pulls her long red hair into a ponytail and sashays past him. She cocks a full hip to one side and white-feathered wings rise from her back, arching over her head.

"Baby!" Max exclaims.

Red blushes at her fiancé's praise.

Kraven examines her wings. "You've been practicing for some time."

A smile sweeps over her face. "Ever since I saw yours the night Rector stole Charlie's soul," she says. "I figured it out a few days ago."

Kraven backs away from Valery's wings and she lowers them. He addresses the room. "Anyone else?"

Nothing happens, and maybe I'm happy for it. I'm proud that Valery got her wings without help, but I kind of liked being the big shot. Not that I'm any less of a stunner now that Red's packing feathers.

Paine steps forward and so does Neco. White wings rise from behind them.

Damn it.

Kraven claps with delight but doesn't smile. It's a creepy combination, though that doesn't really surprise me. "Excellent." His gaze lowers. "We're getting close."

Blue's face burns bright red when Kraven looks at him with a question. He shakes his head.

"That's okay. That's what training is for." Kraven looks at Max, and Max shakes his head like Blue did. "There are seven of us in this room with dargon. And two more liberators keeping watch over something we will need for war."

"What's that?" Valery asks.

He doesn't answer her, and my heart sets ablaze with pride. He hasn't told anyone else about the weapon room, which means even if he didn't tell me about the missing part of the scroll, the dude is totally starting to trust me. I wonder if it'd be weird for me to tackle hug him. I decide to save it for later. This probably means we're like co-leaders, equal power and crap. I'm so money.

"I can help Max and Blue if you want to work with the others," I say.

Kraven eyes me. He nods.

Oh, snap! Did everyone see that? Dante Walker is calling the shots. Pow!

For the next couple of hours, Valery, Paine, and Neco learn how to sweep someone's legs beneath them with their wing. They learn how to throw a body across the room by whipping their feathered appendages across their body. And they learn how to fly a few feet off the ground. The three liberators are far from practiced, but they're learning quickly.

Blue and Max, on the other hand, still can't summon their wings. I spew all the same mumble jumble Kraven did.

Reject the darkness.

Think of something pure and hold onto it.

Blue reaches out to touch my wings. "Why are your wings black?"

I slap his hand away. "You want to grab my junk, too? Keep your nappy hands to yourself."

"Yes, Dante," Kraven says from across the room. "Why are your wings black?"

I glare at him.

Because I don't believe He cares. Because no matter what happens, I won't rely on anyone but myself to fight this fight.

Because my darkness is not something I'll ever release.

When we trek down to the great room to grab dinner, I'm amazed by what I see. The humans are lined up in neat rows of eight. Before them, the jackrabbits demonstrate combat techniques. The humans watch on with the focus of a bomb squad. They're good, better than I ever would have expected. Lincoln has had his hands on these people for one day and already they fight with determination and confidence.

The dude runs things like a general, striding up and down in front of his *soldiers*, monitoring their progress. He even wears a brown militaristic uniform that someone must have made him in the late night hours. It's pretty ridiculous in all honesty, but I can't say I'm surprised to see him sporting it. I just wonder what his father would say if he saw his skittish Goth kid now.

What really impresses me though is Annabelle. She works beside Lincoln, moving the humans into groups and showing them what they're doing right, and what they still need to work on. Seeing her, I laugh so hard my gut aches. That Annabelle; she's been spying on our training sessions. Kraven is grinding his teeth so hard he's going to need dentures.

I grip his shoulder. "Calm down. You should be happy that she's determined to help. And it's good that she knows how to protect herself."

"This war won't happen here." His whole body shakes with fury, or maybe fear. "But when it does, Annabelle won't be anywhere nearby."

"Hey, Paine," Annabelle calls out.

Paine waves and a mammoth grin narrows his features. Kraven stares at Annabelle smiling, Annabelle training, Annabelle flirting. Then he spins on his heel and he's gone. Annabelle's face falls. I don't feel sorry for her. In fact, the person I feel sorry for is Paine. He and his plaid shirts and British accent are going to have a broken heart when this is all said and done.

I follow after Kraven, but take a right turn where he takes a left. Soon after, I step inside Oswald's basement. Charlie is seated in a simple wooden chair in the center of the room. Her eyes are closed and concentration runs so deeply on her face that it unnerves me. Oswald is bending down on her left side, whispering in her ear.

I start to come in, but Oswald holds up a firm hand. He shakes his head *no*, and then continues speaking soft words to my girl. He stands, clutches his dung brown robe, and says, "Try again. Focus."

My stomach flips as Charlie slowly raises her arms. Her hands stretch out in front of her and her eyes remain shut. A perfect harmony rolls over her body, and it's as if she's alight with peace.

"You can do this," Oswald implores.

At first, nothing happens. Then a crackling blue light blooms in her palms and crawls over her fingers and the back of her hands. It's like her entire hand is a ball of blue fire.

"Yes," Oswald says, almost too enthusiastically. "Hold it, now. Hold it."

The blue light vanishes and Charlie slumps forward.

I rush forward and grab her shoulders. "Are you okay?"

Her head snaps up. She smiles that angel smile and I flinch from the pureness. "What are you doing here?"

"I came to see how you were progressing." Even though I'm wary of the energy I saw radiating from her hands, I tug her against me. She wraps her arms around my torso and buries her head into my stomach. Then she lets go and lightly pushes me away.

"I have to keep working," she says. "A few more hours."

My brow furrows. "But it's late. Aren't you hungry?"

Her back straightens. "I have to keep working."

I examine my girlfriend. She's become so strong, so determined. It scares the ever loving piss out of me. Maybe I want her to need me. Maybe I'd hoped that when the morning of war came, Charlie would flee to the darkest corner she could find and hide until it was all over. At least then I'd know she was safe.

But the resolution in the set of her shoulders and the tightness around her eyes tells me I'm dreaming. Charlie will fight, and why not? She cares about the fate of mankind perhaps more than any of us. And she is powerful.

Paine stumbles into the room. "Hey, D, Kraven wanted me to tell you..." He stops speaking suddenly and his mouth gapes open. "Why are there so many lamps down here?"

"I like them," Oswald says in a small voice.

"How did you get them all here?" Paine asks in an even smaller voice.

Oswald blushes. "Some of the staff members made them for me. See, this one is actually made from an old broom handle, and this one—"

Paine's nose wrinkles in disgust and he takes a small, almost unperceivable step back. "I don't like this one bit."

"What's wrong with you?" I ask. "You act like you just saw your mama in a sex swing."

Paine shakes his head. "I don't like lamps."

"Why?" Charlie says without a hint of laughter.

"It's the light bulbs." Paine wipes a hand across his brow. The kid's sweating like a pig on the spit. "I don't like when you screw them in. You never know if the thing is on or off, and then it zaps on right as you make that last twist of the bulb." He shakes his head again. "It's always on. No matter how sure you are that it isn't."

"A fear of screwing in light bulbs," I say in disbelief. "That's pretty jacked up, Paine."

He grins.

Charlie stands from the chair and starts to say something.

But then—

The basement is ablaze with screams.

The four of us search for the source of the screaming, but we don't see anyone. The sound is terrible and bone-chilling, and it seems to arise from inside my head.

"I think it's beneath us," Oswald yells.

The bells start ringing.

"Stay here with them," I order Paine.

I'm gone, racing toward Kraven's chambers, the screams growing louder. I turn once and see Charlie running behind me. Though I hate her being exposed like this, I don't ask her to turn back. At least this way I can keep an eye on her. We run side by side until we reach Kraven's room. When I don't immediately see Kraven, I dive through the fireplace and urge Charlie to follow. I've told her about this place, but she has yet to see it for herself. We run downward until we reach the weaponry room. As we stumble inside, I spot a black hole squeezing closed at the Quiet Ones' feet.

Many of the weapons are gone—even the sparrow—but that's not what bothers me most.

It's the Quiet Ones, heads tilted back, mouths open. Together, they wail this high-pitched cry that seeps into my very soul and slashes it to pieces. It's a sound that says something significant has happened. It's the sound that marks a date people will remember. The noise has no beginning and no end. It just *is*. The two women hold hands and their eyes leak tears onto pink cheeks. And they scream.

They stand with perfect posture, lips curled back, and they scream.

⌖ 30 ⌖

LIAR

Kraven arrives inside the weapons room a beat after I do. He manages to calm the Quiet Ones and sends them to bed. They shake and mumble to themselves as they pass by and slip under the small door. Charlie accompanies them to ensure they are okay.

They spoke. The Quiet Ones spoke, sort of.

I'm attempting to wrap my head around this, and the fact that the sparrow sword is gone, when Kraven grabs ahold of my shirt and throws me across the room. He jerks a finger in my face. "You! I thought I could trust you!" He rears back and lands a blow directly into my stomach. I double over in pain. Kraven shoves my shoulder so that I'm upright and then hits me swiftly across the face. I go down like a ten-dollar whore.

"What are you—?"

It's all I get out before he kicks me into the remaining shields. I finally gather that I'm getting my ass handed to me and go on the offense. I crack Kraven straight in the nose and when he hunches over, I throw an uppercut into his side. He groans and curls in on himself. Then he straightens, his chest rising and falling quickly, betrayal etched into his features.

"I didn't tell anyone about the weapons," I say, understanding at once what this is about.

"Liar," he snarls.

"Only Charlie." I throw a third punch into his gut for good measure. Also, because Kraven's accusation hurts worse than his fists. I thought he trusted me. I thought he saw the good in me, yet as soon as the cards fall I'm the first person he blames.

"You're the only one who knew," he growls, though some of the fight is gone from his voice.

"And the Quiet Ones," I say, "Who, as it turns out, can be incredibly loud. I thought you said they could guard this place. Seems the betrayal may lie with them."

"They'd never give away our weapons willingly."

"What makes you so sure?"

He touches a hand to his lip and his fingers come away with blood on them. "Because," he says, "they are the Patrelli sisters."

My mind spins as I attempt to process what he's saying. "Are you telling me the Quiet Ones, the chicks who heal our wounds and bring us our breakfast, killed themselves?"

Kraven glares at me, and it's all the answer I need. All this time, I thought those two chicks were the weakest of our group. But in truth, perhaps they are the bravest. They knew the war was coming, and instead of considering their work done, they ended their mortal lives to become liberators. Their only task was to guard the weapons that their ancestor created, and yet they've done so much more.

"Holy crap," I say before remembering something. I point at him. "What about you? Were you going to tell me a piece of the scroll had been stolen?"

"It was you," Kraven repeats, ignoring me. "You are the traitor."

"Knock it off, Cyborg. If I were the traitor, I wouldn't be shagging the savior."

"That isn't a strong argument." Kraven moves toward me like

he's ready for round two.

I step back. "Someone must have eavesdropped, Kraven." I glance down. I don't want to admit what's weighing on my heart, but I don't think I have a choice. "Listen, it hurts that you're accusing me. I thought we were, like, comrades in this. I've tried my hardest to trust you. I went to training. I stayed in the Hive because you said it was the best place to be. I left to recruit Lincoln because you assured me you'd protect Charlie while I was away. I ignored the fact that your face freaking *changed* before my eyes.

"I've trusted you with my life, but what's more, I've trusted you with Charlie's. But you…you set me up. You told me about these weapons as a test. And I bet you were relieved to see that you were right. Because that meant you didn't have to trust anyone anymore." I smile. "You know, Kraven, we're not so different."

I slide under the miniature door and take the long walk back to Kraven's room. When I get there, Max is waiting. He seems surprised when I walk in.

"I heard the screaming," he offers.

"Yeah. Kraven's going to explain all about that."

Charlie returns to Kraven's room and I go to her at once. A few moments later, Valery and Neco charge in, and Kraven appears from the fireplace behind me.

"Did you just come out of the fireplace?" Valery asks him.

Kraven mutters a response, but I can't stop staring at Neco. He wears a worried expression, and I don't miss the starbursts of sweat on his grey T-shirt. Neco looks a lot like a guy who just did something he's not proud of.

"Where you been, Neco?" I ask, gripping Charlie's hand.

He shakes his head. "I was in my room."

"I bet you were." I cross my arms. "Right where no one could see you."

"Dante, stop." Kraven goes to the door of his room and closes it.

"War is in four days' time, and we mustn't fight."

"Isn't there a saying about a pot and kettle and their mutual blackness?" I say.

Kraven turns to Valery, Max, and Neco. "Go and inform the others that tomorrow will be the last day of training and that tomorrow night we will feast like true warriors."

No one says a word. Max meets my gaze before he leaves, and I see my own fear echoed back in his eyes.

Charlie and I begin to follow after him, but Kraven stops me with a hand on my shoulder.

"I'd like to show the two of you something." He walks to the table near the far wall and knocks his knuckles against it. I cross the room and stare down at the map I spotted the last time I was in his chambers.

"You see this here?" He points to a circle. "This is the Hive." He runs his hand across the ancient yellowed map to an unmarked area surrounded by illustrated foliage. There are three words inscribed there. "This is a field with tall grasses. It's an empty square mile, and it's where the war will take place."

"*Sa Ligral's Phun*," I say. "The Lion's Hand."

Kraven's eyes snap to my face. "You can read it?"

Charlie is equally surprised. It's the one thing I hadn't gotten around to telling her.

"You trust me, I trust you," I tell Kraven.

The liberator studies my face for another moment and then looks at Charlie. Blood pools in the corner of his mouth where I hit him. His eyes fall to the map, and I may be mistaken, but he appears almost sorrowful. "We must be there, four mornings from now."

"Will we hide among the trees?" Charlie points to the spindly things on the map.

"No, they'll expect that. And if we did they'd do the same. It would turn into a stalemate."

"Then what will we do?" I ask.

"We'll arrive early and wait in the field," he responds.

I balk. "In plain sight? No way, that'll give them the advantage."

"We won't be visible," he says, slowly. "We'll bury ourselves in the ground."

I straighten and inspect the liberator closer. He's serious. He's crazy, but he's serious. This is his plan. It isn't that imaginative, and it will only give us a moment's advantage, but he's shared it with me. I don't expect an apology for his earlier accusations. I imagine this is the closest I'll get to that. And I'll take it.

"They stole our weapons," Charlie says.

"Not all of them," Kraven replies.

Charlie thinks. "Was the one we needed gone? The sparrow among the crows?"

"It was," I tell her.

"Can we defeat them without it?" she asks.

Kraven hangs his head. "We have no choice but to try."

"We have eight liberators, one collector, thirteen jackrabbits with combat skills, and about fifty humans with a day's training," I say. "There are maybe seventy of us against hundreds of sirens, probably many who have been trained. And let's not forget the five collectors."

"We have Oswald, too," Kraven adds.

"You believe we will win?"

Kraven rolls up the map and slides it inside the drawer beneath the table. He looks past me, not meeting my gaze. "We must."

"And me," Charlie says suddenly, surprising Kraven and me both. "Don't forget I will be on that battlefield, too."

⧼ 31 ⧽

BENEATH THE MOON

It's late at night when I wake to find Charlie sitting on the edge of my bed, knees pulled to her chest. She is so small, so painfully small.

"We had weapons," she whispers when she realizes I've woken. "We had *the* weapon. And they took them."

I sit up, but don't reach for her. "We knew this would happen. Kraven said they would try to weaken us before the war. We'll get the sparrow back somehow."

Do I believe that? I'm not sure. What I do believe is I'll defeat Rector with or without a special weapon.

The bedsprings move and Charlie folds her arms around my neck. "One more day of training."

"It'll be enough." I'm trying to feign confidence. If I'm confident, maybe Charlie will feel safe. I've always had the ability to ooze the stuff, but with so much out of my control, and with Charlie's safety on the line, I feel depleted. My heart aches and I'm sick to my stomach. Anxiety courses through me and my muscles twitch with the need to release pent-up nervousness. It's not war I'm afraid of. In fact, I'm itching to face Rector again. What scares me is thinking about Charlie out there. Every moment we're together feels like our last. And I hate that more than anything.

"Charlie," I say in a whisper. "About what the scroll said. The part about two hearts beating as one will make a great sacrifice?"

"I know." She guides me back on the bed. I move with her body like there's no place I'd rather be. She wraps her quiet hands around my face and meets my gaze. "Don't be afraid, Dante," she says, "I won't let anything happen to you."

I flinch. "You won't let anything happen to *me*? No, Charlie, that's not how—"

She kisses me. It's a hungry kiss, one that tells me she doesn't want to let go this time. Kraven said war is in four days' time, and that tomorrow evening we dine. We will fight and we will finally save Aspen from hell's clutches. Tomorrow is the last day of preparation. But tonight…

Tonight it's Charlie and me.

I kiss her firmly, my tongue touching the tip of hers. Pulling back a breath, I bite her lower lip and she tugs me closer. Time slows down, or maybe it speeds up. With Charlie touching me like this, I feel everything at once, every last inch of skin on both of our bodies.

I crawl on top of Charlie and lower myself between her legs. She gasps and I kiss her again. I wish I could keep Charlie safe. I wish I could hold her forever. Her fingers trail up my back and grip my shoulders. I lower my head and lick the sensitive skin along her neck. She entwines her legs around my waist and I nearly howl with lust.

The snap on her jeans pops in my hands and then I'm pulling them down the length of her, one leg, and then the other. My fingers find the outside of her ankle. I run them along the length of her leg and back to her hip. I lie down on her and we move together for a moment, allowing ourselves to imagine what it will feel like when the rest of our clothes are gone.

My shirt comes away in her hands, and then I'm pulling hers

off, my hands sliding over the smoothness of her stomach. I find the inside of her knee and kiss my way toward her hip. Her hands find my hair and her back arches. I move my mouth to her other leg and brush my lips down the other thigh, too. When I get too close to her, she breathes my name. It turns me into an animal, and I feel like I may swallow her whole just to make her mine.

I find the edge of her bra and slip my thumbs beneath the sky blue fabric. Her bra is covered in intricate lace, and the sweetness of it makes me growl with anticipation. I want to protect her.

I want to ravage her.

I want everything she has, and I want to give her everything in return. I unclasp her bra and then my mouth is on her. Charlie throws her head back and leans into my touch. When I can't wait any longer, I rip off my jeans and boxers, and slip her blue underwear off, too.

When I settle myself on top of her, I pause. Her eyes are open and we meet each other's gaze. I take her in: soft blond hair, full pink lips, slight crinkles around her eyes. She is beautiful.

She was *always* beautiful.

"I love you, Dante," she whispers. "Forever."

I kiss her lips once, twice. "Forever."

I touch my forehead to hers and smell the scent of soap on her skin. And then we are together. My mind never strays from the girl I love clutching me tight.

⇥ 32 ⇤

SUNDRESS

Always in my dreams, I see her. So I know that I'm asleep when I spot Aspen's face above me. I sit up and find we are in a field of purple bulbous flowers. They sway gently in the sunlight and the air itself seems to bend and sparkle like someone has tossed a handful of glitter into the breeze.

Aspen offers her hand. I grasp her fingerless gloved hand and pull myself up. "It took you longer to find me this time," she says.

I dust off the back of my jeans. "You won't be here much longer, Aspen. The war is coming in four days."

"Four days," she says through a sigh. Her body sags as if the thought of bearing those ninety-six hours in a place like this is unimaginable.

"Blue thinks about you every day."

Her green eyes snap to mine. She smiles and then covers her lips with two fingers. "He does, really?"

"Of course he does." I'm glad to have made her smile. "He was smitten with you from the first moment he saw you at your father's cabin."

She laughs and her whole body laughs along with her. She touches a hand to her black hair. She's wearing a yellow cotton dress that's unexpected, and the diamond stud ring is gone from her nose. Aspen looks buoyant, as if she could skip to the clouds if she wished.

"We have this guy named Oswald who will help us win. And we've all trained really hard for this day. Once the fighting is over, we'll go and fetch you from hell."

She shrugs and grins. "Just like that, huh?"

"Just like that."

Her smile fades. She points to the edge of the field. "Do you see my friends?"

My stomach plummets when I notice what I didn't before. Six men and women stand in a line, skin ashen, gazes empty. Each person has a dark gash across their throat like a sinister smile. They are the walkers, gone from this world. But why are they here?

"He took their souls," she whispers. "He stole them."

I shake my head. "That can't happen. They have to go to Judgment if their soul light isn't completely sealed."

"He doesn't like those rules."

My blood burns hot and fury claws at the inside of my eyes. "We'll end this. All of this." I return my glare to Aspen. "When we save you, we'll save them, too."

"You must rescue the sparrow. You must remember the beast and the untrained tongue."

"What are you talking about?" I ask.

She covers her face and moans.

"Aspen," I say, alarmed. "Aspen, are you talking about the scroll?"

Her nails drag down her face and red jagged lines appear where she rips away the skin. I go to stop her, but she shoves me back with both hands. I stumble but keep from falling. Aspen presses the heel of her hands to her temples. "You're already dead. Go back to sleep."

"Why do you keep saying that?" I yell.

She gasps and glances around like she's in disbelief that I'm still here. "Don't you understand, Dante?" Tears slip from her eyes and race down the claw marks she created.

"No, I don't understand anything." My voice grows in volume. "Tell me!"

"Shhhhhhh!" the walkers hiss in unison, pointer fingers raised to their lips.

I glance back at Aspen, my own eyes stinging. "Tell me."

Her bottom lip wobbles and tears drown her heart-shaped face. She throws herself into my arms and buries her head into my neck. Then, so slowly I hardly register that she's lifted her head, her lips touch my ear. "Dante, Dante," she whispers.

I close my eyes and squeeze her tight.

"I'm already dead."

• • •

The next day, I can't shake the dream I had of Aspen. A sweet sickness swirls inside me, like eating too many pancakes drowned in syrup. On one hand, I feel invisible from the night I spent with Charlie. I think about her touch, about the way we felt immortal together in that moment.

On the other, there's Aspen. Aspen with her yellow sundress and promises of death. She's not gone, not really. She can't be. We're too close to battling our enemy and coming for her.

I think about the walkers, too, but I know they were a mirage, more trickery that Rector somehow created to make me lose my mind.

But mostly, I think about what she said before. About finding the sparrow and remembering the beast and the untrained tongue. If war is in four days, how will I find the sword in time, or solve the riddle about the beast, or locate the missing part of the scroll.

I pass Lincoln and the jackrabbits on my way to training. They're already in the great room, chairs moved aside, going over drills. Somberness hangs heavy over everything like a pregnant rain cloud. The humans are rapt with attention, focusing so keenly on Lincoln's every word that if I drove a spear through their sides, I doubt they'd notice the pain until he told them to do so.

With Lincoln here, teaching the humans the same things he's learned from his father—how to move without being seen, how to incapacitate your enemy using only your hands--the humans will stand a much better chance on the battlefield. Of course, if memory serves, it was Aspen that taught Lincoln most of what he knows.

Inside the liberator training room, it's much of the same. No one speaks as Kraven teaches us one last thing. Blue and Max have not uncovered the capability to summon their wings, but we must move forward, Kraven says. Today, for a few hours, we study Sector 6, Amplification.

The liberator introduces things that make my pulse beat against my eardrums. Not a question is voiced, not a word muttered, as he paces in front of us, unveiling secrets. We can't comprehend the things he's telling us, mostly because he admits there isn't a way to easily explain it.

"Amplification," he says, in closing, after a day of stories that sound like legends, "is a state of advanced being that you cannot access alone."

He meets my gaze.

I do not look away.

"Tonight, you will pray. You will pray to Him for the ability and courage to access this part of yourself. And when we are on the battlefield, you will believe He has heard you. You *must* believe it."

I wonder if this amplification is what I saw in Kraven the night his face changed. If it's the same thing I experienced that day when I wrestled with Neco. I think back to the night Rector stole Charlie's soul from me. His face changed, too. Is it possible for collectors to experience amplification? I believe it is. When they've opened themselves up to the devil the way Rector has, then yes.

Kraven runs a hand through his dirty blond hair. He appears weathered, and though he's a man in his early twenties, right now he seems much older. "Go and get ready for our feast. The humans stopped their training early today to prepare it for us. Don't forget to show your appreciation."

As we pluck water bottles from the ground and head toward the door, dumbfounded, Kraven adds, "Don't forget what I told you about the collectors. Don't forget what I told you to do."

I won't forget.

❧ 33 ☙

EVERLASTING EMBRACE

As the sun sets, three humans arrive at our suite of bedrooms and usher in a rack of clothing. It reminds me of the night we dined with Kraven, and Annabelle wore that red dress. It was the first time I realized Kraven might have a thing for Anna.

Now here we are again. Annabelle and Charlie choose their dresses and slip away into Annabelle's room. After the humans leave, it's only Blue and me left behind. It's too similar to the time before. Except this go round, Aspen won't appear in her seventies-inspired get-up, and Blue's jaw won't drop in a cliché manner.

As Blue and I inspect the suits, I'm once again stunned by the preparation that went into creating the Hive. It's as if someone knew exactly who would be here and what we'd need. Even finding clothing to fit has never been a problem. It's almost like the person who instructed the building and planning of this operation was all-knowing.

I step into charcoal-colored pants and then slide on a red long-sleeved undershirt and matching charcoal suit jacket. My black shoes are boss like whoa, and I even find a pair of silver cufflinks in the jacket's left pocket. Overall, I'm feeling like a hustler. Like Dante

Damn Straight Walker.

But I forget myself in a heartbeat when Annabelle's door opens a few minutes later. Annabelle steps out wearing a purple dress with a magnitude of sheer layers cascading from the waist. The top of the dress is more of a corset, and a ruby necklace adorns her chest. She's swiped on mascara and her lips are all shiny and oh man Kraven is going to crap himself.

"You look good, Anna," I say.

Blue steps beside me, wearing a navy pinstriped suit with a simple white undershirt. "He speaks the truth. For once."

I punch him in the shoulder lightly and he laughs. The sound is hollow though, and I know just why.

Charlie comes out behind Annabelle, and I close my eyes against the sight of her. My heart thrums in my ears and when I open my eyes again, she's still there. She's still stolen my breath and my mind and I want to keep her in this moment forever. I want to stop time. Right now. Not last night as we lay together, but now. I want to forever see her in this white lace dress that touches her pink toes. I want to study her face—brightened by Annabelle's hand, no doubt—as if she is my own pristine statue. I want to slip my arms around her and become a part of this frozen moment.

This girl, she's turned me into a freaking poet. I'd vom if I could think to do it.

Charlie fingers her white pearl earrings. "Do I look okay?"

I don't hesitate; I just kiss her. Behind us, Annabelle protests that I'm messing up her makeup, but I can't help myself. My fingers run through Charlie's hair and my other hand rests on the back of her neck. Charlie's lips taste like sugar with a tingle of spearmint. She kisses me back and for a second I think that maybe I'll get my wish and we'll stay like this for eternity. But then Blue clears his throat repeatedly and I sense Annabelle standing too close. When I open my eyes, I find that Annabelle's mug is three inches from ours. She laughs so hard I'm afraid she'll split her purple dress.

"That was way creepy, Annabelle," I say.

She raises the flat of her hand to her hairline and salutes me. "Pleasure to serve."

The four of us trail down the drafty corridors of the Hive toward the great room. When I first step foot into the place we'll be dining, I can't believe it's the same room. A gold tablecloth adorns the main table and smaller covered tables pepper the room. Each table has an arrangement of tall, eerie branches set in a vase of red-stained water.

White plates and sterling silverware sit sharply before each chair, and the enormous gothic chandelier's bulbs overhead have been dimmed. Along the main table, in addition to the arrangements, are silver four-pronged candleholders with cream-colored wicks already aflame. A man in the corner coddles a violin to his neck like a newborn babe and plays gentle notes. There's a slight blush to his cheeks as if he's decided that tonight he'll brave an audience for the first time.

The aroma of roasted meats is overpowering. I know the kitchen is nearby, but the musky-sweet smells are so strong it's as if the food has already been served. My stomach rumbles and I wonder how long it's been since I've lingered at a meal, since I've savored the flavors of a well-made dish.

Valery, Max, and Neco sit at the long table. Max whispers quietly to Valery and she smiles like a new bride who's never glimpsed her husband's bed. It's…dare I admit it…*sweet*. Neco fingers the salad fork to the right of his plate and tries to pretend he doesn't hear the two lovers trading endearments. My spine stiffens studying him. I never got to visit the liberator two nights ago, and now I think what a mistake that was.

I suppose I know, deep down, that I'm not entirely sure he's the traitor. Perhaps it seems too obvious. If he was intent on destroying our efforts, why let me know about it? Still, the things he's said and done, the coincidences that seem to indict him, I can't help feeling as if

I'm waiting for that one final push that tells me we've found our man.
Though when that moment comes, I *will* be the one to take him down.

Charlie takes my hand and leads me to the table. When did this
happen? When did Charlie start being the one to lead *me*? I study the
back of her neck as she moves, the muscles working, the soft blond
hairs. I love her neck. I'm so unbelievably smitten that I can't stop
worshiping her *neck*.

What is wrong with me?

I'm a champ.

I'm the ultimate playboy.

And yet…her neck.

I pull out her chair and watch as she tucks the white dress I want
to tear from her body beneath her. I drop down into my own chair
and Annabelle and Blue sit across from us. Neco is next to Annabelle.
He greets me with a glare that could set a nun afire. I flip him the bird
and he sneers.

"I don't like you, Neco," I say.

"The feeling's mutual, maggot," he responds with venom. But
then something happens, something I almost don't catch. The corner
of his mouth quirks. Not in the *I hate you so much it's hilarious* way,
but more in the *I really enjoy messing with you* way. Just as quickly as
it's there, it's gone.

"You don't really hate me, do you?" I ask.

"Dante." Charlie's voice holds a warning. "Please be nice. We're
all in this together."

"Sorry." I tuck a lock of hair behind her ear. When she's not
looking though, I tap my temple and point to Neco like I'm onto
him. He shakes his head. But then…then I'm even more conflicted.
Maybe Neco is harassing me because he figures I won't think he's the
traitor if he's obvious about it, and he almost smiled because his plan
is working.

Right?

No.

I've confused myself.

"How's it going down there?" Max says from next to Valery. I lean back so I can see him, and he leans forward. Then he leans back and I lean forward. Then we start screwing up on purpose, using Valery's body between us as a game piece.

"Stop it," Red says.

"I won't," Max responds.

Charlie laughs beside me, and Annabelle cracks a smile.

"Good God, men," Blue says in a butchered British voice. "Where's your dignity?"

I laugh at that and stop leaning. Charlie squeezes my leg beneath the table and Annabelle bumps Neco with her shoulder. "Cat got your tongue?" Neco sticks it out and Annabel grabs it.

"Gross." He pulls away from her, but he's laughing. Sort of.

The six of us continue joking, suffocating our fear of tomorrow, as dishes clang in the kitchen. Annabelle is about to make another dig at Neco when her eyes catch on one of the entryways.

"Paine." Annabelle stands up.

Paine stands stock still, hands shoved in his pockets, eyes downcast. He's wearing a black suit that's not messing around and a green undershirt. He's freshly shaved and I'd bet my left nut that he's wearing cologne. Tonight's the night he'll nab Annabelle's attention. At least, that had to have been what he told himself as he dressed.

Paine's gaze raises and a smile touches his lips when he sees her. "You look beautiful, Annabelle." There's something in the way he says her name, as if tonight he's come to play ball. He's come to win.

The liberator strides across the room, chin held high like he's reminded himself to have confidence. "I know it's a bother," he says in a true British accent. "But may I sit next to you?"

Neco looks around and realizes this probably means he needs to move. He doesn't.

"Get up, shit bag," I say. "Let the dude sit next to Annabelle."

"Why me? Make the curly-headed fart get up."

"Classy," Blue mutters, realizing Neco is talking about him. And then, being the standup guy that he is, Blue rises and moves one chair down.

Paine thanks him profusely and then takes his seat. He stares at Annabelle and she stares back, like she's uncertain how to handle this kind of rapt attention from him. Also, like she's determining whether, just maybe, things could go smoother if she developed feelings for Paine instead of Cyborg.

Oswald enters with one of the sisters. A second later, there's a bustle near the kitchen as a neat line of humans trail toward our table, their arms heavy with silver platters. Kraven walks among them, carrying a dish of sautéed summer squash and zucchini that drip with butter. He almost smiles as if he's proud to be among the staff.

He smiles, that is, until he sees Annabelle, her eyes on Paine. He stumbles for a moment, his massive frame suddenly a young boy's. Then he recovers with gritted teeth and approaches the table.

"Thank you all for coming to dinner tonight." He glances around. "Where are the…the jackrabbits? Dante?"

I raise my hands. "What? They're my responsibility?"

"We're here," a new voice chimes.

I turn in my chair. When I spot Lincoln and the other twelve jackrabbits, I pound a fist against the oak table and say, "Yes!"

34

PRINCES

My eyes rake over the guys in the entranceway. I am, in a word, delighted.

Lincoln is still dressed in his military get up, but now the other twelve jackrabbits are outfitted in green and brown camouflage uniforms, too. Each uniform has a black rabbit sewn onto the right pocket, and the soldiers stand at attention proudly displaying their new attire. They expect a reaction, and I'll give it to them.

"That is straight up sick, dude," I say. "You guys look *legit*."

"Where did you get those uniforms?" Kraven asks evenly, always evenly.

A young girl in the staff raises her hand. She has peach-colored hair and green eyes; it seems those eyes have forgotten Blue now that Lincoln's here. "I worked on them," she says with modesty. "But others helped."

The girl meets Lincoln's gaze and he fidgets like Queen Anne Boleyn on her period. But I see right through his unease. Dude's got a crush if I've ever seen one.

Lincoln clears his throat and tips his head. "Fall in, soldiers." The jackrabbits step into a row of two, six people deep. Arms are stiff at their sides, faces staring ahead. "Forward march."

The jackrabbits begin marching forward, leading off with the same foot. The way they move, it's like they're one single person.

"Halt," Lincoln hollers. "About face."

They stop and turn to their general.

And then Lincoln gives one final command, "Present arms!"

The jackrabbits' right hands whip to their green belts. They jerk something out of a holster there, flip their hand once, and bring their arm back down by their side. In each of the jackrabbits' grip is a nine-inch blade.

"Oh, snap!" I yell. "Instant G status!"

Kraven moves toward Lincoln. "How did you get those?"

Lincoln brings a stiff hand to his brow and clicks his heels together. "A quick mission, sir. Four jackrabbits stole stone from the ocean's edge, sir."

Kraven holds out his palm. Lincoln retrieves his knife in a quick, sharp movement and flips the handle toward the liberator. He keeps his other hand in a salute. "Uh, at ease."

Lincoln drops his arm and steps back until he's in line with his soldiers.

Kraven inspects the blade. "You created these?"

"Sir, yes, sir."

"Can you get more?"

Lincoln's gaze drops. "We almost lost a soldier out there. But we can try again. We'll do better."

Kraven waves the thought away. "Absolutely not." The liberator puts a hand on Lincoln's shoulder. "You did good, kid."

Lincoln beams like a spelling bee champion, but at the same time, he seems extremely uncomfortable that Kraven is touching him. Kraven seems to sense this, so he drops his arm. He inspects the blade once more and mumbles, "Wrapped the handle in strips of cloth."

"Sir. They can be used to tie off wounds on the battle field,"

Lincoln responds.

Kraven hands the blade back and Lincoln tucks it away so swiftly I almost miss the movement.

Charlie claps her hands. "Brilliant. You guys are just brilliant."

The sound of her voice wakes me from my jackrabbit trance. I squeeze her knee.

"I wish you didn't take that risk, though," she adds.

"We're sorry to upset you, Princess," Lincoln says.

Charlie laughs. "Princess?"

Lincoln flushes. "It's how we refer to you and Aspen. A princess of life, and a princess of death."

Charlie's smile fades. She stands slowly and crosses the room to where he stands. Kraven steps back, giving her space to approach. My breath catches and no one speaks a word. The way she strides toward them, the way that white dress drapes her body—she really does look like royalty.

"Lincoln," Charlie says. "I will be your princess." She walks down the line of jackrabbits and inspects each of them. Then she looks back to Lincoln with solemnity. "But then you must be my princes."

Lincoln's blush deepens, even if the girl with peach-colored hair is not entirely thrilled at this turn of events.

As this spectacle takes place, the staff sets down platters and uncovers lids. They move on mouse feet so as not to interrupt the show, but now they linger a few feet away, uncertain of what to do next.

Kraven motions to the smaller tables surrounding the larger, longer one. "Please sit," he tells the staff. "We are all the same now. And we will dine as one."

The humans are pleased. They spring toward empty chairs like they'd planned out where they would sit long before he gave his permission. I tuck a white napkin in my lap and listen to the violinist again. He's played this whole time, but he became white noise at one point. Now I savor the melancholy sounds he's producing.

I kiss the side of Charlie's head and reach for the roast in gravy drippings.

Kraven's voice stops me. "Let us pray."

Let us whaaa?

Kraven bows his head and everyone follows suit. I roll my eyes and tighten my jaw and, finally, I bow my head. The others stare at the back of their eyelids as Kraven begins to speak. I stare at my empty plate. Am I being ungrateful to a God who gave me a second chance at life? No. I'm repaying my debt. He wants a fighter, I'll give him one. But I won't pretend that Big Guy cares about me on a personal level. Give me a freaking break.

"Bless us this food to the nourishment of our bodies, your Grace," Kraven says. "And be with us in three days' time as we fight a war you knew would come. We will be victorious with your hand. Hear our words as we say together the prayer you taught us." Kraven hesitates, and when he speaks again, voices from around the room rise up. They speak together and a chill races across my skin. "Our father who art in heaven, hallowed be thy name. Thy Kingdom come, thy will be done, on earth as it is in heaven." They continue, growing in volume, growing in confidence. The violin plays along with their voices, turning their words into a fearsome musical chant. The sound washes over me and I feel as if I'm floating, as if I'm sliding out of my own body. It's an experience like I've never felt and I can sense my wings itching to be released.

I close my eyes.

I don't know this prayer, but I close my eyes anyway and feel the effect.

"For thine is the kingdom, and the power, and the glory forever. Amen."

The power.

Forever.

I'll tell you one thing. I've never heard this prayer before, but that's the kind of confidence I could get behind.

35

DANCING WITH THE DEVIL

We serve ourselves that night. We eat as a family.

My plate overflows with tuna tartar, pan seared foie gras, Dijon crusted lamb in a yogurt mint sauce, goat cheese and roasted tomato stuffed chicken breasts, lump crab mashed potatoes, applewood bacon mac 'n' cheese, almonds dipped in honey, and a popover that oozes butter.

"A meal fit for a princess," I whisper to Charlie.

She blushes. "Stop it."

I expected the night to be gloomy, but it's quite the opposite. The humans laugh and urge the man playing the violin to play louder, to play longer. They pass bottles of red wine and champagne from hand to hand and no one's glass goes empty. Even Valery, always the sophisticate, indulges. Blue nabs Neco's wine every time he turns away and pours it into his own. I bust a gut laughing when I catch him and he shushes me.

Though Max and Valery don't coo the way they did before with Kraven present, they still joke and eat and smile like there isn't a care to be bothered with. They aren't allowed to be together, I know that, but anyone can see how in love the two are. Watching them, I marvel at what they've been through. Valery dying and leaving a fiancé, Max, behind. Max perishing soon after and then somehow managing to find her after death. It seems like fate. They must believe it's fate. And yet they must remain physically separated. It's horrible, really.

My eyes slide across Valery's face and I spy something in her I've never seen before: abandonment. She is at home next to Max, and even as he teases Blue, she watches him like he is her life vest amidst a turbulent sea. Valery is a pillar of control and faith, but I don't miss the desperation on her face as she watches Max. The way her fingers twitch to touch him. The way her body arches toward his.

Max isn't the only one who's despaired over the restraint on their relationship.

Valery is in pain, too, maybe more so.

"Hey, Dante," Annabelle says. "You think you're something special?"

"Like a boss," I reply without missing a beat, though my thoughts are still on Valery.

"You're not that hot." She grins. "In fact, you look like a dog."

"I howl like one, too."

"Hey, Dante," Max says from two seats down. "I find you very, *very* attractive."

"Keep drinking, baby," I say.

He winks and tips his wine glass.

"I'm probably the only hot one here." Annabelle's words are slurred, but I'm not buying that she's drunk.

"You got that right," Paine says, quietly.

She points at his chest and eyes me. "You hear that?"

I nod. "I heard it."

Annabelle pushes back from the table. "I'm full. Maybe I want to dance now."

Paine shoots up in his chair, one hand on his stomach. "Will you dance with me, Annabelle?"

She flashes a quick glance at Kraven. "Yes, Paine. Yes, I will."

Kraven slams his fist down on the table. I don't mean he slams it as emphasis like I did earlier. No, home boy brings his fist down like he wants to shatter the wood in half. "Anna," he says.

The violinist continues, and so does the cheerful babble from the surrounding tables. But our table has hushed. All eyes are on Kraven.

"You've been so kind to me, Paine." Annabelle's voice holds a note of realization, like for the first time she's compared the two men and found Kraven lacking. She takes his hand and leads him to a cozy area near a corner.

Kraven doesn't react again. He just lowers his eyes and we all turn to see what Cannonball Annabelle will do next. That girl has gone from no boyfriend to having two guys lust after her, and I know why, too. She's found her confidence here at the Hive. She's learned to fight, stood by a best friend that needed her, and gotten her hands on some seriously amazing dresses. And she's not in a high school environment anymore. That alone can drastically change how an eighteen-year-old girl carries herself.

Annabelle has grown into herself.

And guys have taken notice.

She and Paine dance awkwardly, stepping on each other's feet. It's a sad sight, really. Fortunately, I don't have the same problem. I stand and offer my hand to Charlie. She dabs her mouth with a stiff white napkin before accepting my offer. I'm glad to get away from Kraven's misery and forget about anything that isn't my girl. We move to where Annabelle and Paine are and I lightly touch her waist.

The music suddenly becomes more cheerful and I ask Charlie, "Do you know how to waltz?"

She shakes her head, her bottom lip pursed.

"I'll show you." I hold her hand to the side and count. "One, two-three. One, two-three. One big flat step, then two shuffle steps on your toes. You see?" I'm not sure if I'm doing this exactly right. It's been a while since I attended a gala with my parents. What I do remember is

Dad talking business the whole night while Mom guzzled too much champagne. Both forgot I was there. But no worries. Someone always found me, a woman too old to be ogling a sixteen-year-old, or a girl my age who never stopped staring. I'd dance with either for hours, because they smelled of expensive perfume and laughed fervently and there was nothing better to do.

One, two-three.

Dancing with Charlie is something else, though. Charlie and I moving together is perfect and natural, like we've done it for years and it's still remarkable and where are our children? Probably getting into trouble but I don't care because I'm holding their mother.

I think back to when we danced at the Halloween ball at Centennial High School. She still had her limp and I swept her into my arms so she could sway to the music without discomfort. I think about doing that now, but she doesn't need me in that way anymore. It makes me wonder if she needs me at all. Not to hold her while she dances. Not to protect her. So what then?

Charlie lays her head on my shoulder and breathes a sigh of pleasure.

Oh.

Soon Max and Valery are dancing next to us, and at some point I spot humans rising from their tables and joining in. The first Patrelli sister who came for the meal leaves and the second sister appears for the dancing. Time slips past too quickly. At one point, seven humans race to the kitchen, champagne glasses in hands, laughing wildly. They reappear with chocolate lemon tortes dusted with powdered sugar. We eat them while dancing and Charlie kisses the chocolate off my lips.

"Stop stealing my dessert, girl."

"Never!" She punches her arm into the air, so I dip her low and kiss her throat.

Annabelle breaks in between Charlie and I and the two of them dance the worst dance I've ever seen. Paine and I link arms and swing around as fast as we can go. This isn't a dance either. But with half a bottle of champagne in my belly, it sure feels like it is. Max links onto my other arm and then I spin them both around like I'm the center of a carnival ride.

The music has reached its peak now and I don't think about tomorrow. I think about now and how Charlie's face is alight with bliss and how I've never seen Annabelle look so radiant. I think about Kraven smiling as he watches Annabelle laugh and how Neco's lurking is pretty funny now that I think about it.

I don't know why I do it.

I don't know.

But I release Paine and Max and rush toward Neco, that bastard. I hook arms with him and spin around and around like I did before. He tries to shove me off with authentic frustration, but then Paine hooks his other arm and Max hooks my spare one. We spin around like one big ball of testosterone that's seen prouder days.

"What are you doing?" Neco yells in his Australian accent as glasses clink and people sing and a lone violin plays.

"We're spinning, dick," I yell.

"Why?" he hollers.

"Why not?" Paine chimes in.

Neco continues to try and pull away until we're spinning so fast that we almost stumble. And then there it is.

A smile.

Neco's grinning and now he's spinning with us instead of against us. Look at me! I'm Charlie Cooper with her infectious fun! Neco may be a traitor, but as I watch him laughing, I think, *Maybe he is. But perhaps converting him back to our side is a better battle to win*.

Max reaches out and grabs Kraven. The liberator says it "isn't happening" but Max holds tight and now we're five full-grown dudes spinning in a circle. Charlie and Annabelle grab Valery and they break into the middle and force us to form a circle around them. We spin one way and they spin another and the room blurs.

Everyone laughs and this is the most fun I've ever had and where's the champagne?

Someone trips and we all tumble onto each other, dying with laughter.

"Party foul," Max yells.

"I think the party foul started when the men started dancing together," Annabelle roars.

All around us the humans and jackrabbits continue to dance, but a few of them point to the sweaty mess that is us piled on the floor. Charlie pulls Annabelle up and motions to the violinist. He sees her and stops playing.

"I have an announcement to make," Charlie says. Annabelle begins to move away to give her room, but Charlie guides her back. "I haven't been able to do as much for my charity as I'd like to in the last few weeks. But once we return home, I plan for it to get the attention it deserves."

I get to my feet and clap my support. I'm not totally sure what I'm clapping for, but Charlie's talking so I'm clapping, damn it.

Charlie turns to her friend. "We're a small operation now, but we're expanding with every event we do. I plan for that to continue. When we're home, we'll pick up where we left off. Every Saturday, we'll help people who have committed to help another person in turn. And we'll grow."

Charlie wipes the sweat from her brow and smiles a strange smile. "I want to ensure Hands Helping Hands continues to thrive. And that's why I'm announcing Annabelle as president."

The crowd erupts in applause. They don't know what they're clapping for, but it's a night of happiness so they don't question it. Annabelle's eyes widen with shock, but when Charlie hugs her close Annabelle returns the embrace.

Annabelle always said she wanted to do more for the cause, but

I bet she never expected this. To be honest, I didn't either. My mind goes straight to a dark place because, well, it's at home there.

Why would Charlie need a president?

What will she do while Annabelle is running things?

I raise my arm to shush everyone, but no one stops talking. "Hey, Charlie," I yell while smiling a lie. "Wait, everyone, I need to ask my girlfriend something." A few people realize I want the floor, so they quiet. It takes another few moments before everyone else follows suit. Half the smile I'm wearing slides off my face, and I struggle to keep the rest intact.

"What about you?" I ask.

Charlie grins, but she also fidgets. I don't miss the nervous gesture. "What do you mean?"

"Where will you be when Annabelle is running your charity?"

She laughs. It sounds forced. It sounds like no other laugh she's ever laughed. "I'll be there with her." Charlie glances at Annabelle and her grin widens. "Co-presidents!"

"You know it," Annabelle says.

"I guess I don't understand why there needs to be two."

Charlie stops smiling, and I'm thankful for the honesty. There's a hushed moment between the two of us that's interrupted when Valery moves past me, quiet as a bird. She clasps Charlie's outer arms and stares at her like Charlie is her own child. "I'm so proud of you, Charlie." She lays a kiss on her cheek. "Don't mind him."

Charlie throws her arms around Valery's neck, and the next thing I hear is the unmistakable sound of tears.

"Charlie." I stride toward her. The sound of her crying stirs some primal instinct in me, and I know I'll do anything to make her happy again.

I stop when I hear Lincoln yelling—

When I hear Lincoln calling orders to his soldiers, telling them the enemy has breached.

⇥ 36 ⇤

FORGIVE ME

The sirens stride in through the main entry like they were invited for dinner. They walk in with an air of superiority, as if we're children waiting by the chimney and they've come to explain that Santa isn't real.

"Liberators, Oswald, front position." Kraven's voice is firm and unafraid. "Jackrabbits, second position. Humans, third. Now!"

We've never practiced this before, but what he's asking makes sense, and so with a soft rustle, eight liberators and one collector move to stand between the sirens and the humans. The jackrabbits align themselves directly behind us in a long, neat row. Behind them, the humans stand ready.

"You know you haven't brought the war here." Kraven addresses the sirens directly. "So why have you come?"

The sirens turn and face the entryway.

And Rector walks through it.

He's tall and thin and his eyes are dark. The jackrabbits may conduct themselves like they're part of the military, but Rector *screams* it with his stance. He holds his hands behind his back and his chin tilts toward the sky. He doesn't remind me of a cold-blooded killer. No, Rector has goals. Everything he does is to win Lucille's favor. He wants approval, and that makes him human. Though the time I saw his face change to that of a demon's tells me that a piece of him is buried deep.

Rector wears a smirk as he strolls closer, and when the sirens move in as if they are protecting him, he waves them away. I search for his slick black wings, but they are nowhere in sight.

"Guard the savior," Kraven orders with the same air of calm.

His words barely reach my mind, because all I hear is a fierce pounding in my ears. It drives me mad; it tells me that Rector is here and that he needs to die at my hand. The pounding magnifies until I imagine the only thing that can stop it is wrapping my hands around Rector's throat. I need to find Aspen, and he has her.

I step forward.

"Dante, stop," Kraven says. "Remember the savior."

The savior. Charlie. The girl I love.

I step back, and together with the others we usher Charlie to the center, away from the sirens' stares and away from Rector. For once, she doesn't fight us.

Why can't Oswald just blow them all to pieces? Why wait until this proclaimed *day* to fight? Why not now?!

"You know what we have come for," Rector says to Kraven in his typical clear, clipped fashion.

Kraven's jaw tightens and I see that storm brewing in his eyes that he's buried for so long. "The war is in three days, demon. Are you afraid to see what we will bring to the battle field?" the liberator says. "You scurry into our home every chance you get like rodents. Your lord has agreed to the same rules mine has: we wait and we battle. Yet you continue to intrude. You continue to test me. You continue to TRY MY PATIENCE!"

Kraven yells the last part so loudly my head rings. He's losing it. Kraven once told me he had his own demons, that he did horrible things in his past. It's why he's ever calm, always pushing down his fury. But right now, that fury rears its head.

"Give us the savior," Rector says as if this is a request we should have expected.

"Turn and leave this place," Kraven responds, his voice dangerously low. "Or I will end you here and now."

Rector sighs like this is quite the inconvenience.

Then he motions for the sirens to attack.

Instinctually, we tighten our bodies together like fish swarming. Some of the sirens produce gleaming knives and rush forward, blades swinging by their sides. A burning smell tickles my senses as Paine, Kraven, and I snap our wings to attention. A few of the humans cry out from behind us having never witnessed our capabilities before.

As each siren nears me, I tear my wings across my body like a shield, throwing bodies across the room. They come faster and harder as if gaining momentum. The sirens are easy enough to take down, but there are so many. It's like stepping on an ant hill and trying to brush them from your legs one at a time. With each defensive blow, I peer past the sirens to Rector. I need to get to him. Screw the war in three days. He's here now, and I want my opportunity to take him down.

Rector stands at the back of the room, shoulders relaxed. He's so pacified that he might as well be smoking a cigarette and asking when this *situation* is going to be over.

But that won't last long.

Oswald spins in clumsy, muttering circles. And then his circling becomes cataclysmic. *Go, boy!* I feel like screaming. *Show 'em what you got!* An orange light engulfs his body, growing in volume and flashing with energy. I yell for everyone to take cover just as his powerful charge erupts in a crackling sonic boom.

I know it's over. Sirens will lie dead. Rector will be on his back. Hell brought a battle to us inside the Hive, and it was an enormous mistake.

But when I open my eyes, I see a black inky cloud pressed against Oswald's orange one. It looks like an open sky when a storm is coming, a bold expanse of orange on one side, and a black mass on the other.

A siren stands in the middle of his brothers and sisters, hands raised toward the dark cloud, concentration stitched into his features. I can't believe what I'm seeing, but I should. If powers are awakening in humans on our side, then of course the same could happen with theirs.

Narrowing my eyes, I realize just who this siren with the black power is. It's Easton, the dude who stood outside Charlie's bedroom window mere weeks ago. And there, not too far behind him, is Salem, his cocky older brother. I thought I'd scared those two pricks off, but I guess not.

The other sirens continue their attack after seeing that old man's orange power is offset. A siren lunges onto my wing and I use the other to bat him off. But now the sirens have an idea, so they charge toward my wings at once and use them to pull me toward the floor. Behind me, I hear someone scream, and my mind ticks through all the screams I've ever heard Charlie make. Was it her?

I scramble away from the sirens somehow, but when I twist onto my back, ready to push myself up, I'm struck silent by the blade arched over my head.

A siren holds it tight between two hands, and for some reason, I find that more horrifying than the weapon itself. It's like this guy with his thin face and thinner eyebrows is intent on plunging the knife as far in as it will go. His arms tremble above his head for one terrible moment, and in that same moment, I notice he has spittle at the left corner of his mouth.

Gross, I think.

And then the blade comes down.

Right as it's about to bury itself into my sternum, a pair of glowing hands touch his chest, and the siren soars across the room. He flies so beautifully, like he's done it all his life. The thing I notice as he sails away are his eyes. They don't even have time to widen before he's gone, and then they're just two dark shadows in his face before he's hitting the ground.

"Stop!" Rector roars.

The sirens edge away from us and toward the lead collector, the collector who's smiling and clasping his hands and looking as if he wants to dance to the violin that's long been quieted.

"I was told of what she could do, but that was spectacular," Rector says with a touch of amazement. "A savior with a power like that of a gifted mortal. She will be quite useful."

Charlie stands over me, her mouth open in bewilderment. It's the second time she's ever fully used her ability, and it's no less mind blowing witnessing it a second time. I get to my feet and start to fold my arms around her, but Valery beats me there.

She gently leads Charlie away from the front lines and toward the humans, whose blooming bruises and bloodied lacerations speak to the first combat they've ever encountered. I scan the room for Neco and find him standing next to Kraven. He hasn't taken a step in Rector's direction, and I wonder if he's truly with us now, if all it took was a smile and a sense of being included. Or if I was wrong about him all along.

"I will see you in three days, old friend." Rector raises his arm and points. But his finger doesn't lead to Kraven.

It points directly at me.

I stretch my wings far above my head and my chest swells. *I'll be ready for you.*

Over my shoulder, Valery whispers to Charlie, soothing her worries. I turn to Charlie to assure her that Red is right, that everything will be okay.

My heart stops.

A chill rushes down my body.

Valery's arms are wrapped around Charlie's body, pinning my girlfriend's own arms against her sides. A black hole appears before Valery's feet as she whispers a language she shouldn't know. A language *I* shouldn't know.

"Nobody move," Kraven says.

Rector laughs from the other side of the room, a sound of steel and flames. "Perfect timing, dove!"

"Valery, how could—?" Kraven starts, his words brimming with surprise. He finds his center quickly. "Don't do this, Valery. If you do this, they've won. Remember the promise you made. Remember the vow you took."

Valery shakes her head and her eyes redden, but no tears escape. "He'll never let us be together," she explains, her gaze on Max. "I don't care what side I'm on anymore as long as it's with you."

My body contracts so hard that I can't find my breath, I can't think beyond seeing Charlie thrashing against Valery. She's too small, and her hands are useless at her sides.

"Valery," I force out, inching toward her, afraid to make any sudden movements. "Please!"

Valery closes her eyes and she says in a whisper, "Forgive me."

Then she steps forward with my angel and the two drop out of sight.

INFERNO

"Through me is the way into the doleful city; through me the way into the eternal pain; through me the way among the people lost."

—Dante's Inferno

⇥ 37 ⇤

WE ALL FALL DOWN

The cry that rips from my throat sounds as though it's coming from somebody else. I stumble toward the hole as it closes and tear at it with my fingernails.

"Charlie," I roar. "Charlie!"

As the floor cinches shut, I fight harder. I try to pull the floorboards apart and keep the hole from closing. It's no use. Blood streaks the tired wood. It must be mine. I scream for her and inside my beating heart, a river of sorrow sings like a siren. I can't see. I'm blind. No, I'm crying.

"Charlie!"

I grab the first person I see—Max. I shake him hard and tell him to bring her back, but he's broken like me, yelling for a woman who deceived us all. I turn to Paine, but he has nothing to give, nothing to say. I see Kraven. I see Blue. I see Lincoln. All are scrambling, barking orders, or reaching for me like they can help. They can do nothing. *Nothing!*

"Bring her back!" I yell. "Where is she?"

Then I see him.

I see him and I know I am unstoppable. My legs power across

the room and my wings carry me faster than any human could travel. I collide into Rector like a wrecking ball and the two of us smash against the east wall of the great room.

My hands find his throat and, sweet relief, the terror on his face eases my pain.

"Be afraid!" I roar.

Rector's eyeballs bulge with fear, or maybe from lack of oxygen. I don't know which it is and I don't care. I squeeze tighter and pummel him into the wall time and again. The cracking of his skull is the sound of angels singing, the blood that runs down his face their tears of joy.

"Be afraid," I whisper.

Kraven's voice rings through the room. "Neco, no!"

No other name could've made me stop in that moment. No name but Neco's.

My head spins around just in time to see Neco tackling a siren that was moments from driving a blade into my back. That same knife finds its way into Neco's belly. The siren jerks the blade up and opens Neco like a fish. His insides pour over the siren in a sloshing shower of cranberry red.

I tear away from Rector and grab Neco's shoulders. The siren scrambles out from beneath his body as I drag the liberator toward our people. I don't why I do this. It seems right. Rector rushes into the hallway, the sirens close on his heel. No doubt there's a vultrip not far from here that Valery whispered open while the rest of us danced, ignorant to her muted words.

My wings slide into my body and then Kraven is there, taking Neco from me and laying him down. He's dead. He's so obviously dead. But that's okay; he'll heal once his dargon kicks in. Perhaps new organs will grow, but I don't want him to be out for longer than necessary. Not after what he did for me.

I grab slick red pieces of him and put them back inside his body.

"Dante, stop," Kraven says quietly.

"It's okay," I tell him. "He'll heal faster this way."

Kraven grabs onto my arm. "Stop doing that."

I yank away and try to close the gabbing wound that extends from Neco's chest to his pelvis. "Look, he's barely even bleeding anymore," I say too loudly. Why is my voice so loud? Where is Charlie?

I close Neco's eyes. Their blank stare causes a wave of nausea to roll over me, but that's ridiculous because he'll be back, so nothing to worry about.

"Dante." Kraven speaks my name differently this time. I don't like the way he says it.

I grind my teeth. "Don't."

"Neco isn't coming back," he says. "He's finished his duty as a liberator."

My hands curl into fists over Neco's body. I shake my head. He'll come back. That's what we do. We come back.

Kraven motions to Lincoln and when I see what the jackrabbit hands him, I almost lose my mind. Kraven slides down to Neco's ankle, his blood-splattered white wings folded behind him. He raises the knife.

"What are you doing?" I yell.

He brings the blade down at a right angle, like he's done this too many times to count. The dargon severs, and from there Kraven pulls it away easily enough. He stands, the dargon clutched in his right hand. "Neco's gone now. But don't mourn him."

He's right, I think. Neco is probably inside the heavens already. So why is the feel of his blood on my hands so sickening? Because Neco felt the pain that killed him? Because maybe he didn't know he wouldn't return? Because he died to save my life?

The humans are huddled together. Many are crying, but others appear strengthened by the battle. Blue stands a few feet away, his eyes on the ground.

"Blue," I say. "Where's Charlie?"

I don't know why I say it. I know where she is. I watched as she disappeared into the floor. When I glance back at Neco's mangled corpse, I realize my mind has focused on his death to avoid a more unimaginable truth—Charlie is gone.

"Dante," Kraven touches my shoulder.

"Get off me!" I yell. "What are you going to do? Are we going for her?"

Kraven remains silent. "I won't wait here while she sits down there. I waited with Aspen. I trusted you, and now she—"

"She what?" Blue asks.

"We have to go for her, Kraven," I say. "We have to go right now. *I* am going right now. Are you coming with me?"

"You will not go." Kraven speaks each word like a bullet. "We will pack our belongings, and we will leave for the battlefield. They'll do the same. We'll combat them as it was foretold, and then we'll take back the savior and soldier." Kraven gazes around the room. "It'll require all of us to be triumphant."

My muscles clench in actual pain. My body feels the same way I did when I was mortal and had the flu—aching body, dizziness, fever. I can't live without Charlie. I told her I'd protect her, and now she's gone. And I can't go on without her.

I decide then that maybe I won't. Maybe this is the moment that I kiss my mind goodbye. There was a piece of me, a quiet place Charlie had unbolted in my heart that spoke of forgiveness and compassion. But now, only darkness swims through my blood. It opens its arms in a morning stretch and swallows the goodness. It's amazing how easy it is to tap my rage, to let it consume my every thought. I will not mourn Valery's betrayal. I will not cry for my fallen angel.

I will only seek vengeance.

⇥ 38 ⇤

SPEAK

Oswald comes to my room after I storm from the battle scene. I'm throwing clothing and boots and bottles of water into a bag. I have no idea what I'll need for this war so I just shove everything in with a nervous gut-wrenching energy.

"You need to see something," Oswald says from the doorway.

I continue packing.

"You're upset," the old man notes. "But you do need to see this. Kraven asked me to show you."

Oswald moves aside and motions for someone to step inside. I recognize the guy immediately. It's the siren that almost killed me, the one Charlie blocked with her blue electricity. His face is thin and he has dark, thin eyebrows that rise in a question. It's a face I'll never forget.

I expect to experience fury at seeing him here. But instead, I'm delighted. Oswald has delivered me an outlet for my anger, one I will take my time enjoying.

I smile. "I'm going to kill you."

Of all the things I expect him to say back, it isn't this: "I'm so deeply sorry."

The guy hangs his head and black hair tickles his forehead. He weeps and my nose turns up at the sound.

"What's he doing?" I ask Oswald.

The old man touches the siren's back in comfort. "He's grieving the things he's done."

"Bullshit. That guy's as sorry as a pothead in county jail."

The siren raises his head. He has small lines around his brown eyes that tell me he's older than I am. "She changed me."

This gets my attention. "What?"

Oswald nods to the siren, encouraging him to continue. "That girl who…who shocked me, she *changed* me. I felt like I had this emptiness inside from the things I'd done, but then it was gone. I feel different." The guy offers a sad smile. "I feel happy."

I narrow my eyes at this sorry excuse of a man. Lies. All of it— lies. "I don't have time for this."

"Look at his soul light," Oswald says gently.

But I don't want to. I know what he's implying and I don't give a crap. I wouldn't forgive this guy if he rid the world of loud talkers and felines.

"Please, Dante," Oswald implores. "Just look."

"Jaysus." I spin around and flip on the dude's soul light. Yep, it's as powdery clean as a newborn's asshole. "He has no sin seals. That's great. He still tried to kill me. He still helped take Charlie away."

Speaking her name hurts.

Though I'm going for indifference, I'm stunned by what I see. I've witnessed sin seals dissolving beneath liberator seals. But Kraven told me sirens didn't have souls; that they forfeited them when they agreed to work for the collectors. Though what I'm beholding contradicts that statement. It's almost as if Charlie resuscitated this guy. If before his soul was in the hands of hell, now it's back inside of him, glowing like a beacon of hope.

"Get out of my sight," I tell the siren.

Oswald motions to the sitting area and the siren strides past him and out of my room. The old man closes the door until it's just the two of us.

"You gonna leave that guy out there by himself?" I snap. "He's probably already run for it."

Oswald folds his thin arms over his robe. There's a bluish-green bruise over his left elbow that looks like the state of Florida. "She's changed him, Dante."

"So? He'll just screw up again," I say. "He's like a fat ass after liposuction. It's just a fresh opportunity to wreck that shit."

"I don't think so," Oswald mutters. "Kraven says we're to meet at the front of the Hive."

"What about the siren?" I say.

"I'll leave him to you." Oswald scoots out of my room even as I call for him to get his skinny rear back here.

Then he's gone. And I'm staring at the siren who's trying his damnedest to avoid eye contact. "You think you're redeemed?" My lip curls in disgust. "You're no different than you were an hour ago, fart stain." I step closer to him. "I'll tell you what I'm going to do for you. I'm going to keep you around so that when we get to the final battlefield, I can kick things off with a human sacrifice and decorate my warrior face in your blood."

The dude doesn't respond, which must mean he has a brain.

"For now, you'll be my bag boy." I shove my bundle into his chest and he jerks back from the impact. "Get up. I need to fetch the weapon I'm going to kill you with."

"I'm sorry about Charlie," he whispers. "I was confused."

I close my eyes and breathe through my nose. I try to count backward, and to think of a freshly pressed Armani vest, and to visualize Charlie's face—anything that will help me calm down. But nothing helps. My eyes snap open and I throw my fist into the siren's face. It's a blow I feel clear to my shoulder. It feels like Christmas morning. It feels like the first time I heard Charlie laugh.

"Don't say her name. The next time you do, I'll cut your tongue out." I roll my shoulders back, a sense of satisfaction settling over me. "Now, let's go get that weapon, shall we?"

Fifteen minutes later, I'm at the front of the Hive with the siren and a few blades of glory rearing to do some killin'. When Paine comes into view, I notice he has tightly rolled packs loaded onto his back.

"What are those?" I ask.

He twitches when I address him the same way others have since Charlie was taken. They all believe I'm off the handle.

I am.

Lade-fucking-da.

"Tents." He shifts the weight of them. "Kraven says it'll take a day of travel to get there." Paine notices the siren standing next to me, his bound hands. "Isn't that—?"

"A siren? Yeah. His name is Fart Stain, and I'd appreciate it if you used it."

Paine chances a smile. It disappears when Max enters the holding area inside the Hive's entrance. He's carrying jackets and blankets and looks like a cancer patient, like he's about to call off the whole radiation thing and demand a banana split, dammit.

I don't offer him condolences. I'm not sure why. Maybe because I lost someone, too. And maybe, if I'm being honest, it's because I have a hard time believing he didn't suspect what Valery was up to. Even if he didn't, maybe he should have.

Thinking about Valery infuriates me. Perhaps I should understand her reasons for betrayal, because there's little I wouldn't do to be with Charlie, but somehow I can't forgive her. She was always the perfect student, always the star pupil. It's no wonder she discovered the dead language. And it doesn't surprise me that she taught herself enough to damage our plight. I don't believe she wanted to harm us. Even the fire she started in the library must have been done when she thought the room was empty. It doesn't matter though.

I still hate her.

How quickly I can go from *like* to *detestation*. My ability to embrace hostile emotions knows no bounds. As I'm dwelling on this, my mind whispers *Charlie, Charlie, Charlie.* It never stops. From the moment she vanished, my brain began echoing her name. It's like a ringing in your ear you can't escape; it's ever present and all-consuming.

Charlie.

"We need to leave," I bark. "Where's Kraven? Where are the humans? The jackrabbits? What's taking so long?"

"They're preparing," a new voice says. It's the sound of rustling leaves in the treetops, soothing and tender.

I spin around and find the Quiet Ones studying me. They stand shoulder to shoulder, hair tied back in ponytails. The younger one, the one not much younger than me, is the one who spoke. I know this on instinct.

"They took our weapons," she says. "They took the one we swore to serve." The girl squeezes her hands together and I notice her eyes are red-rimmed and puffy. She and her sister are holding clear tote bags harboring hand shovels. "We won't be silent any longer. We will fight alongside you."

My heart picks up at this new turn of events, but each time it beats with vigor, pain courses through my limbs. *I'm here to remind you she's gone* it seems to say.

"I don't suppose the two of you have any hidden abilities like the old dude," I question.

The girl's head turns toward the woman next to her. They regard each other silently, and then the younger of the two offers a shy smile. "We can do some things."

The sound of footsteps approaching seizes my attention. Kraven strides toward our group, Annabelle, Blue, and Oswald at his side.

Oswald is busy tucking something into his pocket. It looks like a glasses case. I didn't know the old dude wore spectacles, but it doesn't surprise me.

Behind them are the jackrabbits, loaded down with the remaining weapons. Lincoln is sniffing the air for some unknown reason, and the humans are following behind the jackrabbits, all squared shoulders and grit.

The mass of bodies comes to a stop.

Kraven hands me a bag to carry. When I zip it open I see several dozen thin metallic tubes shaped like straws. I have no idea what purpose they'll serve, but I pull the bag onto my back anyway.

"We'll walk to Widow's Nest and stop early evening tomorrow," Kraven announces. "It's a long journey, and what lies beyond it is war and suffering. If you walk out this door now, you are bound to this cause. Anyone may choose to stay behind." At this he shoots a pointed look at Annabelle. "But if you do, there will be no one to protect you should the collectors or sirens return to scavenge our home."

Kraven scans our group, inspecting our faces for any sign of hesitancy.

There is none to see.

We are ready.

✦ 39 ✦

WIDOW'S NEST

The sun rises over the snow-covered horizon in the early morning hours, and we walk. It toggles at midday behind thick purple clouds, and we walk. And even as it arches toward the earth, our muscles tight with fatigue and worry, we push onward.

I keep pace beside Kraven, and every so often, I find it in myself to answer his questions. He's trying to keep my spirit up, though there's no spirit to speak of. I may harbor my soul within this dead body, but it's for naught. I don't need the blasted thing. I can hate this world and everything in it with my mind alone.

What I really keep thinking about, as Kraven speaks to deaf ears and Oswald mutters about his old man knees and Paine ogles Annabelle's ass, is how maybe Charlie being taken was predetermined. Or at the very least, that she suspected it would happen. Why else would she appoint Annabelle president of Hands Helping Hands? Did Charlie know? Or is it worse than that? Was it always Annabelle that was supposed to lead the charity while Charlie was to do something else—like become a martyr so those who loved her would be driven to action?

I shake my head at the thought and fight the nausea clenching my throat. Thinking back, I try and remember what Valery said about Charlie's charity in my Las Vegas hotel room.

Her organization will continue to grow and flourish, and in time, it will change the face of humankind. It will remind people how to love another. It will show them how to care again.

She didn't say Charlie would be the one running things. All Valery said was that the charity that would grow, not who would be behind it. Suddenly I have a new picture of the future, one where Annabelle is poised at podiums and giving radio interviews; one where Annabelle organizes nationwide food drives and suicide outreach programs in her late best friend's name. People will be helped, and they will help others in return, just the way Charlie envisioned.

"Dante." Kraven's voice snaps me back to the present. "You must stay out of your head. It's a dangerous place to be right now."

For the first time on our foot journey, I agree with him. We have to be on the lookout for sirens and collectors who haven't shown their faces, but could at any time. All my mind offers is nightmares and promises of death, and right now I need to become a body, ready for combat and nothing more.

When we reach Widow's Nest, I know it immediately. We've trekked through the forest that surrounds the Hive for hours, snow crunching beneath our boots and coldness nipping at our skin. But now we stand before a glove of damp earth that's cocooned by twisted branches and thickets. Together the mass creates a cavernous tunnel, and when Kraven waves us into the darkness, we follow him in.

The space is maybe twenty-five feet wide and about the same distance deep. There's enough room for us all to fit inside, but not so much that we can spread out. When I stand I'm able to do so without hunching, but when I raise my arms above my head they're met with course moss-covered twigs.

Outside Widow's Nest, swallows call to one another and somewhere in the distance a barn owl hoots. As we walked through the day, the forest floor was still, but now as the sun prepares to slumber, the forest comes alive. Soft rustling sounds greet my ears, perhaps a red fox scrounging for dinner, and overhead a light breeze sweeps through the trees, causing barren limbs to groan against one other. It's growing colder, so we huddle together, thankful for the warmth our bodies bring. The humans do their best to make a meal with what food they carried. Anything would be better than the dried sausage and raw potatoes we ate as we traveled.

As Kraven and Paine work to build a fire, I wonder about the footprints we left behind, but soon the snow begins to fall once more, and this dark snowy day in January proves the perfect day to travel incognito.

When they finish working and a small blaze burns inside the den, Kraven whispers something to Paine and he leaves us.

"Where's he going?" I ask as I breathe in the smell of smoke.

"To set up tents a mile from here," Kraven responds. "He'll light a fire there, too."

"In case they're looking for us?"

Kraven meets my gaze. "They *are* looking for us. But I think leaving so soon after the confrontation bought us some time. They won't have expected it."

I wonder why they wouldn't. It seems that after they took Charlie that that's the first thing we'd do. Or maybe it's just that it's the first thing I would do. Maybe Kraven is more calculative. Maybe he left early because of me. But we were planning to leave the next morning, so I'm not sure what difference it makes.

"We'll sleep in shifts tonight," he tells me. "You'll sleep first, and I'll wake you when it's your turn to keep watch."

"Who else will keep watch?" I ask.

He glances away. "Just you and me. The others will sleep the night through."

I lie down as best I can and listen as Annabelle and Blue whisper to each other. Max huddles in a ball near the entrance, staring at the earth beneath him. He seems lost. If there's danger in losing yourself in your head, it's a risk he's welcomed. The Quiet Ones, who are not so quiet anymore, sit cross-legged near Max, talking closely to each other with absolutely zero hand gestures.

Lincoln sits near the girl with peach-colored hair who I've learned is named Polly. His eyes say he's terrified she'll spontaneously eat his soul, but he doesn't move away when she leans her head on his shoulder. His pierced lips inch upward into a cautious smile. He gently pulls a long black bag off his shoulder and lays it on the ground, careful not to disturb Polly. The jackrabbits crowd Lincoln and the girl, and the humans do their best to find a spot to rest.

Oswald is folding a length of fabric in his hands. It's a scarf that Aspen used to wear around the Hive.

"Why do you have that?" I snap at him more harshly than I intended. "Why are you always taking things that don't belong to you?"

Oswald's cheeks redden and he stuffs the scarf into his jacket pocket. It's the first time I've seen the man in anything but a robe. "When I see something I like, I take it. I'm not hurting anyone."

"Typically you're supposed to wait until someone offers something before you take it."

"Well." Oswald crosses his legs and fumbles with the zipper on his jacket. "Maybe I haven't been offered very much."

I don't know what he's talking about, but my guess is this eccentric old man was severely ignored when he wasn't an old man at all. It's amazing how screwed up parents can make us; Aspen and her fingerless gloves and hard outer shell, me and my anger, Oswald and his petty theft.

I spot the woman with the ever-present shawl. Her name is Laura, and she smiles warmly.

I turn away.

"I won't be able to sleep," I tell Kraven.

He stretches his long legs out in front of him. "Try."

I roll my eyes and lie down, hands shoved beneath my head. Though I don't believe it possible, I find myself crashing into sleep within minutes.

And then I'm standing before my father.

"Dante!" My dad has always seemed larger than life even though he's a quiet man. He pulls me into an embrace, and I realize we're sitting on my bed in our old brownstone. "I knew you'd come."

This time, I don't question the dream I'm experiencing, I just clutch my dad close and bury my head into his chest. "Dad."

"You've done so well," he says. "Things have been hard for you, and you've done so well."

I pull back and inspect my room. Everything is as it was. My made-in-Tuscany bed, my framed chalk drawing signed by the artist, and a row of polished basketball trophies I won before I stopped caring about such things. There's a wicker basket in the corner overflowing with laundry that the maid will handle, and if I remember correctly, a stash of purple condoms stuffed in a sock somewhere in the closet (ribbed for maximum pleasure).

The distinct stale smell of cigarettes hangs in the air, no doubt emanating from my laundry. My parents had to smell it every time they walked in my room. Why didn't they ever say anything? Why didn't they care?

"We did care," Dad says, reading my mind. "We just forgot what was important."

"That sounds like not caring."

My dad takes my chin in his hand. It makes me feel like a child. It makes me feel like his son again. "Sometimes it takes losing the one you love before you truly see them."

"Do you see me now?" My throat tightens.

"I see you, D. I wish I'd seen you the whole time." He touches a closed fist to my knee. "Your mother, she wishes she would have seen you, too."

I turn my face away so he won't spot the emotion welling up inside me. "Are you still watching after her?"

"Every moment. He says if any of them get close to her, He'll intervene."

"How?" I ask.

Dad shrugs. "He's all powerful, right?"

I don't respond.

"You're changing, Dante," my dad says. "Embrace it. Don't be afraid."

I turn to him again and stumble backward in shock. His face is pulled tight against his bones. He looks like a monster.

"Don't be afraid," he repeats, his lips pulled away from his teeth.

40

BROKEN

It's early morning when Kraven wakes me and announces that it's my turn to keep watch. I don't feel as though I've slept enough, but at the same time, I have no desire to return to the place I was. I don't want to listen as Aspen tells me she's dead, and I don't want to pretend that my father's words are real—that he regrets time lost with me.

Kraven falls asleep as quickly as I did, as weird as it is I watch him sleep for a while. It seems like too human of a thing for him to do. I wonder if he's dreaming of war, or if he's dancing with Annabelle in the corner of his mind.

My gaze flicks to Annabelle and I stifle a gasp when I realize her eyes are wide open.

"Is he asleep?" she whispers.

I pull on my earlobe. "Yeah, he's out."

She sits up and tears leak down her cheeks as if they'd never stopped since Charlie was taken. "Annabelle."

"Don't try and comfort me," she says from across the short crackling fire. "I know you're hurting as bad as I am."

I sigh as the pain I'd forgotten while sleeping rushes back. "It's like this big thing has happened, and she's the one I want to tell it, too. But the big thing…is that she's gone. So I just feel—"

"Lost?" Annabelle offers.

I shrug.

Annabelle covers her mouth and says through her fingers. "Sometimes it's like I can't breathe. I think to myself, 'What are my parents thinking? Are the police looking for me?' And sometimes I just wonder what I left in my locker? Like, maybe it was important and it'll be gone when I get back." Her quiet voice quiets further. "*If* I get back."

"Stop. You'll get back. The collectors and sirens have no interest in taking out humans because you guys aren't a threat. No offense. They'll target the liberators and Oswald. Maybe the jackrabbits, but probably not even that. You guys are coming mostly because Kraven realized he couldn't leave you behind, and with the tunnel flooded, it'd be next to impossible to get you anywhere else safely."

I feel like my words should comfort her, but Annabelle cries harder. A few of the humans shift in their sleep, and Annabelle sees them do so.

"I need to go to the bathroom," she says.

"I'll go with you." I get up.

She straightens her back. It does nothing to offset the hurt in her face. "You have to stay here. I'll be fine."

"You can't go alone, Anna."

"I'll go with her," Paine says.

I startle at the sound of his voice. "Okay, is anyone else awake?" When no one responds, I motion for Paine to follow Annabelle and then point to my nonexistent watch, referencing that they should return quickly.

"I would have been fine alone," Annabelle says, but it isn't very convincing, and in truth she seems comforted to have Paine by her side. Before they leave, Paine grabs one of the heavy jackets Max carried and wraps it around her frame. He does the same for himself and they head out into the snowy night.

I second guess my decision to let them go the moment they are gone. But what was I supposed to do? The girl had to pee. I wait for five minutes, which feels like thirty, and start to scratch the inside of my arm.

Where the hell are they?

If this is how I am now, I can't imagine how I'll be tomorrow when we reach the battlefield. After several more minutes, I decide I have to go after them. I consider waking Kraven, but don't want him to think I can't handle something as simple as keeping watch over sleeping bodies.

Pulling a blanket around my shoulders, I head into the falling snow. The flakes touch down on my head and melt into my hair, tingling my scalp. I tug the blanket over my head and think how I must look pretty menacing right now. All I need is a juice box and a plastic sword to play with.

I let the blanket fall down around my shoulders as if this makes me more of a man, and call out for Annabelle. When she doesn't answer, I make a wider loop around Widow's Nest and keep my eyes peeled. As my nerves build, I decide to pull on my shadow.

A noise reaches me.

It's the sound of hushed voices and soft moaning. My stomach turns imagining what I'm about to see. I move closer, hoping on my good looks that I'm not about to see what I think I'm going to see, which is Annabelle getting it on with dude #2.

I duck behind an overgrown tree as the sounds grow louder. I'm just going to ensure they're okay, then I'll scold them like a ninety-year-old grandpa and drag them both back to camp by the ear. The thought makes me smile for the first time since Charlie disappeared.

And just as quickly as it touches my lips, it vanishes.

A sickening ache tugs at my chest. *She's gone.*

I peek out from the tree so I can catch them in the act. Because embarrassing them is the least I can do after they dragged me out into the cold. Besides, I've seen all this PG-13 crap a million times before. No way Annabelle has gone past second base.

When I spot them, I freeze.

Paine has his hand over Annabelle's mouth and his body pressed against hers. She's writhing against him and doing her best to scream for help. She's no match for him though. He whispers fiercely into her ear as she tries to bring her knee between his legs. He blocks her easily enough.

"Let her go!" I yell, before I can think to sneak up on him. Only fifteen feet separate us, and I rush forward, closing the distance as my shadow slips away. Right before I reach Paine, he tears his wings open and tosses me like a discarded toy across the forest. I land on my right side and wince from the impact. The liberator is on me in an instant. He has something in his hands.

A stone!

I bring up my arms to shield myself, but it's no use. Paine brings the stone down on my head and the world spins. I fall back, dizzy and overwhelmed by pain and confused as to why this is happening. Annabelle takes her opportunity to scream, and Paine lunges on her. His hand is back on her mouth. He glances over his shoulder, and when he's satisfied no one is coming and that I'm not getting up, he speaks quickly to her. I overhear bits and pieces as I try and stand. My legs buckle beneath me each time, and I curse that my cuff is taking so long to heal my injury.

"I have favor in hell after the work I've done," Paine says. "We can be together...can be with your friend."

Annabelle shakes her head as Paine lays a kiss along her neck.

Paine mutters against her neck. "So beautiful...we have to go now." I notice that the stone he hit me with is still in his right hand. His left covers Annabelle's mouth. He lifts his right hand up and I see that the stone is wet with my blood. He's going to hit Annabelle with it. I have no doubt he means to knock her unconscious, not to kill her. But I can't lose another person. And I can't stand by as another person I trusted does the taking.

I climb to my feet and though I wobble and the world quivers, I keep upright. I take a slow step toward them. Then another. Annabelle's eyes land on me. They widen.

Paine follows her gaze, and his head whips in my direction. He gasps and there's utter shock stretched across his face.

Kraven touches down into view, his white wings spread in flight.

He snaps Paine's neck.

One moment Paine is breathing.

The next he isn't.

Paine's body slumps to the ground, and in one swift movement, Kraven takes the stone from Paine's limp hand and severs the dargon around his ankle. The head liberator retracts his wings inside of himself and breathes hard through his nose over Paine's body. He stares blankly at the corpse, his lips pressed in a tight line, jaw clenched.

Then he turns to Annabelle. Her black hair is mussed, and Kraven smoothes it down as if that is what matters in this moment. He takes her in his arms and she sobs against his chest. I suddenly feel as I'm intruding.

Kraven turns his head in my direction. I think he's going to yell at me for leaving Widow's Nest, for leaving them all unguarded. Instead, he says, "I saw what he was doing to her."

It's like he's explaining why he was so quick to kill Paine, but he certainly doesn't need to. I understand. Though my mind has yet to accept what happened here. I stare at Paine's face, his eyes wide with surprise, tongue resting on his lower lip. I expect to experience anger at what he did to Annabelle, to all of us. Or maybe sadness. But there's no room in my heart for anything other than the loss I feel for Charlie.

I touch a hand to my head and my mind spins. Paine was a traitor.

This whole time, he was a traitor. How could I have been so blind? How could he have secured a liberator cuff and deceived Big Guy? It wouldn't be the first time He was deceived, I suppose.

This has all happened too quickly. Paine was my friend. Or, he was becoming my friend. He moved around when he was young, and this was going to be the first time he had steadfast friends. He had horrible fashion sense and a kick ass British accent and he wore a fanny pack on the plane to make Max and me laugh. He hated lamps and light bulbs even more. And he cared about Annabelle. Enough so that he tried to talk her into changing sides and being with him. How could he have done this? Was he the one who lit the fire in the library? How much of what happened to us was Valery, and how much was Paine? Did they work together?

Is he the one who stole the last part of the scroll?

Digging my knuckles into my temples, I try and block the questions that clog my brain. My head hurts too much to think on these things. All I know is Paine is dead. He's freaking dead and now he'll spend an eternity in nothingness and silence.

Gagging, I stride over to his corpse and search his pockets. The missing scroll piece isn't there. I jerk away from him and feel Kraven fall in beside me. Together, we walk toward Widow's Nest in silence. He has his arm around Annabelle, and every so often I check on her to see if she's okay.

"Are we just going to leave him out there?" I ask.

Kraven doesn't respond for a long time. When he does, he says only, "This is why I feel like I can't trust anyone."

It doesn't seem like he's waiting for a comment from me, so I don't give him one.

Paine is dead. I try to accept this fact as we crawl inside Widow's Den. I glance around as if I'm going to see Paine there, cozy in his flannel shirt, a ready smile on his face. I thought he was my friend. I thought he was my friend and now he's gone. I want to go back out there and replay what transpired, but I know that's ridiculous.

Kraven pulls Annabelle between his legs and she lays her head back and closes her eyes. She shakes from the horror of what she endured, and Kraven attempts to sooth her. Lincoln wakes up and asks what's going on, but Kraven doesn't say anything.

I tell him to go back to sleep. He studies me and then lies down. I'm sure he fakes returning to sleep, and I wonder how many of the others are wide awake, aware that something big has taken place. Maybe they're too exhausted from traveling to question it, or maybe they spy the look on Kraven's face and don't voice their worry.

All I know is that Paine is dead.

Kraven killed him without a second thought, which makes me wonder how stable the liberator really is. I mean, Paine needed to be brought down. But we could have questioned him. I glance at Fart Stain, who's sleeping in a tight ball near the back. He must have known about Paine. Maybe we can question him tomorrow.

For the next few hours, as the sun rises, all I can think is—Charlie was taken, Valery betrayed us, Neco is gone, Paine is dead in the forest, his neck broken.

And Kraven…Kraven looks like fury has eaten his will to play by the rules.

I nod in his direction, a question on whether we understand one other.

He pauses, looks down at Annabelle. Then he raises his eyes.

He nods.

⟨ 41 ⟩

DO NOT BE AFRAID

When the sun rises, Kraven explains why Paine isn't with us. Well, maybe *explain* is too strong a word.

"He was a traitor." Kraven stomps out the smoldering embers from last night's fire. "And we don't allow traitors to go unpunished. Not when the safety of our people is at stake."

His statement sounds as much like a warning as it does reassurance. I grab Fart Stain by the elbow and pull him to his feet. "Now that you're well rested, let's have a chat." I drag him after me as Kraven leads the way during our second day of walking. "Did you know about Paine?" I ask the siren.

He shakes his head. "I don't know what you're talking about."

"'Course you don't," I snap. "You didn't know Valery would take the savior. You didn't know there was a second traitor posing as a liberator."

The siren holds up his bound hands. "I knew about the one who would take the savior. But I didn't know there was a second person working for us."

I slap him upside the head. "Lie."

He turns his head toward the chalk white earth. "I didn't know his name."

"Seriously?" I stare at the siren in disbelief. "That's how easy you folded?"

"Said I was sorry for the things I done."

I bite the inside of my cheek as we walk and stare at the back of the siren's head. His hair is thinning at the crown even though he's way too young for that. *Did Charlie truly change this guy?*

I decide once again that I don't care. There's no such thing as being resolved of your sins, regardless of what his soul light says.

Today's walk feels even longer than yesterday's. We reach the outskirts of the battlefield at dusk, and Kraven asks us to huddle close. He explains the plan of burrowing ourselves into the ground, and as expected, there are more than a few people horrified by this idea.

"Can't we just be there when the sun rises and wait until they come," a man who looks to be in his early thirties asks. He has enormous nostrils that flare when he gets excited, and right now they look as though they might swallow me alive.

"They will be here tomorrow if they're not already," Kraven explains. "We can't be left out in the open."

"What about our packs?" Polly, the girl with peach colored hair, asks. "What about the food and water and blankets?"

"We'll leave them," I say. Kraven glances at me, and I raise my chin. "You chose to come and fight, and this is the first step. We go under the earth where we won't be seen." I think of what my father said in my dream last night. "Don't be afraid."

"How will we breathe?" Blue rubs a hand down Annabelle's back as he asks this. He knows something happened to her last night, but Annabelle hasn't spoken to anyone all day so he doesn't know the details. Thinking about those details, I consider returning to Widow's Nest and kicking Paine's corpse. Any remorse I had for losing him last night vanished the moment I saw the bruises on Annabelle's arm in the light of day.

Kraven references my pack, and suddenly I understand what the metallic tubes are for. I zip it open, retrieve one, and hold it up so the others can see. "We'll breathe through these."

"And when the enemy is upon us, Lincoln will signal you with a trumpet," Kraven adds.

Lincoln swings the long black bag off his back that I saw him with last night and produces a silver instrument to Kraven. He couldn't be more proud if his prick grew three extra inches.

"When we reach the field, we'll crawl out onto our bellies." Kraven motions to the Quiet Ones. "Each person will receive a hand shovel. It will take many hours, but the point is to conceal yourself as best you can."

Kraven raises his head and examines the lot of us—three trained liberators including him, one collector, two Quiet Ones who've recently broken their silence, one old man with a freaky spin cycle, thirteen jackrabbits, and forty-eight humans. He seems like he wants to say something, but saying something, anything, is not Kraven's forte. "Let's move out."

"Wait." My voice is louder than I intended it to be. Sixty-eight heads turn in my direction. I'm not sure why I ever imagined we were small in number. Look at us. We're sixty-eight strong. But the fear on their faces is palpable. It's so thick, so alive, I can almost taste it.

I think of Charlie.

I think of what my father said.

"We will not be afraid," I say. "Beyond these woods lies a field of tall grass. It's called the Lion's Hand and soon it will fill with blood. My blood, yours. But we will not be afraid. There are humans who are prepared to kill you, collectors who want nothing more than to complete their final conquest.

"They stole our soldier. They kidnapped our savior. They came into the Hive and they murdered your friends. They've taken everything, and yet steady we stand. We will defeat our enemy because we are stronger, we are braver. We've prepared for this moment, we've stayed focused." I glance at Kraven. "And all the while, they did nothing but watch on. All this time, all our training, it has led to this. They believe they will win because they took what was ours, but I tell you this now—let them have our soldier, let them keep our savior."

Blue startles at this, his eyes widening.

"I've counted their hours, and there were plenty. But now they are depleted. Tomorrow morning, when the sun rises, we'll tear our enemy limb from limb. We'll swallow their courage and feast on their fear. Many of us will fall, but do not be afraid. For at the end of the day, we will be triumphant. We will take back what belongs to us. We will drive our enemy back into hell. We will teach them what it means to rise up against those who stand for the heavens. And we will dance for those among us who lose their lives, for they will be the heroes rewarded in the life after this one."

I snap my black wings open and Kraven follows suit. Then I flip on the humans' and jackrabbits' soul light, one by one. I meet Kraven's gaze and then together with Blue and the Quiet Ones, we release liberator seals onto their souls, destroying any sin seals they may have harbored. It takes some time, and when the Quiet Ones explain gently what we are doing, those receiving our seals begin to weep. Even Lincoln, who seems conflicted by what's happening, doesn't ask us to stop.

When the last soul is clean, I turn to the siren. "Fart Stain, are you truly sorry for the things you've done?"

"I am." His voice quivers.

"Are you so changed that you're prepared to join us on the battlefield?"

He turns his face from mine and sucks on his bottom lip. "I won't be afraid."

"That's good." I unknot the ropes that bind his wrists. "What's your name?"

"Frank," he says.

I slap his back. "Oh, man. That's incredible. It's so close to fart."

"It's not really that —"

"It is, Frank," I say. "If you think about it, it really is close."

Oswald seems pleased by this turn of events. He strokes his purple velvet robe, which makes me all kinds of nervous.

"Let's roll out," I instruct.

As I pass by Kraven he says, "Thank you." Then he strides forward like he doesn't want to dwell on his inability to rally his troops. I'm not sure I did the job either, but I do feel fired up.

Too bad this pep talk ends with us digging ourselves into the dirt.

• • •

As we approach the field, I see what Kraven meant by tall grass. It easily stretches to waist level, and a terrifying thought occurs to me: what if the enemy has already done what we plan to do? What if they are already out there, lying in wait?

Kraven gestures to two corners of the field. "Jackrabbits, split into two teams. One team take the right corner, one team take the left. After you sound the trumpet, count to a hundred and sound the trumpet again. At that time you and the humans will show yourselves and join the battle. The rest of us will set up on the other side of the field, liberators and Max in front, and humans behind us."

"Do we have to crawl across this entire field," the older of the Quiet Ones asks.

"It won't take as long as you think it will," he answers.

He's wrong. It takes four times as long as anything in the entire world takes. Crawling across a field, wondering if you're going to happen upon a collector, or in a good scenario, a snake, is something I want no part of. My skin opens on small stones and my face is covered in sweat and grime as I drag my body across the Lion's Hand.

The Lion's Hand.

More the Lion's Nut Sack.

When we reach the opposite side, I pick a place and pull out the hand shovel that's stuffed in my back pocket and begin to dig. It's an absolutely ridiculous task, and I can't imagine how long it'll take me to make a hole deep enough for me to lie in. After a few minutes, I hear someone close by swearing.

"Who's there?" I hiss.

Nothing.

"It's me, Dante," I offer, wondering if saying my name is the smartest thing I've ever done.

The person sighs. "It's Blue."

"And Max!" someone else whispers loudly.

"You're here, too, Max?" Blue says quietly.

"We're all here!" I laugh at how excited I am that I'm not digging in the dirt alone.

"This is a bunch of bullshit," Max says. "But I'm going to do it anyway. Because I can't wait to knock that redhead around."

"You're not really going to do that," Blue says. I can envision his brow pulled together though I can't see him through the tall grass and night sky.

"She was confused," Max mutters. "He'll forgive her."

"I'm thinking about napping down here while the rest of you fight," I yell-whisper.

Blue laughs.

Max does, too.

"Can the three of you please be quiet?" Kraven's hushed voice snaps. I know Annabelle is next to him, otherwise he would have sounded much more Unabomber.

We stop talking, but I feel the grass nearby flutter and realize that Blue is edging close so that his hole is nearer. A smile plays on my lips.

"We're going to be okay," I whisper. Then I dig my hole. For hours on end, I dig. I scoop away piles of dirt with the shovel and with my hands. When I've made it down about two feet, I lie down in the ditch I created. I lift my ass up and retrieve the metal tube out of my pocket and lay my weapon next to my left thigh. Then I start pulling the dirt back over my body.

I wonder again as I do all of this if the collectors aren't already out there, watching, waiting. Perhaps they saw us scurry across the field like mice and slapped each other on the back at the humor of it all.

I'm still not sure I understand what the scroll meant when it said, *Two hearts that beat as one will make a great sacrifice.* Or when it said, *Unconscious words spoken on an unpracticed tongue will drive the beast down.* Not to mention we're missing a crucial weapon and the final piece of that ancient document. But it doesn't matter. We don't have a choice but to fight, with or without those clues solved.

Tomorrow morning, war dawns. And we are ready as we'll ever be.

Ready in our graves.

⇥ 42 ⇤

THE DAWN OF WAR

I always thought war would start with a cannon shot. At the very least, I figured there'd be a line of us, and a line of them, and we'd face off like football players at the Superdome. That's not how it happens at all.

It feels like early morning, my limbs stiff from lying in the earth, when I sense the ground moving. It's a shudder that rocks me from head to foot and sets my nerves aflame. The exhaustion, the fear of losing Charlie, the worry over my friends' lives, it all vanishes in a single moment.

It almost seems like someone is walking beside me, or on top of me. I can't stay down here much longer. I can't wait to seek revenge on the man who kissed my mother, on the man who stole Charlie's soul and tricked me into leaving Aspen behind and caused one of our own to turn against us. I want to squeeze his head in my hands like it's a light bulb, until skull fragments slice into my palms.

The trumpet sounds.

The noise rips through my body like an electric shock and I'm moving. I'm digging through the dirt and pulling myself up like a zombie. All around me, others are doing the same. I spot Lincoln in the far corner, trumpet to his lips.

The sun is quiet in the sky, awaiting its turn to fill our world with light and security. But it's not quite time for that yet. A swatch of red-stained darkness lies over the battlefield. Across from us are the sirens and collectors. They are only steps away as if they walked over our bodies to arrive at where they are now.

I race toward the first person I see.

A siren.

My battle cry mingles with others' and the black wings on my back spring open. I pull the left one across my body and whip it open. The siren flies several feet and then disappears in the tall grass as if swallowed whole. I do the same thing to another siren, and another. They go down easily enough, but there are so many of them. All around me I see other liberators fighting against sirens. They swarm over us like ants would a disruptive beetle. We are agile and better trained, but they have strength in numbers.

I spot a collector, Anthony, and rush forward, pulling on my shadow as I race. The smell of turned soil and blood hits my nose as I run. I love the smell. Want to bathe in it. Anthony is the largest of the collectors, and when I slam into him it feels like diving in front of a semi-truck barreling down an interstate. He doesn't see me coming. He's orchestrating sirens, yelling orders, face darkened by the sleeping sun.

He falls when I hit him, my shadow slipping away. I'm triumphant in this moment. I want to climb on his back and stab a flagpole into his spine and declare this land mine. But he rolls over and grabs hold of my ankle. One quick rip of his wrist brings me down with him. He scrambles over my body and throws his fist into my face. I swallow blood and beg for more. Using my wings, I shove my body away from the ground and Anthony tumbles to the side. I jackknife and shove my heel into his ribcage. A satisfying crack rings through the air. He groans and turns his face to the dirt. I remember the blade in my pocket, born of steel. After taking it in my hand, I raise it high over my head. I remember the last thing Kraven said to us during the training. The two things we are to do today if we are to stand triumphant.

Take the collectors' dargon, and destroy the sirens.

Anthony's ankle is exposed, his cuff poised for the taking. I bring the knife down.

I've almost collided steel to gold cuff when I'm tackled. A siren tears at my face and neck, seeking purchase. I swing the knife wildly, and sense when it takes its first bittersweet taste of siren flesh. The siren falls back, screaming. I kick backward and get to my feet. I don't see Anthony. I have to find Anthony. First though, I should kill this siren. He's here at my feet, and we don't stand a chance of getting to the collectors if we don't dwindle the sirens' numbers.

Kill as many as you can, Kraven said. *Remember, they are soulless.*

But as I look at the siren at my feet, I decide he can't be more than fourteen years old. Some are older, but his one is so young. I can't help thinking of Frank-whose-name-sounds-a-lot-like-fart. Maybe Charlie did change him. Maybe the sirens really can be saved.

Two new sirens grab onto my wings and rip. As agony shoots through my shoulder blades, I decide maybe I don't care about their souls. I only want them off of me. I spin around, and before I can think, my knife finds its way into a siren's stomach. He looks down at it as if surprised he has a stomach at all. Blood spills over my hand and leaks onto the ground, suckled by the Lion's Hand.

The siren I've stabbed is a girl. She looks to be in her mid-twenties and has dark eyes that don't match the sunny color of her hair. The girl falls back, disappearing into the grass. Guilt strikes through me. Why? Why do I care what happens to her? She made her decision and it was the wrong one. Now she has to pay the price, right? The other two sirens drag me away from her, though I doubt it's revenge they want. They only want to accomplish what the collectors have laid out for them. Gather their prize. Reap what is owed to them.

I slash my blade across the space and the two sirens leap back. Others are headed in this direction, and when I glance around, I see exactly how outnumbered we are. The liberators were crazy to assume they would win this war.

But the trumpet sounds again, and now I see thirteen jackrabbits racing across the field. They circled around and now they'll surprise the sirens and collectors from behind. The sirens hesitate, and amidst their rank, I spot two more collectors, Patrick and Zack. They're back to back and surrounded by sirens. They have their eyes set on Max. My best friend is ready for them. Especially with Blue by his side. Especially when a hundred humans rise from the ground and storm toward the sirens.

The humans have fury in their eyes. They remember the walkers, and won't let their enemy forget what they took from them. Laura, the woman with the shawl, leads the charging army of flesh and blood, screaming as if death is something they've longed for.

More than a few sirens fall back, surprised by this sudden appearance of new fighters. The jackrabbits slam into the sirens moments before the humans do. Lincoln swings an axe above his head. In the distance, I see the black ink staining his hands.

J-A-C-K-R-A-B-B-I-T

Damn straight, I think. Then I crack my fist into a siren's face. He drops next to the girl I won't think about as I search for the next siren. The Quiet Ones are in the distance, dragging a human who is already injured away from the battlefield. Cries of pain ring out, sirens scurry over one another, and all around me bodies fight for domination. Amidst it all, I notice something—the sirens are thinning. There are still so many, too many, but some have fallen and others have fled. We're outnumbered, but we're angry and we've been pushed too far and this time we're solid as a tree trunk.

Three sirens reach me together, encircling my body. I'm encouraged by what I've seen though, so I'm ready to play. I wing whip one

38

SPEAK

Oswald comes to my room after I storm from the battle scene. I'm throwing clothing and boots and bottles of water into a bag. I have no idea what I'll need for this war so I just shove everything in with a nervous gut-wrenching energy.

"You need to see something," Oswald says from the doorway.

I continue packing.

"You're upset," the old man notes. "But you do need to see this. Kraven asked me to show you."

Oswald moves aside and motions for someone to step inside. I recognize the guy immediately. It's the siren that almost killed me, the one Charlie blocked with her blue electricity. His face is thin and he has dark, thin eyebrows that rise in a question. It's a face I'll never forget.

I expect to experience fury at seeing him here. But instead, I'm delighted. Oswald has delivered me an outlet for my anger, one I will take my time enjoying.

I smile. "I'm going to kill you."

Of all the things I expect him to say back, it isn't this: "I'm so deeply sorry."

The guy hangs his head and black hair tickles his forehead. He weeps and my nose turns up at the sound.

"What's he doing?" I ask Oswald.

The old man touches the siren's back in comfort. "He's grieving the things he's done."

"Bullshit. That guy's as sorry as a pothead in county jail."

The siren raises his head. He has small lines around his brown eyes that tell me he's older than I am. "She changed me."

This gets my attention. "What?"

Oswald nods to the siren, encouraging him to continue. "That girl who…who shocked me, she *changed* me. I felt like I had this emptiness inside from the things I'd done, but then it was gone. I feel different." The guy offers a sad smile. "I feel happy."

I narrow my eyes at this sorry excuse of a man. Lies. All of it—lies. "I don't have time for this."

"Look at his soul light," Oswald says gently.

But I don't want to. I know what he's implying and I don't give a crap. I wouldn't forgive this guy if he rid the world of loud talkers and felines.

"Please, Dante," Oswald implores. "Just look."

"Jaysus." I spin around and flip on the dude's soul light. Yep, it's as powdery clean as a newborn's asshole. "He has no sin seals. That's great. He still tried to kill me. He still helped take Charlie away."

Speaking her name hurts.

Though I'm going for indifference, I'm stunned by what I see. I've witnessed sin seals dissolving beneath liberator seals. But Kraven told me sirens didn't have souls; that they forfeited them when they agreed to work for the collectors. Though what I'm beholding contradicts that statement. It's almost as if Charlie resuscitated this guy. If before his soul was in the hands of hell, now it's back inside of him, glowing like a beacon of hope.

"Get out of my sight," I tell the siren.

tunnel vision. There is only them. I'm so close to Rector. He smiles when he realizes we're about to collide. It's like that's exactly what he wants.

Blue gets there first.

Great white wings spread out over Blue's head.

On his face is a mask of fury like I've never seen. It reflects what I feel inside with sniper precision. Blue has never been able to summon his wings before this moment, but watching him now, soaring through the air, it's like I can't imagine him without them. All it took was one look at Aspen, and at Charlie, too; one look to remind him what he was fighting for.

He slams into Rector and the ground shudders from the impact. Rector grabs hold of Blue and the two shoot straight into the air like a rocket. Like they're headed for the moon and does anyone else need a ride? I take my opportunity to rush toward the two girls, who seem oblivious to what's transpiring. I'm ten strides from reaching Charlie when Zack, the sixth collector, steps out from behind one of the horses.

In his hand is a sword, something he stole from us, no doubt, but not the sparrow. He circles the stallion and comes to stand at Charlie's side. The sword tip lies at her neck. Zack holds a finger to his thin lips and smirks.

"Shhh…" he says.

Behind me, the fighting resumes. Someone must have hit someone else, and the battle exploded once again. I eye Zack, remembering the way he broke into the Hive. I didn't know vultrips existed before that night.

I bend my wings over my head, ensure he understands what fight he's picking. "If you walk away now, I won't even pursue you."

Lie.

"I'll just get the two of them out of here," I continue. "That's all I want."

I'll get them out of here, and then I'll blind you so that you'll never know who it is that stands over your bed at night. It's me. It will always be me.

The collector shakes his head. "I'm afraid I can't do that."

"I'm afraid I'm going to murder you then." I slice my wing across the space between us, trying to take the legs out from beneath him. He leaps over it like an acrobat, like it's Cirque de Soleil up in here. As soon as he's on his feet again, he jabs the sword into Charlie's neck once again, except this time it breaks the skin. Blood trickles down her throat but she doesn't even flinch. Her mind is gone, her eyes void.

Kraven makes it to the two horses. When he sees Zack's weapon pointed at our savior, though, he backs away and rejoins the fight elsewhere. While there's nothing he can do to save Charlie right now, he can eliminate the collectors still in the lurch. Blue and Rector drop back down to the Lion's Hand, a few yards from where Zack and I face each other.

Rector grabs hold of Blue's ankle and yanks it so that Blue lands on his back. "I already killed you once."

Blue kicks Rector in the gut and the head collector doubles over, gasping for air. My friend scurries to his feet and races toward Aspen.

"No, don't," I yell to Blue.

He freezes when he sees the weapon at Charlie's neck.

We're at a standoff, no one moving, no one speaking. And that's when Oswald starts yelling.

His voice sounds like it's being amplified over a grand speaker at an auditorium. The liberators and humans on our side are nowhere close to him. They must have orchestrated this. Now he stands in the center of hundreds of sirens, his frail arms held above his head.

"If you don't back away from the girl," he says to Zack, to Rector, "I'll destroy your army."

Rector grins, but the gesture is false. "What do I need with them?"

"Without your army," Kraven interjects, "there will be no one to protect you."

The Quiet Ones slink closer to Rector, and so does Max. Rector only sees what's in front of him, and Max is creeping up the back, keeping low to the ground in the tall grass. He has a short knife in his hand. One part of my brain screams for him to stop, but the other eggs him onward.

Rector turns his face to the sky. The moon has finally fallen away, and the first hint of daylight shadows his twisted face. The bones are too sharp in his cheeks, his forehead pushed too far forward. His eyes are dilated and his nose is sunken and he looks similar to the way Kraven did the night of the fire.

Max slithers closer, closer, between the black horses that stamp the earth and plume warm air into the cold. One flicks its tail and slaps Max on the rear. I'd laugh if I didn't feel like screaming.

I look up at Charlie. She looks like a mirage of the girl I know. The happiness is gone from her lips, the thirst for life gone from her posture. She stares straight ahead, the crown atop her head the only sparkle to see.

"Charlie," I say.

I can't help it. She's been gone for such a short time, but ever since I watched her disappear through that hole in the floor I've been eaten alive by hatred. Now that I see her, I remember goodness and hope and all the crap she's taught me that I never understood.

Rector laughs when he hears me whisper her name. As he does, rage returns so fiercely my ears ring.

"I'll be the one to end you, Rector," I say.

Max takes that exact moment to lunge.

CHOOSE

Max leaps to his feet, knife shining over his head.

"No!" a new voice calls out.

Max stops. There's only one person that could have frozen him in his tracks, and she just stepped into view.

"Don't do it." Valery's voice shakes. "The second you touch him, Zack will kill Charlie."

Rector sees that Max was about to stab him. I expect him to retaliate. I expect him to tear Max limb from limb. Instead, he grabs Charlie's leg and rips her from her saddle. The second she slides into his arms—the second Rector does what he's not supposed to do— Oswald explodes.

An orange blast detonates from the wrinkly dude. Even those of us who are out of harm's way are thrown back. Not a single scream colors the air. Not a single utterance of fear. But when the orange light echoes and fades, a hundred bodies lie still along the ground. We could have set this up a dozen different times and failed. After all, it would take Rector one heartbeat to dismember the old man. He was in the exact right place at the exact right time, with our people out of range, and not a single collector or siren noticed him until it was too late.

Anthony appears. He flies across the space toward Oswald, and when I see his wings spread out across the dawn, I gasp. They've been training, too. I always suspected it, but now I know.

Rector has both Charlie and Aspen beneath him. He has a knife. Maybe it's the one Max had. Maybe it's a new one. It glitters between the two girls and Rector's smile glitters, too. This time, his grin lights his face with amusement. He's so happy right now. Look how effing happy he is.

The skin on his face pulls tighter. Veins beat blue blood to his black heart. "I am going to give you a choice. I must sacrifice both in the name of the one true king, but since I consider myself a reasonable guy, I will let you choose who we start with."

The weeks of training I've endured tic through my head. Defense, Shadow in Combat, Incapacitation, Execution, Wings, Amplification. None of them tell me how to deal with this. What am I supposed to do when a lunatic is crouched over the two girls I care most about in this world, telling me to choose which dies first?

I take two quick steps toward him and he raises the knife higher. "No, wait," I yell. "Just…wait."

Rector does something I don't expect—he waits. He gazes at me with anticipation, like he's actually interested in what I have to say. Max stands near Valery, Kraven is behind me, and Blue is out of sight. I don't know where anyone else is. All that matters now is Rector kneeling between the girls. The two lie in the tall grass so that I can't even tell who's who, only that there are bodies in white dresses muddied by the ground.

I inch toward Rector. "Kill me instead. I'm the nuisance. I'm the one who will keep coming for you. If you kill them now, what have you accomplished? If you're lucky, your *king* will get his wish. The scales will tip and demons will pour onto the earth without the need for dargon. But I'll still be here. And Rector, trust me when I say, I'll kill you in the end." My wings fold back, a show of submission. "Spill my blood to please your lord."

Rector drops his head like he's thinking. He wants me gone. More than anything, he wants to silence my tongue forever. When he raises his eyes, my heart catches in my throat.

"Left or right." Rector dances the unforgiving blade between the girls' bodies. "LEFT OR RIGHT?!"

He clasps the knife in both hands and the world falls away.

"Right," I hear someone yell. "Right!"

"Fair enough," he grunts. And then he brings the knife down.

The Quiet Ones scream. It's louder than when they were in the Hive. It's so loud it eats away every thought I have. It eats any mercy that remains inside my body and replaces it with blinding, cancerous wrath.

Rector jerks his arm up again. He moves with supernatural speed, and the bloodied knife stills in the air for only a moment before coming back down.

He's tackled from the side by Annabelle.

She leaps to her feet and swings a mallet through the air. Her aim is true, and Rector falls to his side, clutching the back of his head. Annabelle scrambles in the grass and then gathers a girl in a white dress into her arms, half pulling her. "Don't screw with my friends," she mutters.

I'm on the ground, diving toward the girl left behind.

I can already see Aspen's dark hair, the smooth unmoving skin on her chest.

The Quiet Ones stop screaming and the sounds of fighting replace their wail. A hundred or more sirens are dead, but there are many left. Now they fight with renewed energy, fueled by their leader's triumph.

For me though, all is quiet. Time stops. I cover my face and growl into my hands. I can't do it. I can't see Aspen's lifeless face. Not after the dreams I've had, not after I was sure she was dead and then seeing her again, alive.

When Rector moans in pain, and I glimpse Anthony fighting with Kraven and two other collectors headed in my direction, I know I can't wait any longer. I have to get Aspen out of here. I have to get her off the battlefield so that we can mourn her properly.

I uncover my face, and my entire body burns bright like the rising sun.

Because it isn't Aspen's lifeless face I see lying in the grass—

It's Charlie's.

45

DESTINY

The world ceases to spin the moment I see her. Blood seeps from the wound in her chest and stains her virginal white dress. Her eyes are closed, and her mouth is parted. I gather Charlie into my arms and my emotions flick off. I am a stone figure of the demon I once was.

I can't think. I can't allow myself to absorb this information or I'll crack apart. Annabelle trying to get Aspen to safety is the only thing keeping me sane. Blue touches down in front of Annabelle and takes Aspen from her. He says something quickly to Annabelle and then soars across the Lion's Hand with Aspen in tow.

Anthony charges toward me.

I'm ready for him.

I release Charlie and stand. When Anthony reaches me, I dive over his back, take his head in my hands, and snap his neck. He crumbles to the ground. I retrieve the blade I'd tucked in my waistband, and I stab him. I stab him until he's a human waterfall, a red cascading display. I stab until my arm shakes. I stab until I'm screaming and I have to stop because the emotions are flooding back into my body and I can't handle them.

An arm grabs my shoulder.

It's Kraven.

"Go," he yells. "Get her out of here."

Then he's gone, doing everything he can to keep Rector down. When I see Charlie on the ground, guilt slams into me like a wrecking ball. I forget about Anthony and the cuff I still need to take from him.

I left Charlie on the ground. Look how dirty her dress has gotten. I scoop her up, bend my knees, and I'm off—flying.

A metallic smell hits my nose as I sail across the sky, but I can't allow myself to think it's coming from Charlie. She'll be okay. The Quiet Ones will save her.

Below us, sirens wade through the tall grass. They're everywhere, black spiders building sticky webs across the Lion's Hand, tempting their prey closer. Or maybe they're not spiders at all. Maybe they're bees, releasing pheromones, calling the others to attack. Either way, they're insects and it's impossible to kill them all.

"Retreat," I hear Kraven roar.

Seconds later, a trumpet sounds.

The field divides, good guys running in the direction I'm flying, bad guys giving chase. It's a typical cowboys and Indians showdown, except it's not land we're fighting for, it's two seventeen-year-old girls. And one is still in my arms.

I fly until I can't see the field any longer, and then I don't so much land as I do fall. My legs feel broken beneath me, but I'm happy for the pain. I lay Charlie in a clearing and bend over her body, blue-black wings creating a canopy.

"My Charlie," I whisper.

I lay my head against her bloodied chest and listen, but I don't hear a thing.

I trace my fingers over the skin of her face, her arms, the palm of her hand. She already feels cold to the touch. A movement catches my eye, and my heart leaps into my throat. She's still alive!

When I realize it was her hair sliding off her shoulder and onto the ground, I lose my mind. I thought it was her. For a second, I thought I was wrong and she was still with me, somehow. The severity of this moment lifts me up, slams me back down. My mind screams and my chest explodes in a solar system of hurt. I can hold back my emotions no longer.

"You can't be gone." I shake her body in my arms. "Wake up, Charlie. Please! Stay with me. Don't leave." My voice breaks. "I need you. You're my reason, Charlie. I love you. I love you!"

A sob rattles my entire being. "We said forever…. *You* said forever."

I was supposed to protect her. It was my job, and so it's my fault she's dead. A memory flashes in my mind. Charlie sitting on the edge of the bed, sober acceptance dancing across her face. Charlie spinning in the sunroom, hypnotic, knowing this is how it would end for her.

I never believed it though, not really. Because I knew I'd tear out my own beating heart to save her. But I wasn't given the chance. From the moment she was sucked into that floor, she was dead.

Two hearts that beat as one will make a great sacrifice.

Except Charlie's heart beats no longer, and mine continues, stupidly, without her.

"It was always supposed to be this way," someone says. I spin around and find Valery, tears streaking down her face. "It was her destiny, Dante. Her blood spilled so that our warriors would seek vengeance. Her death will be the catalyst to victory."

A growl rumbles through me. "Get away from me, Valery."

"I loved her, you know," she continues. "But I loved him more."

I lunge at her with everything I have and slam into her body. My hands tighten around her throat though I'd rather tear it out with my teeth. I squeeze until she chokes and kicks and flails. "This is because of you!"

Valery's eyes bulge like Rector's did at the Hive. I want them both dead. Why should they live when she's gone?

I'm thrown backward and Kraven stands between me and the redhead I want to murder. "She's right." Kraven says as Valery gasps for breath. "Charlie Cooper was meant to fall. Her charity will lead to Trelvator, Dante, but it will be with Annabelle at the helm. Right now, you need to let the Quiet Ones take her." He points at Valery then. "And you need to get out of here."

Valery opens her mouth like she might object, but when Kraven takes a quick step toward her, she scrambles several feet away.

Even though what Kraven said is the same thought I had as we journeyed here, I can't accept it. I won't. I crouch over Charlie's body, ready to pounce on anyone who tries to take her from me.

Humans and jackrabbits find where we've converged, and Lincoln mutters a quick, "They've fallen back for now. Regrouping, I think." He chokes on his next words. "We lost four humans, and one of the jackrabbits. My friend."

The Quiet Ones approach. They're largely unharmed and I wonder how it is that they battled without injury. "You must give her to us."

"No one's touching her." I snap at their outstretched hands like a dog that's gone unfed far too long.

"Dante," Aspen says.

I spin to the side. Aspen's eyes still swim in a dark liquid, but some of the green color behind that curtain is breaking through. Blue holds Aspen upright, but never looks away from Charlie. His chest heaves seeing the color leeched from his friend's cheeks. Annabelle is on the ground beside Aspen, head pressed between her knees, howling from the thought of losing her friend.

"Let them have her." Aspen reaches for me, and I break down when her arms circle my neck. "There's nothing you can do for her now."

And that's when it hits me. That's when the truth of the matter spreads inside my brain like an insidious tumor.

Charlie Cooper is gone.

Charlie Cooper is *dead*.

I weep into Aspen's neck and curl my hands into fists. I want to walk this earth with a can of gasoline and a match. I want to burn it all without her, but I know Charlie wouldn't want that. So I move aside when Max takes my arm and pulls me into a hug.

Over his shoulder, I see the sisters carrying Charlie to somewhere I can't see her. It feels like they've stolen the organs from my body. I'm empty now. They say it is better to have loved and lost. I'd like to find the person who said that and murder the one they cherish most. I want to make them write those words on a blackboard over their spouse's lifeless form until their fingers bleed.

"I can't fight without her," I mumble to Max.

He tightens his hold on me. "We've both lost someone."

When I remember who it is he means, I break from Max's grasp and lunge at Valery again. She screams and the sound fills me up. I'm not empty anymore. Max grabs ahold of me without a moment to spare. My hands stretch toward Valery, clawing wildly.

"You did this," I yell. "You're the reason she's gone."

"I made a mistake," she cries.

I jerk away from Max and point a finger into Red's face. "What? We're supposed to forgive you now? Why are you even here? Go back to them. That's what you wanted, isn't it?"

Valery casts her eyes downward. "I thought Max and I could be together as collectors. We'd only seal the souls of those who deserved it. But I saw the place you came from, and I realized I'd made a mistake."

"You realized you made a mistake when you brought Charlie into hell? You are a freaking *genius*, Valery. Didn't you think about what would happen if they hurt her? If she died?"

"I didn't think they'd actually do it," Valery sobs.

I turn away from her. She isn't worth it, and the last word I spoke—*died*—it's like I can't breathe. I search the area. When I don't see Charlie, I panic so that I can hardly stand. "What will happen to her?"

Kraven steps forward. "We'll continue the battle until the last collector falls."

More humans trickle in, appearing from the forest broken and battle worn. They see that something grave is happening and they remain quiet. One of the humans works his way between the people, tending to their wounds, but hardly a word is muttered.

A bolt of grief detonates inside my mind, and I run in the direction the sisters went.

"Dante, stop," Kraven calls out.

He doesn't pursue me though. I stumble when I see the Quiet Ones knelt on the ground, their hands fluttering over Charlie's body. Her white dress has been pulled down so that her wound is exposed. It's a bottomless red hole. My own soul pulses at the sight, desperate to break free. Could I give her my soul and bring her back? If I could, I would without a second thought.

I cringe seeing Charlie exposed, and I don't understand what the sisters are doing. I take one step closer, two. Then I understand exactly what I'm seeing. They're cleaning her body, using moss from the trees and moisture from the snow.

This sight—of my dead girlfriend being prepared for burial—is the last thought I have.

Something strikes the back of my head.

And it's lights out.

⇥ 46 ⇤

CUT THEM DOWN

I wake and the sun has fallen. I've been out all day. I was *knocked out* all day. Searching the area, I find liberators and humans and jackrabbits sleeping along the ground. In the distance, I spot Kraven. He's keeping watch over the group, but he's too far away to notice I'm awake. I know it was him that hit me over the head.

I thank him for it.

I want him to do it every day for the rest of my life.

Lincoln is snoring so loud there's no way our enemies don't know our location. It sounds like he's speaking in tongues. It sounds like someone clubbing baby seals. I've never heard anything like it. Except when Max sleeps, that is.

Lincoln snorts and his eyebrow ring twitches. Polly is sleeping nearby. Any inkling of romantic connection they could have dared hope for will die if she wakes up and hears this.

A rustle steals my attention.

I look up.

Charlie.

Her bloodied torn white dress hangs open so that I can see a slip of skin from chest to belly button. There isn't a stab wound.

She's barefoot, and around her ankle, is a gold liberator cuff. I know instantly whose cuff it is she's wearing. I still remember the way the Aussie died, and how Kraven took his dargon before he'd been dead ten minutes.

Charlie's hair doesn't shine. Her skin isn't flawlessly smooth. She is my Charlie again, my old Charlie with imperfections, and she's breathing.

"Am I dreaming?" I ask.

She doesn't smile, but I can imagine her quirky, crooked grin all the same. I want to see her cheeks redden with excitement more than I've ever wanted anything. Charlie shakes her head.

"You're alive?"

She doesn't answer. On the surface, she looks like the same girl I met in Peachville, Alabama. But there's something very different about the way she stands before me now.

"I'm going to cut them down," she says evenly. "They'll pay for the things they've done."

A chill races across my skin upon hearing her words. Her chest glows, and I spot her soul glittering inside her; the one Rector placed back inside her before parading the princesses onto the field.

Charlie turns and walks away. It almost looks like her feet don't touch the ground, like she's gliding above unconsecrated earth. Her body moves swiftly between the trees, and I jump to my feet, heart racing.

No matter how fast I chase her, she's too quick. With fog swirling about our bodies, Charlie disappears from sight. I search for hours, though I don't dare call out her name. The collectors could be close, and I can't lose her again.

Finally, I return to camp, to the popping fire. To the humans and jackrabbits and liberators sleeping in the snow. Then I turn back to the forest. The trees are heavy from the frost and the ground is frozen solid. Charlie is alive. They brought her back using Neco's dargon.

I don't know how I feel about this, and I don't know why I never suggested giving her a cuff. My cuff. Anyone's. Maybe because I don't want her to be a part of this fight any longer. Charlie seems too good for this battle. I want to lift her above it. I want to be *her* savior.

But the girl I saw step out from between the trees tonight doesn't need saving.

Charlie Cooper looked different. She looked angry.

And I wonder what that will translate to on the battlefield.

ᔡ 47 ᔥ

UNBREAKABLE

The next morning, before the sun has risen, I smell something delicious. It isn't bacon, but it's close enough. I open my eyes and see the sisters cooking quail over the fire. There are a half-dozen birds along the snow beside them and ten rabbits near those.

"You catch all those?" I ask.

The youngest one smiles bashfully.

"I want you to be my bride."

"There are two of us," she says.

"Exactly."

Snow crunches, and I hear, "Divide the meat evenly between the people. Wake them soon. We have to strategize." Kraven the Buzz Kill leans against a tree as I sweep the area, searching for Charlie. "She's with Aspen."

I get up and dust the snow from my pants. "Where?"

"Don't disturb them."

"Where?!"

Kraven sighs and points to my left. "Quarter mile in that direction. Don't sneak up on them."

I'm moving in the direction he referenced before he can utter another word. I stomp through the snow, moving like a herd of elephants over land mines. I couldn't be louder if someone strapped a megaphone to my mouth and I barked the happy birthday song.

I hear Aspen's voice first. "But then we'd have to wait out the day. I say we attack now and with as much force as possible. Every second we wait is another second they have to recover."

"We must be patient." Charlie's voice is gentle. It contradicts the storm I saw in her eyes last night. "We're outnumbered, so our only chance is to outthink them. We've already lost some of our people. I don't want to lose more."

My stomach turns thinking about Lincoln's friend who will never return, and the humans we lost this morning as well.

Aspen holds up a closed fist. "But that's exactly why we should attack immediately. Our troops are angry. They want vengeance."

Watching the two girls, it's like they've been waging war side-by-side for a millennium. I wonder what the two went through in hell together. They must have relied on each other to keep their spirits up. To stay alive.

Realizing I'm being a total creeper by spying on them, I walk into sight.

The girls move unimaginably fast. They stand shoulder to shoulder, knees bent, defensive stance. Aspen has whipped two blades from out of nowhere and holds them hip level. Charlie's hands face each other like she was thinking about praying but changed her mind. Between her palms a blue light crackles and flicks. The light looks like electric strings firing across the distance.

Their brows furrow.

Their lips are pulled back.

They look terrifying as hell.

"Whoa, there," I say. "Professor Xavier called. Said you two are out of control and need to head back to the X-Mansion. Personally, I think a dose of your favorite demon will even you out."

"Dante!" Aspen cries.

She relaxes out of her death stance and runs toward me. Her entire body slams into mine. It feels a bit like running into a brick wall on a unicycle. I crush her to me and revel in this moment.

"You're okay," I say.

"I'm okay."

"I should never have—"

"Stop." Aspen pulls back. "You did the right thing. You have your own soul. There must be a reason for it."

I want to ask her about the dreams; if she remembers them, or if it was all in my head. Part of me doesn't want to know though.

Aspen releases me and walks away, but not before sharing a silent exchange with Charlie. Once she's gone, it's only Charlie and I left. Alone. I cross the distance between us, almost afraid that she'll reject me the way she did when I left to liberate Aspen's soul. She believed I wanted her to change, that I wanted her to be more like me. Nothing could be further from the truth, and I hate myself for ever saying anything that made her think so.

When Charlie doesn't move away, I raise my hand and brush the side of her face with my knuckles. She closes her eyes and reopens them. She's wearing glasses like she did when I first met her. These are different though. Heavy red frames that make her look like a naughty librarian. I wonder where she got them until I remember Oswald tucking the small black case into his pocket at the Hive. If I wasn't sure he knew more than he let on, now I am.

Charlie realizes I'm staring and says, "I don't care what you think."

"What?"

She takes a small step backward. "I know I don't look beautiful anymore, but I don't care. I've moved past such trivial things. I am built of the same things you are. And I am strong. I don't need beauty."

My heart clenches. Does she think so little of me? "Charlie, what happened to you out there... I tried to save you before you disappeared through the floor. I tried to save you again out there on the Lion's Hand. I couldn't get to you. I couldn't..." I shake my head.

"You think I care what you look like? I only want to touch you. When I saw you last night, alive, I hated myself. I hated myself because I was so unbelievably happy to have you back. I thought I'd lost you forever, and now you're here, and I'm glad. I'm glad and that makes me selfish. You should be at rest now." My voice breaks. "You've already done so much for me, for everyone, and you don't deserve to go through more hardship."

"It's not me who will go through hardship." Charlie's voice has a deadly edge.

"Don't go back out there. Please, let me protect you this time. I won't fail you again."

Charlie lays a hand on the center my chest. "It is me who will protect you now. Don't you understand, Dante? This is how it had to end for me. I knew I would be taken. I knew I would die. Oswald told me. It was written on the last part of the scroll, but he unlocked it." She swallows. "*The girl of blue light will fall and be reborn before the final battle.*"

"Oswald knew you would die, and he let it happen? What about Kraven? Did he know, too?"

"And Valery, though it wasn't why she took me below. She did that selfishly. Though you know what our king says about casting stones."

Learning without a doubt that these people knew what would become of Charlie infuriates me. I'd been honest with them, and they hadn't done me the same favor. My breath comes faster. I want to take my anger out on someone, and if that outlet happens to be in the form of a little old man or a twenty-something with a penchant for the color white, so be it.

"Just stop. Stop being so upset on my behalf. It was my decision to not fight back. Because I knew the day for fighting would come, and when it did, I'd be ready. We couldn't tell you before it happened. We all believe that the scroll is guiding us, and you'd have stood in the way of this final prediction if you knew."

She's right. I would have done everything in my power to prohibit her from coming to the Lion's Hand if I knew this was her fate. I acknowledged there was a chance she might get hurt, but I never accepted it as fact. Of course, I suppose Valery took away any chance I had to protect her.

I move my hand from her wrist to her waist. "Charlie, what happened when you…?"

"Died?" She looks down and smiles. I get a glimpse of that peculiar smile, the one I've missed so badly. "I had a dream. In it I was unbreakable. I was lethal. And it felt good."

"Charlie…"

"Go back to camp. Tell Kraven we'll wait until dusk. I want two jackrabbits on guard, and Blue in the trees. If they see the army encroaching, we are to retreat farther into the woods immediately."

"I'm not leaving you alone."

"You'll do as I say, Dante. And you won't hesitate when I ask you to do something more. You will believe in me as I have believed in you. Is that understood?"

My eyes travel over her body. "You are damn hot, woman."

"Yeah, well, I make dead look good."

I wince. "I don't like that joke, but I do like the confidence."

"Baby, I got swag for days."

I touch a finger to her chin. "That's my line."

She smiles. "Go now. I'll be there soon."

I'm going to follow her orders even though I can't wrap my head around this concept. But first I grab her and dip her low to the ground. I kiss her long and hard and ensure she'll never question again how beautiful she is. And yeah, to show her that I'm still her man even if she is all fierce now. Our lips move together, and Charlie swims her fingers through my hair. One of her hands travels over my back, over my hip, to my butt. She squeezes, and I growl. "You want me to leave, or you want me to ravage you?"

"Leave now, ravage later."

Her words are teasing, but she's already returned to that untouchable place I can't reach. Her gaze is locked on the earth, and I can practically see the thoughts swirling in her head, battling for her attention like hungry orphan children. She takes a step away from me, and I see that old limp in her step. The one she got in the fire that killed her parents. The one I took away with the soul contract.

I turn to go but before I leave, I say one last thing. "I'm sorry for what happened to you. It may have been predicted. It may have been your destiny. But I didn't want this life for you."

I walk away, thinking about how last night Kraven said Charlie would spend eternity in the heavens. What he failed to mention was how many years of service she'd put in before then. I wonder how long Big Guy will leave the dargon on Charlie. A day? A year? Will I be there with her? Could we really have forever?

No.

Big Guy doesn't want me for anything more than a weapon. I know that. Still, I can't help wishing things were different. That he found favor in me the way he did the other liberators. Kraven said He forgave him for his indiscretions. But I could never be forgiven. For all my talk of being amazing, down deep, in a place I never venture, I know the truth. I am despicable.

I wasn't a good human. So why would Big Guy ever want me as a liberator after this war is over?

The answer: he won't.

I see the light of the campfire as I approach, and as I do, a new thought occurs to me. If Charlie spends a century liberating souls, what could that mean for mankind? I don't believe another liberator like her has ever existed. She won't just reward souls for the good they've done, she'll guide them in the right direction so that she *can* reward them. Those people could change others.

What would it look like with Annabelle leading Hands Helping Hands, and Charlie acting as the greatest liberator to walk this earth? Would it look like change? Would it look like peace?

Would it last a hundred years and garner a name people would remember?

Would they call it Trelvator?

⟴ 48 ⟴

STING

Charlie and Aspen continue to whisper to one another. The rest of us do what we can: we rest, we eat, we make fun of Blue's newly sprouted wings. Aspen hasn't so much as looked in his direction, but all he does is stare at her, mouth agape.

Oswald hangs out with Lincoln. They are a mismatched pair of friends if I've ever seen one, but Lincoln is mystified by Oswald's orange burst of light, and Oswald likes having an admirer. I, on the other hand, verbally abuse Oswald for never telling me about the last thing he read on the scroll. Even now, I finger the piece of scroll in my pocket he gave me as proof; one little scrap of paper proclaiming that my girlfriend would die.

I hate Oswald, the weasel, especially after I found out it was him who called for Rector to kill the girl on his right. Then again, maybe I don't hate him. One of the two girls was going to die, and he was only ensuring that death followed the scroll's prophecy. I know he didn't want Charlie to get hurt. And it's not really his fault she died.

It's mine.

The anxiety never leaves my body, even as we rag on each other and try to keep our spirits up. Yesterday morning, we lost soldiers on the battlefield, and I can't forget that. I question Kraven repeatedly when I can get him alone. If yesterday was the day of reckoning, what does that make today? He seems stumped. Valery suggests that perhaps yesterday was merely the start of war. Wars can last months, after all. Years.

I still remember the trumpet sound Charlie and I heard over my impeccably chosen dinner of red foods. It was a declaration of war. Their king had received word that we wanted to tango, and they were accepting the invitation. Yesterday, the actual war started, and it's anybody's guess as to when it will come to a close.

An hour before dusk, Charlie appears with Aspen by her side. Valery is sitting across from Kraven, scowling at him. She doesn't even see her best friend appear. The two girls have long removed Rector's crowns from their heads, but a new tiara sits in its place. The Patrelli sisters wove them from gnarled branches, and it looks wicked cool on top of Charlie's hair.

Her blue eyes shine behind her glasses, and her cheeks are red from winter's bite. She walks tall, as if Aspen has taught her how. I can't believe she's a liberator. She's like me now. Immortal. Eternal. A slave to the cuff around her slim ankle.

When the humans and liberators and jackrabbits see the two girls approaching, they quiet. A risky fire flickers in the center of our campsite, casting forlorn shadows across the princesses' features.

Aspen raises her hand as if asking for our attention. "The savior and I have spoken at length about how to proceed in this war. And we've decided the most effective thing we can do at this point is to initiate sting operations."

Charlie steps forward. "We're grossly outnumbered, but we can weaken their spirits and rattle their confidence. If we do it well enough, some of the sirens may abandon their posts. Even if we don't, it'll instill fear into their ranks."

"We'll strike like vipers," Aspen says.

Lincoln stands up. "Or like jackrabbits."

"Do jackrabbits really strike?" Max scratches his chin. "I mean, they don't have fangs or anything."

"Dude, shut up," Lincoln says.

Aspen comes to stand before Lincoln. "Are you volunteering?"

Lincoln's face falls, like how could she even question him? I suddenly remember these two have been friends for a long time. It was Lincoln who took care of Sahara, Aspen's younger sister, when Aspen got lost in her own head. It was Lincoln who stood by her as others took everything she had to give.

He knew she was damaged, but he cared for her anyway.

"Can you act with stealth?" Charlie asks him.

"No more than a panther."

"If you're caught…"

"We won't be."

Charlie and Aspen regard each other before turning back to him. It's like they already decided this was the best possible plan, and only needed him to accept the undertaking. "You'll take two others of your choosing."

Kraven stands up and I smell a slight burning. It's like his wings are begging to make an appearance. "I don't know about this. It should be the liberators who do this. We can protect ourselves if captured."

"What about me?" Oswald opens his arms like he's preparing to make a blood donation on either side. "If I could be snuck in, I could kill many of them at once. You saw what I can do when surrounded."

Charlie shakes her head. "You can only do it once before having to restore your energy. No matter how many you take out, the others will swarm. We can't lose you."

Oswald grins as if Charlie valuing his life is the best thing to happen in his eight hundred years on this planet.

"No offense, Crave," Lincoln says to Kraven, "But you guys are about as quiet as Max sleeping."

Max's brow furrows with confusion.

"You snore," Valery says. "Like a grizzly bear being smothered."

I want to laugh, but then I remember that I hate Valery.

Lincoln continues. "Even flying, you're too loud. But us? We've been trained how to perform covert operations. You couldn't hear us coming any more than you could hear a butterfly beating its wings."

"That was poetic," Max says. "Prick."

"Take the trumpet." Aspen searches the ground until she finds it. "If you run into trouble, sound the instrument and we'll come for you."

"I won't need it, but okay." Lincoln gazes at his fellow jackrabbits. "Rosen, Polo, you'll come with me." When the other jackrabbits appear upset that they weren't chosen, Lincoln adds, "There will be other missions. You'll all get a chance to come along."

I can't believe how brave these emo kids are. Their military moms and dads must have done a number on them. Or maybe they just always strove to emulate their seemingly indestructible parents.

Lincoln looks to Aspen and Charlie. "We'll need time to discuss our strategy."

The girls motion for the three to follow them. I glance at Max like, *What the H are we, chopped liver?* Charlie turns once before leaving and smiles reassuringly in my direction. My chest swells and I realize just how ridiculous this makes me. That one smile from a girl who doesn't know she's beautiful can fill me with pride.

I remember a time when I pushed booze into her hands. A time when I encouraged her to perform petty theft and party it up in Vegas. I was the reason she sinned. I was different then. Dare I say I was a douchebag?

I dare not.

I've always been awesome.

Even if I was a self-centered dick, I was an *awesome* self-centered dick.

Now I'm a dude that waits on Charlie. I want to be her protector, but something changed after she became a liberator. I'm on the outside, wishing I were the soldier by her side. Aspen is still human, after all. Even if she can kick some serious tail, she's still mortal. It should be me protecting Charlie. It should be me protecting Aspen.

Lincoln, Rosen, and Polo return an hour later. They seem properly strategized, I suppose. Lincoln walks like he's lord of this here land and shouldn't we be offering to wash his dirty ass feet?

No more words are spoken.

Lincoln takes the trumpet that managed to make it back to our base camp after the first battle. He hands it to Polo, a dude built like a pencil with long black hair tied back in a super-masculine ponytail. Polo has a blue ribbon tied around his pony. I shit you not—a ribbon. Dude thinks he's Casanova, and you know what? Mad respect. Any guy confident enough to rock a ribbon is A-Okay in my book. Pow!

Rosen is small. I want to put him in a pocket. In fact, I seriously think about doing just that. My left pocket is free. My right one has some random crap in it, but my left one could be all his if he wanted it.

Once Ribbon Dude has the trumpet bag strapped over his back, the three crouch low and scamper across the ground. They move like the breeze. Like a virus. As they disappear from view, the smile leaves my face. I don't want them to go. Or maybe it's that I don't want them to go without me.

"What if something happens to them?" I say to no one in particular.

❖ 49 ❖

DREAM OF YOU

It's late in the night and the jackrabbits still haven't returned. Their friends look out with obvious concern, and I can't stay still. I switch between pacing and hugging Charlie. I want to know she's safe. I want to know she doesn't hate me for not protecting her.

I want to know if her liberator boobs feel differently.

Charlie is unnervingly quiet. I try to make small talk, but what is there to say?

At some point, Annabelle ralphs. If I weren't trying to maintain my dignity, I'd blow chunks right along with her. There's been little to eat since the battle ended almost two days ago, and our stomachs are unsettled. If someone offered me a baked potato right now, fully loaded, and said I had to murder Blue to eat it, I'd walk over his carcass to my reward.

"How you holding up?" Aspen says, startling me.

"Me?" I point to myself. "I'm fine. I was born for this, doll."

"Drop the front, Dante."

"I feel like ass crack."

"There we go."

I sigh. "She's really gone."

Aspen bumps my shoulder with hers. "No, she's not. She's standing right over there. Look, I know this is hard. You had visions of Charlie growing old and you being the one to ensure she was always warm in her bed. You'd be her lover, and then her friend, and finally, her caretaker. But now you can be this."

"What's that?"

"A liberator that works alongside her. Her equal." Aspen sees I'm still fretting. "You know why people fear death? Because it's painful, and because they don't know what awaits them on the other side. Charlie had neither pain nor the fear of the unknown. When we were up on those horses…?" Aspen looks at me like she's confirming that's indeed what they were on. I motion for her continue. "When we were up on those horses, it was like we were swimming, heads never rising above the surface. It sounds scary, but it wasn't. It was some in between place, I suppose."

"And what about before that?"

Aspen stiffens. She still has the diamond in her nose. It doesn't shine like it once did, but it's there. "I don't ever want to talk about what happened when I was down there. I doubt Charlie will either."

Aspen looks at me for a long time, ensuring I understand. I want to push her for information. Maybe I believe if she tells me, I can somehow make it better. In the end though, I don't. If it hurts to discuss it, then I'm leaving it alone. But there is one thing I must ask. "Aspen?"

She cocks her chin.

"Did you ever see me down there? I mean, did you sleep and dream and stuff?"

Aspen diverts her gaze. "I dreamt."

"And did you ever see me in them? Because Aspen, I saw you in mine. A lot."

"Maybe you have a crush on me," she says, but she isn't smiling.

"I'm being serious."

When she looks back at me, I know the answer. It's right there on her face. Something happened while she dreamt. She may not remember the details, but she knows that somehow we connected.

A sound rips me from my conversation with Aspen. When I realize it's Lincoln and his two comrades, I nearly jump from my skin. Those little bastards are creepy as hell.

"Wanted to show you how quiet we can be." Lincoln isn't smiling. He doesn't seem proud and so I assume he failed at infiltrating the enemy's camp. Then I see the blood on his jacket.

"Damn near invisible, too." I nod upward. "Blue and Valery are in the trees and didn't spot you. You okay?"

A rustling sound says the two liberators—if I can even call Red a liberator—are touching down. Kraven arrives with a rabbit slung over his shoulder. Before he can ask what happened, Lincoln says, "We killed one of them. A collector."

Lincoln tosses something onto the ground.

It's a human foot.

"We had to cut it off to get the cuff." He's shaking. "At first we were going to crack the cuff and take it, but it would have been too loud. Ended up having to knock him out and then cut off the entire foot. It took some time, but the blades you gave aren't like others I've seen. They're strong. Strong enough for bone."

Polo drops to the ground and sits cross-legged. He doesn't seem nearly as upset by what they did. "It was the big one. They had him standing guard. He was slow."

I swallow. "Did you see the others?"

"We saw 'em," Rosen says. "All but the one who did the girl."

I flinch and my blood burns with anger. "Do you mean Charlie? Do you mean you didn't see Rector, the one who *killed* Charlie, my girlfriend?"

"Dante," Charlie says.

Polly strolls around the perimeter of the campsite like a cat seeking scraps. She's eyeing Lincoln, ensuring herself that the blood isn't his own. Another human nearby looks at the foot and says, "He had small feet. For being so big, I mean."

Max laughs and then covers his mouth.

It isn't funny, but this isn't usual and we're nervous. I worked for the devil for years but never cut off someone's damn foot and carried it back with me like a carnival souvenir.

"You'll need to go again, immediately." Charlie's voice is gentle.

"So quickly?" I ask, but I'm glad for it. Nothing is worse than sitting around. And what the jackrabbits did—it's progress. It's victory. Thirty minutes ago, there were five collectors. Now one of them— Anthony, the largest—is dead. I stabbed him repeatedly on the field. But they killed him. What if next time they catch Rector? The sirens won't fight without a leader, will they?

"It's imperative that we strike repeatedly in fast succession so they don't have time to plan a proper defense against our strategy." Charlie touches Aspen's shoulder like she's just thought of something, but it's more like she wanted to reassure herself that she was there. "Someone will come to relieve the collector soon and they'll discover that he's dead. We want to be there when that happens."

"What do you think they're doing out there?" a human asks.

We gaze into the distance. It's a question I've asked myself a dozen times. Why aren't they pursuing us like we are them?

Aspen squats down next to Lincoln, who doesn't seem to be able to stand. "Can you go again so soon?"

Though Lincoln nods, I can't help thinking this is brutal. Lincoln is a human, who weeks ago was lounging in his father's apartment in Denver. Today, he cut off a foot. He killed a collector and stole a piece of dargon from the devil's own collection.

Lincoln gestures to two new guys. They stand up, ready to serve our cause. "This time, we could stay close to their camp. We don't have to come back between each sting. In fact, it's probably better that we didn't. They could follow us back. Right now, we could be anywhere. But if they follow us, they'll sense your dargon and know just where to find you."

"No," Aspen snaps. "We need to know you're safe. We also need to keep count on our end of how many collectors, or sirens for that matter, remain."

"We'll never be able to keep count of the sirens," Annabelle interjects.

Aspen grimaces. "My point stands."

Kraven drops the rabbit and comes to stand beside Lincoln. "Are you ready?"

Lincoln steps back. "I said I was."

And just like that, Lincoln and the two fresh jackrabbits head into the false security of night, across the Lion's Hand, and into enemy territory.

After they're gone, Aspen fidgets. She seemed confident the first time they left, but now something feels different. The collectors may have already found Anthony's body. They could be laying a trap for our jackrabbits now. To keep her mind off Lincoln, I tell her we need to come up with a more impactful plan.

She asks what I mean.

What *do* I mean?

Valery closes in, and I fight the urge to yell at her. She's been belittled, ignored, and ridiculed by almost every member at camp, and she repeats the same thing over and over. "I was wrong. I made a mistake, and I'll spend the rest of my days as a liberator protecting the soldier and savior." She says Rector came to her in a dream and presented an offer. Before she woke, he told her what she had to do, and what word to speak to open the vultrips. I'm not sure anyone believes her, but I do. Valery prays a lot now. Kraven encourages her when she does this. Personally, I think it adds insult to injury. Does she think Big Guy will forgive her? I've got her answer right here: No.

Big Guy is not the forgiving type.

"Dante?" Charlie's attention gives me confidence. We need a plan. A better plan for when the collectors and sirens realize what we're up to.

I stride back and forth in front of the fire like it's my stage. Like these people are my audience, and what I'm about to say is Shakespearean. "What the jackrabbits need is a larger weapon."

"I'm listening," Max says. Except he says it like, *I'm liiistening*.

"What if we built a platform of sorts?" I suggest. "The jackrabbits could carry Oswald on top of it so they're still quiet. After Oswald does his orange magic trick, then one of the jackrabbits can sound the horn and I can fly in and get Oswald. The jackrabbits could scatter and hide. They're good at that. We hit the enemy from a different angle every time. They'll never know where we're going to strike next, and we'll take out hordes of sirens, and maybe some collectors, at once."

Aspen's eyes enlarge. She's excited by the idea. "The jackrabbits could take cover when Oswald attacked, and if collectors are knocked out, Lincoln could have just enough time to remove their dargon before the liberators appeared."

"Liberators?"

She motions toward Kraven, Blue, and Valery. "The three of them could get the jackrabbits while you snatch the old man."

"I resent that," Oswald says, "but I like where this is headed."

"We can't all go," I say. "Someone would need to be here to protect you two."

Charlie grimaces. "Protect *us*?"

My head drops to one side, imploring her to understand. "You've only been a liberator for two days, Charlie. And you and Aspen have been through hell, literally. I know you think you're strong enough to—"

"You have no idea what we're strong enough for," Aspen whispers. "Something happened when we were down there. When we were together."

"Aspen!" Charlie glares at her friend like she shouldn't say another word.

Kraven runs a hand through his hair, nervously. "What's she talking about? What happened?"

"We awoke," Aspen says. "That's all."

I'm staring at Charlie. She's staring at me. "You awoke?"

"It's a good idea," Oswald says. "The part about carrying me back. I trust Dante."

I tear my gaze away from Charlie and look to Oswald. My heart grows three sizes. "You do?"

He pounds a cane-like tree branch into the snow. This means *yes*, I think.

"We have a plan," Kraven says.

"We start small and gradually get more aggressive as their numbers dwindle." Charlie touches a hand to her crown of twigs.

Her fingers are still fluttering there—an unconscious gesture—when the trumpet sounds.

⇥50⇤

YOU ARE LOVED

Aspen begins calling orders. "Charlie, by my side. Kraven and Dante, I want one of you on either side. Jackrabbits, line up directly behind us. Humans will remain here as we analyze the situation. Valery, Max, Blue, Oswald, Annabelle, and the sisters, you will stay with the humans. If you hear a second trumpeting, charge the battlefield, half to one side, half to the other."

In a flash, we are positioned exactly as Aspen instructed. There's no time to argue about who the leader is. The way Aspen speaks, it's like no one can imagine anyone being in charge besides her.

We're about to move out when Charlie turns and looks at the humans and the remaining liberators. "Do not be afraid. In war, the unexpected is expected."

Her words are firm, reassuring. Relief floods the humans' faces as they huddle together, seeking the weapons they fled the field with. It's then that I realize how perfectly balanced the two girls are. One calls for action, the other calms the troops. We can't lose with Charlie and Aspen at our helm, even against countless sirens.

I glance back at Max and a silent acknowledgment passes between us. Blue is already instructing the humans, so he doesn't see me watching him. I'm proud that he's my friend. I hope he knows that.

We race through the forest, weaving between spindly trees. When we reach the edge of the Lion's Hand, we hunch over and hurry through the field. About halfway across, I stop short. Aspen and Charlie stand up. The rest of us do, too. We all see what the collectors want us to see.

Patrick has Lincoln's head between his hands. Zack and Kincaid stand on either side of him, holding the other jackrabbits' heads in their hands as well. One of the jackrabbits still clutches the trumpet. I wonder if the collectors encouraged him to blow it.

"One movement," Patrick roars, "and they're dead."

"Don't hurt them!" Polo yells from behind me.

"Quiet," Kraven says coolly. "It's not them they want."

My heart hammers in my chest. We were so stupid sending the jackrabbits to do our bidding. We should never have involved humans. That's the collectors' style, not ours. But then I think back to what Charlie said. War is messy. The unexpected happens.

I take a deep breath and remember it's the long game that matters. I remember who I am, the confidence I harbor. They're threatening to kill my friend and I already watched Charlie die, but I've got the confidence of a tornado. And my name, as it so happens, is Dante Fucking Walker.

I fill my lungs. "Tell us what it is you want."

Patrick laughs. I'm going to pull the tongue from his mouth. I may eat it, too, A-1 sauce and all. "We want the girls. Send the rose first."

The rose. Bile burns my throat remembering Rector's nickname for Aspen. "I have a better idea. The two of us. One on one."

Aspen squares her shoulders. She's trying to act confident, but I can see the way she shakes. "You'll kill him the moment you have me."

"Maybe. Maybe not."

Charlie is about to call out, when suddenly we're surrounded.

Twenty sirens appear from the tall grass in near silence. The jackrabbits could learn a thing or two from their approach.

Immediately, the wings explode from my back. Kraven's do as well. Along with the jackrabbits, we push Aspen and Charlie between us, shielding them with our bodies. It was a mistake to come here without the others. We need Oswald. We need every liberator and human we have. I know why we didn't bring them all, but now I feel sure it was a mistake.

Night hangs over us, intrusive, blinding. The sirens move through the grass, and in one fluid movement, the girls break through our protective barrier. Aspen pulls her arm back. I don't know what she's doing but a siren is charging toward her with a blade and she's going to be killed.

I take flight, pulse pounding, head throbbing. I can't watch her die, too.

Aspen's right arm pulls back farther, farther. Her left arm stays straight ahead like she's pointing at the siren.

You!

Charlie is a step behind her, whispering quiet words.

Kraven takes flight beside me, and then I see it. A green pulsing light extends from Aspen's left hand all the way back to her cocked right hand. As I watch, the light sharpens at the tip. It's almost like she's holding a—

A neon green arrow soars through the space, appearing from an invisible bow between Aspen's hands as if by magic. It drives straight through a siren. The guy is thrown back, and the other sirens scatter. Now that they've seen what Oswald can do, they want no part of the green light.

Charlie rushes toward the fallen siren, and I fly after her, calling for her to fall back. She drops to her knees beside the siren. The guy gasps for air as the arrow in his chest slowly dissolves. There's no blood, but the siren is clearly in pain.

I touch down beside Charlie. "Get away from him."

Big surprise, she ignores me.

Instead, she lays her palms upon his chest and closes her eyes. Energy explodes from her hands like paddles on a heart attack patient. The siren's back arches and his teeth clench down. No one makes a move as his body shakes and then quiets. When the siren opens his eyes, there are tears in them. He grasps at her wrists, her forearms, anywhere he can touch her.

Charlie lowers her head and says something that makes my chest constrict. "You are forgiven. You are loved."

The siren weeps openly.

"Come and join us," she says, "And we will call you family."

The siren gets to his feet, trembling, and Aspen looses two more arrows into the backs of fleeing sirens. Others dash away, out of her aim. But one, one stands with arms open, as if he's waited for this moment.

"Charlie..." Aspen lowers her arms and the green light snuffs out.

Charlie sees the siren that didn't flee and heads toward him.

Kraven has touched down and is inspecting the three collectors in the distance. They appear terrified, and I know why. Our darkness is something we relish. As much as it hurts to hate ourselves, to work for the embodiment of evil, it's easier than facing the things we've done. So when Aspen turns on the collectors and fires toward them, Zack lets go of the jackrabbit he's holding. They may not understand completely what it is Charlie is doing out here, but they see that something has changed in the two sirens standing nearby.

An arrow pierces Kincaid's thigh and he screeches. Not out of pain, but out of shock. His cry is enough to make Patrick release Lincoln. The three jackrabbits race across the field, and Aspen continues to shoot flaming arrows produced from thin air.

Following her lead, I attack. I launch toward Patrick, and feel the beat of Kraven's wings behind me. I'm almost to the collector when I see humans advancing from the shadows. I figured the sirens were at a campsite hidden in the forest. But they're here. All of them. Among them is the one with the black magic, Easton, and his brother, Salem. Easton wields the power cloud above his head, waiting for the right moment to strike. Patrick raises his arm above his head, and then waves it forward.

They attack.

I stop midflight and soar toward Lincoln, who has made it to Aspen's side.

"Do you have the trumpet?" I yell.

Lincoln motions to one of his friends and they search the ground. They find it. They bring it to their lips. They blow and a sharp, urgent sound fills the air. As the sirens rush toward us, the jackrabbit drops the trumpet into the tall grass. It may very well be the last time we hear the instrument's invocation.

The sirens slam into us. I fight them with renewed vigor. I fight them with fury. They helped murder Charlie, even if it did fulfill her destiny, and I want retribution. I grab a siren by the middle and slam him to the ground. He tears at my eyes, but I beat my fists into his face until he blacks out.

Charlie offers forgiveness.

I offer penance.

Two sirens leap onto my back, and I fly into the air. The sirens stop fighting and instead hold onto me for dear life.

"This is the last moment of your life," I say, because I want them to know.

I spin in tight circles until their fingers peel from my skin and their bodies drop like atomic bombs toward the earth. Watching them fall gives me an idea, so I swoop back down and grab another siren. I fly into the sky and drop him, too. They die quickly, one after the other. But it's like there's no end to their numbers. Kraven sees what

I'm doing and he follows my lead.

Below, the humans and remaining jackrabbits storm the Lion's Hand. Valery, Max, and Blue run before them, a warrior cry tearing from their throats. The humans carry weapons, and the jackrabbits do, too. They clash with the sirens and battle fiercely.

Oswald is surrounded on both sides by the Patrelli sisters. Sirens charge toward them, and then something happens. Their bodies fly backward as if hitting an invisible force field. It isn't Oswald's doing. It's the sisters'. That's how Oswald managed to get inside the circle of sirens two days ago without being hurt. That's how the sisters weren't harmed. This even explains why Kraven thought they could guard the weapon room. They have an ability, too, though I suspect they'll tire soon enough, especially since the siren with the black, dancing cloud is headed their way.

It feels like I've been fighting for an eternity when I touch back down to search for Charlie. When I find her, I can hardly believe my eyes. She's surrounded by sirens. At first I believe she's in danger, but when I look closer I realize that's not it at all. Though most of them are confused and scared, they seem to be guarding her against their previous adversaries.

She's truly changed them. She somehow brought their souls back into their bodies, and now they don't want to leave her presence. I want to turn away from this strategy. To be merciless sounds much better. But even I can't deny how effective this could be. I'm trying to kill sirens one at a time, while she's turning them into soldiers.

My optimism raises as Aspen strikes arrows through sirens' hearts and Charlie revives them. I can practically see the white light of their souls streaking from the ground, through the soles of their feet, slamming square into their chests. Heads fallen back, mouths open.

Forgiveness.

Change.

I grab the next siren I see. Not because I care, but because this is the way to victory. I toss the guy more roughly than necessary at Aspen's feet. She glances up and grins. She salutes me. I salute her right back. Then I fly through the air and find Valery, Blue, Max, and Kraven. I tell them what to do. *Move the sirens toward the girls*.

I point toward Charlie and Aspen to drive my point home, and my heart stops beating. The veins in my body collapse. The two girls—the savior and the soldier—stand shoulder to shoulder, their hands clasped. Their hair flies wildly around their heads. They walk, ever slowly, through the mass of sirens, claiming them as their own. They look like the princesses we claim they are. They look lethal, unbeatable.

That's the moment I believe her.

Charlie doesn't need my protection.

She only needs me to be her partner. And so I will be. With a roar ripping through me, I sail toward Patrick. As I fly, I call to Lincoln.

"Knife," I yell. "Knife!"

Lincoln steals a blade from a jackrabbit and tosses it into the air. *Perfect throw, Goth kid*. I catch it smooth and fly hard. Then I slam into Patrick with the force of a tidal wave. He won't walk away from this fight. Not when we're winning this war, not when I feel inexorable. He hits me once in the stomach. I don't feel it. I'm above pain. I clock him across the jaw so that his whole body spins like a Tilt-A-Whirl. He hits the ground and I land on his back. Tossing the knife, I catch the hilt and slam it into the back of his skull. He's out.

Ripping his pant leg up, I search for his dargon. I'll take it the same way Lincoln did Anthony's, but without a morsel of regret. I search his left ankle, his right.

It's gone.

He's not wearing dargon. I sit back, flabbergasted. I don't even have time to think on what this means.

Because Charlie is screaming.

51

HERE THEY CRAWL

This entire time I'd wondered where Rector was, but I was too busy fighting to dwell on it. Now he shoots through the sky like a rotting star. He burst from the ground like a cicada killer wasp and now his arms are around Charlie and he's flying, flying.

Her screams quiet, and I see a flash of blue against the dark sky. The two plummet to earth, and Rector takes a knee on the ground, Charlie leaned over his lap like a willing lover. He stands. His leather wings spread out. He keeps one hand on Charlie, who doesn't struggle, and uses the other to withdraw a long sword from over his shoulder. He places the tip directly above her dargon. Charlie closes her eyes.

She's whispering words I can't hear, but they do nothing to lessen Rector's grip on her.

Rector grins in my direction. "I'm going to give someone here the chance to save this girl. Sacrifice yourself, and she'll walk free."

I open my mouth to elect myself though I know it will do nothing to stop Rector from taking her dargon.

I'm interrupted.

"Take me!" All eyes turn to see Valery striding forward. "You gave me a chance to work for you. You promised me a life with my love. You promised me forgiveness for my fiancé. And I betrayed you. I don't know why you want a willing sacrifice," she says, continuing to move forward, "but take me."

Max races after Valery, but she knocks him back with one sweep of her white wing.

There's no way I'll let Valery do this. Even if I do hate her, she's mine to hate. Her stupid self will stay with us for as long as I say and bear the anger I have to give until one day, maybe, my anger depletes. What I *will* do though is let her serve as a distraction. As Rector eyes Valery, licking his lips, I circle around behind him. He doesn't see me. Not yet.

Charlie lays her hands on Rector's chest again. Flame ignites from her palms and she mutters words, but nothing happens. His soul has been dead too long. She can't restore his humanity any more than I can change the fact that she died before my eyes.

Valery is so close to Rector. I spot Kraven on Rector's other side. He slips through the grass like me, trying to reclaim one of our two most useful weapons in this war.

Déjà vu.

It's a funny thing.

Three days ago, we fell into Rector's trap so easily. He pulled the two girls from their horses and we were helpless to do anything. Now here he is again with Charlie, and here we are, our hands bound.

What broke the moment last time? Who saved us?

Oh, yes.

Annabelle appears from the grass behind Rector. She has a blade in her right hand and radioactive fury written across her face. She's already told him once. She's already warned him to stay away from her friends.

My heart is in my throat as the fingers on her left hand linger unconsciously over her stomach. There's protectiveness in that subtle touch. And through that one small gesture, I understand…everything.

It's Annabelle.

All this time, it was her.

Two hearts that beat as one will make a great sacrifice.

She raises her arm over her head and screams and the world breaks into a thousand pieces.

Rector turns and drives the sword clean through Annabelle and the unborn baby living inside her. Charlie cries out and the blue light that explodes from her hands is like nothing I've ever seen. Rector whips through the sky like a forgotten scrap of paper on the wind.

Blue is there with Annabelle and I'm there with Charlie.

Annabelle isn't moving. She's not moving and the ground is rumbling and Kraven is growling like the demons he's ignored for a decade have resurfaced inside him, hungry. "Annabelle!" His entire body shakes. His wings grow in length. His face contorts, bones spreading. "Annabelle!"

Annabelle is breathing, choking on her words, and Rector is fleeing. The Patrelli sisters rush toward her, and Blue pushes Annabelle into their arms.

"Get her out of here," I say.

The sisters dodge the sirens in their retreat. They won't be able to hold their shield up for much longer, and so the four of them, including Oswald, will have to seek the forest's shelter. As they withdraw, Rector moves farther away. But there's no way Kraven will let him flee and neither will I. I don't want to leave Charlie's side, but I will because I want Rector's head right now more than anything.

Rector has Annabelle's blood on his hands. He paints his face with it and growls toward the moon. Kraven will get to him first, but I'll be there a heartbeat after that. Together, we'll pull him limb from limb.

A ripple rolls across the Lion's Hand. I feel it even in flight. Though I'm unsure as to where it stems from it does little to slow my strike. When a second ripple hits the earth though, I hesitate in the air, wings beating. Kraven does, too.

Rector opens his mouth and yells. His words feel like acid rain pelting my skin. "Blood of the savior. Blood of the soldier. Blood of the sacrifice. Come into me, king. I have done as you commanded!"

I search the field for Aspen and spot her. She's holding her arm, the same one she injured in hell on our journey to save Charlie's soul. Blood seeps between her fingers. Rector must have cut her before he shot into the air with Charlie.

The ground rocks with even more enthusiasm, and I call for Kraven to go to Charlie and Aspen. He's got arsenic in his veins though, and the only thing that will satiate him is Rector's death.

I fly toward him and shake his shoulders in the air. "Go to the savior and soldier. Fight with them. I'll kill Rector. I swear to you."

When he turns and looks at me, a shiver climbs up my spine. His face, and the bones in his body, they aren't right. I've seen it before during the night of the fire and during our Amplification training and on Rector's own face, but it's jarring all the same.

"Go, Kraven! Do it for Annabelle."

I'm not sure what convinces him, but he roars and sails toward a pocket of sirens and begins throwing them toward Charlie and Aspen. He's an unstoppable force, fighting with a darkness liberators shouldn't possess. No one will get past him now. Not sirens, not the remaining collectors. He is ruthless in his worry over Annabelle.

The earth shakes a third time, and I turn back to Rector.

He picks up his knees one at a time like he's skipping rope. He laughs. He screams at nothingness and his eyes leech of color and behind him, a massive fissure opens in the earth.

Out of it, the demons crawl.

52

I THEE WED

There are hundreds of them. Black-and-yellow-scaled things with arched backs and heavy heads. They whistle and hiss and turn their demon bodies toward our troops. Tongues dart out from between sharpened teeth, and clawed fingers twitch.

The hair rises on the back of my neck, and the humans who fight with us scream out in horror. They were prepared to fight other humans—*sirens*—and winged men. But not this.

This is why they didn't attack again after our first battle.

This is the grand finale they were busy planning.

I don't understand how it's even possible until I see them—rings. Gold rings are fitted around the monsters' fingers like they're moments from walking down the aisle. I understand at once why Patrick wasn't wearing a cuff. They removed his dargon, and probably a couple of the other collectors', too, and welded the material into rings so they and their demons could crawl from hell and onto the Lion's Hand.

No one is whispering the vultrips open anymore.

That betrayal was completed, and Rector spilled what blood he needed to in order to open a last and final vultrip.

As Rector dances in place, elated with his performance, red smoke wisps from beneath his feet and surrounds his body. He bows to it, and soon I can't even see him the scarlet fog is so dense. The demons pour toward the humans and liberators and jackrabbits. They tear into them, and they tear into the sirens, too; those who have been changed and those who haven't. The meat tastes the same to the black and yellow monsters.

I race toward the fog, no longer caring what hides behind its veil.

That's when Rector steps into view.

He is larger than he was before, and his body is covered in black scales like the demons he unleashed. His eyes burn red and his face is coated in black tar. Muscles bulge from beneath his scaled armor as he steadies the sword, still coated in Annabelle's blood, toward me.

Wings like an ocean unfurl from behind his back, and a sinister smile twists his gaping mouth. I know in this instant that it's no longer simply Rector I'm fighting. Not really. It's Rector empowered. It's Rector possessed.

He flies toward me.

I fly toward him.

Our bodies collide and the universe trembles.

He narrowly misses my abdomen with his sword. I grab his right wrist to keep the blade from doing any damage, and he bites down on my neck. I scream with agony and bring my knee into his stomach. It does nothing to lessen his teeth sinking into my flesh. Only when I slam my head into his does he let go. I fly away from him and dive over his head. Hooking an arm around his throat, I pull back. He's too strong though, and he quickly tears away from my grasp.

Rector swings his sword and it catches me on the right thigh. I whip out of his reach and hear someone yelling from several feet below. Glancing down, I see Max waving a sword over his head.

My boy, Max!

I swoop down to get it, but Rector slams into my side and jams the butt of his sword into my ribs. A crack reaches my ears and tells me he's done real damage. I throw my fist into his face and into his neck. He barely flinches from the impact.

Once again, I fly down to meet Max, but Rector intercepts my attempt. I can hear Max crying out in frustration as Rector grabs hold of me and sails straight up, away from Max and the weapon he holds. I kick my heel into Rector's shin and remember the defense Kraven taught me.

Curling my wings around myself, I spin. It does the job and I break from Rector's hold. Pulling on my shadow, I plunge fast toward the earth, but he's there in a second, and I barely dodge the sword from opening me across the middle. Rector pulls to one side and brings his elbow across my face. My shadow falls away and blood pours from my shattered nose. Before I can think, he brings the sword around his head. It comes slicing toward my neck, the same place where he bit me moments before.

I spin and fall again, and he swipes empty space where my head once was. I have to kill Rector, and I won't stop until one of us dies, but I don't know how I can win. Not without a weapon. I should have thought to grab something before I took off after him, but there wasn't time.

Rector crashes into me and this time pain explodes in my left leg. I don't know how he hit me or where, exactly. He blasted into me and left just as swiftly. With his heightened senses he's faster than I am, and my injuries drive the point home. For the third time, I hear Max's sounds of frustration. Then his voice grows closer. I don't understand what's happening until I spot Max soaring toward me, grey-feathered wings spread over his head.

The look on his face is one I'll never forget.

Pride.

Excitement.

My best friend finally found his wings.

He tosses the sword to me—and one second later, one heartbeat after my hand closes over the hilt—Rector drives his sword through Max's chest. It enters through his back and appears again directly below his right collar bone.

The smile crumbles from Max's face. He screams as Rector shoves his boot into Max's back and pushes my best friend's body off his sword. Rector swings his sword unnaturally fast and cuts Max's foot off above the ankle, dargon separated from his body. Max falls.

"No!" I dive toward him, blood ringing in my ears. This can't be happening. Not to Charlie. Not to Annabelle. Not to Max.

He'll heal.

We'll replace the dargon somehow and he'll be okay.

Rector crashes into me again, and a vicious snarl tears from my throat. I fight to get away from him, to save my friend from hitting the earth. But Kraven swoops in out of nowhere and grabs Max's falling body. The two skid along the ground and I breathe a sigh of relief.

I rip free of Rector and set my gaze on his ankle. I point the tip of the sword Max gave me toward his dargon.

I'll take it before the sun rises.

Nerves fire through my body when I realize what it is I'm holding. A sword no different than any others on the battlefield. No different, expect for the yellow gemstone in the hilt. No different, except for the feel of it in my hand.

I'm certain Max has no idea what sword he stole.

Weapons are scattered across the Lion's Hand, and he must have simply plucked one from the tall grass.

It almost seems like a heavenly force has sidled into my corner.

Because in my hand is the sparrow among the crows.

I release a bone-chilling battle cry and charge toward him, wings beating the night sky. My sparrow catches him in his shoulder, but the blade doesn't break through his glossy scales. I close my wings and plummet toward the earth headfirst. Then I make a tight turn and soar toward Rector. I plunge the sword into his shoulder blade, and Rector startles like the weapon surprised him. The blade has only sunk about two inches into his ghastly armor. I jerk the sword free and Rector catapults my body through the air with a smack of his right wing.

He pulls his own sword to his side and grins. The blackness coating his face stretches like rubber. Even his nose and brows are only an outline in the thick gummy material. I wonder if the mask he wears over his face is a sort of armor, too. I blast straight upward and grab my sword with both hands. If this doesn't work, I don't know how I'll ever defeat him.

I think of Charlie.

I think of Annabelle and Max.

I think of the fate of mankind all over the world and set my sights on the flat space behind Rector's neck.

I fly downward with every ounce of power I have and focus every firing nerve in my brain on that one spot. Kill him. End this. Save the world.

The blade comes down on the back of Rector's neck. It should drive straight into his flesh and lay flat against his spine. It should spear him through and give me the time I need to break the dargon from his ankle.

It does neither of those things.

The sparrow bounces off and flies from my hands. I tumble through time and space trying to grab it, but it freefalls out of reach. After all that worry over a weapon cited in the omniscient scroll, it didn't do anything. And now it's gone.

Rector's own sword finds my forearm. My skin peels open. Blood rushes down my arm and into my open hand like a hand shake.

How do you do?

I swing with my uninjured arm toward Rector, functioning on pure adrenaline. He dodges my attack as easily as if I was a toddler and then he bites into my other shoulder. The biting thing is getting old, so I punch him in the stomach. If my sword didn't harm him, my blows do little more than tickle his immense body.

When Rector raises his head, his teeth are laced with blood and bits of my flesh. I'll heal, but he'll keep coming at me until he gets what he wants. I manage to shake him loose and fly over the Lion's Hand with Rector close on my heel.

Below me, the battlefield is stained red as demons crawl over humans and jackrabbits. Sirens fight against sirens, and collectors clash with liberators. Valery is crouched over Max's body, screaming. In one hand she has his severed foot, and she's trying to reattach it with the other. The Patrelli sisters, Oswald, and Annabelle are gone from the field, and Charlie and Aspen are standing behind a wall of sirens. The demons pummel past their bodies, moving ever closer to their prize. They want the princesses, and if I don't do something to stop this, they'll succeed.

My mind branches into countless paths. I should touch down and fight the demons. I should continue battling Rector so he's distracted from leading his troops. I should call for retreat.

The problem is I can't imagine doing any of these things successfully.

Snow trickles from the sky, floating ignorantly to the blood stained field. It cloaks the monsters' shoulders in a white cape. It's a false promise of hope when there's nothing to be hopeful about. I can't defeat Rector, Charlie and Aspen can't save the souls of those too far gone, and our soldiers are no match for the demons.

We'll be defeated on this battlefield. Even with the savior. Even with the soldier. Even with the sisters and Oswald and the jackrabbits and humans risking their lives. Even with liberators who know what we stand to lose, who have trained for weeks for this moment.

Even with me.

Unless…

ᗒ53ᗕ

WE ARE MONSTROUS

I dive across the field and land in the tall grass. When I look up, I see that against all odds, Rector has lost sight of me. He searches the skies, and when he doesn't immediately find what he's looking for, he flies in the opposite direction.

I take a knee.

I think about Charlie praying at the dining room table and how sure she was that He was listening. I think about Valery praying for forgiveness and Kraven supporting that endeavor. I think how Aspen was ordained to help save the world even though she lived a sinful life before Charlie came along. I think about what I felt in that training room with Neco. I think about the soul that lingers inside of me.

I rub a hand over my chest and feel blood there. Broken bones and bruises assault my entire body, but my soul is still intact. Why?

I wouldn't be the only liberator to ever keep his soul, unless there's a reason for it.

I gaze once more at the ravaged battlefield, at my friends fearful, at humans dying. I've never looked outside of myself for help. Never thought there was anything I couldn't do with my own damn hand. I am Dante Walker, and I didn't need anyone—*anyone*—to do a thing for me. Until now.

I bow my head.

I know you're up there watching this, and I know you don't want hell to win this war. I never lived a good life, and I've turned my back on you more times than I can count, so there's no reason you should listen. But this battle will kill us all without you.

Please help Charlie and Aspen so they can use their gifts to the best of their abilities. Please help the liberators remember their training. Help Oswald and the jackrabbits and the humans fight bravely, and help the sisters to heal those who are injured.

When nothing magical happens, I start to stand. Something hangs heavy in my heart though, so I take a knee once more.

Forgive me the things I have done. Help me this night. Please.

I open my eyes and search for Rector. When I locate him, one last thought blasts through my mind.

I can't do this without you.

The legs are knocked out from beneath me, and this time I'm on both knees. A yellow mist surrounds my body and wraps me in sweet perfume. I try to see past the fog, but I'm hit a second time by an invisible force. Pain explodes behind my eyes as my body grinds against itself. Bones lengthen and muscles expand and my face is torn apart. My skin rips and my limbs elongate. The pain consumes every thought I have. Every thought except one.

Charlie.

I always imagined the color of God was blue. Blue like the seals I now use. Blue like running water and a clear summer sky. But the yellowness that surrounds me feels right. It seeps into my pores forcefully, as if reuniting with an old friend lost so many years ago. There's a current engulfing my body and I can't name this thing I'm becoming. I'll try—

Dominant.

Invincible.

Terrifying.

Not for me…for others. I am not afraid.

But he should be.

I'm blinded by the power rushing through my bloodstream and I'm certain this is far above anything Kraven has ever experienced. Heat rushes through my fingers and my insides transform into gears and springs. Tick-tick-tick.

Boom.

I touch my face. Slickness coats the features there. And my body, it's larger and covered in a thin, gray material that shines like silver. I'm a knight dressed for battle. A forest fire raging. I cannot be controlled. I cannot be intimidated.

In that moment, I realize I was wrong. God is merciful. He may not want me after this war is over, but right now he does. He's forgiven me enough to sink his own teeth into my body. But there's something else I sense rolling off of him.

Anger.

Fury.

He isn't happy about what Lucifer and the collectors have done.

Neither am I.

I stand and find Rector on the back of a demon, riding it as if there's a saddle between his legs and reins in his hands. He's pumping his fist in the air and cheering his demons forward. He no longer has his sword. Overconfident prick.

I unfurl my wings.

The feathers are black as death. But there are new ones among the old. Yellow like the color of God and admonishment and castigation. Yellow like the color of fear. I stretch them upward and roll my shoulders back. I crack my head to the side and search the area until I find it. Leaning down, I take the sacred sword into my hand and point it straight upward.

For you.

Then I point it toward Rector and a growl begins deep in my core. It builds until my entire body becomes a rocket, flames practically shooting from my feet. I blast across the sky. Rector sees me a second before I collide into him.

The smile falls from his mouth, and in his eyes is something that fuels my rage—panic. I rip him from his demon and sail straight upward, wrapping my wings around our bodies. Darkness presses down on us, and I whisper one word to him.

"Die."

I hit him, my fist a cannon of demolition. His blood covers my silver hand. I pull my sword back and slam him in the chest with the hilt. A snapping sound fills me up. Rector scrambles to flee, but his attempts are in vain. I'm stronger. I'm faster. I'm more everything, and he knows it.

I keep him near with the use of my wings and steady my sword in both hands. Swinging with everything I have, I slice toward his right hand. It severs in one blow and falls to the earth. I pull my wings back and grab onto him. When he sees his missing hand, he cries out in shock. Then he screams in pain as his body comprehends what's happened. I take the sword and arc it toward his other wrist.

Down the left hand tumbles, a pink starfish against the night sky.

Rector hollers again. He's calling for the collectors, for Patrick and Kincaid and Zack. A quick glance down tells me they won't answer his call for help. The yellow fog rolls across the field, swallowing the black. Our warriors seem larger than life in its midst. I spot Oswald appearing onto the field, unafraid. He lights the area with his orange bomb and demons explode into red-scaled chunks. Kraven fights with one of the collectors—Zack—and I can tell he's winning with ease.

And Charlie and Aspen—

Seeing them, I release Rector. I can't do anything besides stare. Aspen sends green arrows into sirens, and Charlie sucks their souls from hell and returns it into their bodies. Their eyes are glazed over and filled with a creamy white texture. And their feet, they don't touch the ground. Every step they take is on air. They look ethereal.

They look monstrous.

Our humans race toward the demons and slash with confident blades. Rings are severed from the creatures' hands and plucked from the ground. The Patrelli sisters are on the field now, too, healing out in the open without the use of their shield. Slowly, our troops drive the demons and sirens back, the yellow mist giving them courage.

Rector flies across the field toward the forest. More than once, he falls to the ground and appears again in the sky. I drive toward him, a snarl starting from my feet and vibrating against my tongue. I catch him from behind and snap his head backward. Then, remembering all the things he's done, I lay the tip of my sword above his cuff.

This is the guy who kissed my mother.

Who nipped my father's penny from my pocket.

Who forced Charlie to fulfill the contract.

Who stole her soul from me, and took Blue's life.

The guy who tricked Aspen into staying in hell and turned Valery against us and killed Charlie Cooper. He hurt Annabelle. He hurt Max. But he won't hurt anyone else ever again.

I spin in a circle, and my aim is true. Rector screams as his foot and cuff separate from his leg and somersault toward the earth.

"No!" he screams. "No, no, no!" He turns around and faces me, a man with one foot and no hands. "No. No. No. Nooooo!" He continues repeating himself, but the word begins to have a mocking quality to it. "No. No-wah. Nooo-wah! Ha, ha! Nooo! Don't take my dargon, Dante. What ever would I do then?"

Rector is cut in more places than I can count, but there's one place I haven't thought to strike. One place I know he won't laugh at. I pull my sword back, breathe in, and drive it straight through his chest. His mouth opens in a perfect circle of nothingness, and even though he's grunting against the pain, he still manages to beat his wings and laugh.

"Don't you see? You can't kill me." He points a bloody stump at my shirt, tight against my new larger body. "I melted one of the rings down. I melted it down and I drank it."

My heart races upon hearing his secret. I shake him off and he plummets downward. He may still be alive, my sword speared through his chest, but he doesn't have the strength to fly any longer. Could it be? Could Rector be truly immortal?

If I severed his head, would he simply reattach it? Or maybe he'd keep moving forward without one. I shudder and take off after him, unwilling to accept that it comes down to this. I can hear the cries of victory on the Lion's Hand, and know that we're coming close to winning this battle. If I can bring our enemies their leader's lifeless body, they'll surely surrender. No one else needs to die today, save for one.

Rector is crawling through the grass. I touch down and walk after him, thinking. He finds something in the field and turns to show it to me. It's his right hand. Then again, it may not be his. He's not the only one who was cut down today.

I stare at Rector, the smug smile on his face. He pulls the sword from his chest and falls back, laughing. Hearing his happiness, I become the embodiment of rage. I am wrath. I am light.

I am sharp eyes for hunting, broad shoulders for fighting, strong hands for gripping a weapon. I am built for this. I will protect Charlie and Aspen and all of mankind from scum like Rector. There's nothing I wouldn't do for my girls, and I have done it all. Blood has spilled, and I spilled it without a second thought.

I am a machine.

There's one last nuisance that must be exterminated for me to sleep easy, and he sits before me, sputtering. He drank the dargon. It's a part of him. It races through his bloodstream and the only thing I can think to do is burn him until there's nothing left.

But there would always be something left, wouldn't there? Ashes. Great, sweeping piles of him carried on the wind. How long until the flakes converge and multiply? Until he rises from death like a god and walks the earth once more?

Hot blood pulses through me and I breathe hard. I'm remembering something. Rector is talking to me about winning, but I'm remembering. I'm remembering the first time I saw the strange words on the scroll. I understood them even though I shouldn't have. I searched the library and found others, and every last one of them my mind relished like a pleasant memory. I remember what Oswald said about the words having other uses we don't yet know.

I remember something else, too.

Aspen with spiders crawling the length of her hair. Aspen with holes in her head where her eyes once were. Aspen with legs that rooted into a lonesome island. We spoke to each other in our dreams. I close my eyes, not caring about Rector's threats. Not caring that he's rising to his feet and that my sword is clutched precariously between his dripping wrists.

Tell me what to do.

But He doesn't have to. I know. The dots connect in a glorious constellation of understanding.

Unconscious words spoken on an unpracticed tongue will drive the beast down.

It's the final message on the scroll I never comprehended, until now. My tongue is unpracticed. And the beast lies before me. It's only a matter of translating the correct words to end his reign.

I open my eyes. I jerk the sword away from Rector. And I press the tip of it against the existing wound in his chest. Rector smiles again. He thinks I've come to the same conclusion: he can't be killed. But anything that lives can expire. And tonight, as the snow falls over his shoulders, Rector will die.

I pull the sword back and, thinking of all the dreams I've shared with Aspen, I repeat her words, "You're already dead. Go back to sleep."

And then, my soul vibrating within my body, I repeat the words in a language only I can understand:

Vu frade darta. Ja paik ta sal.

I drive the sword home, and yellow light erupts from Rector's body. It shoots from his open mouth and his ears and nose. It eats his insides like a thousand ravenous maggots. His body begins to collapse like a slowly deflating balloon. The black scales encasing his body fold over on one another and he screams.

And he *screams*.

He screams so loudly that those on the battlefield turn and gawk. They watch as their leader, their foe, implodes. Somewhere in the distance, I hear Kraven ordering our troops to attack with force. The sound of cries and colliding weapons reach my ears, but I can't tear my eyes away from Rector's body. Organ by organ, cell by cell, the yellow light eats away at him. In the end, all that's left is the shadow of his face, lying in a pool of black liquid. His mouth moves in a silent plea. And then his features are swallowed by black.

There's one final burst of yellow light and then he's gone. Nothing remains. As the snow falls on the place Rector once was, I feel as if a part of myself has died as well. Rector was the embodiment of everything I hated about my past, and by killing him, it's as though I ended that piece of me, too. It feels good, liberating. But it's also mystifying. Without that side of me, what remains?

I'm eager to find out.

I turn back to the battle and storm toward the first demon I see.

54

GOODBYE

Once Rector has fallen, the remaining troops are unstoppable. They overcome the demons with hundreds of sirens fighting alongside them. Some of the remaining sirens flee, while others seem to linger, awaiting their turn to regain their soul. Easton, Charlie's old neighbor and the siren who wielded a powerful black cloud, and his brother, Salem, are among the sirens who ask for redemption.

As my body returns to its natural shape, Blue rushes over and tells me that both Annabelle and Max are in bad sorts, but that both are alive and are with the Patrelli sisters. I breathe a sigh of relief even though I shouldn't. Max won't survive much longer without a cuff. The only reason he's still alive is because his injuries aren't as severe as Neco's were when his own cuff was removed. And Annabelle lost so much blood, and she couldn't have been more than a few weeks along.

Kraven strides over as well and says Zack and Kincaid have fallen, and that only Patrick remains.

He asks if I would like to do the honors, but I shake my head.

"Ask him whether he wants be absolved of his sins and work for us. If he scoffs, sever his dargon." Patrick will never agree to it, and even if he said he'd changed, I'm not sure we have liberator dargon to give him and I'm certain I wouldn't believe his sudden change of heart. But it seems like a slap in Big Guy's face not to offer a second chance after I was given one.

Kraven stares at me. So does Blue.

"What?" I ask.

"You killed Rector," Blue says, "even after he turned into that *thing*."

I glance around at the dying battle. "We all did. Besides, I kind of turned into a *thing,* too."

Keeping an eye on Charlie, I call Lincoln over and instruct him to make a pass over the field with his jackrabbits. He tells me he's lost two more of his friends, and I'm stung by the news. When we return to the Hive, our mourning will be long. The worst part is that the jackrabbits who fell have family and friends who will never know where they went. They'll never know how bravely they fought or that they helped prevent the balance between heaven and hell from tipping in hell's favor. The demons they helped kill here aren't a hundredth of what waited in the shadows.

What would have happened if they'd won?

What would happen if demons had been able to walk the earth without the use of dargon?

I head toward Charlie, my legs moving as if on their own accord. She sees me coming and stops her work on a siren.

She throws her arms around me.

We kiss.

We kiss and all is right in the world and everything will be okay.

I'd fight a thousand battles to rewind the fact that Charlie died, but I don't believe she'd change a single thing. Not when she kisses me like this.

Charlie sees that I'm hurt and panic lights her face.

"I'll heal." I hold up my arm to show her how the wound has

stopped bleeding. "The same will happen to you if you're ever harmed."

Her face falls. When I lift her chin she says only, "Annabelle and Max, and all the others. Will they be okay?"

I don't know what to say to ease her grief, and I don't know the answer to her question, so I don't say anything at all.

Aspen fires off two more arrows and then turns toward me. "The demons have fallen. All of them."

I nod. "We need to get our wounded back to the Hive where the sisters have more supplies. Ask the remaining sirens who wish to be changed to follow us. Two days' journey in the snow. It'll do them good to wonder whether we'll still be forgiving when we arrive."

"And the sirens that fled?" Aspen asks.

Charlie answers her. "Let them go. Their leader is gone. If they don't want forgiveness, it's not our place to force it on them."

Aspen grimaces and mutters, "I was asking if we should kill them."

Charlie nudges her and tries to smile, but she's too exhausted and too afraid for our wounded friends. We all are. I don't know how the humans are standing upright. I wave Kraven over and tell him that we should get moving. We'll carry the injured if we have to. For the first time, I see fatigue on his face, but he agrees we must push onward.

It won't be as hard to march when we know we're going someplace safe, the idea of victory fresh on our minds.

$\bullet\ \bullet\ \bullet$

It takes less time to reach the Hive than it did when we traveled to the Lion's Hand. Blue and I carry a platform, and Max groans softly the whole way. The Patrelli sisters keep snow packed on Annabelle's wound and have applied what small bit of salve they brought to the battlefield, but it's anyone's guess as to whether she'll survive.

We are much fewer in number when we reach our odd charismatic estate, but there's also visible relief as we step through the three sets of doorways and land inside the great room. Much of the place has been ransacked, but Laura, the woman who wears the gold shawl, appears from the kitchen with a quick step. "There's food and tea. I'll need help making both." She's addressing the other humans, and they seem glad for the mirage of normalcy.

The Patrelli sisters order us through narrow hallways, and Blue and I navigate the board we carry Max on between the walls. Finally, we set him down on the floor and then lift him onto the bed. As we do this, my eyes travel down Max's leg to his missing foot. My stomach rolls. He's my best friend. If we don't do something, he'll die a final death. No hell, no heaven. Just an eternity of nothingness.

Kraven says he must pray through the night and hope Big Guy provides direction. Charlie was always meant to be a liberator, he says, but he can't make Max one without instruction to do so. I consider saying *screw that* and giving Max a piece of my dargon anyway. But I'm learning to trust something bigger than myself, so when one of the sisters shoos us out, insistent that she needs space to work, I exit the chambers.

The other sister follows Kraven, who has carried Annabelle every step of our return journey. Charlie, Blue, Aspen, and I are on his heels as he takes her to his bedroom and sets her on his bed. There are tears in his eyes, and when I ask if I can do anything, he roars for me to leave.

I want to tell him to back off, that Annabelle was my friend long before she was his heart. But if it were Charlie clinging to life, with our child in her stomach, there's no one that could stand between us. I squeeze Charlie's hand and send a second and third prayer to Big Guy. Then I turn and leave the room because I'm about to lose my mind.

. . .

It's several hours later when I'm woken by a kiss. Charlie's lips are still on my forehead and I reach up to keep her there a moment longer.

"Kraven has received word on what to do about Max," she says.

I pull back and meet her eyes.

She's crying.

"No way." I stand up, frustration beating in time with my heart. "After everything Max has done, this can't be his fate. He'll die, Charlie, and it'll be forever." I don't know why I say it like this, like it's her fault, but I'm dizzy with fear and need someone to blame.

Charlie wraps her arm around mine. "Just come with me."

I want to pull away and race toward Kraven's room. I want to pulverize the dude who claims he receives messages straight from Big Guy. I'm the one with the soul, right? Why not speak through me? I follow Charlie anyway, because I want to see Max right now. Part of me is terrified he's already gone, and that there's nothing I can do now.

Charlie raps softly on the doorway and we enter the room. The younger sister is sitting next to his bed, touching a wet cloth to Max's brow. When Max turns his head and attempts to grin, I sigh with relief. My legs shake as the sister stands and points to her chair.

"You can sit here, Dante," she says. "Keep the rag on his head."

I rush toward the chair, relieved she's given me something to do. Charlie comes to stand on the other side of the bed, and the sister excuses herself from the room.

"Why so glum?" Max croaks.

I shake my head. "Don't joke."

"It's my party and I'll joke if I want to."

"Bastard."

"Tool."

I raise the hand not holding the washcloth and give him the finger. He does the same to me though he can't lift his arm for long. It falls back to the bed with a thud.

Max cranes his neck away, motioning that he doesn't want the rag on his forehead any longer. "What's the verdict? Am I to liberate the world and spend an eternity kicking your ass in that regard?"

He's messing around, but I don't miss the hopeful lilt to his words. I glance at Charlie. I can't be the one to tell him. My throat burns as it is, and I'll be damned if I cry in front of him.

Charlie smiles. It's a sad smile, but not too sad. My heart twinges with hope. "Are you sorry for the wrongs you've committed, Maximillian?"

Max shifts in the bed and his eyes enlarge. He studies Charlie like she's the answer to every prayer he's ever spoken. For a dying man, he nods eagerly. I choke up when Charlie lays her hands on his chest and clenches her lids shut.

A moment later, the blue light glows from her hands and Aspen quietly enters the room. Her eyes blaze as sweat coats Charlie's brow. There's a tugging in my own chest as she works, and I find myself willing this to happen. It *must* happen.

Max gasps and his head is thrown back on the pillow. And then, just as suddenly, his entire body goes still. He gasps for air and Charlie wipes at her face. Aspen comes to stand beside the bed and asks, "Is it done? Did it work?"

Charlie grins. "Yeah, it did."

I leap from the chair. "You got his soul back? So he's going to live?"

Aspen's face falls. "No, Dante. That's not what she can do."

Max fumbles for my hand. It's such a strange gesture for him, but there's nothing I can do but take it in my own. "I'm going to die. But now I have a chance to go to Judgment. Is that right?" He looks at Charlie and she nods.

"They've removed Valery's cuff," Charlie says. "She won't be allowed to liberate any longer."

Max squeezes my hand and I glance down at him. "But hey, that means she'll be where I'm going. And if I get in, I'm going to spend an eternity punishing her for what she did to Charlie."

Charlie lays a hand on his shoulder. "She did what she did for *you*."

"I'm going to teach her a lesson anyway." And then Max does what Max does best. He winks. He makes a sexual innuendo about Valery, he winks, and then he closes his eyes and doesn't open them again.

I sit by Max's bed for another four hours until the sisters tell me he's gone.

In that time, I tell him he's my best friend. That I don't know what I'll do without him, and have I ever said how much I loved him?

Because I do.

✦⚶✦

PERMANENT ASSIGNMENTS

Before Valery passed, I went to see her. I was still angry for what she did to Charlie. Ultimately, it was her fault that she died. But I put myself in her situation and asked myself what I'd do if someone had kept me from Charlie for months on end. I'd do my best to follow orders, I guess.

And then I'd drag the entire world to hell and become a collector again if it meant being with her. Not saying it's right, but love makes you wear an idiot badge with pride.

So I stood at Valery's bedside. I thanked her for helping me and Charlie before her brain fart, and I said goodbye. Red was mortified by what she'd done, and I'm sure she'll be shoveling angel dung for a long time upstairs, but I'm happy knowing Max will be there to call her (sexual) names as she works.

I also said goodbye to Lincoln and the jackrabbits who survived the war. Aspen hugged Lincoln for a solid minute, which is probably a record for her. Lincoln eyed Polly the entire time Aspen embraced him and promised he'd be back to visit. I told the dude to be sure and get a few more facial rings to commemorate the war, and then he scurried toward the entrance with his friends like the lovable freak he is.

Two nights after Valery passes, I'm sitting in the great room with Kraven and Charlie. We're discussing the Hive and whether we should use it as a liberator headquarters, or if we should set up smaller locations across the world. I can tell Kraven's thoughts are only on Annabelle, and the baby he didn't know about until the war ended. I don't blame him for being sidetracked. I still don't know what I'll be doing long-term, and it feels like I'm living on borrowed time. So yeah, it's a bit hard for me to concentrate as well.

It's late in the night when something sounds at the end of the great room.

We look up and see her.

Annabelle.

One of the Patrelli sisters is helping support her and apologizing and saying that she told the girl ten times not to get up. It doesn't matter. We're all on our feet. Kraven's steps eat the ground between him and Annabelle, and he takes the sister's place. Gently, he moves Annabelle across the room and sits her down in a chair. Annabelle is pale and thin, and I can see the bulk of gauze beneath her nightgown.

Kraven kneels down and lays his head on her lap.

Charlie rushes to her friend's side and hugs her head. "I'm so glad to see you okay."

"You and me both," Annabelle manages.

"Annabelle—" I say.

She wraps her palms around Kraven's cheeks. "Guys, can we do this a bit later? I'll be around. Promise."

Charlie and I force ourselves to leave the room. As we walk away, I hear the sisters explaining to Kraven that they can't be sure the baby will survive, but that both are doing well for now. I imagine what Annabelle and Kraven's baby would be like, and how it's even possible. One is technically dead and can sprout wings. Will the child be able to do the same? I shiver thinking of the child sassy Annabelle and brooding Kraven will produce.

It also makes me think of Charlie and me and our future together, if there will be one.

I'm still thinking about this as Oswald turns the corner at the end of the hallway. When he spots me, he goes to flee.

"Stop in the name of Hugh Hefner," I say.

Oswald freezes, and then turns slowly around. "I'm sorry I didn't tell you what the scroll said about Charlie."

Charlie gives me a look of warning as we approach the old dude. When I get an arm away from him, I reach out a hand. "You trained Charlie to do what she was meant to do, and you performed bravely on the battlefield. I'm honored to call you friend."

"We're...we're okay?"

"Sure. We can swap wardrobes sometime. Maybe you could try out pants. Crazier things have happened."

Oswald smiles. It's a horrible thing.

And wonderful.

Losing Max—and yeah, Valery, too—is still raw, but seeing Annabelle out of bed has lifted my spirits. I slap Oswald on the back and lead Charlie toward our room. Once I get her inside, I shut the door and pull her onto our bed. We haven't slept a full night since the war started, but it's early evening, and now seems as good a time as any to catch up on sleep. To get started on what time we have left before Big Guy sends word on what's to happen to us.

For the first time since the dawn of time, I don't have *business* on the brain. I only want to hold Charlie, and to fall asleep with her safe in my arms.

She inches backward until her back is pressed into my abs. I force my right wing out and wrap it around her. The yellow feathers are still present, and Charlie strokes them, sending goose bumps racing over my skin.

Charlie and I have discussed the battle. We've discussed our friends and loss and the tragedy we've seen. And we've dissected her death and rebirth as a liberator. It feels good that those things are out of the way. Now we can be real again, boring.

"Do you like cats?" Charlie asks.

"What the hell did you just ask me?"

"Cats. Do you like them? I've always thought it would be nice to have a pet. And since we're a couple, and the war is over…"

I try to control my breathing. "Charlie, if you want a pet, I can be that for you. Or we could get a dog. How's that?" A shuffling sound comes from the bathroom, and Charlie giggles. "Charlie?" I ask, as my liberator girlfriend laughs harder. "What is that noise?"

"It's a kitten."

"No."

She jumps up, testing a smile, seeing how it feels after everything we've been through. "Jezza found it outside, and I said I'd—"

"No. And who's Jezza?"

Charlie cocks her head. "She works at the Hive. Don't you know everyone's name by now?"

"I call them The Humans."

"You need to learn their names." Charlie gets up and walks toward the bathroom.

"Don't you do it, Charlie. Don't you dare bring that blasted creature into this room."

Charlie squeals and runs back to the bed with something black and furry in her hands. I'm so disgusted I could retch. The creature climbs out of Charlie's arms and into my lap because it *knows* I hate it. "Get it away from me! It's sucking my soul out."

Charlie laughs so loudly that I feel a grin pulling at my mouth.

"It's probably got herpes, Charlie," I say. "That stuff is contagious."

She pets the kitten's back and the devil creature begins to purr. It kind of sounds like it's angry, even though the petting has to feel pretty awesome. Anger during pleasure. Hmm. That's all right, I guess.

Charlie scratches under the kitten's chin and says, "Thought we could name him Max."

I give her a look, because that's a cheap shot in trying to get me to like him. And then, as if to earn his namesake, the kitten starts licking my hand. I grimace. "Looks like he's got an oral fixation."

Charlie groans and leaves the room to get a glass of water, though I think in truth she's trying to give me and the monster time to get to know each other.

"Look, cat, you and I are never going to be friends. She's going to call you Max, but I'm going to call you Shit Head. And if you think for one second—" The cat lies down in a tight little ball of nastiness and falls asleep. "Oh, please. Make yourself at home by sleeping on my scrotum." I peek out into the sitting room area that connects to the four bedrooms, and then glance back at the kitten. Releasing a sigh of discontent, I pet Shit Head with one finger. He purrs extra hard, and I find myself wondering if I could train him to do things. Every hero needs a sidekick, and I'm nothing if not a Grade-A Hero.

• • •

I'm asleep, the horrid kitten on my side of the bed, when Kraven comes and wakes me. I tell him not to wake Charlie or I'll sic Shit Head on him.

Kraven can't stop smiling. Annabelle and his unborn baby are okay, and so everything makes sense again. "I have something to tell you."

"You're attracted to me, I know. Everyone is. Don't start second-guessing your sexuality. It's just a Dante Walker thing."

"You and Charlie are to remain liberators for the foreseeable future. And you're both to retain your souls as well."

I can't breathe. I can't speak. Damn cat probably stole my tongue. Does that really happen? Oh God, it probably does. I swallow hard and take a moment. "I don't have to turn in my dargon?"

Kraven shakes his head.

"Because I'm amazing?"

"What? No, he just said—"

I jump out of bed, and the kitten meows this tiny meow. It's damn cute. I hate him for being cute. "He said I'm supposed to lead the Hive and all the liberators?"

"He didn't say anything like that."

Charlie wakes up. "What's going on?"

I practically dive onto the bed and hug Charlie close. "Big Guy said we're both staying here, and that I've been promoted so that Kraven is beneath me."

Charlie bolts upright and hugs me back. "It'll be like Kraven is our child. We'll have to raise him."

"I'm leaving," Kraven says.

Aspen and Blue appear in the doorway as he shoulders his way out.

"What is everyone getting so excited about?" Aspen asks.

"I'm staying here!" I yell. "I'm a legit liberator for good."

Aspen rolls her eyes. "Yeah, you were the only one who ever thought you wouldn't be. Is that a cat?"

"Aspen?" Charlie says. "Were you in Blue's room just now?"

Aspen turns three shades of red and grumbles something about needing a snack.

I grab Shit Head and lift him above my head. "I absolve you of your disgustingness, cat! I'm not going to kick you out. You have a permanent place here." I put the kitten down as Aspen and Blue return to whatever things they were doing that I will not think about. Then I move toward Charlie. I must have that look on my face, because she starts laughing and shaking her head.

"It's late." She holds her hands up to stop me.

"Don't care."

"We'll scar the kitten."

"He's not looking." I crawl over Charlie until she's flat on her back and I'm hovering over her. I brush the back of my hand over her beautiful face, the one I first saw in Peachville. Charlie leans into my touch, and the features on her face morph from happiness into lust.

"Forever," she says, wrapping her arms around me.

I press my mouth to her and whisper against her lips—

Forever.

❖⧾ Epilogue ⧽❖

It's Easter, and Charlie has it in her head that we should do an egg hunt. I'd rather fling myself into the horrid ocean, but I'm a chump who will do anything to make her happy.

She hoists her long yellow dress up, and I glimpse the gold cuff around her ankle. I also glimpse her calf, which is enough to turn me on. Don't judge. Annabelle runs after Charlie and together they hide eggs in the grass outside the Hive. Every once in a while, the two turn and yell at Kraven, Blue, and I to stop looking.

"How would we be able to find them then?" Blue is purposely trying to get on the girls' nerves. I approve of his strategy.

Charlie puts a hand on her hip and mockingly purses her lips. Aspen has been doing Charlie's hair and forcing makeup and contacts onto her. With or without those things, she's so extraordinarily sexy I could scream.

Annabelle stumbles on a rock and almost face-plants on the ground. Kraven is soaring across the space in an instant. "I swear on all that is holy, Kraven." Annabelle holds a finger up like she means business. "I'm pregnant, not paraplegic."

He assures himself she's okay, and then strolls back toward us. We rag on him pretty hard. Blue especially, until Aspen walks into view.

"Tell me they're not hiding eggs," Aspen says.

Blue straightens, trying to appear taller. "Pretty dumb, huh?"

She shrugs. "Actually, might be fun."

"Well, yeah. Dumb, but fun."

Kraven and I look at each other and roll our eyes. It's obvious to anyone with a brain that the two dig each other. But for some unforeseen reason, they still have yet to admit it out loud. Not that it stops them from creeping into each other's beds at night. I've seen both do the dash of shame across the sitting area that joins our rooms more times than I can count.

Aspen looks at the sky. It's a clear day with a subtle breeze rolling off the ocean. "Lincoln will be here soon. He's bringing a couple of the jackrabbits with him. They can only stay for the weekend, but it should be cool."

I perk. "Wait, so the dudes are going to outnumber the girls? Sounds like we'll finally get started on that man cave."

Ever since the liberators set up permanent placement inside the Hive, the humans—whose names I now know—have been busy fixing the place up. But there's one room we've argued over for months. The girls want a new library, and the guys want a cave to do cave-like things in.

"How are your studies going?" Kraven asks Aspen.

"The sisters are good teachers. We should all have our GEDs soon." Aspen seems proud of herself, but I can tell thinking about the future brings up memories of her sister, Sahara, who she hasn't seen in months. And Annabelle, she basically called home and said she had decided to get her GED and attend college in London, and that she'd come visit when she could. There wasn't much they could do since she's eighteen, but I know she misses her family more than she admits. Kraven says once we're a bit more settled in our roles, there's no reason we can't go home for visits.

I study Charlie and the concentration on her face as she hides the eggs. She's done such great work liberating souls already, and Annabelle and Aspen have collaborated on expanding Hands Helping

Hands nationally, with a goal to make it global within five years. It's an aggressive plan, but one I believe they'll meet. Although we've been liberating locally in order to give ourselves a break, Kraven says soon we'll need to branch out and hit other areas.

Charlie doesn't know this yet, but I want to take her to college. It would be fun to act like a normal student for once, and Big Guy knows there'd be a ton of souls there we could help keep on the straight and narrow. Well, Charlie could do that. I could order pizza. With toppings.

Something tickles my ankle, and when I glance down, I see Shit Head rubbing against me. Charlie says when he does that it means he wants attention. I say it means the cat is marking me, and that an assassin is just around the corner awaiting Shit Head's signal. I sigh and pick him up.

Oswald calls from the front door of the Hive that lunch is almost ready. Kraven, Blue, Aspen, and I turn in his direction. The wind catches his orange robe, and we get a full frontal shot.

"Ohhh!" we yell at once.

Oswald grins and shuffles back inside. He's not even embarrassed. Hell, it may have been planned. I hand Shit Head to Blue, who curls the animal close to his chest. Unlike me, Blue enjoys him a demented ball of fur. The kitten purrs happily, and I furrow my brow.

"Don't be getting any ideas." I scratch under the cat's chin. "You're *my* waste of space, for better or worse."

"Dante!" Charlie yells, overhearing me. She's smiling though, because she knows I've fallen for the stupid cat. Can't even sleep now without knowing where that bag of bones is.

I cross the distance between us, and Charlie waves for me to get lost. She's trying to hide hard-boiled eggs, damn it. I don't care. I wrap my arms around her waist and spin her in a circle. Her toes leave the ground, and she laughs the same laugh I heard almost a year ago as we strolled toward her school, pumpkins littering porches. As I hold her, I think of all the memories we share.

The first time I saw her, and how blind I was to her beauty. The first time Charlie's face lit up outside the journalism room. The time I carried Charlie from the forest during a cruel game of hide and go seek, and the way Charlie looked at me in Las Vegas when she said she saw the good in me. I remember hauling her ass out of a barn after she kissed Blue, playing spin the bottle, and leaving her to go to Denver to liberate Aspen. My heart twinges with pain recalling the distance between us when Charlie believed I wanted her to be more like me, and less like herself, and how mind-blowing it felt the first time we were truly together.

I remember Charlie rushing down the stairs of hell to save me, and watching Rector drive a blade through Charlie's chest.

I remember when I saw her again, heart beating once again.

I remember thinking she'd never looked so stunning, back in her old skin, glowing with confidence.

I can't wait to make new memories with Charlie Cooper.

For starters, I can't wait to give her the two ridiculous plastic eggs I have hidden under my bed. The first one is filled with Skittles, and I can already see her turning it upside down and spilling every last one of those candies into her mouth and laughing as her tongue turns red and green and blue.

The second egg holds a ring.

It's not an engagement ring, but rather a thank you for the change she's brought my life, and for the change she and I will bring to thousands of people across the world, many of them never realizing it. But it's not only a thank you, it's a promise. A promise that I will always love her.

A promise that one day I will stand before our friends and make that girl mine forever.

And a promise that one day we'll try and have little Dante Walkers of our own.

Because wouldn't that just be the shit?

Pow!

ACKNOWLEDGMENTS

A big thank you to fellow young adult authors who keep me sane: Wendy Higgins, Jessica Brody, April Genevieve Tucholke, Page Morgan, Lindsay Cummings, Mari Mancusi, and Mary Lindsey. I heart you girls something fierce.

To the team at Entangled Teen who helped mold this story, Publisher Liz Pelletier, Editor Stacy Abrams, Copyeditor Melanie Smith, and the publicists who work so hard to get Dante Walker the exposure he expects—my deepest gratitude.

Thank you to literary agent Laurie McLean, who sold the Dante Walker trilogy and kick-started my career. Dante would still be chilling in the slush pile if it weren't for you. And he is not a slush pile kinda' guy.

Big hugs to the V Mafia! You continue to wow me with your dedication to my stories and characters. And to my super fan and assistant extraordinaire, Jessica Baker—my books would never make it to the shelves without your support and time. Thank you!

To my family, who is there for the good and the bad. With you guys by my side, I can (pretend) to do anything. Special shout out to my mom, Vicky, and my sister, Tyse, for reading an early version of *The Warrior* and providing valuable feedback. I love you, I love you.

Finally, always, to my husband, Ryan. You carry me when I'm

weak, dry my tears when I am sad, and love me when I am at my lowest. But mostly, you are *you*, and I thank God for putting you in my path that one, random Tuesday evening. I told you I'd give you my number if you danced with me in the rain. And you know what?

You did.